ALSO BY MARCOS M. VILLATORO

MINOS

A ROMILIA CHACÓN NOVEL

MARCOS M. VILLATORO

A DELL BOOK

MINOS

A Dell Book

PUBLISHING HISTORY

Kate's Mystery Books hardcover edition published 2003
Dell mass market edition / March 2005

Published by
Bantam Dell
A Division of Random House, Inc.
New York, New York

Library of Congress Catalog Card Number: 200354624

Dell is a registered trademark of Random House, Inc., and the
colophon is a trademark of Random House, Inc.

ISBN 0-440-24221-5

Printed in the United States of America
Published simultaneously in Canada

www.bantamdell.com

OPM 10 9 8 7 6 5 4 3 2 1

Minòs . . . conoscitor de la peccata
vede qual loco d' inferno è da essa;
cignesi con la coda tante volte
quantunque gradi vuol che giù sia messa.

Minos, great connoisseur of sin, discerns
For every spirit its proper place in Hell,
And wraps himself in his tail with as many
    turns
As levels down that shade will have to
    dwell.

—From Canto V of Dante's *Inferno*

Kill them all. God will know his own.

—Bishop Arnaud de Cîteaux

Para las girlfriends de Romilia Chacón,
mis estudiantes de Mount St. Mary's College.
For my students at the Mount.

MINOS

Alas—that sweet conceptions and passion so deep
Should bring them here
The Inferno, Canto V

AUGUST, 1994

Planning makes this easier. He's learned that the hard way. Do something, do it right. Makes sense. He so enjoys when the logic kicks in, when he has to make no more decisions regarding right or wrong. Take this woman before him, Catalina, who's been coming into the coffee shop for over a month now. He liked her immediately. On her first visit she asked his name. "Bobby," he said. She never forgot it. Sometimes he thought she was flirting with him, such as the time she ordered a mocha cappuccino with extra whipped cream, "Come on Bobby, pour in a little more cream, this waistline can take it!" She lifted her T-shirt, pinched skin the size and color of a roll of pennies, right there, right in the coffee shop. She has that way. Everyone follows her whim, gets seduced by her good humor, that smile. So does Bobby. He even thought about asking her out, but then shied away. Too complicated. Still, the idea piqued him, and he almost asked her out on a date. The thought became a pressure, right behind his ears, a headache without the pain. He's relieved when she comes in one afternoon, orders her coffee, then leans over the bar and tells him about her new boyfriend, a guy named Jonathan. "You know him, Bobby. Comes in here three, four times a week. Once came in with his wife?" She winces at that thinly disguised confession, sticks her tongue's tip between her teeth.

The logic clicks in, perfect cogs. When it does, the pressure eases off the back of his skull. It's all clear. He's clear. "That's not right," he says. At first she says nothing, obviously startled. He gets clearer, more specific, like talking to a child. "Catalina, you should know better. He's got a wife. It's adultery, pure and simple." The clarity slips from his mouth. He stands firm, on the edge of a ring, a pool of conviction. He doesn't budge, even when she says, "Maybe you should mind your own business," and walks out.

He wasn't born yesterday. The world has changed, it's stretched the rules. Give every girl a chance to mend her ways. Always room for reconciliation, here in the dark woods. But she mends nothing. She returns to the shop, lover in hand. She orders two coffees from the other barista, a cappuccino for her, not mentioning the extra cream, and a regular Colombian for Jonathan. Then she turns to Bobby. "Hey. *¿Qué tal?*" she says, saying words she taught him earlier, when she came in almost every day, when, he thought, her flirting was just for him. Yet now he knows that's just the way she is with everybody.

"*Bien*," Bobby says, "I'm *bien*." That's the end of their little joke. She looks at the counter, then takes the coffee to the small round table, where Jonathan waits.

Bobby turns, looks around. Now the shimmer of

nine circles takes the coffee shop, ripples over the folks walking down Peach Tree Boulevard, weaves around the corner of Ponce de Leon Avenue, covers the entire city. Somewhere between the second and fifth circles sits that guy, the one who ordered the Colombian.

The nine circles, one inside another, appear only when they have to. Only when there's a need.

If Catalina had not returned, this planning would not be necessary. Bobby would have let it pass. But this is too much: the two of them sitting there, sipping their coffees and talking as if what they do is normal, and she, approaching Bobby with her *¿Qué tal?* as a way of hoping for his recognition, his affirmation. It's just wrong. People marry, Catalina. That is order. Your walking in here with your lover, ordering coffee like you always do, then sitting in your favorite spot and forcing upon everyone the normalcy of your affair, that just won't do.

"Bobby. Hey Bobby. Wake up. I need a decaf latte, man." The manager pops him in the small of his back.

"Yes. Coming right up."

Jonathan smiles across the table at her. He has polished teeth. His ash blonde hair is cut short and perfectly groomed. A real looker, though all in the face. His body is thin, like a tennis player's. No real definition, just sleek. There are the books Jonathan teaches, stacked on the edge of the table. From this distance, standing behind the coffee bar, Bobby can make out one title: Henry Fielding's *Tom Jones*. Bobby read it two years ago. He knows the erotic plot, Tom's sexual exploits. So appropriate, that they would discuss that book, only to set it aside and pick up their coffees and read no more.

He takes off his apron, tosses it in a plastic barrel.

"Going home, Bobby?" Catalina asks. She dares to ask.

"Yes. My shift's over."

Jonathan looks up to see who she's talking with.

"So, see you tomorrow?" Catalina says, hoping for that recognition, a seal of approval.

"No. I've got stuff to do."

The last time was a mess because he had not thought everything out. Back then he was exhausted by the time the sun rose. Still, he had done it, and although it may have lacked art, it was full of meaning. He's saved the newspaper clippings. He ironed them into a spiral photo album, pressing them onto the thick black construction paper, as if to take out the wrinkles of the action itself, a final clean-up, guiding the iron over the clippings, creasing them, folding them away. Pure justice, those killings. The moment he had done it, when that woman, Eileen, lost her final yelp in a wheeze that blew from her opened lung and over the broken cola bottle, Bobby had spilled in his pants. That had been a surprise. He couldn't simply ignore the ecstasy in the act. It was more than just sexual; more like God. No, that was not enough to explain it: he had wanted her to believe *he* was God.

Now that he knows what happens, planning makes all the difference. After an hour and a half workout in the weight room at the YMCA on Ponce de Leon, he showers and dresses and says goodnight to Madeline at the front desk. He's tired, though tomorrow would be worse, as Tuesdays are his heavy aerobics day: running, swimming, and Stairmaster, half an hour each.

Today he makes the Home Depot run.

"Precut metal poles. Tell me what kind you need, son," says the worker in aisle seven, an older gentleman named Willie who was bored of retirement so now works part time at the Home Depot and obviously just loves it. He rubs his round chin, his thick fingers just a bit more ebony than his face. "What you need it for, piping? PVC pipe's better for that. Much lighter, they're like plastic."

"Oh no, I'm working in the back yard. I need to dig some tiny holes to put some trellises up. For my roses."

"Oh. You got some of those vine roses, the ones that take over the place, I bet."

"You got it."

"Yeah, they're like kudzu, only prettier. Trellises . . ." More chin-rubbing. "What you need is some stake poles. Just drive them in the ground, pull them up, you got your hole. One will do you. Maybe two, in case the first one breaks."

Willie means to take him to the Outdoor Garden section. On the way they pass through Garden Tools. There Bobby sees tall, black spears, piled vertically in a small stand.

"What about those, Willie?"

"What, leverage bars? You don't want them. They're for heavy jobs, like breaking up concrete."

But Bobby walks to them. Willie follows. Bobby stares at the black bars, as tall as he: six feet, or as it says on the rack's sign, "Seventy-two inches of pure iron." The shank itself is a good one-inch thick, a hexagon, the six sides easy to grasp, the iron not completely smooth, its rough edge making for a tight grip. At one end of the bar there is a flat chisel, used to break up cement, which does not interest Bobby. It's the other end, what the sign calls a "Pencil Point," that catches his eye. The sign shows all the varieties of leverage bars that Home Depot offers. One in particular is called a

"Diamond Point." It looks even sharper than the pencil point.

"Do you have any of those?" he asks Willie.

"Diamond Points? Let's see here. No, don't think we do. Just the pencil points. But they're just as strong."

The sign says each pole weighs seventeen pounds, so he doesn't bother with both hands. He lifts one from the rack, pulls it out easily. "Damn, son. I figured you for a weight lifter. You handle that bar like a real pencil."

Bobby chuckles. He examines the pole. It's what he needs, though he wishes it were that sharper Diamond Point. But he'll make do. It's on sale for $18.95. "I'll take one of these."

"All right. Anything else today?"

It's a slow moment at Home Depot, which is rare. Willie likes this young man, the way he speaks, with a "yessir" from time to time, something Willie hasn't heard from a white boy in a long while. He looks white. Though that dark black hair on the boy makes Willie think Greek, or Italian. Bobby has a list with him. He calls off the items, "Let's see . . . duct tape, forty feet of nylon rope, and a small, one-hand crowbar."

He then flips the leverage bar around, touches the Pencil Point with his index fingertip. It's just not sharp enough. "One more thing, Willie. I should pick up a metal file."

"Hardware and tools will have all that."

Willie shows him the large spools of rope on aisle eleven. Bobby chooses a 5/16 inch in diameter of solid braid white nylon. It's soft, but does not give nor stretch. It can hold one hundred ninety-two pounds, an overkill of course. And it's a bit more expensive, at twenty cents per foot. But it's the softest of them all.

In tools he picks a four-in-one hand file, with both

double cut and rasp cut. "That it?" says Willie. "Go on over to Ellen, she'll ring you up. Good luck with the roses."

Willie walks away. Bobby pays Ellen, then turns and sees Willie approach another customer. Bobby smiles, a satisfaction, seeing clearly how much order is in Willie's life. Willie has no need for the logic of circles.

Six days later, once they break down the door of Bobby's home, the police and the detectives will find, in the cool, humid basement, under a lone lightbulb, three king-sized mattresses stacked one atop the other. The bulb shows easily all those puncture marks in the top mattress. A woman from the Scientific Investigation Division probes the holes. In the shallower ones she finds three thin, iron filings, along with a pinch of iron dust. The filings, of course, will match the iron of the murder weapon. The puncture holes in the middle of the mattress are uneven, of various, superficial depths. The rest are much deeper. The detectives will create theories: the deeper holes were made later. Whoever did this was practicing.

He will be gone from this southern city. He collected his last check at the coffee shop two days before breaking into Catalina's apartment. Not that he needs it.

By the time they find the dead lovers locked together in a forced embrace, he has checked into a Best Western in Marietta, just northwest of Atlanta. When they match the iron filings and dust to the pole, he will be somewhere in the southernmost hills of Appalachia, those rolling mountains that bleed into Alabama. He has rivers to cross, gates to open, towers to see.

Somewhere between the Georgia border and Birmingham, the proprietress of the small bed and

breakfast is kind enough to fry the Spam that Bobby
has brought in with him. Her name is Janie. She smiles
when she serves it to him, cut up into small chunks,
fried with onions and garlic before tossing in the
beaten eggs. "My daddy ate a lot of Spam," she says,
"when he was in the Navy. Can't stand it now. But my
mother never fixed it like this. She just cut it into thick
slabs and fried it. Is this the way you meant?"

"It's just right."

"I'm sorry I didn't have any pineapple chunks."

"No problem."

A television is on, the volume turned low. Janie
turns it up when the morning news moves to an update
on the killings in Atlanta. CNN is hungry for it, as it
is in the city of their network headquarters. Still, they
use the same tired, lethargic syntax to explain the
event: disturbing, tortuous, horrendous act of double-
murder. References to bondage, S/M gone awry, un-
speakable acts of torture.

So prosaic, he thinks. He chews the Spam.

"That's just so god-awful," says Janie. She shakes
her head, turns away from the television and to him.
She smiles. "Boy, you finished that off quickly. You
must like the way I fixed it. Let me cook up some
more." She's flirting. He knows this. She has no wed-
ding ring, though she's a bit older than he.

He hands her the plate. "Just like my aunt used to
make."

She turns up the volume with the remote, then
walks back to the kitchen with his plate. He sips coffee
and watches. The camera focuses on a taped clip of two
women, one of them older, an obvious mother who
weeps as she walks from the precinct door and through
the gaggle of newspeople. She speaks, but Bobby cannot understand her. No one can, for that older woman

utters her cries in Spanish. The other is much younger. She is familiar, too familiar. Bobby pauses between sips, stares at the girl-woman. She does not cry. Her head is down slightly, but he can see her eyes. Yes, of course, she looks much like her sister. The cheekbones are the same, as are the lips, the thin jaw. Yet the ebullient nature, she just doesn't have it. Is it due to the theme of the newscast? He thinks not. They give her name, Romilia Chacón, younger sister of the murdered Catalina Chacón, and a senior at Emory. Romilia is darker than her sister. Not in skin color; of that they are the same: light coffee-colored, a soft brown cream. Like fairly new pennies. But she is darker in her eyes. Her look casts shadows like a black net. Still, she's young. Darkness over youth; it does not age her, but rather moves her into a world that is familiar to him. Is little Romilia being shaped, right now, as she leaves the police department? He thinks so. Will she speak with phantoms too someday, will long soliloquies embroider the quieter moments of her days? Of course. For now, she walks through a forest of chaos, as Bobby once did. But she has that look, casting a shadow over her gaze. So he will need to keep an eye on her.

"Here you are, darling."

Janie sets the second helping of Spammed eggs before him. He smiles and thanks her. She lingers a bit, rests her fingertips on his table. Behind her, the newscast moves on to other items of the day.

DECEMBER, 2000

I'll never get used to it.

That's when I cried, of course, standing before the mirror. I'd been home from the hospital for three days. I unwrapped the loose dressings from my neck, alone, with no help, pulling the gauze from the cut. There it was in all its glory: twenty-four bindings total. From this angle I could see only six of the twelve outer staples. They pulled the skin of my neck tight over the ten concealed interior stitches, along with the two that pulled together the nick on the external jugular. It was all clean now, little discharge. Ten days of antibiotics had taken care of any infection. A week in the hospital had made me stiff from idleness, my only movement picking at the food they served, sometimes finishing off a tamal that Mamá sneaked into the room.

In the hospital the nurses had done the bandaging. To change them they had combed and tied my hair back, pulling it tight into a pony tail then hooking the tail to the crown of my head. This freed them up to change the dressings. No chance of a loose hair falling and sticking to the cut. The taut hair pulled my scalp and my scalp pulled at the skin of my neck and I felt the pain. Then I knew, but did not say, that this was something I would not get used to: a rip in the cloth of skin that covered my head.

After putting on the third dressing, the nurses washed my hair for the first time since the attack. They had to do all the work of lowering me backward, holding my head and upper back to keep me from tensing any muscles, especially all those from my shoulders to my ears. "Got to keep an eye on that sternocleidomastoid," said Betsy Anne, the head nurse. She smiled. She had shown me that muscle before, on a chart, how it was the two-headed string of tissue that connected my skull, behind my ear, to my sternum and clavicle, just under my chin. Though not completely severed, the knife had cut partway through. Internal stitches held that muscle together now. I couldn't turn my head, left or right, without a dull throb swallowing the side of my neck.

Betsy Anne and I had been friends since my second day in Vanderbilt Hospital. During one of her afternoon shifts I had flung a fourteen-karat diamond ring into the trash can, then told her to take it home and cash it in. She did. A man named Tekún Umán, a local drug runner now on the run, had sent me the ring for saving his life. His would-be killer had given me this cut. I didn't want either; but I could only get rid of the ring. Betsy Anne took it and walked out of a pawn shop four thousand dollars richer. She took good care of my sternocleidomastoid.

She hoped to take care of more than that. Her

washing my hair was nothing less than a full head massage. She rubbed every inch of my scalp at least three times. She told me how lovely and thick my hair was, it was no wonder why that young Tekún Umán had fallen for me. She actually got the pronunciation right. Most of Nashville could pronounce that drug lord's Mayan nickname, having heard it so much in the news.

Betsy Anne was trying to prepare me to see the slash. My hair, thick and brown and beautiful; my eyes, round and awake and dark when angered ("Girl, you could bust a telephone pole in half with that look!"); my age, twenty-eight, which Betsy Anne, a decade my senior, said she coveted. After the wash she dried my hair, combed it carefully, let it fall to my left shoulder. She moved and tucked it, no longer a nurse but a private hair stylist. She kept tossing it over the front of my shoulder, in a way I had never worn it. "There. Call Mr. DeMille. This girl's ready for her close-up."

I stared at her beauty work. In the hospital mirror across the room, the loose dressing around my neck looked like a thick white choker, something I could have worn with any color if I were a woman who tended toward scarves. But it was obvious what she meant to do: with my hair fluffed over the front of both shoulders, you couldn't see either side of my neck. Just the front of the white wrap against my brown skin, like the collar of a monsignor.

Betsy Anne couldn't come home with me. Before I left Vanderbilt Hospital, she had preached to me the ways of walking (Not too fast), of turning my head (Don't), of lying down (Have your mother lower your head to the pillow). I couldn't put much pressure on any part of the neck, for although the inner stitches held the muscles and jugular tight, the strings would soon dissolve. I needed to give time for my neck to stitch back together, before starting physical therapy.

My doctor, a young fellow named Clancy, told me I was one lucky woman: my attacker had cut only the external jugular vein, not the interior jugular nor, even worse, the carotid. I only heard the word "jugular," and that it had been cut. Dr. Clancy explained, "The external jugular drains blood from your scalp and your face. The internal jugulars drain the blood from your brain. That's why you didn't pass out completely when he cut you. Good thing you were here at the hospital already. You went into hypovolemic shock. And I bet your whole head tingled."

It had, but I paid little attention to the tingles. Before the symptoms of the shock took me over, I had the opportunity to see Tekún Umán's would-be killer put a pistol to his own left eye and pull the trigger. He was known as the Jade Pyramid Serial Killer. He had left a small wake of bodies in the streets of Nashville before killing himself. He had almost killed me. Instead he left me with the image of his eye socket punched with blood, and the sound of his dead body dropping sack-like to the floor. A memory I tried to turn away from, literally, physically, until the damned pain in my neck stopped me, reminding me that I could never turn away.

I waited until Mamá left the house, with my son Sergio, before taking off the bandage. I had my eyes closed when she was getting ready to leave. *"Voy donde Marina,"* she had said, meaning Marina's Taquería and Grocery Mart, the first Hispanic-run market in Nashville, over on Nolensville Road. "They say it's going to snow tonight. We better stock up on supplies." Meaning, of course, masa harina, beans, rice, tomatoes, cilantro, cumin, and another CD of *norteño* music, which *doña* Marina had introduced my mother to. "You going to be all right?"

"I'll be fine." I kept my eyes closed. "Could you pick up some bourbon too?"

"*¿Qué es* bourbon?"

"Whiskey."

"What kind?"

The first name from college years came up. "Wild Turkey. There's a large bird on the label."

"*Ay, el chompipe,*" she smiled. "I think your father liked that one."

He did, as did my sister, Catalina, who used to sneak it as a teenager.

Mamá did not mind that I drank. She probably made little connection to the pain medication that I was on. But I had. Bourbon and codeine. A fine combination.

I wanted to be alone when I changed the dressing, because I didn't want to scare my son. Sergio was three, would turn four in less than a week. He had visited me in the hospital only twice. Both times I could tell he was frightened of me. Not of me, but of the bandage, the unseen scar underneath the gauze. He had said little. Mamá had to coax him to come near me, to place a kiss on my cheek. Then he darted back to his grandmother and held onto her waist.

I was afraid. I had reason to be scared, due to a game of Frisbee Catalina and I had played one afternoon, when I was twelve. She was sixteen. I was barefoot at the time. She had launched the Frisbee on a long flight, and I went chasing after it, looking up at the disc, not seeing the high concrete sidewalk with the sharp edge. I kicked it with the full force of the run. The sidewalk's corner cut deep, a string of blood shot

toward my shoulder with each limped step I took.
Catalina had rushed me to the emergency room, her
voice trembling between fear for her little sister and
anger over me bleeding on her upholstery, "I just vacu-
umed the floor mats, *¡Ay la gran púchica!*" Caty had carried me into the emergency room. My head bounced
against her shoulder. I could feel her breasts (always
larger than mine) pressed against my left arm. I told
her she didn't have to carry me, I was fine, though I was
getting awfully sleepy.

The doctor patched me up with four stitches.
None of that bothered me. It was a childhood adventure.

What disturbed me was the healing afterwards.
When my mother took me back to the doctor, and
when he unrolled the bandage and pulled off the gauze,
Mamá was the first to respond. Her hand went to her
mouth, "*Ay jodido*, what happened?"

It looked malformed, as if the healing had gone
wrong. Perhaps some awful disease, like gangrene, had
set in. But my toe was not green nor black with rot.
Rather, it looked like a hard pus had dried over the root
of my toe, a solidified jell of bumpy, confused skin, not
tan like the rest of my body, nor white like a wound. It
was an unsightly tissue, as if in that one half inch area of
scar, my skin had turned inside out.

At first the doctor said nothing about it. He instructed me to wiggle my toes. I did. Nothing hurt. He
happily declared me healed.

"But, but what about that scar?" my mother said.

He shook his head, acknowledging her concern,
yet obviously not wanting to make a big deal of it.
"That's called a Keloid Scar. Some people are prone to
it, though we don't know why. We see it a lot in ethnic
people. You're Mexican, right?"

"Salvadoran," Mamá said. She hated it when people couldn't tell the difference.

The doctor didn't catch her rancor. "A Keloid Scar's an abnormal proliferation of tissue over a wound. It's as if your body overcompensates, puts too much scar tissue over the skin to make sure the lesion closes up. It's not very pretty. But it's nothing to worry about." The doctor washed his hands at the sink.

My mother stuttered through some English, then turned to me and asked what she wanted to ask, in Spanish. I translated, "Is it going to look like this forever?"

"Afraid so. Not much you can do about it. If we had had a plastic surgeon on call the day you kicked the sidewalk, we may have been able to do some corrective surgery, maybe tuck the skin a little. But I don't think your insurance would have covered that." He looked at us both, at our obvious worry. "Oh now don't be too bothered by that little Keloid. You're too pretty a young lady to get upset by one scar on your foot that no one will ever see. Why I bet even a pair of sandals would cover it over." He had smiled, then ended with the phrase that now, sixteen years later, sounded like nothing less than a curse, "If you're going to have a Keloid, better that it happens where you'll rarely ever see it."

So as my mother and son shopped for cilantro and sweet breads at *doña* Marina's, I stood at the bedroom mirror, pulled the tape from my neck, and peeled away the gauze. The new me in the mirror cried, seemingly harder than I did.

Caty, at such a moment, would have known exactly what to do. Sometimes I can see her in the mirror, right behind me, pushing my thick hair over the cut, then whispering into my ear, "Now's a fine time to smoke some fine shit."

And that's exactly what we would do. While Sergio ran between the wooden stands of tomatillos and jabanero peppers, and my mother caught up with gossip from *doña* Marina, Caty and I would have rolled a nice fat joint and walked out on the back porch of my little house here in Germantown. We would have looked out on the new Promenade that Nashville had built nearby, north of downtown, an outdoor structure of specialty shops and restaurants that had doubled the value of my property in one year. While getting thoroughly ripped Catalina and I would have talked away from the scar, then slowly back to it, with Caty leading the conversation. Just like she did when I broke up with some creep white guy in high school back in Atlanta, or when some of the girls in our old neighborhood ragged on me about how much I hid behind books. Caty had that way. She would have said something perfect, like "That *pendejo* coward who did it to you is dead. And you're alive. You don't deserve the scar. But you do deserve to live." Something like that. Something, somehow, perfect. Made perfect by her voice.

But Caty's not smoking grass with me. I don't see her in the mirror. She never entered this house. All because of another killer six, no . . . almost seven years ago. The one they call the Whisperer. The one who got away.

My son Sergio never knew his aunt. He's only seen her in photos that I've hung on the walls. He's only caught a glimpse of her soul in the anger of my eyes. Maybe that's why he never asks about her.

All these men in my life: two serial killers and one drug runner.

The Whisperer is not dead. According to Memphis police reports, he's very alive.

The Jade Pyramid killer committed suicide, which made me Nashville's newest heroine.

Tekún Umán took off.

Though we have no idea where. The Drug Enforcement Administration's Public Website is just that: public. General information. Though new to the internet, I learned quickly that it took some work to find real facts on anything that was worth researching, such as the whereabouts of a now-famous head of a regional drug cartel.

I'm new to computers. A week before I took the bandage off my neck, two men visited me: my boss, Lieutenant Patrick McCabe, and Jacob "Doc" Callahan, the Medical Examiner who worked directly with our Homicide Department. They came bearing an early Christmas gift: a black cloth case that held a very thin, very light laptop computer. Doc unzipped the case, pulled out the laptop, and placed it atop the blankets that covered my legs.

"Is this a joke?" I said.

"Not at all," said Doc. His accent was a bit clipped, as if he were from the upper class neighborhood of West Nashville. "The word is out on how computer illiterate you are, Romilia. Patrick and I have decided to take advantage of your condition. We're bound and determined not to leave you in the past millennium. You *will* learn the Internet."

"You bought me a computer."

"Not really," said McCabe. He rubbed the back of his balding head, shoved his other hand in a pocket, like an embarrassed little boy. "The lion's share of the gift comes from Doc."

Doc clarified. "I'm a doctor. Wealthy. I covered the

computer. Pat's a cop. He's poor. He got you the first
two months of AOL."

Lieutenant McCabe didn't stay long. He was ready
to get home. I wondered if he still shied around me because of the Jade Pyramid case, because of how close I
had gotten to getting killed under his watch. He also
knew me, better than others did in the force. He had
my file from Atlanta, which held two incidents that lay
like blots of shame on my record. My reputation as a
hot-head had followed me to Nashville, but luckily I
had a boss who kept that reputation locked in his file
cabinet. It was up to me whether or not others would
learn about those previous incidents, the time I
slammed a suspect against a wall and gave him a nice,
light concussion, and the other fellow whom witnesses
had claimed I had pistol-whipped. I still have a different angle on that, but my angle doesn't echo much in
McCabe's file cabinet.

Still, McCabe respected me. I had solved the Jade
Pyramid Serial Killings that had haunted Nashville this
past autumn. The Mayor of Nashville, Winston
Campbell, had congratulated me. So now, while visiting me in my house, McCabe acted a bit sheepish, as if
he wanted to become paternal toward me. But he
pulled out of that quickly, became my boss again. "Get
better. I want to see you back in the office soon." He
made to touch my foot under the blanket, but that was
too intimate for him. Instead he tapped his index finger
against the bed's footboard three times.

Doc stayed. This was no surprise, and in fact
pleased me. Though he was old enough to be my father, sometimes I wondered if Doc had a crush on me.
He plugged in the computer, hooked it up to my
phone. "I'll set up the programs for you," he said.

I slept. When I awoke, Sergio was standing next to

Doc. Both of them stared at the screen. Doc allowed Sergio to move the internal mouse with his finger, then taught him the art of clicking, "Now put the arrow right on Buttercup's head, and click. Then it'll give you, see? All the information on her and the other Powderpuff Girls."

"Powerpuff," said Sergio.

"Oh. Right. My granddaughter corrects me on that too."

"They get mad if you call them Powderpuff." Sergio then clicked on Blossom.

I closed my eyes again, listened to them play. Sometimes the laptop chirped, or the voice of one of the cartoon characters giggled and invited Sergio into a game room. After twenty minutes of this, Sergio asked, as if it suddenly had occurred to him, "Why did you get this for my Mamá?"

He whispered, "Oh, because she's my girl."

"Really?"

Doc chuckled. I kept my eyes closed.

Sergio was much more enthused about the laptop than I. An hour later Doc had the computer on my lap, and he took me through the same steps of point-and-click. He sat on a chair, leaned over the bed, staring at the screen, showing me how to sign in an email name, how to check my mail (all I had so far were welcome letters from AOL). He wasn't that old. In his late fifties, still handsome, with a strong jaw and very blue eyes and a thick though cropped head of gray hair, once honey-brown. A widower, I had heard from the other detectives. I liked him. Sometimes I wondered if I was, in fact, in need of a father figure. He had a strong, agreeable cologne on, though it could not completely cut the scent of formaldehyde off him.

A father-figure. Or a man. Was I in need of a man?

That thought, if spoken, would have thrilled my mother. Sure: I'd love to have a man here, next to me. Doc Callahan? How about that young fellow, Doctor Clancy, who had bandaged me up at Vanderbilt Hospital? How about any guy who could live with a mutilated woman? *Jodido*.

An hour after Doc left, I was still on the computer. I was clumsy at finding websites, but started to get the hang of "surfing." At one point, while looking at a web page on a García Márquez fan club out of Ecuador, the computer spoke up, telling me I had mail. It was from Doc. "I've tried to call, but seems you're still online. I'm glad you're enjoying the computer. Doc." Then his full name appeared below, very formal: Dr. Jacob Callahan, along with his home address. I wrote him back with the "Reply" button, "I'm looking at photos on a *Playgirl* website." I was joking, of course . . . then after sending Doc the note, I moved the arrow to the little white Search Box and typed "Playgirl" in. A slew of website names popped up. It took some clicks, but finally, there I was. So of course right when the young, dark brown fellow with the stomach of Michelangelo's *David* popped up and came into crisp focus, I heard from the side of my bed, "Who's that? He's sure got a big penis." I slammed the laptop shut.

I tried to turn my head, and managed a smile, even with the pain. "Sergio, *mi hijo*. Why aren't you asleep?"

He answered with a shrug of his shoulders. His eyes darted toward the bandage, the one I had yet to pull off. Then he looked at me again.

He smiled, the first smile since I had come home. Perhaps he had seen something relax in me, for which I quietly thanked Doc. His gift had taken my mind off things for a handful of hours. Sergio saw this.

"*¿Querés acostarte vos?*" I asked.

"*Sí,*" he said, and his grin broke open. Then I no-

ticed something about him that I had not paid attention to in days, a detail of his childhood: he twirled his
hair with his left index finger. He climbed into bed with
me, stretched out underneath the blankets, pushed his
toes over my hip. His head lay in the crux of my arm. I
had to look at him without turning my neck. "*Te quiero,
mijito,*" I said. He reached up to grab my entire head
and kiss me, as was his habit. "*Ay, cuidado,* careful there.
Don't pull." I forced a smile, not to scare him away.
"Just reach up, kiss me on the cheek. There. That's
nice." He settled back down and soon was asleep. My
mother would carry him to bed soon, but I was in no
hurry. Though I was curious: After assuring myself that
Sergio slept, I pried open the laptop, touched the "Re-
sume" button. The liquid screen came alive again,
right where I had slammed it closed on that lovely man,
and . . . Wow. Damned if Sergio wasn't right.

The real Tekún Umán had been a famous Mayan Indian of Guatemala who had died in hand-to-hand combat with the Spanish Conquistador Pedro de Alvarado in the sixteenth century. He was a Central American folk hero. This guy, displayed on the DEA web page, with the name "Rafael Murillo" typed underneath the photo, once told me that *la gente* had given him the indigenous nickname. All because he took care of poor folks through his store-front façades of nonprofit corporations. The nonprofits not only hid his drug operation, they helped people turn a blind eye from his illegal source of revenue. Tekún had started selling cocaine in Atlanta. That's where he built his first homeless shelters. It was four-star charity. Tekún didn't serve soup, but steak, brown rice, fish, sautéed chicken dishes, and fresh-roasted coffee. His homeless shelters had HBO in every room. On Sunday nights all his rooms were completely filled, with homeless men and women sharing beds and chairs to watch *The Sopranos*.

The mayor of Atlanta lost a lot of voters when he decided to shut down all of Tekún Umán's nonprofits soon after Tekún left Atlanta and moved to Nashville. It didn't matter how many times he reminded the news media about the connection between the Central American drug cartel and the homeless shelters, how cocaine was keeping these luxurious nonprofits afloat: the papers grilled him, brown and crisp, on the editorial page. Nashville's Mayor Campbell had escaped such embarrassment, as Tekún had only recently arrived in our city when I outed him as a drug lord. Tekún had yet to set up a fully functioning charity program. That's why Mayor Campbell loved me; I had saved him from the news editorials of shame.

I clicked onto Rafael Murillo's face. His photo took over most of my screen. The basic information was listed to one side: his name (and here, in parenthesis, his Mayan nickname, or as the DEA said, "Other Aliases"), age (thirty-seven), race (Hispanic, though I knew that while his father was from Guatemala, his mother was a white woman from Chattanooga. Thus Tekún's connection to the American South). Height: five feet eleven inches. Weight, a slim one hundred sixty-five.

It said nothing of his Armani and Versace suits, his one hundred dollar cologne, his thousand dollar earring, the aromatic, subtle hand cream from Italy. Those were things I had remembered.

Unlike the Most Wanted mug shots of other fugitives, all grainy and rough, this one showed the handsome look Tekún could strike. The photo had come from *The Cumberland Journal*, a local Nashville paper. He wore a silk tie under one of his Versace double-breasts. He smiled at the camera. His short beard was perfectly groomed.

Drug running, money laundering, dealing mostly in the fledgling yet growing Guatemalan branch of the Latin American cartel. Considered armed and dangerous.

I knew the details behind that last remark. We couldn't charge Tekún for murder; but any court could have charged him for torture. He had a way of making sure his victims never forgot their sins against him. He was a good speller with a knife.

Even though I blew his Nashville drug market, Tekún never came after me. I had saved his life. The Jade Pyramid Killer had managed to put two bullet holes into Tekún. Then I had stepped in, got cut, but ended the killings. Tekún survived, then his people flew him out. Now he was hiding out somewhere in Central America.

After he fled, he sent me the letter and the gold ring, proclaiming his undying love for me. *Mi amor*, Tekún had said. No other man had used that line on me. "If it were not for you, I would not be alive this instant, writing this letter. It is because of you that I exist. And now, my existence desires only to think of you." Something I don't believe now. And if Tekún were here right now, standing beside my bed, looking at this scar, I doubt he would either.

Only when my mother is asleep do I flip the computer on and log onto the Internet and type into the white Search Box the words "Serial Killers."

Not Jade Pyramid, of course. But the Whisperer. A name I never say around Mamá.

Obsession becomes easier, more fluid, with the Internet. So many web pages devoted to the careers of

Ted Bundy, John Wayne Gacy, Charles Manson. And there are details: Bundy's apartment of dismembered, cooked victims, Gacy's hidden cemetery of little boys, Manson's photo, complete with the swastika cut into his forehead.

There is little information on the Whisperer. Just those same three cases, in Bristol, Atlanta and now Memphis. Just the names of the victims, small biographies of their lives, the manners in which they were all killed. All murdered with different M.O.s, but the Bureau had decided to lace them together. Obviously something tied the three together, but the specialists at Quantico weren't telling the world everything.

Until recently I had been able to let this go. That was when there were only two cities, Bristol and Atlanta. Then came the news leak while I was still in the hospital, that the murders of three men from Memphis last fall were now considered by the FBI as an act done by the Whisperer. Six years after killing my sister, he resurfaced once again. Six years that had allowed me to believe he was somehow dead and gone.

There are the three little boxes with the cities' names. Just a click away and I can read all about them.

"Here is your *Chompipe Loco*." Mamá placed the bottle of Wild Turkey on the dresser drawer, on the other side of the room, away from the bed. She walked to my side, snatched up the bottle of pain killers and tossed them into her purse. "I will be more than happy to fix you a drink. In about twelve hours." She placed a bottle of apple juice where the medicine had sat.

"Mamá, a little drink won't hurt now."

"You think I'm an idiot. Look, *mi hija*, you can change pain killers if you want, from pills to *trago*. But you won't mix them. Tonight, around ten o'clock, I'll fix us both a nice highball."

"But the pain will come back before then."

"So you'll enjoy your drink more. Besides, it's time you got up and walked around a bit. It will be good for your circulation. I got a call from your physical therapist. She told me to remind you that you can't stay in this bed forever."

Mamá was changing roles, from spoiling caregiver to drill sergeant. She helped lift me from the bed. "The doctor said it's okay for you to sit up. I moved the rocker to the front window for you. You can keep an eye on Sergio and watch television at the same time."

"Where is he?"

"Outside. Playing in the snow."

"He shouldn't be by himself."

"He's fine. He's with little Roy. Come on, up."

She took me to the living room, where a new fire blazed in the hearth. A cup of hot chocolate sat next to the rocking chair. Through the window was my son, tossing a snowball at his friend's head and missing Roy by a good twenty feet.

"Now you just relax here awhile," she said to me. So the caregiving role wasn't completely over. She went to take a shower, which I know would keep her busy for a good thirty minutes. Enough time for me to sneak back into the bedroom and drop a shot of bourbon into the hot chocolate. That first sip was oh so good, rich in chocolate and whiskey. This would be a better day. Perhaps I'd even go outside and try to pop Sergio with a snowball. Little Roy, Sergio's age, would get in the fray. But Roy had a much better aim; his daddy already had him in Pee Wee baseball. Beautiful, to see my son laugh, see his teeth, as he stumbled through the snow with Roy behind him, both boys brown and dark brown against all that white. I was getting soppy. It was the whiskey's fault, making me weep slightly over all that damn joy outside. Even the laptop got happy. I had forgotten to sign off from the Internet. It chirped at me in that white fellow's voice, "You've got mail!" Doc, of course. Probably getting back to me for an update on my porno-surfing. I walked to my bedroom and clicked on the mailbox again. It wasn't Doc's email address, but rather some other name, Cowgirlx14, or something like that, on a different web server. I opened it.

> *Mi amor,*
> *How are you? Convalescing? I hear Wilson left you quite wounded. Nicked in the jugular, and yet you live. Marvelous. No doubt it's that Salvadoran blood of yours. Just too strong, or stubborn, to die that easily.*
> *Tell me, are you the one checking in on that horrible Serial Killer website every fifteen minutes?*
> *There are too many moments in a day, Romi; too many empty opportunities in which I am driven to think of you.*
>
> *tu*

It was all written in Spanish. Even the accents were there, perfect grammar. And so the lack of an accent on the final word, the signature, was no mistake: he had chosen to use his nickname, or at least the initials of his nickname, Tekún Umán.

Of course, "tu" without an accent also means "yours."

I replied. The only thing I asked was, in English, where that arrogant shit was hiding. "Show yourself, you coward. Come on back to Nashville, so we can finish up business."

An hour later I got a reply, from Cowgirlx14, "Excuse me, but I don't think I know you, and I'd appreciate you not calling me names. And I've never worked in Nashville."

I wouldn't hear from Tekún again for another six weeks, when he sent me the package with the drawings from Atlanta, Bristol, and Memphis.

Tekún Umán is alive and well and sticking his tongue out at me." I dropped the hard copy of the email onto Patrick McCabe's desk.

McCabe looked up. "What are you doing here?"

"Just visiting. I promise." I smiled, though I wanted to wince; sitting, and standing, and tossing the email at him, all of it hurt my neck.

"How'd you get here? You didn't drive, did you?"

"My mother's out in the parking lot. I told her it'd only be a minute."

McCabe looked tired. It was still morning. No big cases were up on the white board. Numerous black lines were crossed through old cases. "Jade Pyramid" was under my name, with four victims written under that umbrella case. Gladys, our full-time temp, stared at the whiteboard and input the data into a new computer program the department had acquired.

When I first entered, a few other detectives on the day shift had walked by, said hello to me, poured themselves coffee. A slow morning. Yet McCabe still looked worn out. Perhaps he was over-caffeinated, as was his way. He walked around me, poured himself another cup, offered me one, which I took.

He gestured me toward a chair. "You've still got a few rest days coming to you. What does your doctor say?"

"I can get behind a desk by the end of next week."

"How's your neck?"

"It hurts. But it's fine." No lie. It was fine, even though it still was sore. In fact, it was healing too well. Just like my damn foot in childhood, an over-compensation of a wound. My mother said it was a Salvadoran thing, a sign of how strong we were, that even our scars showed our resilience. That was whenever she got in her revolutionary mood.

Instead of sitting at his desk, he took the chair opposite me, giving us an equal, relaxed footing. Something that never happens when I'm on duty.

"Stapleton over at *The Cumberland Journal* called yesterday. Says he wants to do a follow up on you. An after-the-case human interest story on Nashville's young heroine, Romilia Chacón."

"Not interested."

"Just what I told him. But Anthony can be a mule of an editor. He'll call you soon. And don't get on his bad side. Say no nicely." McCabe donned his reading glasses, read the printed email. I told him about my verbal attack on Cowgirlx14.

McCabe's brow furrowed. "Could be he's got some sort of computer device to hack in on someone else's email address. Or it could be Tekún *is* Cowgirlx14, and he merely wrote back the response on your reply, pretending to be an innocent waif in Idaho. I'll get Gladys on this, she's our hottest geek now. You never answered my question."

"What's that?"

"Why you're here."

I glanced to the left, at a pile of newspapers on his coffee table. "I got bored in bed."

"You could have gone to the bookstore, the movies, the Opryland Hotel. I hear a really good Liberace impersonator is over there now."

"Yeah, but they closed down the amusement park. No roller coasters to ride on anymore. Just a big ugly mall."

"Right." He lowered his head, looked over his reading glasses, which I hate. Anytime a man, especially an older man, does that to me, I believe in his complete authority and want to punch holes in it. "So *have* you been checking out some serial killer websites?"

Bringing him the email may have been a mistake. But staying in bed with codeine and bourbon a reach away was a bigger error. I wanted to go to the gym. I longed for a Stairmaster and the free weights. "Just a little. To see if there are any updates."

He sighed. "Romi, those are civilian websites. Guys obsessed with serial killers. You won't get much real info from them." He paused, then said, as carefully as possible, "And I don't know how wise it is to dwell on him."

Him meaning the Whisperer. Neither of us had to be specific.

"I don't dwell, Lieutenant. I investigate. She was my sister. I have the right."

He didn't argue. He turned back to the email.

"Besides," I said, "right now my head's crowded with Tekún Umán." Not exactly true; but not a complete lie.

"Why?"

"Because he and I have some unfinished business."

"Oh. I see. The boy, right? What was his name, Gato Negro?"

I looked down at the floor. "Yes."

"The kid you couldn't protect from Tekún."

I said nothing.

"So this is a vengeance thing," he said.

"No. It's a legal thing. Tekún Umán tortured that boy, cut him up." And then the images flashed through me, of a sixteen year old boy who trusted me with information on Tekún Umán, and that same boy, a week later in a hospital with one less eye and the Spanish word for *narc* cut into his stomach, all because I was careless: Tekún Umán had found out about Gato Negro, because of me.

McCabe interrupted my guilt. "But the boy hasn't talked, and I doubt he'll ever file charges."

"He might if we bring Tekún in."

The sigh pushed through his nostrils. "Who's got files on Mr. Tekún now?"

"Atlanta narcotics was the first to peg him. But they haven't got much. When I first started investigating him for the Diego Saenz murder, they didn't even know about his nickname. I think we knew more about him than the Feds did." I paused, then made my way toward a specific hint, a need, "Still, DC may have some files on him that could be helpful to us locally."

"Oh. So you want to go to Washington? With that?" He motioned to my cut.

I faked a chuckle. "Not at all. I was thinking that, if I just had a little more access to the DEA computer files . . ."

"That you could work from your home." He actually rolled his eyes. Perhaps he cursed Doc for giving me the laptop. All those hours in bed had given me a lot of time to practice web surfing.

"No. Not my home. From the office. Investigating Tekún is work, sir."

"You're on sick leave."

"My physical therapist says I've got to get moving again, or the muscles will atrophy. I'll shrivel."

"So shrivel. Stay home. You've busted a big case. Rest."

"I don't want to rest." That may have sounded testy.

"Why? Tekún's gone. He's a federal case, not local."

"Not necessarily. Tekún was setting up camp here. I'd be interested to know how much business he got going before he cut town. Obviously enough to get his name known on the street."

"So what do you want?"

"Well, every time I check into the DEA website, I notice there's this little box where you can type in a password code. I guess it's for law enforcement agents working on cases, a way for them to have access to more information, data that's not shared with the public."

"You want a pass code."

I smiled. The tourniquet around my neck seemed a bit tight.

"I've got one," he said. "You can't use it. I can petition for one for you, under mine. That'll take a day or so. But listen up: you can't use that pass code to web surf anywhere you want. They can monitor you. You have to keep to a specific case, or they'll slap your hand hard enough to draw blood. Then DC will come after me for trusting you with a code. I don't want problems with the DEA. And if you breathe anything of what you learn from the DEA's web to somebody like Anthony Stapleton, I will personally see to your demotion."

That was a bit strong. Obviously my wounded neck, the tourniquet, and my best smile could not win over my boss completely. Then again, McCabe had gone to school with the newspaper editor. There was an animosity between the two, a rivalry, that I had felt since my first case here in Nashville.

I promised: no communication with Stapleton nor any of his reporters.

"So, when do you get back to the office?" he asked.

"Thursday."

"I'll ask for a temporary code. We'll see what we can do."

I thanked him and left his office. He returned to his thick coffee and his computer screen. I was actually happy. Soon I would be back at my desk, tracking down a lovesick druglord who playfully thumbed his nose at me. It was something to do. Perhaps McCabe understood this: I needed to keep busy. Besides, I might surprise my boss by actually finding Tekún. McCabe was right, I could dwell on things. Obsession, it's part of the job, right up there with forensics and psychological profiles. I could focus it: I wouldn't get my boss in trouble by trying to use the pass code on other websites, such as the Behaviorial Science Unit at Quantico. I would be a good detective: focus on Rafael Murillo, aka Tekún Umán. Keep my sight focused, that was the way of keeping me from going under.

Cindy, my physical therapist, twisted my head left, right, back and forth, forcing all the face, scalp and neck muscles to stretch. She worked with and against the pain, using my grimace as a barometer. Though it hurt when she turned my skull certain ways, I could tell the muscles around the wound had become more supple. I could look over my right shoulder now. Though not without pain.

"You can be back in the gym in two weeks," she said. "Until then, I advise some solid fast-walking."

I took the advice. Every morning I woke early, put my head through the therapy motions Cindy had taught me until the stiffness born in sleep worked itself out. I ate cereal with Sergio, then, with my running suit on, hit the sidewalks of my neighborhood and made my way to the downtown Promenade. The weight I had gained in bed, I hoped, was mostly fluid. I longed for the gym.

After a shower and patching the scar, I drove to work. No more need for pain killer: my head was clear. Even the bourbon was a little less tempting. I had work to do, something to keep me occupied.

McCabe's temporary pass code slipped me into a deeper layer of the DEA world. Though sitting at my desk in downtown Nashville, I spent an entire morning staring at computer files housed in a Washington database. Once Tekún Umán made the DEA's Fugitive List, a number of files opened under his name. According to one, Tekún's flight from the law began the night a number of his "cousins" came into Vanderbilt Hospital and checked him out of Intensive Care, just a few minutes before midnight. I had been asleep two floors above him, in my own recovery room, and would not hear of his departure until late the following day. I heard none of the ruckus between the cousins and the nurses, the latter who said it was too dangerous to move a patient with gunshot wounds. But the cousins won out, and flew him in a private jet out of the Nashville airport, heading toward Atlanta, where it never touched down. Only one report followed out the lead: Tekún's plane apparently turned southwest, and flew into an airport in Leon, Mexico. That was the last they heard of him.

Tekún had not left Tennessee with nothing to show: the DEA proudly recorded that, out of the one hundred six clandestine methamphetamine laboratories that they had seized last year in an operation called Ice-Breaker, twenty-nine of them could be traced to Rafael Murillo, Tekún Umán.

This did not surprise me as much as did the first number: one hundred six labs, all of them cooking

speed. Or better known as ice, crystal. In my first years
as a cop on the beat and then as detective, I had seen
my share of stash, plastic bags filled with the clear
chunks of crystals that looked like rock candy. I had
seen the outcome of a smoke of ice, the euphoria it at
first causes, then the lightning of violence born out of
overuse, the schizophrenia, a sixteen year old boy picking at the skin of his forearm with his fingernails until
he bleeds. Withdrawal from high doses brought on
loaded depressions; I knew of two teen suicides back in
Atlanta linked to their using ice. Still, meth was becoming more popular among the young crowds, taking
cocaine's place for many of them. Perhaps that was due
to its local manufacturing. It wasn't that hard to set up
a local lab in your utility room.

Sometimes, when I read such reports about the
newest drug of choice, or saw some punk white boy
with enough needle marks in his forearm to look like a
bruised constellation, I thought about my own kid,
Sergio. But he was only three, going on four. I knew
what kept him safe: the women in his life, me, and especially, his grandmother. He was safe for now. In a
couple of years, however, I'd have to start talking with
him about school, and with that, of course, about
drugs. The more I saw on the street, the more I considered home schooling.

I wanted to call home. Here I was, one day back on
the job, and I wanted to have my mother put Sergio on
the line, so I could talk with him and imagine him
twisting that lock of hair around his finger.

Tekún had too many names: Tekún Umán for the
street; Rafael Murillo for the public; and Rafael Murillo
James for his family. This last one I learned from his
birth certificate. Though Guatemalan on his father's
side, he had been born in Chattanooga, Tennessee. The

father of the family must have insisted on giving his boy the names of both his parents, a true Latin American tradition. The certificate said that the mother, Ruth James, was from Chattanooga; perhaps that family name was old to Chattanooga, and there were still some James' around.

There were. A few phone calls to information got me the number of one Ruth Anne James, with a phone listing.

I called. Ruth Anne did not answer. Her sister, Kimberly, did. "Who is calling, please?" Her voice was southern, upper middle class, white. There was money behind that cadence.

I introduced myself, my profession, where I lived.

"Yes. And what is this in regards to?"

I gave her the name of her nephew, Rafael Murillo.

She paused long enough to tell me I had the correct family. Then, "I'm sorry, I have no connection with him."

"No ma'am, I didn't think you would. But I was wondering if I could ask you some questions."

"Such as?"

"Well, I'm afraid your nephew is under an investigation."

She laughed.

"I'm sorry?"

"Detective Chacón, that is no news to me."

"Would you mind answering a few questions?"

"Yes I would. To be honest, I do not like speaking on the phone."

"May I visit you?"

She sighed. She spoke straight, which I appreciated, though her very tone had a way of putting me two rungs below her Saks Fifth Avenue shoes. "I do not mind. You may visit. But if you're hoping to find Rafael, I'm afraid I won't be of much use to you."

"How about if I talked with Mr. Murillo's mother, Ruth?"

"Ruthie will be of even less use."

"I'm sorry?"

"My sister has Alzheimer's. She'll probably think you're her cat."

"Oh. I'm sorry."

"Still, Ruthie likes visitors. She can plug you into her childhood. Come on down. Tomorrow is fine. Or the next day. We're not going anywhere."

My only visit to Chattanooga was when my mother and son and I moved from Atlanta to Nashville. I drove the Ryder moving truck, Mamá followed behind in our Honda. In Chattanooga we took a lunch break, then Sergio crawled up in the Ryder with me and we pretended to be truckers all the way into Nashville.

The James' lived in one of the nicer neighborhoods of the city, perhaps the nicest. These were homes of the old rich; they certainly did not look like housing for drug runners. The plantation-style columns on the large front patios, the three-stories of bedrooms and servants' quarters turned, no doubt, into private studios and offices, the lawns manicured by the ubiquitous Mexican landscapers, all spoke of money that had passed through centuries, that had changed labor forces from African American to low-income white to Latino.

A young maid showed me into a library. She spoke

Spanish, though it sounded simple, with grammatical mistakes a child would make (*Dicieron* for *dijeron*, or the common *haiga* for *haya*, similar to our *ain't*). But she was not a simpleton; Spanish, I could see, was her second language. She looked Aztec, or Mayan. She left me. Five minutes later she brought me an iced tea, and told me that *doña* Kimberly would be with me shortly.

Fifteen minutes later Kimberly James wheeled in her sister, Ruth Anne. They were twins. It was as if a full-length mirror moved the wheelchair toward me. I stood. They were both beautiful women, in their late sixties or early seventies. They did not dye their hair, though both had the long locks pulled up into perfect buns. They wore different clothes: Ruthie, in the wheelchair, had been dressed in a long purple skirt that covered her to her ankles, and a cream colored blouse with light embroidery around her neck. It was a bit lower cut, showing the pink skin of her throat and collar bones. Kimberly wore pants, a similar blouse, and perfectly white tennis shoes. As they entered the library, if it hadn't been for the wheelchair I would not have known who was the sick one.

"Once I told Ruthie that we were having a guest, someone who was friends with Rafael, she just insisted on dolling up." She wheeled her sister to one side of the coffee table, came around and shook my hand. I stood. "Take a seat, Detective. Well now, it's been a long time since I last talked with Rafael, but I bet if I did, he would certainly remember you."

I blushed; and I twirled my hair over my neck, the beginning of a habit that would haunt me the rest of my life. "So even though Mr. Murillo lived nearby, in Atlanta and then in Nashville, you didn't visit with him?"

"I haven't seen him in a good four years."

"Where is Rafie?"

The Alzheimer's became apparent immediately. Ruthie James looked about the room, trying to catch sight of her son.

"He's not here right now, Ruthie. You just talked with him last night, remember? In the bathtub?"

"Did he take a bath?"

"Yes he did."

"Very dirty. He swings in those trees too much. Dammit."

I had never seen the symptoms of Alzheimer's before. Kimberly seemed very poised, as if the difficulties and strains that accompanied the disease had not affected her. She explained, as if knowing I was pondering this, "It's not her sundown time. I can move her thoughts a bit more easily now. Come night, though, and she's hell on wheels." Kimberly chuckled, but it was filled with a certain weariness that I had not known. "We've had her on various cocktails: Tacrine, Donepezil, Rivastigmine. Galantamine is the latest, it seems to have the best effect, better than the others. It keeps her somewhat lucid, until sundown. And Vitamin E, of course, though I'm not sure how much good it does. She's still slipping away from me."

She was a woman who knew more about a disease than she ever wanted to. And she was exhausted.

We sat. Though an old southern belle, the southern hospitality chatting did not last long. After asking how my drive was, and if I had ever been to Chattanooga before, she launched, "What would you like to know about my nephew?"

"Perhaps you know, Mrs. James, that he's under a national investigation."

"Yes, for connections with the drug cartel, and now, as a fugitive from the Drug Enforcement Agency."

Her bluntness surprised me. "Do you think the allegations are correct?"

"Does it matter what I think?" she looked at her sister, then turned back to me. "I am no witness. I have never seen my nephew do anything bad, or illegal. But I'm not blind. I know what my sister lived through. Why do you think she ended up with this sickness?"

She spoke as if Ruthie were not there. Was it because she knew Ruthie would forget; or that Ruthie had no capacity to forget, since she had no ability to remember, the way she once remembered? Kimberly's tone could have been mistaken for the voice of a callous twin sister, were it not for the obvious care she showered upon her sibling: the dress, the well-combed hair, the perfume that placed Ruthie in an air redolent of dignity.

"Ruthie lived through too much in Guatemala. She saw too much. The tension wrecked her. No one in my family has had Alzheimer's. I do not fear getting it. I never lived in that jungle."

"What jungle?"

"The Petén. I visited a few times, after my short-lived acting career. Just enough to see that there are still savage places in the world. Some corners of the earth still live in a primitive state."

I was not sure what to do with this. It smacked of racism toward Latins. I tried to mollify, "You were an actress?"

"Yes. In New York. Off Broadway." She smiled, remembering those off-Broadway days; then she became a bit softer regarding Guatemalans. "The people there, in the Petén, some of the finest, most welcoming souls I have ever met, even to a stranger like me. As much as they've suffered, you'd think they'd learn not to trust anybody. Especially their own military. But you've not come here to talk about Guatemalan politics. You're looking for Rafael."

"Yes. I would like to learn more about your nephew."

"Why?" This time, when she looked at me, she saw something that only the elderly can see: they spot in us what we can't see in ourselves. "Yes. You know Rafael, don't you?" Her question made me shift only slightly; my eyes left hers, barely, then came back to her. All that was enough to tell her something that I had not thought possible to see.

Again, a self-realization, that I was very young, in many ways.

"Yes ma'am, I did speak with him a few times." Did my voice shake? Just a little, not enough to be noticed. "I had to. You see, I was the investigator about the Jade Pyramid Killings, up in Nashville? I'm sure you may have heard something about what happened. . . ."

"Oh yes. All over the news. And so you're the one who saved my nephew's life."

". . . Yes."

"Tell me, Detective: has Rafael been in touch with you since he flew out of Nashville? Did he write to you?"

"I received a thank-you note. Yes."

"A thank-you. Any more than that?"

Did she know about the gift? How could she know that? She couldn't; all she could know was what all family members, even those separated for decades, know about one another: their ways.

"He sent me a present." She stared at me, waiting for the detail. "A ring. A little ring." Worth four Ks. I didn't say that.

She laughed.

"Excuse me?" I said.

"Oh Lord, Detective. I don't know if I'd want to be in your shoes."

• • •

Kimberly wheeled her sister into the dining room, where the maid, whose name was Carlita, took care of feeding her. Before Kimberly and I left the dining room I looked back. Carlita whispered kindly in an odd language to Ruthie, while feeding her the soup. Then she broke into Spanish, "*Cuidese doña Ruthie, está bien caliente,*" to which Ruthie said, "Oh it's not too hot. *Ay*, my favorite *caldo!*" I could have sworn that, within that refined southern accent, I heard a perfectly toned Guatemalan voice.

"Ruthie goes in and out," said Kimberly, her own voice now allowing itself to become more tired, relaxing into a reprieve. "During the day she does quite well. The cocktail, you'd start to believe in it. She even talks with Carlita in Spanish. But at night, it's just so difficult. She walks around the house, sticking the iron in the freezer or putting plates in the garage. I woke up one morning to her wristwatch in the sugar bowl. I was lucky to get five hours of sleep last night."

"Do you take care of her full-time?"

"Oh yes. Some of my cousins and I have talked about putting her in a home, and we probably will, perhaps in the next six months or so. But I don't want to. She's my sister. Twins, you know, joined at the hip. All those years she lived in Guatemala, sometimes I think I'm just trying to make up for them."

We walked into a solarium. Even with the cold outside, it was more than comfortable in the glass room. Plants grew in pots; a long trough of black earth housed a half dozen bougainvilleas. "We'll transplant those in March. I'm trying to get a Bird-of-Paradise going over there," she pointed to the far corner of the solarium at a weak, bent plant, "but I'm not having much luck. It just knows it's not in Santa Barbara."

We sat at a table. Another maid, a white woman, brought in a pot of coffee and cups, along with a small plate of sugar cookies. Kimberly lit up. The thin, brown cigarette allowed her to slip into a deeper relaxation, no matter how temporary.

"So. Tell me about your relationship with Rafael."

I laughed, "We don't really have a relationship."

"Excuse me. Please tell me about your encounters with him."

So I did. Considering the quick insights she had caught hold of, I thought it safe to tell her, though scantly, about our conversations. How I had first met him, in a coffee shop, interviewing him for the investigation of the Diego Saenz murder. How it seemed clear that her nephew was involved in the drug trade. Then, how Tekún Umán (as I referred to him, at first accidentally, then continuously, as she waved me on, knowing well the nickname) reacted to my arresting some of his people for selling false immigration papers to Mexicans. He had threatened me. Had threatened to kill me. The tale ended, of course, with the letter, the ring, and me tossing it into the trash.

"So. Now you know that a man who announces his love for you and the man who promises to end your life can be one and the same man."

"Do you live under any threats?" I asked.

"Not at all. I'm his aunt. He respects the family lines. More than that: he loves me, and I him. For that reason, he knows not to have any communication with me."

"Why?"

"Because he knows how much we disapprove of his trade."

"The drugs?"

"Of course." She stabbed the cigarette into a green, glass ashtray. "Just like my brother-in-law Jorge."

"Tekún's father."

She shook her head, drank some coffee. "Don't get me wrong. Jorge was a good man, and I was happy when Ruthie said she was going to marry him. We all were. He came from good stock, a farm-owner in Guatemala who was a fair man, paying his farm workers a third more than any other bossman in the area. Our family, who were all Democrats, liked this. Rafael worshipped his father. So it was hard on him when Jorge was killed."

"What happened?"

"Bullet through the head. He was drinking a scotch and soda at the time. Rafael was a teenager. He remembered how good his father was, how he treated the workers. He also knew Jorge was getting more involved in land reform issues, which is the kiss of death in Guatemala. It was easy for Rafael to believe that his father died for the cause of the struggling workers."

"He didn't?"

"Not at all. Jorge was making a deal at the time with some Colombian traffickers. They were all killed in a restaurant in Guatemala City."

Again, her clarity, her blunt statements regarding kin, threw me. I had to stop, question, "How do you know all this?"

"My dear, some families prefer to be blind to the ways of their relatives. Others see their relatives as all screwed up. Our family, the Jameses, were not ones to gild the lily, even if it was our own kin. I had visited my sister enough down in the Petén to see what was happening. Why in the world did my brother-in-law need to build all those warehouses out in the jungle? He had three new storage facilities built by the time they killed him."

"What were they used for?" Though I was sure I knew.

"Do you know how many tons of cocaine make their way into the United States each month? You need a place to store all that en route."

"Why do people really call him Tekún Umán?"

She lit another cigarette. "Rafael was born on February 20. That's the feast day of Tekún Umán. The Indian women in the house called him that, believed he was some special babe who would do great things. He certainly was a bright little fellow. Spoke three languages: English, Spanish, and Q'eqchi'. Ruthie was proud of that. She knew that language meant power, and that knowing more languages would help the boy, even if one of the languages was Indian. Then they sent him off to that elite military school, what was its name . . . Adolfo Hall Academy. Strange place. You've got fifteen year old kids learning the most god-awful things. Still, they gave him a good education. He was headed for college, but before he enrolled, decided to spend a year in the Guatemalan Special Forces."

"Why?" I poured myself more coffee.

"I'm not sure. Maybe because he learned what his father was really involved in, that Jorge wasn't such a pure man who worried over the plight of his nation's poor. I think Rafael was confused, he was looking for answers. He was a boy still, though precocious. So he joined the Special Forces, trying to make some sense out of his life. Trying to put some order into it.

"That's when his mother started getting sick. After his military training he came home to a mother he did not recognize. And worse, she didn't recognize him. She'd become frightened of the maids and the workers. She didn't remember the trees or the macaw that she had fed for six years. She kept calling it a strange rooster. So

Rafael flew her home, here to Chattanooga. That was the last time I saw him."

"Where did he go?"

"Back to the *finca* in Guatemala. And from what I hear, he whipped it back into shape, and then some."

"Where do you think he is now?"

"My dear, I have no idea."

This seemed an honest answer. Still, I asked for clarity, "Do you think he returned to his home in Guatemala?"

"I'm sure the DEA has staked out a place outside his *finca*. But as far as I know, he could be in Italy. He loved Florence. Tell me, why are you so interested in him? This seems out of the jurisdiction of a Homicide Detective."

"He hurt a boy in Nashville. I need to make amends."

"I see. Vengeance."

"No. Justice." But that sounded cheap, the moment it came out of my mouth.

She said nothing. She just looked at me, smiled slightly; not mocking me, but enjoying something, perhaps a moment of levity in a life that had become heavy with the loss of her sister's mind.

I meant to fill the silence, "What did you mean earlier, that you wouldn't want to be in my shoes?"

She paused, smoked, then spoke. "You'll never catch him. He's too elusive. He's been trained. The Guatemalan military, especially their Special Forces, is a surreptitious bunch. And violent, that goes without saying. And the world of drug runners, it's a world none of us wants to believe in. You won't catch him. I don't doubt, however, that you'll see him again."

JANUARY, 2001

Small prop planes had flown into the dusty Poptún airport for the past five weeks. Small planes that Tekún Umán did not believe in.

On the thin, streamlined fuselage of them all was painted "Pyramid Travels." A blue abstract drawing of a Mayan temple trailed behind the words, toward the tail. New paint. This was supposedly a new company. Rafael Murillo had heard about a private tourist company in the States starting a new branch of business here, in the northern jungles of Guatemala. The owners of Pyramid Travels catered to the rich and adventurous: the tourists visited the ancient ruins of Tikal, one of the oldest indigenous sites of Mesoamerica, while maintaining a level of comfort in a private plane, fine hotel rooms, safe drinking water. None of which Murillo believed.

"Why come here?" he asked *doña* Celia, an old

woman who sold black beans in the northeast corner of the marketplace, right next to a bike repair shop. They spoke in Maya Q'eqchi'. "Tikal is still a half-day's drive away."

Celia shrugged her shoulders. "Our cousin Memo says they want to have an adventure. So they fly in here and drive one of those black trucks north, to Flores."

"Yes. The black trucks with the air conditioning and the shockproof CD player. Don't you think that's strange?"

Celia smiled. She had a CD of marimba music playing right behind her. Murillo had given both the player and the disc to her two months ago, when he had first returned home to Poptún. "We think the ways of most gringos are strange," she said.

Spanish is not her first language. Q'eqchi', like the twenty-two other Mayan languages in the country, tends toward the first person plural, as if there were few individuals in Celia's world. Though he is fluent in her language, at times Murillo forgets this; he has spent most of the last few years in the States. His business has a way of forcing him to think as an individual, to be alone. That's why he visits Celia in the market: to remember.

She asked, "How is the shoulder?"

He twisted his arm in a circle to show that he could move it more briskly, with less pain. "It still pinches at times," he said, "but it's much better."

"And the one in your belly?"

"No food is leaking out."

"And you are alive," she said. "So even bullets cannot bring down Tekún Umán."

He grinned, a bit sheepishly. Though the nickname meant more to him here than it did in the States, as it was spoken by the people who had first given him the name, he had doubted, in these past weeks, how much he had deserved it. It was no act of heroism that had him give Celia's cousin a job as a janitor of the local airport watchtower. That had been an act of necessity, a pawn move of survival. Celia's cousin was more than happy to be an *oreja*, an ear, for Tekún Umán. Nor had the bullets that cut through his shoulder and gut failed to kill him because of any warrior tactics on his part. Detective Romilia Chacón had saved his life. He had barely escaped both death and the DEA. He felt little kinship with the ancient Mayan warrior. Yet Celia here was not mocking him. She meant it when she called him Tekún Umán.

He did not believe the logos on the new planes. Too few tourists walked in and out of them, most of them men, a few of them women, all relatively young. Though some wore large sunglasses and billowy, flowered shirts, he could tell, even through his binoculars, how in shape they were: runners, weight lifters, martial artists. The DEA agents were not good actors.

Tekún's accountant, computer expert and *padrino* was an older man named Rosario but whom everyone called "Beads," due to his holy name and his alacrity with math. Beads helped dismantle Pyramid Travel's lie. He was a city boy from Zone Ten in Guatemala City who preferred to live in the world of numbers. People were too inconsistent, while numbers never vacillated. They were the only truth. He spoke to Tekún Umán with a matter-of-fact voice that he had always used on his godson and boss, ever since Tekún was a teenager. They spoke in English. "In '99 we were up way over two hundred percent. You had a production flow of two planes a week into Florida and California with a cargo averaging a thousand pounds of premium each. It all sold before the weekend. Retail in L.A. and Tampa couldn't hold it. Now we're down to half in premium, we have to rely on selling the cheaper smack because of the drop in the Dow—people are going back to purchasing crack again. Can you believe that? I don't think we'll see the gains we made in '99. Not for awhile, anyway, until the new crystal labs start a regular production and keep a steady consumer base."

Beads looked up from the books. Tekún frowned. The accountant, as if woken brusquely from a sleep, knew why: Tekún permitted no one in his charge to speak the name of his merchandise. Not even his godfather.

"Sorry about that," said Beads; not out of fear, but rather a respect for the dead. Beads had been a *cuate* to Antonio Murillo, Tekún's father. He was Tekún's godfather. Pure *Compadrazco*.

Tekún turned away, lifted the binoculars again, peered out the window. A Pyramid Travels jet, already landed and geared down, opened its doors. The man who stepped out turned his face away from the jungle's sudden heat, as if he regretted stepping out of the air conditioning. He carried a small brown briefcase. He looked about at the adobe homes with their thatched roofs, all scattered to each side of the runway, then turned to the anomaly of a military control tower, with its antennae and radio controls hidden behind sheets of dark glass. It was obvious he did not want to be here, in this tropical heat, in the dust of a ragged Guatemalan town. His was the look of a man who had chosen the wrong vacation package, or had accepted the wrong assignment.

"Beads," said Tekún. The accountant walked to the large window and took the binoculars, then adjusted the focus. Tekún turned away, as if bored or on the verge of a sigh. "Is that who I think it is?"

"Which one? The balding white guy?"

"They're all white. Well, almost." Tekún glanced once more out the window, remembering that one person who had disboarded, a woman, was African American. "The one with the brown briefcase. Look familiar?"

"Not really."

"I do believe . . . yes. That's agent Carl Spooner."

"Who's that?"

"Worked for the DEA in Atlanta when I was living there. He and his people were always on my ass. I believe I upset him when I left for Nashville. And now he's here . . . Check him out please, Beads." He lowered his binoculars, then left Beads in the den of his home, passed the bar, the Monet, and the small marble statue of a woman playing a harpsichord, which he had outbid the Getty Center of Los Angeles for. He retreated to a far room, below the ground, where it was perpetually cool, and a series of computers was always on.

The amount of production flying from Colombia through Guatemala to Florida and California, though a concern, was not his highest priority. This business always meant a maintaining of vigilance, something he had known since his youth, when Beads, now turning gray, had a mop of brown hair. A certain boredom always laced itself into the stress, a constant waiting to get caught. The arrival of someone like the balding young man in the Pyramid Travel plane could at times be a welcome relief from the pressure, a nemesis to focus your attention on. Sometimes the chase, itself thrilling, could shake one from the anxiety of ennui.

Now, however, was not the time. Since getting shot in his new offices in Nashville two months ago (offices that the Nashville Police had since shut down), Tekún had little desire to take on any authority. This was hiding, and he knew it. He had never planned to be brought down by a rookie homicide detective in a Tennessee city. So much work had gone into Nashville, a place where he could cultivate a large, consistent and respectable clientele. Street kids and high schoolers, of course, for they were the main consumer base for ice. But there was also the well-to-do of West Nashville, the doctors who didn't mind peddling cocaine directly to their patients, the professors of both elite and state-run universities, who understood well the role of cocaine in American life: it was ordinary. It was American, in the most mundane, prosaic way you could say it. By the time Tekún had moved to Nashville to set up shop, the price of an ounce had been cut more than half; yet the lifestyles of his colleagues had not faltered one bit, had in fact grown. Nashville had promised to be an easy market, until Romilia Chacón started her investigation of serial killings in the state's capital.

She had surprised Tekún in a number of ways. Once she broke the serial killing spree, her investigative acumen had become front-page news. Tekún was actually surprised that Romilia had figured those cases out, considering the anger she harbored so closely inside her chest, the rage that added a hot beat to her heart. He recognized it in her during their talks, when she questioned him about the Jade Pyramid Murders. Yet while she asked him about the recent victims, how their necks had been opened and a piece of costume jewelry, a plastic, green pyramid, had been pushed into the wound by the killer, Tekún silently studied her: she was angry, all the time. He knew that rage, having lost his own father, the death he believed had thrown the web of Alzheimer's over his mother's brain. He knew how rage can blind you, can actually keep you from reaching the source of the anger, the reason for your loss. Indeed, it had already gotten Romilia in trouble; amazing that she had kept her job.

Thus he was thankful for the military, for his time in the Special Forces. Romilia's anger could be blunt, like a club. His was more sure, precise, like the infinite edge of a razor.

Beads walked into Tekún's office, reading off a pad of notes. "Carl Spooner. DEA Agent, once in charge of the Atlanta office, now recently moved to DC. This is his first overseas assignment. He's never taken a basket up to this point—one of those guys who wants to get through the department bribe-less. He's thirty-two, got two kids, both of them girls, ten and seven. There's one on the way, a boy, due in April. They just moved to Fairfax, close to George Mason University, where his wife teaches in the Biology Department. And yes, he is going prematurely bald."

"That's his grandfather's fault, on his mother's side." Tekún did not look up from the large computer screen, though he did reach for his cappuccino.

"So you were right. Pyramid Travels is a front."

"A front that's growing. And they've brought in someone who's got the hots for me."

Beads knew what his godson and boss referred to: three Pyramid Travel planes had flown into the area in the past two days. The DEA was getting ready for something, and in doing so showed a bit too much enthusiasm, flying in two planes in one day. And the tourists who departed the planes carried far too much luggage for a weekend in Tikal.

"So why is Spooner after you? You do something to him?"

"Not at all." Tekún turned around, looked at Beads with incredulity. "All I did was leave town."

"And he had nothing on you."

"Nothing was to be had."

Tekún always speaks as if his business were completely legal. *The legitimacy of the people,* he likes to say. *Once the government recognizes how common our product is in American homes, they'll do the quaint formality of legalizing it.*

Now all he said to Beads was, "Inventory?"

"All the bodegas are emptied out except for number four, which they've fronted with dry corn from the last harvest."

"Once Agent Spooner and his troops storm number four, have the corn distributed through the Church in town. Then fly the last of the inventory to the AFO in Tijuana. Tell the Arellano Felix Brothers it's a gift from their fledgling Chapín connection." Tekún surfed through two websites.

"You're going to start doing business with the AFO?" said Beads. "That's nothing but trouble. Ramon Arellano Felix just made the FBI's Ten Most Wanted. Besides, Spooner's not after the inventory. He's here to get you."

Tekún chuckled. "What, extradite me? I'm not even here."

"Exactly. You're not here. So don't put it past them to snatch you here, fly you to Texas and have the press snap pictures of them picking you up in the streets of El Paso."

"My dear Rosario: That would be kidnapping."

Beads rolled his eyes.

"Fine, Beads. I'll get ready." Again he sighed. He'd been doing that a lot lately. "Besides, them bringing in Spooner means they're serious. Bulldog training. This should be fun."

"Okay. Where to?" and before Tekún could answer, Beads knocked off a list of destinations: Managua, Jalisco, or, if he wanted to stay in-country, Chichicaste-nango was nice this time of year.

Tekún barely heard the list of regions. He mini-mized the web page that highlighted John Wayne Gacy, Jeffrey Dahmer, and the Whisperer, which then maxi-mized the one web page of *The Cumberland Journal*, Nashville's paper. There, on the front page of a three-month-old column, stood Romilia Chacón. An old shot of her, without the neck wound (*How does she fare now, with that cut?*). "Detective Ends Serial Killing Scam." Again Tekún pulled up the Serial Killer Homepage, clicked, once again, on the Whisperer. No scam there.

"So. Where to?" Beads said again.

"I'd like to visit my mother."

He had not planned such an abrupt departure. The past three months had been fruitful regarding the research he had done on Romilia Chacón. Thanks to the array of counterintelligence equipment that Beads had acquired in the past few years (some of the same computer technology Beads had used to enter the DEA databank to get the background check on Agent Carl Spooner), Tekún Umán had lots of access. Sometimes he wished Beads were not such an intelligence-gatherer, but rather worked more in shipment and handling. Tekún had heard that Pablo Escobar himself, while alive, had owned an armada of small, computerized submarines, with no sailors on board, only the digital chips that guided each underwater vehicle and the large storage space in its belly. The submarines were programmed to make their way through the Gulf of Mexico and dig into the beaches of Dolphin Island in Alabama, where moving trucks awaited their arrival. They were small enough to pass under the sonar of any U.S. surveillance ship. But Beads was a personal computer professional, a post-nerd hacker who still relied on airplanes and cattle trucks to take cargo from one place to the next. Still, just about any piece of information could be found, with Bead's little set of personally tailored viruses. Take the Whisperer. That Serial Killer Web Page had very little data on him, and the FBI's public website gave only scant references to that name. The Whisperer, of course, was not on their Ten Most Wanted List, for they had no real idea who he (or she) was. According to these public sites, there was absolutely no data on the killer's height, skin color, age, place of birth. Nothing.

When Tekún had first returned to his *Finca* Ixaba, he had requested a laptop. His private nurse did not allow him to place the computer on his lap. "You start typing on that, you'll strain your abdominal muscles." Beads had to do the typing for him in those first weeks. The accountant showed Tekún how to ride a virus planted in an email into a number of judicial websites, including that of the FBI. Beads shoved his carefully burned CD into the laptop. "Give me a second. I'm going to route the worm through a personal PC in Idaho."

"Who do you know in Idaho?"

"Her name's Yolanda. Goes by the screen name Cowgirl. I met her on some lonely women's chat room. She thinks my name is Henrietta. Her computer will get us into the Fed's database."

"Can't they trace down where this is coming from?" Tekún's voice strained in those first days; he still ached from the gunshot wounds.

"Oh they'll trace it all right, all the way to Cowgirl. But then it'll bounce over to the Police Department in Pocatela, Idaho. That way Cowgirl's computer is safe to use for awhile."

A week later Tekún would send his first email through Cowgirl to Romilia Chacón on AOL.

"But you've got to be careful," said Beads. "The Feds will start asking why a cop in Pocatela is so interested in the Whisperer. They'll think the killer has shown up in Idaho. Once Idaho says they *haven't* been gathering info on the Whisperer, the Bureau will start a hunt for the hacker. You've got to get offline before that happens. Delete and wipe, with this." He held up another CD. "Separate yourself completely."

For the first three weeks of his convalescence, Tekún web-surfed, reading old newspaper reports of the past seven years, plugging "Romilia Chacón" into the Search Box to see what the engine would find. Very little, except for the recent closing of the serial murder cases in Nashville.

A physical therapist came in from Guatemala City, and started working Tekún as vigorously as his body could withstand. She was impressed. "You're in good shape. That helps quicken the healing."

Tekún still squinted as the therapist helped him move his arm in wide circles. But he never complained. Even after the therapist retired to her private room on the *finca*, he continued to move his arm in a wide, full circle.

Three weeks later he sat at a desk. A maid brought him coffee and sweet bread. "*Bantiox*," he said, thanking her in her native Q'eqchi'. She smiled, walked out of the room. He took Bead's CD, slipped it into the laptop and made his way to the FBI website. The virus allowed him into the interior records with no need for

a password. For the next four hours he read about the
Whisperer, downloaded files, printed documents, and
surmised that the Feds had no idea who the killer was.
They did, however, have data. The devil was purely in
these details.

From the walled safety of his home in Ixaba, and from the safety of distance, of a certain objectivity, Tekún read about the killing of Catalina Chacón and her lover Jonathan Grassey in Atlanta seven years ago.

He studied the digitized photos on his computer screen. The woman tied to the bed was Romilia Chacón's older sister. The photos taken by the Atlanta Homicide Division, which the FBI later procured, showed numerous angles of the crime scene. Tekún's computer was fast; his took half the time of a regular PC to download the files of photos, which he then burned onto a CD. He drank coffee as the hard drive did its work. He nibbled on a *bolillo*, one of his favored breads; not too sweet, just enough to balance out the coffee.

After the photos, the computer downloaded the written reports, which took less time. Atlanta had

been thorough: the pictures, the reports written by
the detectives on duty that night, and the medical examiner's write-up all gave a detailed account of how
Caty and her lover left this world. It happened in
Caty's apartment near Emory, a one-bedroom that
she had been living in for two years. By the time the
police found them, their facial muscles, no doubt taut
as pulled cloth during the slow killing, had passed
through the initial rigor mortis, and had settled into a
look that makes us mistake death for peace. Jonathan's
head was nestled under Caty's chin. Her face was
turned to one side. Their wrists and ankles were tied
to the four bed posts, he on top of her, their arms and
legs pulled directly over each other in a double-X position. She lay on her back, he on his stomach, the full
weight of his nude body atop hers. Both their clothes
lay piled to one side, in a heap on the floor. It had
been January; both had worn sweaters, which were at
the bottom of the pile. Tekún, when first downloading the photos, leaned into one, adjusting his reading
glasses while staring at the vertical javelin that hooked
the two bodies together. Underneath the photo were
words, written quickly, partly crossed out, "Leverage
bar, ~~diamond point~~ pencil point. Iron filings may
mean a sharpening."

There were four dry puncture holes in the mattress: two on each side of the victims' heads, about six
inches away. Unlike the holes in the mattress that was
found in the perpetrator's abandoned apartment, which
they surmised to be signs of practicing, it was clear that
the holes in Caty's bed were made before the killing,
perhaps as a way to show the victims what was to happen to them. Squares of duct tape, four inches long,
were found to one side; the gum on the victims' faces
matched the glue on the tape's backing.

The final report surmised that the perpetrator had surprised both victims, entering through a window that he had broken in the bathroom before either of them had come home. He held them captive, and although no trace of an armament was found, may have held them at gunpoint in order to instruct them. According to theories constructed after the procedural, he had thought it out thoroughly: he had told both to strip. He ordered Jonathan to take the precut pieces of nylon rope and tie Caty to the bed (this, from the residue of dust found under Jonathan's fingernails, which matched the dust collected from the nylon fibers of the ropes). The Medical Examiner's report said something about a drug called Alprostadil, that it had been injected into Jonathan's corpus cavernosum, which resulted in an involuntary erection. This confused Tekún, until he read the full of the report, that Jonathan's penis showed signs of being well into Caty at the time of death.

The killer tied Jonathan right atop Caty. Once both were secured, he went around the bed, loosened each rope, retied it: the uniformity of the knots and the tautness testified to this. Jonathan was in Caty, forced to push deeply by the commands of his killer, until he ejaculated, at which point the killer lifted the leverage bar and plunged it through Jonathan's lower back.

He was strong: the tip of the pencil point, sharpened with a metal file, pierced through the bottom of the bed, stopping three inches from the wooden floor.

Both died from vast hemorrhaging through double-openings in the dorsal and abdominal regions of their bodies.

It was when Tekún looked at the photo of Catalina, alive, smiling at the camera during a birthday party (a good head shot that the Bureau had asked to have from the family), that he placed his coffee to one side and left it to cool. Then the distance closed in against itself, like dirt caving in to a soft space, an empty cave under the earth: she looked too much like her younger sister. A forced imagination took hold of him: there she is, under her lover's body, looking up at her killer as he climbs above them both, iron javelin in hand. He places his feet to each side of their bodies, near their waistlines, positions himself, thrusts the iron to the left, then the right of their heads, ripping dry through the top mattress. They watch him, watch the iron pole right next to them, penetrating the hard cloth. He talks to them; what does he say? Obviously an instruction into Jonathan's ear, to thrust, to make love. How does he say it? Is he crude, does he curse them, does he laugh? Or does he merely instruct Jonathan to do what a man is built to do, to push, harder and deeper until it's done? And then it's done, and Caty watches over her lover's shoulder as her killer lifts the iron spear one final time.

That was enough. Tekún turned away. He picked up the coffee cup, looked at it, then put it back on the oak table. His computer clicked, then chirped. It had continued downloading. Half a minute later a sign popped up on the screen. *File's done.*

It had left one final report, entitled "Death Note 2." Tekún searched through the files for a "Death Note 1," but found nothing. He opened this file. A close-up photograph of a sheet of paper, cream-colored, appeared. Its message, carefully written, had been done almost as a drawing, with shades of red and black ink.

The addendum attached to the note, written by one of the detectives (a woman named Jacobs), said

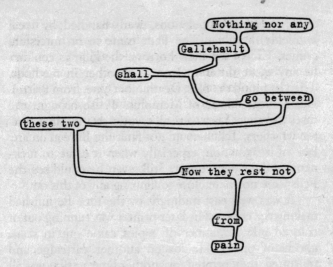

that they had found the note on the floor, at the foot of the bed. It had no fingerprints.

The only fingerprints found in the apartment were those of Catalina, Jonathan, and a few others traced back to visits from Catalina's mother and little sister Romilia. Except for a small amount of marijuana found in a ziplock bag underneath a couch, the rest of the Crime Scene report showed the average lifestyle of an average twenty-six year old woman living alone in Atlanta.

"But this, they called 'Death Note 2...'" said Tekún, mumbling. In the newspaper reports, there had been no mention of notes left in any of the cities where the Whisperer had killed.

He still had Bristol and Memphis to look up.

Two more hours of illegal downloading would reveal to him not only why the Bureau had referred to the killer as the Whisperer, but also why the FBI had taken on these three cases in the first place. Murders, espe-

cially in urban populations, were handled by local
homicide divisions. The Feds came in on interstate
crimes. Except for their horrors, the killings couldn't
be any more different from each other in methods.
Then he found the files: Death Note One, from Bristol.
Death Note Three of Memphis. These brought the
cases together. They were all cryptic, strange, like written whispers. Tekún could not fault the Bureau on any
lack of imagination, especially when it came to nick-
naming their perpetrator. Still, even he could see the
Feds were nowhere close to figuring any of this out.

It was well past midnight by the time he finished
making the copies. His laser printer was running out of
colored ink; a number of copies came out in scant
ghosts of prints. He loaded another cartridge and
reprinted, then printed for another hour until it was all
done. His body told him this was a mistake: he was
overtired. A malaise took him. He wondered if it was
from his own healing wounds or due to a night dedi-
cated to studying the macabre wake left behind by one
serial killer.

With a few mouse-clicks he directed the CD with
the refractor virus to break the connection from the
Behavioral Science Unit and skim away any residue of
tracks he may have made in the cyber forest.

The following day, after sleeping in, he felt more
refreshed. He ate a breakfast of black beans, eggs and
tortillas with Beads, then retired once again to his office, where he tried to make sense of the downloaded
files. A half hour of pouring over the pages gradually
dulled into fifteen minutes of flipping, hoping that
something, "a clue," he muttered, would pop up and fly
out at him. But he was no detective; this he himself had
to confess. And besides, as Beads reminded him, he had
business to attend to, a departure to arrange.

• • •

As Tekún carefully gathered all the procured documents and arranged them chronologically by case and placed them in a cardboard document box, Beads prepared the *finca*. Tekún took an hour of an early morning to compose a letter on handmade stationery, created by the Cartiera F. Amatruda in a fourteenth century paper mill at Amalfi, one of the oldest centers of papermaking in Italy. The deckle-edged parchment, made from cotton rag, was difficult to come by, though he had been fortunate to find a thin box of the pages, along with their handmade envelopes, on his last visit to Florence. It was a pleasure to write on. The paper itself had a way of making him slow his pen and his thoughts. He could block, for the moment, all the movement that Beads was in charge of outside. Tekún had to refer to his worn paperback copy of *El amor en los tiempos del cólera* to finish the letter. Though he owned a Spanish first edition of *Love in the Time of Cholera*, signed by the author himself, Tekún would never dare crack it open to search for the name of a certain character. Of course he remembered Fermina Daza; who wouldn't? The most beautiful woman of Márquez's novel, and as hard-nosed as Romilia Chacón. But Fermina's daughter, what was that girl's name?

He finished the letter, carefully creased it into a fold, and tucked it into its envelope. Then he placed it atop the document box, sealed the box with tape, shoved it into a courier envelope. He walked across his *finca* toward Beads, who was instructing a crew of workers to go to each bodega and, with high-powered water hoses, wash down any dust (particularly white) from inside the empty warehouses.

"Please make sure this gets mailed," said Tekún. He handed Beads the package.

"From where?"

"St. Paul. Do it fourth class. That will take more time."

"Something you haven't got," said Beads.

Tekún Umán owns no personal gun, though all his workers do. He carries with him, at all times, a Sorcerer's Apprentice. He sheathes it in the small of his back. He is a thin man; his muscle fiber, after three months of therapy and exercise following the gunshots of last November, has healed well. Certain movements still hurt, but he has learned to move around and through the pain.

The knife weighs ten ounces. Its blade is mirror-polished stainless steel. It's shaped much like a Harpy Knife: its tip curves forward into a clean, needle-like hook. What at first attracted him to the knife was its black, African gazelle horn handle, and the green jade ring that connected the handle to the blade. A hearkening back to the original continent, with a touch of Mayan. It cost him six hundred dollars. So taken was he with its beauty, he had not bothered to deal down the

San Diego seller. He placed six one hundred dollar bills onto the glass case and walked out of the showroom with his new purchase.

Many knife owners test the hone of their blade on paper, to see if the metal, with its own weight, slips through the sheet like a razor. Tekún does the same, only on sheets of leather. After sharpening, he drops the hook onto the oiled sheet, then palms the blade. Its weight opens the skin.

He enjoys the old ways, the indigenous forms of combat, of survival. It's a hobby of sorts, one that he developed in the Special Forces. On a visit to Bolivia last year to meet, face to face, some new suppliers, his host greeted Tekún with a gift: a blowgun set hand-carved by a Guarani woodsmith. At first he was disappointed; Tekún had always enjoyed Andean music, and had hoped to acquire an original *quena*, the flute played by the Bolivian Indians. Then Rex, his new business partner, showed him how the blow-gun worked. "Even my five year old boy can do it," said Rex. "Watch."

The dart was a needle-like wooden shaft the length of a pencil, though much thinner, sharper. Rex loaded it into the ornate blow gun. The gun itself was made of a dark wood similar to the mahogany that Tekún saw cut down and dragged out of his own jungle every day. He made a dry statement about its beauty, still thinking about a flute. Rex said, "I thought you'd like it. It's an original. And watch how accurate it is."

Rex puffed his cheeks and blew once, a quick, short, solid burst of breath. Tekún barely caught sight of the dart flying. It popped into a wooden target that Rex had no doubt made specifically for this game, perhaps for his boy. He had hit the bull's-eye.

"How about that?" said Rex.

"Oh. Impressive. Indeed," said Tekún, trying to sound impressed. "You've obviously been practicing."

"Not really. It's not that difficult, if you're just playing darts. But out in the jungle, it's different."

Rex turned to the bar. They were all outside on Rex's patio. Two men stood at the only door to the house. A gardener, an older man who probably, Tekún thought, spoke more Aymara than he did Spanish, tended to a bed of thick, blue and pink flowers. A German Shepherd wandered through the garden and onto the patio. The dog's presence at first startled Tekún, which made the animal turn and look at the visitor. When Tekún settled back into his chair, the dog turned away.

Rex lifted a small receptacle from the back of the bar. The wood of the vessel matched that of the blowgun, dark, like mahogany. It was small enough to fit in Rex's palm. He lifted the lid and carefully dipped a dart into it, then pulled it out. The dart's tip glistened with a thick liquid. Some of the honey-like substance dripped back into the vessel. "I heard of your antipathy toward guns," said Rex. For a moment, but barely a moment, this statement disturbed Tekún. He took a quick, defensive inventory: The guards at the door carried no guns, not even a pistol. Was this in respect to his visit? He concluded that yes, it was: Rex aimed the blowgun toward the yard, at the dog. He blew. The German Shepherd yipped with the sting, swung its head toward its flank, where the dart had entered and where it now bounced about, like a spear in a bull. The dog took one step, then another. Its legs buckled and he collapsed.

Tekún looked at Rex, who was smiling, and who then motioned him toward the dog. Both men walked to it. Tekún almost asked, *You killed him?* But that sounded too accusatory; for they were still new partners. "Is he dead?" he asked.

"Looks like it, doesn't it? But not at all. Not only is he alive, he's awake. Look at his eye. Relámpago! Here boy!"

The dog's eye swirled toward its master.

Tekún drew back. He turned his head to one side, studying the animal, its eye; was that fear in there?

"In fifteen minutes he'll jump right up. He'll shake off the paralysis quickly. Of course, in the jungle, that gives a hunter enough time to tie the animal, or gut it." Rex handed the blowgun to Tekún. "It's all wood. You'll have no problem in any airport. But be careful with this," he handed Tekún the vessel of poison honey. Tekún smiled; he thanked his new associate, shook his hand, admiring the blowgun and its small quiver of darts. He thought little more of not getting a flute.

Beads had learned the schedule of the DEA's raid: Celia's cousin at the control tower, who feigned his bad Spanish and acted completely ignorant of English (though he had studied in Ossining, New York, for two years), heard an American agent say to another gringo, four A.M. on Tuesday. This was Sunday night. The *finca* was clean. The trucks had left. The corn from Bodega Number Four would be delivered to the local priest on Monday morning. "We can leave now," said Beads, though he knew his statement was in vain.

Tekún wore a dark green running suit. The nights were always cool here. The suit was a good idea for an evening jog. His running shoes, new, were Nikes; he had peeled off the reflectors. "I'll meet you in Machaquilá at eight forty-five."

"That's a seven mile run," said Beads.

"Yes, and I usually run ten. Come on now, Beads,

quit that worrying," Tekún's voice turned southern, borrowed from his mother's side, though still badly wrought. "I'll be fine."

"Your father wouldn't approve."

"My father hesitated. That's why he's dead." Tekún sounded angry, something rare. "His lack of entering fully into this business is what got him killed. He died with regrets. Something I plan never to do."

"But *Chico*, you don't have to leave your mark wherever you go." Beads knew his voice sounded desperate.

Tekún turned and looked at his godfather. He laughed and slapped Beads on the shoulder. "Of course I do."

Carl Spooner and four other agents lived in a rental adobe cottage in the middle of town, about five blocks east of the market. The market was now closed. The rest of the town was following suit, except for both bars, *Mi Oficina* and *Donde Siempre Me Encuentran*. Both were far enough away from Carl's window that he heard only the suggestion of mariachi music that blasted from one of the cantina's windows. Sometimes a neighboring house held a party, usually a *quinceñera* for a daughter who had just come into womanhood. Then the noise level on the street peaked, until a couple of the agents went over to complain and, when that failed, to take up the father's invitation and join the festivities.

In his two weeks here, Carl had visited no parties. He had walked through the marketplace a couple of times, enough to see that he was a minority here. The

Indian women and the Ladino men who sat in their
kiosks never looked him straight in the eye, though a
number, including Celia, tried to answer his questions
regarding the fruit that they sold. He could hear them
mutter to one another after he passed, though he understood none of it. They used one term over and again; it
sounded to him like "la seeya, la seeya." That sounded
familiar, and then he remembered, *chair*. Why in the
world were they all talking about a chair? Maybe they
thought they should have offered him a seat. Later that
day one of his housemates, a fellow they called Chico
who was from La Joya, California, explained it to him,
"No Carl. Not *silla*. They're saying *La CIA*. C-I-A."

"What? They thought I was a CIA agent?"

"They think every gringo's a CIA agent. Even the
missionaries."

Carl did not understand. How do small-town folks
living in a remote area of a Central American jungle
know about the Central Intelligence Agency? There
was a certain history here, one that he was not privy to.
This ignorance picked at him each day he walked
through Poptún, and made him feel an emotion that he
had not allowed himself to feel for a long time: Doubt.
This was not good, for doubt led to dread, and dread,
with all its trappings, was a worthless and dangerous
sensibility.

Once, all he wanted was to nail the bastard Tekún
Umán. Now he wanted only Jessica. Fourteen days,
only two weeks since he last saw her; and yet those
were fourteen days during which the new life inside her
had grown, had developed more features, the embroidery of a heart valve, the weave of a thumbprint. Perhaps his son-to-be was already sucking his thumb: he
had seen that in Sandra's sonogram, when the tiny
creature pulled into itself, the thumb snug in its mouth.

Fourteen days. Two days until the raid, then five days of surreptitious travel to Texas, processing, paperwork, all in Dallas of course, a shake-down of their extradited fugitive. Staying focused was necessary. But at night, while he waited, sitting in his little bedroom, with the curtains of the glassless window barely moving for lack of a breeze, staying focused was impossible. All this seemed a logistic mistake.

But it was more than that. This was an emotional mistake. Carl should not have left home, should not have missed one day of his wife's pregnancy. That's what he thought, sitting here at a wooden desk, writing in a journal, drinking a shot of scotch: regret. He could be home now, helping Sandra with her spelling words, because she always has a spelling test on Monday. Sandra had been reading *Charlotte's Web*, so she could spell "salutations," but her teacher demanded more, had the whole class learn how to spell "agriculture" and "aggravate." That's the word Carl had been helping her with the night before he left. Sandra always wanted to spell it with an "i," "agrivate," "Just like the other word Daddy! Agriculture, agrivate, see?" He had laughed at that, just as he chuckled over it now, when the bee stung him in the nape of his neck.

A silent bee he thought, *a bee that makes no sound.* This is a jungle. Possible, he thought. He could think a lot, even as his body separated from itself, dropped itself atop the desk. The scotch spilled; its tumbler rolled toward the lamp.

The bulk weight of his chest pulled him over the desk's edge. Someone caught him. He felt the pressure of strong, bony hands under his armpits. "Careful there now, Agent Spooner," said a low voice into his ear from behind.

The legs do not work, nor the arms nor fingers;

not even the mouth, nor the cheek muscles; and not even the eyelids work, though the eyes, they seem to obey. They swirl one way, another, as if turning in a gyre of mud the size and depth of his entire body, looking for the voice that lays him out on the floor and calls him by name. This is not his body anymore, never was his body and he's just waking up to that fact, waking up into a nightmare where he cannot scream, not with this useless, frozen throat.

"So Carl Spooner. How's it going? Did you sell that split-level townhouse in Atlanta?" Tekún smiled down at him. "Oh by the way, don't worry about the paralysis. It's temporary. Lasts only twenty minutes or so. You'll pull out of it quickly. And with absolutely no side effects." He spoke like a promising doctor.

Tekún lay next to Carl, propping his head in his palm. "I know this means little to you and your colleagues, but the United Nations, along with the World Court, has declared extradition illegal. The next thing you know, that new Republican president of ours will be dragging Fidel out of Havana."

Tekún sat up, but kept talking in a low voice so that the agents in other rooms heard nothing. Carl heard everything Tekún said, about the Pinochet case, how even Spain had to deliver that dictator back into the hands of the Chileans. And he, Tekún, was no dictator; he was just a businessman in a business that showed no signs of diminishing, and the quicker Carl Spooner understood that, he said while unbuttoning Carl's shirt and pulling it back to expose the full of Carl's stomach, chest, his bellybutton, the better off we'll all be.

"Man, you work out, don't you?"

The Sorcerer's Apprentice fits perfectly in the palm, making it easy to twist the wrist in quick turns, for curves in letters, the belly of "d," the two swipes, pulled inward, that make an "O."

Though the Uruguayan elixir worked well, thoroughly, it could not stop the body from responding, even if only slightly, to entry wounds. "Easy now," said Tekún, his head directly over Carl's as he worked, just slightly bent over, writing.

"How are your girls, Sandra and Angie? A handful I bet. And one on the way. Isn't it time you considered family planning?"

The Sorcerer's Apprentice whispered through the cloth of Carl's jeans.

The Guarani of Uruguay, who use the elixir only on game, probably never pay any mind to the circular muscles around the eyeballs, the ones that rotate the sphere of sight, the same ones that squeeze up against the lacrimal gland, that make certain mammals weep.

It takes Tekún Umán about seven minutes to run a comfortable mile. It took twenty-four minutes for the elixir to wear out of Carl's blood. By the time the other agents ran into Carl's room, called in by the scream that lurched out of him, Tekún was a good two miles north of Poptún, running on a foot path known by the Q'eqchi'. As they cleaned Carl's wounds, and made out the word on his stomach, one that needed no translation (the "a" in *idiota* seemed superfluous), and as they checked Carl's blood soaked pants, ribboned from the blade, Tekún slowed his pace and knocked on the Land Rover's door. Beads unlocked the door. His boss climbed in. In thirty minutes he was in a private plane. Within the hour he entered Mexican airspace. His shipment traveled another route. "You've made things worse," said Beads, as if it were his duty to say so. To which Tekún responded, "No. I've made things clearer."

Three-headed Cerberus, monstrous and cruel,
Barks doglike at the souls immersed here, louder
For his triple throat.

The Inferno, Canto VI

SEPTEMBER, 2000

Sometimes the plans are simple. This time Bobby
needs few supplies: rope, a pit, duct tape, and a dog.

A sense of place. Technique. Actors. This is how
he sets it up, in his mind, before anything takes place.
He sees it clearly before anything has been done. He
must begin with the character, for the character is the
reason.

There are many characters here. Plenty to choose
from. This is a relief; at times he has wondered if the
right people will appear along the way. They always do.
For everywhere there are people, leaving a trail of sins.

This is not just a city; it is *the* city, the one with the
tower, alongside the river. It is all perfect, just as he had
routed it in the book and on the road map. It comes together clean, everything fits. True, the glass tower is
more Egyptian than he would like; but it is grand
nonetheless, and it points the way to the docks, where

ships wait, taking lovers and retirees and group rates up and down, from Dubuque to New Orleans.

The pyramid is a sports arena, not a temple of choice for him. Beyond the pyramid, in the center of downtown, he finds his players. The financial district. Small, in comparison to New York, even to Los Angeles. Still, there is activity here, the same desires, the very same sins. Here they gather, gluttons, spenders, hoarders all. They signal to one another with a click of wrists, the snapping of fingers, the high and low signals kicked over the floor. He watches them from above, from the glass room where tourists and other curious sit, watching as men and a few women make decisions on the floor, yelling choices and commands to someone ten heads away. They never look very happy. Stressed out, some would say. They are tired; yet here they are, every single work day, giving signals, staring up at the digital belt of red fractions and company symbols, hoping for a rise, a bull.

After several days of watching them, he sees something in them that they cannot see: they want relief. Confession is what they crave.

There is no hurry. There can't be. During down time, when the stocks close and all the workers in two hundred dollar warehouse suits head toward drinks, gyms, supper, Bobby trolls. He stays away from the usual tourist sites, such as Graceland and Beale Street, the self-proclaimed Home of the Blues. Bobby opts for icons off the worn path, such as the house on Audubon Drive, where the King lived before he made it big. It's a modest house, privately owned, a white-brick ranch style in a neighborhood near Audubon Park. A lone flamingo, pink, stands on one plastic foot that's sunk into the yard. Bobby leans up against the black wrought-iron fence, puts his foot atop the white brick that is the fence's foundation. He sings, *But I can't help falling in love with you.*

A young mother walks by, baby carriage before her. She smiles at him, at his singing. His is a good voice. A natural baritone, little strain.

The only time he goes to Beale Street is to follow some of the men who have left the Financial District for the day. Their favored hangout is a Blues Coffee House down from the Hard Rock Café. This will not do. He will have to get to know them, and from that, he will invite them to a quieter place.

They are many. Legion, he wants to say. Some gather in groups of five, way too many. He figures three is the apt number. Three can make for an inarticulate din.

There. Those three men. Always together.

After the second week of sitting in the booth, one of the three working the floor looks up at him. The man, a fellow in his late twenties, looks up and makes eye contact with Bobby. The man smiles; it is pitiful. This one, Bobby knows, is the most desperate among the bunch. His friends are in the small crowd, though from his perch, Bobby sees that the other two young fellows have worked in their own favor, loading the first boy down with lousy stocks. Dumping, in order to loosen themselves up from the weight and put their money to another purchase. This is not malice; it is simply the way of gluttons, hoarders, spenders.

Their names: Sam, with the pitiable smile; Larry, and Raymond. All young, late twenties, though Raymond looks like he's pushing into his thirties. Perhaps it's the paunch of Raymond's stomach that makes Bobby think this. Larry is the opposite. No doubt that, before making it to the floor at eight A.M., Larry has a thorough early morning workout at a local private gym. His chest and arms make curves in his J.C. Penney dress shirt. The only curve on Raymond is the growing circle above his belt line.

And yet it is Larry, the svelte one, who is the glutton. Larry, who buys quickly, sells quickly in order to buy more, getting rid of stocks like a bulimic teenager gets rid of food. Larry is insatiable, and thus, he never gains.

Raymond is the hoarder. He holds the goods for way too long, making sure no one on the floor takes what is his.

Then there's Sam, the loser. Sam the loner, though he doesn't know it, thinking the other two are his friends. Sam, who spends like a bad cliché, like there's no tomorrow; Sam, who jettisons stocks as quick as he gets them. Wasn't Sam the one who dumped a load of Fed Ex, and here, in that company's home city? Dumbass Sam, who's losing any sense of place in this world he has entered, in this third circle of pure incontinence.

Bobby takes them out for drinks in a quiet bar off of Beale. They wonder who he is, this man who is so prodigal with his cash, who pays for Sam's scotch, Larry's light beer, Raymond's two beers and refried potato skins. Sam's voice is as slight as his little body. It shakes, as if a wind through the bar's front door caught the strings of his lungs, "So Bobby, what are you doing, sitting up in the booth all day?"

"I study the movement." Bobby smiles. Then he explains, "I'm a personal financial consultant, my offices are in St. Louis. Most of my time I'm dealing with clients throughout the midwest and the south. But sometimes I pull back, pick a financially plugged-in city, go there, study what's happening. That's why I'm here now. Memphis is cooking. Sure, Fed Ex keeps the city hot in a bull run." He looks at Sam, whose eyes turn down. "But then you've got entities that at first might appear ancillary, like the Memphis Grizzlies. Every time they score a good season, watch the tickets on the street. Basketball and an international courier company. Tie that with tourism, Beale Street, Graceland, you've got one cooking city. You fellows are in a good place. So I visit a city like Memphis. And I ruminate. I do something that hardly anyone else in this business does: I meditate on the movement."

Larry eats while he talks. He's very good at it. "What, so you're up there in the booth, doing some damn zen-sitting?" he laughs, while he eats. He can do that too.

"Exactly, Larry. That's just what I do."

At first they are not sure; but then Bobby smiles, which gives them permission to laugh. They like Bobby. He's that easy to get close to.

He explains to them: the ways of the market may seem capricious, and in many solitary moments, they are. You never know: on a Friday the Nasdaq composite index may post a quarterly gain after four straight losing quarters; the following Monday Wall Street's bears attack this glimmer of hope with their grim outlooks on global recession, which leaves everybody scrambling to dump. Nothing helps: the Federal Reserve board slashes interest rates with abandon, the president offers a tax-rebate program; still, the bears will predict recession and doom.

He stops, takes a sniff, interrupts himself, "What's that cologne you're wearing?" he asks Larry.

It takes Larry a moment to respond, so caught up is he with Bobby's voice. "Oh. It's called *Hom*. It means 'the juice of the sacred plant of Persia.' Or something like that. Raymond here swore up and down it'd get me some thigh meat, but so far it hasn't worked."

The others laugh at this. Raymond makes a reference to a woman they work with, one who's so horny
she'd probably leave a trail like a snail if she didn't have
legs, but even she's not interested in Larry. Larry tells
his friends to fuck off. "Ignore them, Bobby. They're
assholes from the get-go. Just tell me, how do you
make your money?"

"He's trying to tell you how he makes his money,
Fatback," says Raymond. "You've got to get used to the
market's mood swings. Isn't that right, Bobby?"

"But it's more than mood swings," says Sam, finally
adding something to the conversation. "I mean, how is
it you become a consultant? You've got to have a reputation for knowing the market, don't you?" He looks to
Bobby for affirmation. "But it all seems, I don't know,
so whimsical."

It's not that whimsical, Bobby explains. Again, his
voice is low, a baritone that has a mesmerist's purr and
moves like a warm fog over their table. At one point
Sam thinks that the young girl serving them drinks, just
by approaching their table for another round, could fall
under Bobby's voice. Bobby tells them how you have to
study politics in order to know what's happening to the
market. But it's not that simple either. Did Clinton create the swelling of a bountiful economic time in the
nineties, or did he merely ride the wave? Will we go
into recession next quarter, depending on what happens with the current president's war on terrorism?
Follow the National Bureau of Economic Research,
the official arbiter of U.S. business cycles. Watch what
they watch: industrial production, manufacturing and
trade sales, employment, personal income. Which are
up, which have fallen? Watch out for the three big en-
gines: The United States, Japan, and Europe. If they're
standing idle at the same time, then global activity's go-

ing to suffer. Get knowledgeable about everything imaginable on Wall Street and Tokyo, just as Bobby has done in order to bring these three men together in this bar, each of them leaning over the table and listening to every articulate word that Bobby has to say concerning a business that he really doesn't care about.

"But then," he says, "you've got to study the floor."

He looks at each of them. What he means, of course, is you study the men on the floor. The ones making the hip-shot decisions, taking directions from someone over the ear-piece, watching the digital belt and signaling to a friend across the other end of the room. They are not peons, Bobby tells them; they are the troops that make this whole outfit work.

"Right," says Larry. "But if we're not peons, why is it everybody on the damn floor's looking to move up?"

Larry is the first to show his avarice. Avarice and gluttony; are they not cousins?

It is here where the conversation can begin to turn. They have worked all day; they have drink in them; they are hungry (even Raymond), and thus are just weak enough to be moved to what they thirst most for: the confession. Something we all crave, something Bobby is more than willing to give. He will find what these three need to say. Already he has some ideas. Larry wants a woman, Raymond seeks narcissistic perfection. Sam, he needs to escape the bubble of solitude that surrounds him. Bobby will learn more, as he takes them out for dinners, one at a time. He will hear them, learn the names of their parents, a brother, an uncle with groping fingers, lewd, embarrassed thoughts about an older sister, the first smoke of a joint, anything that will make them come closer, trust him. Then he will set them free.

The nearest Home Depot can supply him with only so much. He must look elsewhere for a dog.

He travels away from the city, through small towns like Collierville and Ripley. He drives into poverty: the trailer parks on county highways, the stucco Habitat for Humanity houses built three decades ago, made to last a good twenty years. It is not enough. More poverty awaits south, in the neighboring state of Mississippi. He drives the rental car through towns called Red Banks, Potts Camp, Ecru, all towns of few populations, agricultural, tobacco and tomato fields. Migrant workers bend over the crops next to the county highways. They never look up.

There are no accidents in his life. He drives through Oxford, salutes the bronze statue of Faulkner on a sidewalk. From here, he will leave a trail, the slightest map, read by one person only.

In small stores and on park benches he strikes up conversations. He says he's looking for guard dogs. Attack dogs, to be more specific. He's got some property he'd like to protect, a waste management facility (junkyard, he explains to them with a wink) up in Memphis that was recently robbed. What the thieves steal is not so important as the property damage they leave behind. The cost of highly trained guard dogs, he explains, is ludicrous; he knows that good folks such as themselves who have raised all sorts of animals, especially dogs, know just as much as a professional trainer who's bought a diploma at the veterinary school at the university.

The four men standing about in the country store in Hickory Flat, all of them over fifty, those who drink coffee in stained ceramic cups and a couple of them who smoke, understand his concerns. "What kinda dog you looking to buy?" asks the eldest gentlemen on the other side of the stall.

"German Shepherd maybe. Or perhaps something a bit more aggressive. Pitbull, Rottweiler. A dog that won't hesitate."

"Some dogs're born aggressive, but ain't none of them born mean."

All the men agree with this. They know dogs, just like they know most any mammal in the territory. Under the right hand, dogs can be made into something they are not.

"So is there anyone around here who's got the right hand?" Bobby smiles.

They mention a couple of names. Jimmy, down near Ecru, he's got some hunting dogs and a couple of Pits. Hank's got some dogs, but they're all German Shepherds, for fox hunting.

"But didn't Jimmy give away one of them Pitbull pups, to Blevins?"

They all remember, and they regret the memory. Jimmy owed money to Blevins over a card game. He paid Blevins in dog.

"Who is Blevins?" asks Bobby.

"Lives outside of Abbeville. Not far from here. Don't know if you want to meet him, son. He's been in and out of jail since the first President Bush."

Bobby laughed when they spoke of Blevins' jail record. Now he does not laugh. He does not know Blevins' world, the yellow and white trailer that is fairly new yet is already showing signs of wear, the weeds that grow in tufts around the trailer's corners, the metal spike with the empty chain in the front yard. The pole is in the middle of a dusty oval, made by an animal that has wrapped the chain around the iron spike, then, with constant practice, had learned to unwrap it. There is no dog. The place is not familiar, though something in the air is. It's Blevins. Bobby knows Blevins. He can see who Blevins is through the eyes of Blevins' daughter, that white girl, eleven, perhaps twelve, who sticks her head out the window. She has short blonde hair, straight. She has eyes that should not be on an eleven year old. In the back of her a television plays. They have satellite TV, the steel black satellite is bolted to the top of the trailer. He hopes she is eleven. Yet Bobby knows that age will make it all worse. The girl will grow, and her very growth will be her loss. Still, she looks nothing like Maggie. Nothing like Maggie.

"What you need?"

Blevins wears a white, buttoned shirt, brown pants that are worn but clean. He wears brown boots. His hair, though thinning, is well combed, held with a lotion, a mousse. It is quite blonde, as if he works under the sun. His skin also gives this away, tawny, on its way to being leathery, a tan that makes him handsome. His hands are in his pockets. His eyes do little work; they rest upon the world, hold the world down with an invisible weight. Though he is Bobby's height, Blevins, to Bobby, seems taller. Blevins will always be taller.

Bobby has many questions. Where do you work? Why do you dress like that, yet live in a trailer? And out here, away from everyone? Where is your wife? The girl's mother, where is she? Yet all these questions, these probings, make Bobby's mind shake, and with that shaking comes a shimmer that throws the nine circles of his world out of focus.

If there were a boy around, younger than the girl, then Bobby would fall. His knees would hit the ground, and he would shatter.

But there is no boy. There is no mother. That is why this is not familiar, why this is not his. Not just the poverty of the trailer, nor the used Dodge truck with the covered bed parked alongside Bobby's rented Camry. It is the absence of others that makes this unique, and allows Bobby to come out of the shimmer, awaken once again into clarity. He shakes the man's hand, introduces himself.

"I'm looking to buy a dog."

"What makes you think I got a dog to sell?"

This is a challenge. Yet it is the challenge of men who know they must take on anything that comes into their territory, especially another man. The question is an invitation to battle lightly, smell each other out, piss into the corners.

"I know you've got a dog," says Bobby, kindly, but clearly. A clatter of nerves erupts in his stomach, but he swallows it back. He motions to the spike in the ground, the slack, empty chain running from it in the dust. "And from the size of those links, I'd say it's a fairly big bitch."

Bitch. A word he'd never use. But his voice, his very language must change here.

Blevins barely smiles. "Not a bitch. Male. I put him out here at night. Daytime I put him in the shed."

"Sounds like a tame one, if you can move him around like that."

Blevins turns away, toward the shed, but his right eye stays on Bobby. "He's only tame with me." Then his eye pulls away with the walk toward the woods.

There is no mother. But yes, there is a boy.

The Pitbull is alone, no doubt as it has been all its life with Blevins. Pitbulls are social dogs, more at home in groups, families, siblings. Loneliness turns their innate energy another way. This one does not bark, even when Blevins enters the shed. "Wait here a sec," he says to Bobby, and shuts the door.

Through the thin gap between two boards, Bobby watches Blevins. The man does not hesitate, but walks directly over the hay and the dirt as if walking through the hallway of a home. The dog watches him. It does not pant. It does not open its mouth. It stares. This dog will not do; the men at the grocery store had it wrong. The dog is way too passive for what Bobby needs. Just look at the way Blevins snaps the chain to the dog's collar, the way the dog turns away, as if avoiding the man's eyes, the lack of words. Look at the new, short brown fur that has grown over the rivulets of scars along the dog's back. It is a broken animal; it is a boy, one that makes this entire scene familiar. Bobby's armpits burst a sweat, toss an acrid smell into the humid air.

Mississippi heat carries pheromones like tiny

steaks on tiny plates: wet air falls on a wet nose. It is a specific hormone, fear. Fear means protection and protection means either attack or flight and the dog knows this. "Come on in," says Blevins, but Bobby's odor floats in before him. Before he pushes his weight against the wood of the door the Pit has already launched. Bobby sees the dog midair, a leap that is perfect, that is power, one that propels that face and that bulky, muscular jaw forward, that shows Bobby fangs that do not hesitate, saliva that sprays. Then that guttural, wet roar, it too is familiar. It is all there; the dog is the boy.

The chain hitched to the back wall snaps tight. The dog plummets, hits the loose hay on the floor. Yet it does not yelp. There is no barking, for barking is weak, empty. The snarl is akin to meat being torn. Bobby stands at the doorjamb, held at bay. Blevins, his hands in his pockets, stands behind the dog. At times the chain slaps against his left leg, but he pays it no mind.

"This the kind of dog you need?" he says.

"Yes."

At that moment there is an understanding between the two men. For Bobby stands tall, while the dog snaps away at the air between them. Though the air is filled with his fear, it is an old fear; he no longer feels it. He negotiates with Blevins. Within a minute they have a price. They talk calmly to each other, as if the snarls were not there, like two parents ignoring a bratty, razor-wielding child.

Bobby says, "May I borrow your truck? I'll pay extra."

Again, they negotiate. Blevins knows Bobby will not go far, having that rental car here on his property. Bobby knows Blevins will not steal the rental, not

wanting to get involved with a man who has bought
such a dog. There are papers behind rental cars, a trail
of credit card numbers. And Blevin's isn't a Camry
man. He needs his truck. He needs money. One hundred dollars for twelve hours' use of the truck to carry
the dog away, plus a full tank of gas upon return.
Blevins doesn't say it, but he thinks it: you sure can't
beat that with a stick.

Blevins takes the chain and pulls the dog to the
truck. The Pit keeps snapping at the air in front of
Bobby, but he does it less; Bobby's skin doesn't throw
off the scent. Blevins makes the dog jump onto the
truckbed, then closes the gate. "Keep the little windows here open on the cover, else he'll cook." Blevins
shoves them open. The dog's snout pushes through the
one on the side; the wet nostrils suck in air. The curiosity is too much, even for Blevins, "How you going to
get him out, without him tearing you up?"

"We'll be fine."

It's too curt an answer. Blevins' eyes load up.
"You'll be fine. Right. You open this door, the first
thing it goes for is the neck. It knows the neck is the
weakest spot on a man, besides his dick. You'll be just
fine."

Bobby looks down, toward the oval dirt of the dog's
old running ring. The shimmer begins again, a confusion of two worlds, two ways of thinking, one old, the
other the present. When this happens, he almost thinks
in old ways, in ways that most of us are familiar with: he
wishes he could kill Blevins, as if killing this stranger
who has, in an hour visit, become too familiar, would
have ended all this, would have laid down some peace
somewhere in his head.

But the old ways of thinking are the destructive
ones: down that path leads death and chaos. He used to

ask why all this has happened to him; but that was a useless question, one that neither he nor Maggie could answer.

Maggie in the window. Little girl with blonde hair, with eyes that should not be hers.

Bobby has made too many decisions. The choices, they were what cleared up the shimmering before. The nine circles, one inside the other, spiraling all the way into the pit; *they* make sense.

Farther north, just above Memphis and near Meeman Shelby Forest, Bobby opens the back of the truck and pulls the Pitbull out by its hind legs. The dog is limp, his eyes closed. The Promethazine Hydrochloride he rubbed into the raw steak, then punched into the middle of the meat, has taken full effect; the dog will sleep well, for several hours. It will wake up to three bowls of water, all of which it will drink upon waking.

It's the winding dirt roads that make for this isolation: this old, large shed, once used for storing canned goods and dried meat for a family that lived and died out here seventy years ago, is a good half hour away from any home. There is a good fishing hole nearby, which concerns him. But as many times as he's come out here on hikes in the past month, he's never run into any other soul. It's a beautiful location; he's not seen so many dogwoods and poplars all in one place.

It took him some time to dig out the pit in the middle of the shed's dirt floor. Then again, three days of digging a well that's fifteen feet deep and six feet wide made for a full workout. His back ached, which helped him see which muscles to focus on the next time he went to the gym. He used a hatchet against the poplar roots that crisscrossed the earth. He became agile at filling the large buckets, climbing the rope tied to one of the shed's thick rafters, then hauling the buckets out with their own ropes. He tossed the dirt outside, next to the door.

Now he is careful, placing the drugged Pitbull over his shoulder, lowering himself and the dog into the pit. He lays the dog on its side. He pets it, whispers to it as if he's known it all its life. Naming it makes this all complete, "Easy, Cerberus," he says, "easy now." He takes off its collar, puts on a new one, with three words scratched into its leather.

He pours water from a canteen into three metal bowls. Then he climbs the rope and walks to the truck.

"Here kitty. Come here now."

The brown tabby has tried to hide under the truck's seat. It's still frightened, even though the drugged Pit quit growling miles back. Bobby coaxes the cat with Meow Mix. He picks it up carefully, strokes its back. Bobby sits on the passenger seat of the truck. As the cat calms and sits on his lap (it's still confused: the smell of Pit on Bobby's shoulders, the waft of food in his palm), Bobby adds one more odor to the mix. From the glove compartment he pulls a tiny bottle: *Hom.* Just two slight sprays, over the cat's back thighs. The cat eats.

Bobby strokes him, carries him to the shed, drops him into the fifteen foot shaft. The cat lands on all fours, right atop the Pit's flank, then leaps to a far corner. For now the Pit sleeps.

MARCH 2, 2001

Weeks had passed. I had kept busy with my investigation of Tekún's whereabouts, and then at night, while Sergio was asleep and my mother read a novel in bed, I was busy on the computer.

I was healed now, though to talk with Mamá Celia, you'd think differently. I could tell she was pissed at me, though at first I wasn't sure why. She moved toward the subject matter indirectly, which wasn't always her way. Since she had checked me out of the hospital six weeks ago, she had been more careful with me. The scar on my neck was it: she didn't want to disturb me anymore, didn't want to hurt me in some way. I missed her directness. But the more my neck healed and formed the thick Keloid scar, the more she approached me with caution, like a stranger.

She could beat around the bush only so long.

"You certainly spend a lot of time behind that little

machine," she finally said one night. "What's so interesting about it?"

"Oh, just web surfing."

Though we spoke in Spanish, I used the English term, which she did not understand. "I'm just flipping through the Internet," I explained. "It's fun. Like changing television channels. You see all sorts of crazy things in here."

"So interesting that you keep notes?"

She pursed her lips and, in Salvadoran style, pointed them toward the yellow notepad next to the laptop. There were a good ten pages of paper folded back, all filled with pencil markings, sentence fragments. I moved to cover the notes; but she had already seen the words. She knew what, or rather who, I was looking for. And it wasn't Tekún Umán.

Mamá said nothing more. She walked away, grabbed a copy of *El amor y otros demonios*, and retired to her bedroom.

Two days later she picked up the conversation. "You don't read as much as you used to."

This sounded like a scold from childhood. Yet it wouldn't have been my childhood; Mamá never had to reprimand me for not reading. If anything, she had to remind me to close a book, get outside, breathe some fresh Atlanta-air, play with the kids in the barrio.

"I'm reading," I said. My voice clipped itself. "Just not books, not now."

Then she did something to show me how much I was missing, how much I did not see. She set the bottle of whiskey on the table in front of me. The oily liquid, which filled the bottle half way, sloshed; that's how hard she set it down.

With that, she became the Celia Chacón who I've

always known and loved, the one who could piss me off quicker than anybody alive. "We need to talk," she said.

She sat down. The hairs on the back of my head raised, which, I knew, meant that my skin was tightening. A muscle was pulling back there, preparing me for defense, to take on my mother. It pulled so tight, I wondered if my beloved Keloid would get hauled back to my hairline, maybe disappear. That'd be a hell of a neat trick.

"You come home after a full day's work of I don't know what. You barely eat, barely talk with your son. You certainly don't play with him anymore. Then I get him to bed, and when I come out of his room you're behind this bottle and that *jodida* computer and I can't get one sentence out of you."

It was not like her to curse. She always reprimanded me for using words such as *jodido*, Salvadoran for "fucked up." She was mad. But so was I. "This is my home, you know. I can spend my time the way I want."

"Looking for someone who you'll never find? Aren't you the one who once told me how impossible it is to find a serial killer?" She turned away. Those were tears she tried to hide. We both thought of her other daughter, the woman who used to zip through our lives loudly, who was the smarter one, funnier, who made outlandish statements before our mother about men's small penises and inflated egos and her desire to be a lesbian, only to get a laugh from *doña* Celia. Catalina had gone against the first child syndrome. You'd think she was the youngest brat of the house, the one who always got away with everything. That was supposed to be my job, not that I was ever resentful about it. Caty never let me get too pissed at her, but chided me until I came around, laughing. She made us all laugh. She made us loud. In death she had left a silence in our home, no matter where we moved. Sometimes I wanted to blame Catalina for the silence. For even though my mother walked through this world like the Salvadoran posterchild of survival, having lived through Death Squads, INS raids, widowhood, and the murder of a daughter, I knew how much all that had shaped her. She was a good mother, always had been; she was a grandmother any child would want. But she had become too clear in her answers, her way of thinking, as if clarity, a certain orthodoxy on the suffering of life, kept her sane. She still felt pain, still turned away and, momentarily, tried to hide. And yet she could turn back and show me her Salvadoran core, the hot, enraged blood of Central America, "You're not doing yourself, or anybody else, any good. And God bless your father's soul, Romilia, but you're drinking more than he did."

That did it. "If you don't like the way I'm living my life, Mamá, maybe you should move back to Atlanta. You've never liked Nashville anyway."

This was a mistake, for she had an answer, "Believe me, daughter, I would, except if I did, my grandson would be lost."

I was a creature of habit: my house and car keys were always placed, at the end of the day, on the small wooden table next to the door, where an old plaque of the Sun God of Teotihuacán stood. My coat hung on the second bolt of the coat rack. Both of these I could grab quickly, without stumbling or dropping the notepad. Neither the anger nor the alcohol could keep me from walking out quickly, almost soberly, from the house. All I heard was the *"Ay hija, no te vayas vos,"* but then the door, flung behind me, slammed hard against the intimacy of that Spanish.

I left the house before *la propaganda* began. Even Mamá called it that: *propagandizar*, to indoctrinate someone, an old, vibrant word from a past world of guerrillas and armies. She laughed about it; but she was also dead serious about it. Mamá had a way of making sure I never forgot who we were, *guanacos*, Salvadoreños, people of the tiniest country in Central America, *la gente industrial*, harder working than those neighboring Nicaraguans, more focused than the Panamanians. And don't get her started on the Mexicans. I once dated a young guy named Raul from Monterrey whose jawbone was like a sculpted rock but whose accent Mamá picked out in a second. She accused me of seeing Raul just to spite her, and of course she was right. Raul and I didn't last, even with that hard jaw that matched the rest of his body. Of course, his family had fed him a headful about Central Americans as well.

In the car I punched through five radio stations before settling into Queen's *Another One Bites the Dust*. That song got me all the way to Charlotte and Seventeenth, where a new coffee shop, Serious Grounds was still open. A young white woman standing in a crowd of young, good looking men and women (all of them Vanderbilt students, no doubt) looked at me slamming the steering wheel with my open palm to the song's beat. She was one of those blonde beauties with silicontucked tits and retro-eighties hair. No cuts on her skin. I sang right at her. She turned away.

A pissed-off Latina woman in Nashville, wearing the latest in slit throats. Surely one scary-looking bitch.

The music in Serious Grounds pulled the mood another way, though it didn't lose momentum. A piece by Palmieri. Some good jazz. Very good. Strong coffee sounded good.

And just like that, away from the house, out here, in a coffee shop whose very air smelled like sobriety, I considered my mother. She was probably right. I'd have to rethink the Wild Turkey every night. Shit.

The Palmieri changed to Miles Davis' *Sketches of Spain*, though I didn't notice until well into my second cup. There were three of us in the coffee house. A young man named Tony sat at a small, round table, working at a laptop. He was a regular, just like me. He looked up at me, saluted, then returned to his short story or article or whatever other piece of literature he meant to sell. Which of us was the more obsessed, Tony with his short story, or me, with my pad of notes?

The notes. An entire yellow notepad, filled with information I had collected from the Internet. As many times as I had gone over them, I failed to see how the three murders were connected to the same killer. The FBI was holding out on the general public, not showing us all their information. Bristol, Atlanta and now Memphis. Since the leak about the Memphis killings, the Feds had referred to the three-city connection as tenuous. Earlier reports and clues pointed to a possible linking of the sites and the victims, but as the investigation continued, they could not be so sure. "These could be random acts of violence, ones that have no relationship with one another whatsoever," said one agent in Memphis.

There was reason to believe this. What did a child day care manager and her husband in east Tennessee, a graduate student and her boyfriend in Atlanta, and three young Wall-Street wannabees in Memphis have in common?

I knew these people much more than anyone should. Both their deaths and their lives. Steve and Eileen Masterson had opened their SafeWorld Daycare ten years ago in Bristol. According to the newspapers, SafeWorld wasn't as safe a world as they claimed. Within their first year of business, Bristol Police arrested Steve, thirty-four, on three counts of possible sexual molestation.

The couple ran SafeWorld out of their home in a quiet middle class white neighborhood of Bristol, on the Virginia side of town. The Mastersons were true entrepreneurs: while Eileen ran the daycare, watching over twenty and, as her business flourished, thirty dropped-off kids at a time, Steve built websites for individual clients throughout the country. Many times he was on the road, attending internet conferences in the midwest and in Florida. When he was home, he holed himself up in a small, windowless office upstairs, while the children played in the upgraded, air-conditioned basement. Whenever Eileen needed a break or just had to separate the kids into smaller groups to better manage them, Steve was more than happy to leave his computer and play, sometimes taking one of the more rowdy kids into his office to show them a computer game. Bailey, age four, a boy with red hair and eyes as green as pine needles, had been taught to say words that most of his preschool classmates did not know, such as *penis*, *anus*, *inappropriate*, and *No!* That *No!* stopped Steve, then echoed out of the computer room all the way to Bailey's parents, who did not hesitate to call the police. Once Bailey's *No!* hit *The Bristol Harold Courier*, Janice's and Lila's parents came forward. The families' lawyers promised that the children's separate testimonies were enough to convict Steve and shut down Eileen's business. Under a harsh cross-examination, the police learned that Eileen knew about her husband's craving for children. Yet she not only kept the daycare open but continued to have children visit Steve's computer room. They arrested her for complicity. The media frenzy kept Bristol in a perpetual shock: a woman opens a daycare to feed her husband's pedophilic tendencies. SafeWorld was a harvest house. No one in the Tri-Cities thought it could get any worse, that the shame and the horror could mount, until the morning the city woke up to the bloodstains on the Masterson's bedroom wall, the ribboned bodies of Eileen and Steve, their wrists tied to the bedposts, their bodies tossed off the bed, hanging toward the floor. A broken cola bottle, its thick, sharded ends stained with the couples' blood, lay on the bed. It had clear fingerprints on its neck, a complete palm print, locked into the dried blood. The prints matched no one on record.

Each time I read over the notes of the Masterson

murders, I could only think that this was no whisper of a killing. It was an enraged scream.

I followed my trail of notes to Atlanta. The coffee helped me read through the pages regarding my sister's death. The whiskey had helped to quell the sick anger I felt, about my sister being connected to the deaths of a pedophile and his consenting wife. Yes, my sister had been in an affair with a married man. We all knew that. The papers and television news told everyone. Sometimes I wondered if I had really given up on the shame behind that knowledge, as I had once said to the reporter from *The Atlanta Constitution*, when I was still in college. There's my quote, "Is it anybody's damn business who my sister slept with?" I still agreed with myself, though that edgy thought, *What if she hadn't been sleeping with Jonathan? Would she still be alive?* still rolled in my head.

Similarities in the two cases: the killer, in both circumstances, entered through a window. He had cut the glass pane in Catalina's apartment, then easily flipped the window lock. In the Masterson home, he had jimmied the window pane and entered. He had probably entered the homes beforehand, while the victims were out, and had hid somewhere in the house, waiting for them. The victims were tied to beds. He had to have kept them at bay, which means he may have held them at gunpoint or with a knife; and he must have had one tie up the other. Eileen Masterson's bound wrists were tied with a clumsy square knot, while Steve Masterson had been bound most efficiently with tight slip knots. Duct tape on their mouths, left there after the killing. The cola bottle was from their own kitchen. The killer had tapped the bottom off on the hard edge of their formica countertop, had left the broken bottom on the floor.

In Atlanta, Catalina Chacón and Jonathan Grassey, tied together, forced to make love, then javelined.

I ordered another coffee. Tony, the writer, smoked. I borrowed a cigarette from him. He lit it for me. I hadn't smoked since college. It took little time to relish the hit.

Then the three young men from Memphis, killed last autumn. Found in an abandoned shed in a deep woods north of the city. Three men tied upside down by their ankles, hanging together from the same rafter, their hands bound in the small of their backs, and their bodies dropped into a deep hole in the dirt floor, where a starved Pitbull stood. The dog had killed two, having gripped them tight at the neck, crushing their throats. The third man, the one named Raymond Price, had a clean slice through his neck, halfway decapitating him.

I left the coffee alone. It turned cold. I borrowed another cigarette from Tony. Smoking kept me from rubbing the scar.

When three boys from a nearby town found the bodies, the dog was not in the hole. All they found were three dead men with white maggots moving like curtains in and out of their skins. It was the smell that had stopped the boys from fishing that day.

But there was no dog. The Memphis Police found the dog buried behind the shed, in a shallow grave about fifty feet away.

On the bodies the forensic entomologist found evidence of the birth of a generation of blowflies: empty pupae casings, where the larvae had metamorphosed into adults. The casings revealed the birthing process of one generation, which takes seven days to complete. There was more than enough blood at the site to bring on the larvae immediately after death. The fishing boys found the bodies on September twenty-ninth, which meant the men had been killed on or near the twenty-second.

Sodium phenobarbitol in the dog's blood. A veterinarian's common drug to put an animal down. They sleep, then die.

Sometimes I mumbled aloud, "'Also slight, inert traces of Promethazine . . .'"

When the Federal agents cut down the bodies, they found bruises all throughout the victims' chests, their foreheads and shoulders, and some on their legs. They looked as if someone had beaten them with a light stick. Then a detective figured they had beaten themselves: hanging upside down like that, their hands tied behind, and panic running through them, their bodies had swung like weighted balls on strings, banging against one another while lowered into the pit. Of course they could not scream; the duct tape on the dirt floor and the matching glue on their mouths proved that.

Prints lifted from the Crime Scenes in Atlanta and Memphis rang no bells in Washington: the Automated Fingerprint Identification System had nothing to match. Nor did any prints match with the few left in Bristol. These last two killings were carefully planned.

The Mastersons were charged for crimes. My sister was no criminal, though she had broken someone's moral code. These three men, what had they done? Stockbrokers. What could be more legal, more boring?

Over at his small, round table, Tony closed up his laptop, drank the last of his coffee. He headed home. As he passed by he placed the pack of cigarettes on the table. He smiled. Nice face, though a little old for me. And the smile looked sincere. I thanked him, reached for another one. The taste of the first two was still in my mouth. Whiskey, black coffee, and now, cigarettes;

you wouldn't guess I was the type of woman to work out daily in a gym, pressing free weights and meaning to strip the gears on a Stairmaster. The moment I got cut and had to spend weeks in physical therapy, I went from Workout Queen to Oral Fixation Girl in one night. All because of a scolding mother.

No. That wasn't true. The whiskey had come on before *doña* Celia had. The cigarettes were just a natural follow-through. I couldn't blame her for where I was. And Tony's kind smile must have been born in pity: no doubt I looked like shit.

The coffee, however, helped me scan one more time through the notes, which helped me see something I had not seen before: where had the dog come from? According to my notes, there was nothing on the dog's kennel life, if it had lived in a domestic situation, or if it was a trained attack dog, nothing.

A dog that rips the throats out of bound men has a history. But the FBI had said nothing about it. Hadn't they followed through with the Pitbull?

"Sometimes I wonder if they care," I muttered. I reached for the cigarettes. Then I thought better of it. Or perhaps it's more precise to say, right then I started to think better. Besides, Serious Grounds was getting ready to close. I was the last customer. I said goodnight to the proprietress, took Charlotte Avenue to the middle of the city, headed back to Germantown. I walked into my quiet house, walked past my mother's room. She was asleep, Garcia Marquez's book spread over her chest. I turned off her light. I almost woke her, but thought it better to wake early the next morning, surprise her with breakfast, surprise her with a kiss on the cheek and an apology and a good *sobremesa* before I headed to the office. Maybe I'd call in late for work. Maybe we'd sit and drink coffee (though my stomach burned with caffeine now) and make the amends that were common in our lives, more common than the arguments.

For now I found my boy's room. He was asleep, with a Powerpuff stuffed doll (*Which one is she? Buttercup? Blossom? And is he in love with her?*) under his arm. I undressed to my underwear, pulled over to his side. Mamá probably wouldn't approve, a mother in her bra and panties, snuggled up to her son, face to sleeping face. But I'd remind her that he was the only man in my life I could trust. The coffee in me just couldn't hold up to the tranquil rhythm of his breaths. His closed eyes mesmerized me for a long time, as did his smooth cheek, his lips. I barely remember, before drifting off, considering the idea of not just calling in late tomorrow, but sick.

Making amends with my mother did not mean giving up on this case.

"You're going where?" she asked.

"Memphis."

"When?"

"This weekend."

"And why? To look for a *chucho?*"

"No, the dog's dead. I'm looking for its previous owner."

We had made up our differences. Morning has that way, burning away the anger of the night before. By the time Sergio got up, pulled off his wet night diaper, peed, dressed and climbed up to the breakfast table, we were talking about her latest Márquez novel ("It's about this girl in the sixteenth century, in Colombia. They think she's been bitten by a rabid dog. But she's just in love"). Sergio had migrated to my lap, and was chewing on a piece of sweet bread, when I brought up my trip to Memphis.

"I thought you just said you were over all this."

Funny, how a mother can interpret a daughter's words. I had to correct her, "No, Mami, I said I was sorry about last night, and that you were right about," and I shepherded Sergio off my lap, allowed him to go turn on the television, "you know, about the drinking. I've just been down about this," I half-pointed to my neck, "but I'll pull out of it. And I won't be playing with the computer so much. A waste of time, really." Then I leaned over the table, over my coffee, "But Mami, I never said I'd give up on Catalina."

She turned away with a clearly pitched *Ay*, said nothing more, then turned back. Sergio walked by, opened a drawer next to the stove, pulled out a small package and headed back toward the living room. I stopped him. "What's this, *mi vida*?" I asked, taking the package from him.

"*Piedrecitas*," he said. He already had a piece in his mouth, sucking it. Little gravels, also known as Salvadoran Rock Candy. I opened the bag. The small, clear crystals lay in a loose pile of sugar granules.

"Oh Sergio," I said, "this stuff's nothing but tooth decay. Come on, spit it out."

"Where did you find it?" my mother asked him. She seemed most innocent.

"Where you put it, *abuelita*," and he pointed, with his lips, toward the drawer next to the oven.

"*Ay*, you're faster than a rabbit," she said, smiling. She took him and put him on her lap. "Always getting to the goodies before I can stop him." She tickled him hard. He belted a laugh. She smiled. Then she turned to me, sighed. "Just call me when you get there, please?"

• • •

There are three hours of Interstate Forty between Nashville and Memphis. Plenty of time to play with my scar.

It was a new habit, rubbing my middle finger on the tip front end of the scar. There was a thin lump there, one that I could feel, like a tiny nerve that stuck out from underneath the Keloid. Rubbing it was my way of trying to erase it. These days I gave people I talked with my right profile, never looking at them head-on, but turning just to their side, hiding the false nerve of the cut. Either that, or I kept busy flicking the full weight of my hair over the left side of my neck. It was more than aggravating. The movements around my neck became something I had to fashion my life around: my driving, eating, the way I spoke with my boss, the way I tried to hide the scar from Sergio. Only with my mother could I rest: I could look her straight in the face, somehow, and not think about the cut.

When she wasn't around, I thought about Wild Turkey.

"That's enough, girl," I said while walking across a gas station parking lot in Jackson. Across the street stood a liquor store. I shut the door quick and drove off.

My hands: they had to keep busy. My silent coffee buddy, Tony, from Serious Grounds, helped out. I pulled his half a pack of filtered cigarettes from my purse. That old lighter in the Taurus still worked.

My mother would not approve. But perhaps, once she saw how little I fiddled with the scar, she'd cut me some slack.

Looking for the dog's owner was more than a long shot; it was a desperate attempt to put a face on my sister's killer. But this was my time, the weekend, and I could spend it any way I wanted to. This would not happen every weekend, I had promised Mamá. I had even offered to bring Sergio with me. But she didn't care for that idea. "I'm sorry, *hija*. Knowing his mother is a policewoman is enough. He doesn't need details." She kept him at home. She had plans to help set up a carnival that a local church in west Nashville was having on Sunday, a fund raiser to benefit one of the county's drug rehabilitation facilities. Sergio would go with her, play with the other kids while she and the adults set up the water dunking games, the huge bounce-castles, the duck shoots. That, I knew, would be much more fun for Sergio than listening to me badger some local Memphis cops.

And badger them I would. Why wasn't there more information on the dog? A dog with a history, a dog who had looked into the eyes of my sister's killer.

"You should have just stayed home, Detective," said the cop at the front desk of Memphis' main station downtown. "TBI has the files on the Shelby Forest case."

"Shelby Forest?"

"The bodies of the three men were found in a shed near the park, just a few miles from the Mississippi River." His name was McDaniels. He was older, with a little gray hair. He was nice enough, but he didn't look me much in the eye, nor the neck. "Memphis PD was called in because the three men were from here. But like I said, TBI knows more than we do."

The Tennessee Bureau of Investigation. In Nashville. This, he thought, was a waste of time, coming down to Memphis. "Was there anybody on your watch involved with the case?"

He picked up his phone. "I'll see if Darla's here. She was the blue who tied the ribbons at the crime scene." He called, talked with Darla, hung up. "Back near the window facing the Sports Arena. Best view in the house."

Darla stood from her desk, shook my hand, smiled. McDaniels was right. When she turned, Darla could see the glass, triangular Sports Arena, just north of her window. "Pleasure to meet you, Detective," and that seemed very sincere, with a sense of awe, in fact. "I kept up with the entire Jade Pyramid Case. Some amazing work there."

I thanked her, then asked the obvious, as there was a copy of Hans Gross' *Criminal Investigation* on her desk, well thumbed, "Are you interested in Homicide?"

"Yeah, sure am." She offered me a seat. "Gross' work is dated, but it's fascinating."

"He was the first guy to form a system of investigation. He turned it into a science."

We talked about Gross' theories for three, four minutes. She turned the conversation, "You know, I wouldn't mind chewing your ear about how you brought that killer down. You in Memphis long?"

"For the weekend."

Her eyes lit up: perhaps an invitation to dinner or a cup of coffee was coming my way. This was good: having her automatic respect before I had even come through the door would help get some questions asked. She was about my age, and still in blue; this could have created jealousy had it not been for the success of my last case. I was also Latina, and she African American. Again, yet another factor to consider here, in the South: one ethnic minority making it before the other. Yet Darla did not act pulled one way or another by that.

She told me about the Shelby Forest case, how they had been called in to canvass areas where the men had lived. "I never saw the bodies, but I read all the reports. A god-awful way to die."

"What did you learn from the canvasses?"

"Not much. Just the guys' lifestyles. They were in that yuppie world, you know, financing. It was the first time we ever did a DNA dragnet. Swabbed just about every mouth in their three neighborhoods. Didn't have any problem until we starting Q-tipping the victims' coworkers downtown. Then they called in the ACLU, and that was that."

DNA dragnets had finally come to Memphis. Used all over Europe, the practice hadn't settled as well in the States. The idea was simple: take DNA samples from every single person you can who may have a connection to the victims. It's a long, expensive process of elimination. Cops go around with boxes of cotton swabs, taking samples of people's saliva, rubbing them onto tiny plastic matting. It's that simple, until the watchers of Civil Liberties get a whiff of it.

I didn't care for the practice, but not because of civil liberties. Dragnets are the shotguns of investigation: you're just hoping you spread enough buckshot to hit somebody.

"What do you know about the dog?" I asked.

"Just that it was buried outside the shed, with mud packed into his mouth. It was drugged to death."

"Why do you think the perp did that?"

She engaged: a homicide cop was asking her opinion. And she had one. "Well, he put the dog to sleep. Didn't shoot or cut it. It was a 'kind' way of dealing with it, you could say. I think the perp liked the dog. I don't get the mud in his mouth."

"Was the dog male or female?"

"A male, I believe. Yeah. Popeye, yeah."

"Any idea where it came from?"

"No."

"And what about . . . wait, what did you call it? Popeye?"

"Yeah. That was the dog's name."

"How do you know that?"

She looked quizzically at me. "It was on his collar."

"The dog had a collar. And a name?"

"Sure did. Scratched right on the leather band."

"Not a little nameplate?"

"No. I thought that was weird too."

So did I.

"And they never found the dog's owner. Where did they search?"

"I think they canvassed the area around the murder scene, all the little towns around there. Nothing. Then they came around Memphis, checked into dog training schools in the area. There are a couple of guard dog camps here. The owners of the camps weren't too pleased. Said that this sort of killing just lends itself to the prejudice against guard dogs."

"Well, he *did* rip the victims' necks open."

"A true guard dog won't do that, unless it's being attacked. These boys were hanging from their ankles. I think the dog was abused and trained to kill like that."

I wanted to see the dog's collar. She gave me the address to the Memphis offices of the FBI, on Humphreys Boulevard, then showed me on a map how to get there. This was a Friday, which I had taken off in order to get a head start on my weekend. The Feds' offices would still be open until five. Then came the invite: she got off at five, and knew a good barbecue joint on Beale Street, and did I like the Blues? We agreed on six o'clock.

The FBI tries to maintain good relations with local police departments. This always helps whenever a case comes up and it's questionable on whose ground it falls, federal or local. Local Homicide gets upset whenever the Feds come in, muscling into the work we've already done. Who can blame us?

The Memphis Feds were housed in a cumbersome building of glass and brick, jutting up from a grove of evergreens. I got through the front door with little difficulty. The fellow at the front desk of Suite 300 balked, but once I showed him my badge and identification, he softened a bit. "Nashville. A little out of your backyard, aren't you?"

"Just a little."

"So what is it you want to see?"

"I'd like to check the evidence bags for the Shelby Forest Murders."

"That was Agent Burkett's call. He worked with Memphis PD on it. At first they took it as a local killing, but then they tied it to that Whisperer fellow."

"Any idea why they did that?"

"You'd have to ask Agent Burkett." He reached for the phone. The way he phrased his words to Burkett, I could tell I had the front desk man in my court, "There's a Homicide detective here to see you, sir, has some information on Shelby Forest."

An all-out lie. I was looking for information. But this young fellow knew I wouldn't get in without having something to offer. I could turn his lie into a certain truth: I *did* have something, though not necessarily a clue. I had an offering that hopefully would draw sympathy: that I was a Homicide Cop because of the perp who Burkett sought.

Burkett looked young, barely in his thirties. That surprised and bothered me: why had local Feds put such a young guy on such a big case? Were they that stretched? Still, he was pleasant enough. He saw through the front desk's lie, then kindly yet directly asked, "So how can I help you, Detective?"

I told him, to mollify his suspicions, "Catalina Chacón, the Whisperer's second victim? She was my sister."

That got me into his office. We talked awhile, though I was in a hurry to get to the Evidence Room. He allowed for that, though hesitantly. "I'll have to go with you. The dog collar is there. No offense, but we just can't have outsiders going to Evidence without one of us with them, even law officers."

He called ahead, asked for them to pull the bags on the case, then said to tag-out the dog collar. "This way," he said, standing from his desk, opening the door for me.

Just like in our own Evidence Room in Nashville, I had to sign the tag on the collar, then date it, all this after showing my credentials. The collar had already been dusted for fingerprints; according to its long Evidence Tag, it had also been checked for fibers and hairs, both canine and human. Burkett talked as I took the bag, but at first I did not hear him. The moment I unzipped the plastic, the faint smell of leather, fresh, hit my nose. It did not smell of dog. A bit of dirt, miniscule clods of earth, collected in a corner of the plastic bag. Dirt, I presumed, from the grave where they had found the dog. And I smelled that as well, the stale resonance of dirt. But the odor of leather was much stronger.

Burkett read from a file that came with the tagged collar. "Let's see, we didn't get any fibers from the collar. Only a couple of hairs from the dog itself. Then of course there's the name burned on the collar. We tried everything, but couldn't make heads or tails from it."

The moment I read the entire name, I could see why they were thrown. Darla had been partly right:

Popeye lay dying

I smiled; I hoped Burkett wouldn't see my smile. There was a rush of thought that took my head, a torrent. I love torrents. Especially the ones that whip through you during a case, meaning to rush you right up next to the killer's side.

I asked, "Did you run the phrase through your database?"

"Of course. Lots of references to the cartoon character, Spinach, Olive Oyl, that sort of thing. Which got us into some gourmet cooking websites. The fact that he lies dying, well, it's the dog. It's dead. Nothing much we could use."

"Any cross references you could try?"

Burkett looked at me, glanced over to my left. I figured he was ignoring my scar, which, again, I covered with my hair. "There was nothing to cross reference it with." He looked back at me.

That was fine. I was ready to leave. This was a bit scary, so sure was I about the flood of possibilities. I had to see Darla. We handed the evidence bags back to the clerk, walked to the front of the building, toward the lobby. "Thanks so much for your help, Agent Burkett." I shook his hand. He seemed truly sincere when he said he was sorry he couldn't help me more, though he promised to stay on the case. That was sorrow in his eyes; had he seen pictures of my sister? If so, he had seen the resemblance between her and me. His sorrow may have been enough to blind him from the hope I now felt, the one that may have made my smile too thankful, too ostentatious.

I waited until our beers came to tell Darla, "The dog's from Mississippi. Near Oxford."

She dipped a breadstick into some hot barbecue sauce, careful not to spill it onto her green blouse. She looked much more soft out of her blue uniform. Men walking by noticed her. More than they noticed me. She smiled at me. "Now tell me how you figured that," she said.

I leaned onto the table, and began telling her about my love for Gabriel García Márquez. "That's one old man I wouldn't kick out of bed." I had to take a roundabout way toward my theory, telling Darla how sexy and political and surrealistic García Márquez was. Then I noticed I was losing her. She got that glazed look others get when I start a roll about Gabo. "Anyway . . . Márquez has always been a big Faulkner lover. So, of course, I read everything Faulkner wrote. Did you know García Márquez's first novel, *Leafstorm*, is a replica of Faulkner's *As I Lay Dying?*"

The title pinged through her. "Yeah, I read that in college. *Lay Dying* . . ."

I waited just a moment for that to sink in. "And it so happens that Popeye is the main character in Faulkner's *Sanctuary.*"

"'Popeye lay dying . . .' Wait a minute . . ." The images shimmered through her, in and out of focus. She understood, but wasn't sure. "So you think the Whisperer has some thing for Faulkner?"

"Maybe. But it tells us a couple of things: The Whisperer is a reader. He's smart. And, he wants to be followed. He's giving messages to the world."

"I don't get it."

I told her about the smell of leather that puffed out of the plastic evidence bag. "The collar had been in that bag for seven months. The plastic contained the odor: it still smelled like new. The dog hardly had worn it. The killer must have bought the collar just to put that message on the dog."

"So you think the killer got the dog in Mississippi."

"Not only that. I'd bet you dinner he got it some-where close to Oxford. That's where Faulkner lived. It makes sense: they found traces of Promethazine in the dog's blood stream. A sedative. That wasn't meant to kill the dog, but have him sleep awhile. He must have drugged the dog in order to transport it to the crime scene."

"But why would he leave such a cryptic message like that?"

"I've wondered that myself. Either he wants us to follow him, or he wants to be stopped, or he's torment-ing us by leaving a clue like this behind. Sometimes I wonder if he's a goal-oriented serial killer, you know, the type who wants to achieve some result from his killings. That makes sense when you look at the first two cases, involving the pedophile couple in Tennessee and my, my sister, with her lover. But it doesn't make sense here: how has the Whisperer made the world a better place by killing three market consultants? He's domineering. He likes to see his victims suffer, that's obvious, especially in my sister's case and this one. And leaving a signature, like putting the collar on the dog with the Faulkner reference, that's a sure sign of a domineering killer. It taunts the authorities, makes him feel he's more in control. I don't see a lot of sexual overtones here, though it's obviously S/M based. He could be thrill-seeking, though again, usually you see more sexual overtones, ripping out a man's genitals, cutting off a woman's breasts. He's not delusional, that's for sure: these crime scenes are not in disarray. They're well planned, they're getting better planned each time. So I don't think he's hearing voices. And a delusional killer doesn't have a particular victim targeted, but rather just kills whoever is nearby. No, this guy, he's got targets. He hunts them, gets to know them. He's got a purpose in life."

I stopped. Darla was looking at me. She was concerned: for me, or for her, I couldn't tell.

The following morning her worry was gone. At least, she must have tucked it away. She met me in the hotel lobby. She had asked if I wanted to go up north to the crime scene, but I passed. No need to go to a place where two seasons had pushed through. The leads would be dead there. If there were any living witnesses they would be south of here, in Mississippi.

We drove in two cars to Oxford, having traded cell phone numbers before leaving Memphis. Two bathroom breaks later, we were in the land of Faulkner. And he was everywhere: bronze statues of him in the center of town, signs leading toward his home and the museum. I wanted to go there; rumor had it that Márquez, while visiting Washington, DC, during the Cold War, when the U.S. Immigration gave him a very limited visa into the country due to his leftist politics and his friendship with Castro, borrowed a car and sneaked down to Mississippi to visit the home of his literary mentor. Supposedly Gabo had made his way into Faulkner's house and signed his name in the visitor's book. I wanted to see that signature. But there were other things I wanted more.

Faulkner wrote about the fictional Yoknapatawpha County, based on this real county called Lafayette. I'm sure Darla thought it was not only a waste of time, but an act of desperation, for two women to try to canvass an entire county. But it was the only lead we had.

We focused on public places: churches, small stores, gas stations. We separated, Darla in the north section of the county, while I went south. The morning hours gave us nothing but head shaking. Sometimes, when I said that I was related to one of the victims, I received sad, hard looks, the anger that comes with sudden empathy. "You poor child," said one woman at a QuikMart. "I remember reading about that. Just terrible." But she knew little about dog trainers, except for a woman named Grace who, in her hair styling salon, also trimmed poodles and terriers for just twelve dollars.

At noon Darla and I met back in Oxford for a quick meal. She was tired; I bought lunch. The thought occurred to me that I had put too much strain on this new acquaintance, but she brushed that away after ordering some coffee, "Well, let's do round two," and she was up, ready to go.

I was in Springdale, near Water Valley, when my

phone rang. "Head up to Abbeville," she said, "take the Seven all the way to the edge of the county. I'll be at the Texaco, right at the southern edge of town."

"What'd you get?"

"An asshole who doesn't like black women."

"I hate to say this, Darla, but that could be a lot of people here."

"Yeah, but this cracker's got a dog chain with no dog."

At the Texaco she explained how she found the man named Blevins. "Some older gentlemen over at that store," she pointed to a coffee shop across the street, "the moment I started talking about the case, just about all of them walked away. I thought it was my perfume. Then one of them came back, a little white guy named Andrew, had a really scruffy beard. He sat down and said, real prissy like, 'Ma'am, you didn't hear this from me.' And then I heard it from him, the name Blevins. He said that shortly before the three Wall Street guys got killed, a man came through here, asking about attack dogs. Someone pointed him to Blevins. Andrew said they were all sure it was Blevins' dog that did the killing."

"Why didn't anyone report him?"

"Seems like Blevins has a reputation around here. I haven't talked with him yet."

"Oh. How do you know he doesn't like Blacks?"

"Andrew. He said it'd be a waste of time for an African American to approach Blevins. But I still drove by his place. There it is, right in front of the trailer: the empty dog chain."

That too seemed like a long shot. Like the Crime Scene near Shelby Forest, finding an empty dog chain seven months after a murder was nothing if not tenuous.

I was wrong. This was the place, and this was the man, the one coming out of the trailer. I knew we had found him, not so much because of the empty dog chain, but because of the girl who played with two Barbie dolls outside on the edge of the yard. The bruises on her calves told me that this was the place.

Little scruffy Andrew, Darla's new squeal, was right. The first thing Blevins did when he stepped out of the trailer was stick his hands in his well-ironed pants pockets. He looked back and forth at each of us, looking down, as he was taller than us both. "Black and brown. The damned Rainbow Coalition."

Darla had her badge out first. I took mine out right behind her, a redundancy of authority. He read them both. So he could read. "Memphis and Nashville. Way out of your jurisdiction." He knew a word like jurisdiction. Learned, no doubt, in court.

"You're not under arrest for anything, Mr. Blevins," said Darla. "We're just looking for some information."

He didn't say anything. I piped in. "We're looking for attack dogs."

He smiled. He knew why we were here. The girl in the dirt, with her two Barbies, shifted. She turned as if to look at another spot in the yard, but really she was turning to hear us better. Her hands stopped real play.

She simulated play, moving the one Barbie over the dirt like a svelte ghost.

"I don't keep dogs," said Blevins.

"But you used to, didn't you?" I pointed to the chain. "What happened to the one you had here?"

"He up and died on me."

"What killed him?"

"I don't know. I think it was, a disease."

"I see. Is your wife here?" Though I already knew the answer to this. Andrew had filled Darla in on Blevins' manslaughter charge, dropped for lack of evidence.

"I'm afraid she's passed away."

The girl shifted again.

"What's your daughter's name?" I asked.

"None of your business."

"Mind if I talk with her?"

"Yes I do."

"Why?"

He said nothing.

There have been a few times in my life when I've looked into a face and wondered, does it have a personality besides malice? Does it think in any other way except through the stare of hatred? I believed that my sister's killer had such a face, one that could not shift to another emotion, one that could never evoke empathy. Such was the face of Blevins. And the mouth on such a face would give very little of what we wanted. He was stone. I could not break through him by hitting him directly. But I bet, if I worked through something he, not loved, but coveted, I'd have a better chance.

So I turned away and walked toward the girl. She shifted. I wondered if she would bolt, run into the trailer, where I would have no chance of seeing her again. But now, out here, I could say, "Hi little lady,

those are nice Barbies you have there. Is that one
Surfer Barbie?" I talked sweetly, even with the protest
behind me: not only Blevins, but Darla as well. He
cursed; Darla just kept saying my name. I ignored them
both, knelt down and quickly stroked her hair. "My
name's Romilia," I said, smiling. She looked up at me,
smiled back, as if for a moment the sudden intimacy I
created blocked out the other two adults, even her father. I asked, loud enough for him to hear, "Tell me,
honey, did you ever have a dog . . . oh goodness child,
what happened to your legs?"

His shadow gave him away: he was directly behind
me. The shadow also showed how he hurt his daughter.
His leg swung back. I turned, just in time to see it
swing toward me. I caught it, just above his boot, with
both my hands. I used his own momentum to toss him.
He fell back onto his shoulder blades. Once he blinked
from the fall, he could see the back of my nine-
millimeter parabellum, pushed up against his ear.

"Who'd you sell the dog to?"

"Fuck you, Spic cunt."

And so I hit him. Just once, on the chest, with the
butt of my gun. The girl yelped. Darla said my name
again, this time with panic in her voice.

These moments have happened before in my life.
In Atlanta, before moving to Nashville. They were
very clear moments, the clarity as solid as cut glass.
They have all been recorded and filed away.

You'd think I would have learned. But in the moment, it's the clarity that guides me.

The slam on his sternum caught his attention. He
looked at my barrel with a bit more respect, especially
now that I had it on the bridge of his nose. And so I was
wrong. This *pendejo's* face could shift to another expres-

sion. Though he still evoked no empathy, he could, like
any man, shit in his pants with fear.

Everyone turned silent, which gave me the chance
to ask again, "Who bought the dog?"

"Some guy. Young. Black hair."

"Race?"

"White. White kid."

"Kid?"

"No, about, I don't know, late twenties. Early thirties."

"Why'd he want the dog?"

"He didn't say. He just wanted a wild one. One
that'd attack." I saw something in Blevins' eyes, something I had seen in a man who I had pistol whipped in
an alleyway in Atlanta: that certain sense of panic and
awe, wrapped together, seeing a woman with such a
look, such a stare.

"How'd he take it?"

"What? He drugged it, gave it something to eat. It
fell asleep. He took off."

"In what?"

"Truck. My truck. He left his rental here, drove
away in my truck, came back the same day."

"How'd you know it was a rental?"

"I looked in it." He was still breathing hard, but his
eyes began to lose their fear: a shadow of anger slid
over his irises. This was not good. I had to do something, before losing this trail of information.

I cocked the hammer back.

"Jesus, Romilia!" Darla raised her arms. The girl
screamed, ran into the trailer. That was okay, for all
that brought back the hot droplets of fear on Blevins'
forehead, a man who I had thought felt only one thing.

"So what did you find in the car?" I asked.

And he told me something he had never forgotten.

For Blevins was an intelligent, quick man. He knew
that someone buying a dog from the likes of him was a
man up to nothing good. So he jimmied the rental and
looked for something that could tell him more about
the stranger, information that maybe he, Blevins, could
someday use. He was right; today he used it, as he
would believe, to save his life from the trigger of a
crazed Hispanic cop.

I like clarity.

"What?" I asked, insistent, "What did you find?"

He told me, Nothing except a name: PriceRight
Auto Rentals. Memphis, Tennessee.

We had driven to Blevins' home in the same car. On
the way back to the Texaco station, Darla said nothing.
And so I figured our fledgling friendship was just about
to end.

I was right. At the Texaco she got in her car and
drove off. I thanked her as she opened the door, told
her I couldn't have done it without her. "Please don't
tell my superiors that," she said before slamming my
car closed.

I felt bad about this. I liked her, liked her style.
She'd make a good Homicide detective someday.

Before the end of the day I was at PriceRight Auto
Rentals, a small Mom & Pop on the edge of town, near
the Memphis airport but far enough away to distinguish it from the Hertz, Enterprise, and Budget rentals
crowding the terminals. I worked quickly: I showed my
badge, told the employee that I wanted a list of names
of people who rented cars between September 18 and
25 of last year, three days before and after the Estimated Time of Death. I got the names, along with their
credit card numbers. Luckily the young employee
didn't know better: he should have just given me the

names. Now I could cross reference, see which of the numbers were forgeries.

That same night I drove home. It was Saturday. How nice, I thought; I'd have Sunday with Sergio and my mother.

My mother called right about then and told me I'd be spending the night at Vanderbilt Hospital.

"It was an accident," she said. She was crying.

I yelled into the cell phone. All Mamá said was Sergio, overdose, an arrest, and Intensive Care. I broke the speed laws, all the way to Nashville.

Dr. Clancy promised me it was not a coma. But I had a hard time believing that, the way Sergio lay there, the drip punched into his thin arm, the oxygen tubes hanging from his nostrils, his eyes closed, never responding to any of my words, my touch.

Clancy had been good to me before, when I was the one in the bed a few months ago. Mamá said he was off duty, but he was hanging around, making sure our boy would be okay.

"It's not a coma," he said again. "It's the 'crash.' He'll come out of it. It'll be rocky for him, but he'll pull through."

"What do you mean rocky?" I looked up at him. Did the wet mask of my eyeliner scare him? Or was this just my usual stare? "What's a crash? What's going to happen?"

"He's gone through the worst of it. I'm glad you didn't have to see it, but he's . . ."

"My mother saw it."

"Yes. I know. But that's over. The tremors, the fighting. He also had a fever, but we've managed to bring it down. And the aggression, that should be over with too."

Aggression. He said it so easily, well-trained in the diagnosis of symptoms. My mother would never forget that aggression, her only grandson coming at her the way he did.

"Meth is highly unpredictable, Detective. Different people react to it in different ways. And we're not used to seeing children come in here from an overdose."

"So it was an overdose?" My voice rattled.

"Well, yes, we have to call it that. He's only four, and his weight, thirty-seven pounds . . . his body absorbed more than what it could handle. And it's methamphetamine, it affects the central nervous system."

"How? What's going to happen? Will you please tell me what is going to happen to my boy?"

I was out of my chair. The next minute we were outside, in the hallway, though I don't remember Clancy trying to gently push me through. Out there, beyond the darkness of the room where my boy lay, we argued.

He held my shoulders, until I shook his hands off. He held his fingers in the air, near my arms, and spoke calmly, clearly. "Listen. Sergio will be all right. He's not going to die. He will wake up in a few hours, maybe four, six. And he will be depressed. Probably cry a lot, or maybe just stare at you. To be honest, I've never seen a little boy come down from methamphetamine, but I'm willing to bet he'll sink for awhile. The worst that may happen is what's called 'tweaking,' in which he won't be able to sleep for two, maybe three days. He'll be irritable, paranoid, afraid. And he'll want more meth. I don't know how he'll try to say that, but his body will crave it again, to get back the high. In adults, the craving can lead to more aggression, violence. With Sergio, well, we just need to keep him here until he passes through all that."

This broke me. I cried. Cried in front of Dr. Clancy, hating him for the tears, knowing later I'd probably thank him, though he'd never know that.

I went back inside. Clancy left me alone. One of the women from the West Nashville church had taken my mother downstairs for a cup of coffee. This had been a good move. The moment I had burst into Vanderbilt Hospital, I had the look that no grandmother wants to see from her daughter: blame. I had to check myself on that, for I would soon learn how wrong it was to blame my mother. Celia Chacón would crush the world just to cuddle her *nieto*. And she would have crushed everyone in that church, had she known what was in that girl's purse.

When she came back from her coffee, I'd sit with her and look at her as her daughter. And then I would get the full story. That way, I could be the one to do the crushing.

My mother held an ice pack on the left side of her jaw. "What do the gringos say? Never trust a book by its cover."

I meant to correct her, ". . . Never *judge* . . ." But her phrase was more accurate.

My mother, unlike me, was a practicing Catholic. This, of course, meant that I had Sunday mornings to myself. Sergio would go with her to church. He didn't mind. Sergio had a crush on a teenage girl named Brandy, who worked in the parish daycare on Sunday mornings.

And Brandy was the book my mother referred to.

She was a straight A student at a private high school that sat on seventy acres on the edge of the city. Brandy would graduate in a year; no one doubted her position as valedictorian, nor her acceptance into Vanderbilt or Stanford or NYU, having applied to all three. The school promoted her as one of their best leaders: she was president of her class and editor of the yearbook. She planned a career in journalism; no teenager watched CNN more than she. The few times she took care of Sergio when Mamá and I went out for dinner or a movie, we always came back to the television tuned to the news station. No one connected her high energy to a diet of meth.

For now, I only heard the breakdown of what happened on Saturday afternoon, while my mother helped set up the carnival at the church. "Brandy and I were hanging up streamers around the duck-shoot. She's the one who saw Sergio at her purse. It was open, that's where he saw it, the bag of that stuff, you see," her voice shook as she spoke, for here, I knew, she thought I would blame her. "Looked just like the *piedrecitas*, the candy. He didn't know. Even when he started sucking on it, he thought it was some of the *dulces* I buy him, *ay* . . . I just don't understand, he didn't swallow any of it. Just sucked on it, until Brandy got to him."

I knew why. No need to ingest a drug, when the lining of the mouth is the most direct way to snatch a high. However long he had it in his mouth, it had dissolved enough to get under his tongue, shoot straight into his system.

"Brandy didn't say anything. I looked over, there

she was, fussing with Sergio. I did see him spit something out. But then she was cleaning out his mouth, standing over him. She pushed something else into his mouth. Then she came back, started helping me again. She just said he had gotten into her purse, looking for candy, so she gave him a Certs. I stopped and scolded him for getting into her stuff. He felt bad, but you know, he's still learning about keeping his hands out of other people's belongings.

"Everything was fine, we all got to working on the other kiosks. But then he yelled for me. I won't forget that way he yelled, kept saying *Abuelita, Abuelita*, I had never heard him so scared. Then that shaking, *ay Dios . . .*"

The shaking, the tremors. Increase of heart rate, blood pressure, the rising of body temperature, the erratic breathing. All in the body of a four year old. He got hyper, which anyone could see as normal at first, in a little boy who's eaten one too many Krispy Kreme Doughnuts, who's having fun at a carnival set up in a church, a church for Christ's sake. He even looked happy, too happy. But to be so hyper was not Sergio, not the grandson she knew, so she stopped him as he ran across the gym floor, held him. "I looked into his eyes, and knew something was wrong. His eyes, the black part, they were too large, like a doll's eyes. I thought they would burst open."

That's when he hit her. Took his little fist and slammed it against his grandmother's jaw. She fell back. The church volunteers, many of them members of the youth group, ran through the doors after him. They caught him on the other side of West End Avenue. Two cars had to slam their brakes. They took him back to the church, called 911. She rode in the ambulance with her grandson, who was screaming; my boy, screaming.

Something I have never heard, never want to hear. It was horrible, imagining it, indirectly, through my mother's words.

At Vanderbilt they separated the two, took care of my mother's bruised jaw, took him away. They asked her what had happened, and she did not know. They had given him no sedative, seeing the signs of some drug intake, not wanting to risk any contraindications. They just strapped him down.

Once Mamá told the doctor about the incident at the purse, they tracked down Brandy. She was still at the church in the bathroom. She was smart to flush the plastic zip bag along with the rocks. But being a teenager, she wouldn't have known what I and my mother would know: that a boy leaves his trail of crumbs everywhere. He had eaten the meth, had not liked the taste, and so dropped the remaining rocks from his palm back into the bag. A four year old's hand does not worry about precision; two tiny pieces of the ice fell to the bottom of the purse, which the police quickly found.

Brandy had studied enough to know that she had rights, and she had watched enough *Law & Order* to know that they needed some sort of warrant to look through her private belongings. But the cops knew more than she about authority, that a boy had taken some substance, most undoubtedly dangerous, life threatening, and they had to track it down to save his life, unless she wanted a second-degree manslaughter charge slapped on her.

She opened her purse.

When Mamá stopped telling me all this, she looked straight at me. *"Hija, lo siento mucho. Ay, mi corazón . . ."*

It could have been her heart hurting; or perhaps

she referred to her grandson, her *corazón*. But that's a foolish distinction: they are the same.

Again, the clarity. I leaned over, took her head in my hands, "Mamá," I said, in our language; sometimes, in such circumstances, Spanish is the only language there is, "It's not your fault. You are his world."

My mother has been strong for me, all my short, brutish life. It was my turn.

I spent the night beside him. I wanted to believe the rhythm of his breath was normal; at least, it was continual. His heart still punched the green light on the monitor, too quickly for my comfort. But he slept; or at least, he was out. He did not know the pain his body pushed through.

At least that's what I wanted to believe.

He turned. His face dropped slightly to the right. I almost cried, right then and there; for that was a sign of no coma, something Clancy had been telling me all night. Not a coma, but a crash.

With his head tilted, I could see both Sergio's eyelids, the full of his face. For a moment I could ignore the thin plastic tubes running from his nostrils to the oxygen tank, and could see, just for brief seconds, his father. I had not thought of César for awhile. César, my mother always said to me, should be the reason I believed in Heaven, for there had to be somewhere for a man like that to spend the rest of these days. Sometimes I believed Mamá was more in love with my husband than I was. César was her example of the *hombre cabal*, a man someone like Fidel (one of Mamá's biggest heroes) would see as truly revolutionized. All because César cooked *pupusas* and cleaned the kitchen, sometimes in the same evening. And he did iron his own shirts, though he had trouble creasing pants. César's family was more Indio than ours was, coming from the northern mountains of El Salvador. César, though born north of Lake Ilopango, did not speak Nahuatl nor Pipil, not like his grandmother did. But he kept a clean house.

There was César, in our boy's sleeping face.

Brandy was caught off guard by me coming through the interrogation room door. She probably figured, or hoped, they would have sent in another cop, one who would be more objective. Surprise.

I spent little time with her. She had already lawyered-up. Considering her pedigree and her father's ownership of a local golf club, she wouldn't spend too much, if any, time in jail. She'd get counseling, rehab; maybe she'd be able to spend some time in that clinic that St. Elizabeth's Church was raising funds for.

I told her this.

She said nothing. She didn't look at me, even though I sat directly in front of her, on the other side of the table in the interview box. The lawyer said something about not having to put up with such snide remarks, that it was a form of harassment. I looked at him, told him it was my boy who was coming out of the meth-induced coma. This was news to him. He shut up.

"Where'd you buy the meth?" I asked.

"She didn't buy any illegal substance."

"Then where did you get it, Brandy?"

"She doesn't have to answer any of your questions."

"Would *you* shut the fuck up?"

That was a mistake, of course. He walked out the door, called for the Lieutenant in charge of the watch. It happened to be McCabe. Even though he had given me permission to interview her, my boss would be at the door within the minute, pulling me out. I had to shake her quickly.

"You've got a lot of hopes for your future, I understand," I said. "My mother always talks about you, your plans for college, Ivy League, a career in journalism. You're smart, brilliant, articulate. You've planned to go far. You can probably still go far, if you just tell me where you got the meth. I'll go to bat for you, ask the judge to be more easy, though I can't promise the charges will be dropped. But you can keep with your plans." Or part of them, at least.

Two women, staring each other down, weighing out what was needed from the other. All before McCabe got here.

She spoke. "Dale Cartwell. My boyfriend. He deals."

That was quick.

"Come on, Romi."

That was my boss. He stood at the door. His voice was easy, the only voice at this point who could get me to move. I stood, got up, walked to the door and followed him. Before I left the room I turned to her and gave her information that she had not asked for, which, of course, told me a little bit more about who she was. "By the way, Sergio's doing better. They're still keeping a close eye on him."

"He's ruined my life, you know."

Her tone actually meant to evoke pity. Pity, from the mother whose son almost died the night before. Through the window I saw the lawyer, who jumped as I slammed the door.

Dale was pretty stupid. He ran. I'm sure it was the image of two blue uniforms along with a plainclothes detective coming to his door. His stupidity came out in his mode of escape: he dove out of his bedroom window, which was on the second floor. The scraggly bougainvillea bushes, though cushioning his fall, held him snuggly until the two cops and I came around the house. We pulled him out of the bush.

"Look Dale, I just want to know one thing," I said, pulling a broken twig out of his long blonde hair. "Names of the boys you buy from."

"I don't know who you're talking about."

"No, you don't know who you're talking *to*," I said. And then I told him: I was the cop whose kid got the overdose. I let his imagination do the rest, regarding how mad I was, how much I meant to tie his balls in a sling, etc.

"Okay. All right. My mom's gardener."

I smiled, ready to pelt him. "Come on, Dale."

"Serious! He's a short Hispanic guy, works this whole neighborhood."

"Your gardener deals in ice."

"Yeah but he works this whole neighborhood too, I mean he mows yards, with a group of those illegal immigrant guys, you know?"

"Name?"

"I don't know, they call him Duro . . . Jurassic . . . something. He said it's a fruit. He mows our yards on Wednesdays. His crew always eats lunch over there." Dale pointed to a nearby park.

A fruit that sounds like Jurassic. I've had to do this a lot in Nashville, guessing locals' derivations of Spanish words they've recently had to learn. "You mean *Durazno*?"

"Yeah. That's it."

The perp in question: Peaches.

"Where does he live?" I asked.

"I don't know. I just buy from him on Wednesdays. But don't let him know that, man. Those friends of his

are big guys. I'm sure they're all into the meth shit."
His voice trembled.

"Good boy, Dale," I said. I turned away as
Barrington, the white cop, cuffed him. They took off
in their patrol car. And I took off in my Taurus.

Some ice-houses are just too obvious. This one was not
in the richest neighborhood of Nashville, nor the
poorest. Once I checked the map, I wondered if it was
in Nashville at all. I was on the outskirts, on the east
end, near the airport. A lot of the houses looked the
same, with that HUD nuance about them. It was night.
No kids outside playing, few cars driving by. These
were the homes of families watching television and
cleaning up after dinner and finishing homework.

A Lexus was parked in the driveway. A Montero,
new, was parked alongside it. Another SUV was in the
street.

Two hours later I returned, better dressed.

I knocked. A little guy came to the door. Peaches.
The fuzz on his chin gave away his nickname. He left
the steel-mesh door closed, locked. He spoke through
the metal mesh, "Yes?"

It was dark in the house. All I could see was his outline, the thick curls of hair. He smoked a cigarette.
"What you need?" he asked.

"Oh man. I am in bad need of a hit." I smiled. My
hair was thick over my neck, falling before my shoulder. My voice was as feminine as I could possibly make
it. I sounded horny. My dress enhanced the effect: a red
skirt that stopped a good five inches above my knees,
with a red stretch top over my cupped red bra. All the
clothes my mother didn't know I owned. All in my
favorite color. It was chilly; I wore a thin white jacket,
with a wide open collar. My breasts aren't the most

perfect of Hollywood silicon, but they can do the trick; this I could see by the way they pulled down Peaches' eyes.

He finally looked up. "I know you?" he said. He smiled.

"My name's Megan. And I'd like to get to know you. Would you be . . . Peaches?"

"I'm sorry, but I can't see anybody right now . . . Look, why don't you come back later? Bring somebody I know, you know? The guy who told you about Peaches?"

I was losing him. "Sure. I can do that. But how about a drink? You got any beer? Or whiskey? I'm a Jim Beam girl myself."

"I can't let you in now, this ain't my house."

Someone yelled from the back, or from downstairs. He yelled back to them, *It's all right, just a girl,* in perfect Spanish. It was night. I had spoken in my regular, Atlanta-tinged English. He did not know.

"What'd you say? Can you talk French?" I asked.

"What? No man, that's, that's Spanish."

"I like it."

"Yeah?"

"Yeah."

He looked down. Breasts floating in red cups. A skirt half a foot wide, tight on the ass. Not the most comfortable. I should have stood on a serving plate. He looked back up at me.

"So. How about a little something for the road?" I said. "Just you and me." This was getting ridiculous. But I played it out. I could tell his pants were doing the thinking for him.

"Okay okay, just a little drink. But it's a nice night, let's have it outside." He walked away, came back from the kitchen, quickly. What did he hope for, a quick plug out on the front lawn? He had two glasses with him, a bottle. "I got some don Pedro, that's a brandy."

"Sounds good," I said. I reached back as if stretching—more pleasure for him, more signals to show how women really are, we're just hungry for it. We shove our boobs right at you. Just enough to unbuckle the holster strapped to my lower back.

He had to put down the glasses to fiddle with the dead bolt. "Yeah," he said, and I could almost hear him smiling, "old don Pedro's always welcome at any *fiesta.* . . ."

I punched the door with my shoulder. The edge of the metal door slammed his nose and forehead. The bottle fell. He stumbled against a couch, dropped onto it, holding his bleeding nose. He may have heard the click. I had my hand on his neck, the barrel to his sight.

"Where's the lab?" I asked.

"Oh shit, *hijo de la gran puta* . . ."

So I made it clear, *"Oyeme bien, buey, si no me dices donde el hielo, te machuco los huevos y te mando con la migra para que te jodan en el culo día tras día por el resto de tu vida miserable."*

My mother has told me that, when I get angry and righteous at the same time, I sound a bit like Monseñor Oscar Romero on the day of his last homily, when he ordered the army to stop killing the peasants. She should know: she was in the church at the time.

Of course, Romero died two days later, a bullet through the heart.

"Abajo," he said, *"en el sótano."* He barely pointed, with his left finger, toward the basement stairs.

I cuffed him, left him on the floor. A voice from downstairs, *"Durazno, qué te pasa?"* I followed the voice.

When I was halfway down the steps, Peaches made a decision upstairs. *"Raimundo! La Chota!"*

I heard a curse from downstairs, followed by the breaking of several small glasses.

I rushed the stairs, hit the concrete floor with both high heels, raised my parabellum right at the man and said "Freeze! Police!" followed immediately by "I'll be damned. . . ."

The man raised his large, thick arms. He looked straight at me, having to look down, due to his height. "Detective Chacón. How are you?"

There, in a loose web of orange rubber tubes dangling from thick plastic beakers, with the other ends dropped into a red cooking pot sitting on an electric eye, and with plastic bottles filled with iodine, a box of rat poison on a table, a sack of lye next to it, and numerous little bottles of over-the-counter cold medicines, stood a man I knew.

Raimundo Salgado, though nervous, smiled at me. He held two five gallon gas cans that were tied together with duct tape. Their nozzles had been taped together as well, in a solidified pucker. He stood in a basketball-tossing position, ready to pitch them out an open basement window. So then I learned that the man I once nicknamed Godzilla from Guanajuato had more than one vocation in life. The last time I had seen him, he was a bodyguard. Now he was a chemist. I expected him to give me greetings from his old boss, Tekún Umán.

nlawful entry," said McCabe. He disliked the phrase so much, he said it again, "Unlawful entry. What were you thinking?"

"I was thinking about my son."

I sat in the chair in front of his desk. He leaned back, as if meaning to relax. Or perhaps put a harder gaze on me, a boss' stance. It wasn't working, not like it used to. Perhaps he sensed this. He scratched the bald of his head. "How is Sergio?"

"I've never seen a kid go through delirium tremors."

McCabe winced at that, shook his head. He let some silence fall between us before giving me an update. "Your little friend Francisco 'Peaches' Nevara is now with Immigration. No papers. INS has him in Atlanta now. They'll work it out with DEA to see who has jurisdiction. I've got a feeling Immigration will hand this one over to the feds."

"And Raimundo?"

"Lawyered up."

I laughed. "I caught him with meth beakers in his hand."

"After you broke Peaches' nose. Raimundo's a U.S. Citizen, Romi. He knows his rights. Even with the local DEA office taking over the case, Raimundo's threatened to press charges."

A crock, I wanted to say, but instead, "Peaches let me in. He opened the door. I had grounds to suspect a meth lab in operation, and I acted on that suspicion."

"Without backup. And you stormed the lab. You know how dangerous that is? You don't know how Raimundo keeps a drug house. Poisons all over, crystal dust everywhere. It takes the Feds a full day to clean out and sterilize a meth lab."

He was angry, but he had also worried about me, knowing I could have gotten hurt by a small explosion of Raimundo's chemicals, or taken down after accidentally absorbing meth traces from a broken glass beaker. McCabe liked me, which I could use to my advantage. Again, my mother came to mind. *There are words back in the old country for women like that*, she would say.

McCabe couldn't help but add one more update. "Stapleton called. *The Cumberland Journal*. You bent his nose by not returning his previous calls. Now he insists on a story on the meth lab bust."

"What did you tell him?"

"I kindly told my old college roommate to hold his horses."

I turned the conversation. "So what's DEA think about all this? It's one more lab closed down."

"Actually, they're more animated about your find

than anyone else." McCabe moved to his coffee pot, poured us both a cup. I lit a cigarette. He stopped, looked at me with obvious surprise. "I didn't know you smoked."

I stuttered a bit, as if my father were questioning me. "Is it okay?"

"Everybody else who comes in here lights up. Why not you?" But he didn't sound convincing. He was disappointed in me. I thought about stubbing it out. But my fingers were going toward the scar, and I didn't want to be picking at it in front of him.

He continued, "DEA would really like to pin this on Tekún Umán, even with Raimundo swearing his operation has no connection with his old boss. Seems the DEA's got the hots to bring Tekún down."

"Of course. His cute little cartel is getting bigger."

McCabe chagrined. It was a look that showed how naïve I was. "Romilia. You make them sound like superheros. There's no federal agency more like Sisyphus than the DEA. Going after a stone that will always roll down the hill again." He looked down at his desk, glanced back up at me. "They're after Tekún because he cut one of their own."

I knew what he meant by 'cut.' It was literal.

"One of their agents down in Guatemala. Young fellow named Carl Spooner. Tekún sliced him. I heard from a friend in the agency that the man's got kids, a wife."

"He's dead?"

"No. But maybe wishes he was. I don't know." McCabe's glance took in the whole room, a man feeling a horrible empathy for another man. "You remember how Tekún is with a knife. He didn't cut off the man's testicles. Just, well, sliced into them, damn. Like a surgeon. He cut Spooner's scrotum, sliced up his vas deferens, then popped his bag open. Shit."

He talked as if he needed to tell me the details in order to get them out of his head. But getting them out meant seeing them again.

"DEA took Raimundo. They've got him at TBI downtown. They'll hold him for questioning."

"So they had Tekún cornered in Guatemala. And now?"

"No idea. He got away."

I thought about what Tekún's aunt had said, that she didn't doubt I'd see him again. That seemed most impossible when she and I had talked.

McCabe looked hard at me. "You shouldn't have stormed that house alone. You're right: Peaches let you in. So you'll get out of this one. But Stapleton's onto it, and since you ignored his last request for an interview, he's got a thorn up his ass. He'll eat this one up. Be prepared to hit the papers soon." He paused, let that sink in, then plunged one more warning into me. "I don't keep Lone Rangers on my watch, Romilia."

His tone changed. The reprimand was harder than what I expected.

"Look. I know it's difficult, what happened to Sergio. But it's not going to help you to fly off the handle, taking things into your own hands. They'll say you can't handle the job. And I don't think I need to remind you, how some guys think about women on the force: that a woman lets her personal life get in the way of her work."

He didn't need to fill in the blanks. If a man had done what I had done, he'd be one tough bastard, somebody you didn't mess with. They may have slapped his hand, like McCabe was slapping mine. But then he'd walk out of the boss' office to other men who slapped him on the back. I didn't need to tell this to McCabe. He knew. There was something about his look: he'd never want to say it, but he'd gone to bat for me a number of times. Lucky for me I had solved a big case under his watch; but I couldn't tell how long the shine from that success would protect him, or me.

"Go home to Sergio," he said. "Take the day off. Tomorrow too, if you want. It's slow here now. I've got some of the guys helping out over in arson, on that warehouse burn downtown. I've even shepherded out a couple of detectives to Robbery. Go home."

An offer I didn't refuse.

An hour later I was sitting next to Sergio, watching Cartoon Network. Sometimes he channel-surfed like an old man, flipping between the cartoons, the Family Channel, Disney, the Food Network, back to the cartoons. Why the Food Network? Why get so fixed on sautéed eggplants? But I didn't ask him. I just played with his hair, twirling it the way he did, which calmed him, made him look vacuously at the television. I hoped it was my twirling that made for that stare.

That's when the package came.

"Who's it from?" I asked Mamá as she handed it to me.

"Some woman in Minnesota. Friend of yours?"

"I don't know anyone in Minnesota." Today was March 9. The package had been mailed over three weeks ago, book rate. I tore at the brown wrapping, looked at the name, Ofelia Urbino, which scarcely rang a bell. According to the label, she worked at Ruminator Books in St. Paul. Sergio was not curious. He kept staring at the fried eggplants. That bothered me; Sergio always loved getting presents. Whenever a package came from Atlanta, he was the first to spot it, the first to start tearing into one side while I worked on the other. Now he just looked at the screen, his mouth closed, his words gone.

No. Not gone. As bad as it was, it had only been one hit of meth. Not enough to destroy all his brain cells, or too many of them. This, I prayed for. Yes, I surprised myself: I prayed. Mamá and I had blindsided ourselves, believing he was okay. He may have been okay, according to Dr. Clancy. But he wasn't back yet, not completely.

Inside was a ream box, the type that held large manuscripts. On top was taped an envelope, its edges ragged, like papyrus. I opened it. Then it came to me: Ofelia Urbino. Urbino. Her father, Doctor Juvenal Urbino.

Mi Vida,

As you felt it impossible to accept my last gift of an engagement ring, I do hope you may consider the contents of this package something that may not only benefit you, but also may reveal to you my heart.

It seems that our federal protectorate against interstate violence, the FBI, has indeed held out on you and the other families who have suffered from the ways of the Whisperer. Honestly, I don't see how you or anyone could have figured out why they call him that. Nor how the Bureau connected all these killings, putting them under the aegis of the same man.

*The drawings are strange, are they not? I
couldn't make heads or tails of them. Then again, I
am but a layman, a civilian. You may have better
luck.*

*I hope all is well, Romilia. I've had to make a
few sudden changes in my itinerary. The freedom of
the quetzal, it is no longer mine. I've decided to retire to Ofelia Urbino's hometown. Perhaps there,
I'll be able to touch what was out of her father's
reach.*

Siempre
Tekún

I retreated to my bedroom, closed the door. Before
I shut it completely, I looked at my son. He had not
moved, had not even turned to see me leave him.

I spread out the contents. I read. My eyes clung to
each sentence, swinging from one line to the next. My
thoughts bolted between the documents and the
knowledge already in my brain. This was a hinging of
information, a slamming away at the unknown, beating
it with a sledgehammer of clarity.

And still I did not know.

But there were these drawings, these notes, left by
the killer. The notes, which accounted for his nickname, explained why the Feds, those fucking Feds, had
strung these murders together.

First there was the note found in the mailbox of
Steve and Eileen Masterson, in Bristol.

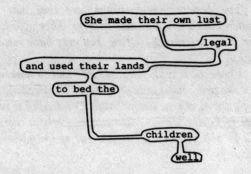

At the foot of my sister's bed:

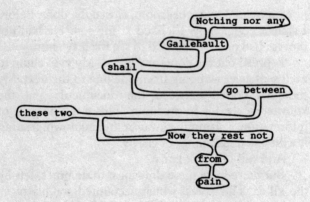

The third, found next to the pit where the three men hung from their ankles, told me how much bull-shit I had received from Burkett, the good little fed agent in Memphis.

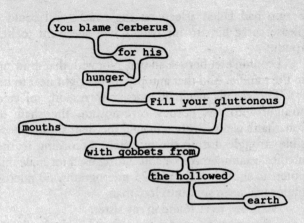

A second balloon of words was on this same page, somewhat different from the other phrases,

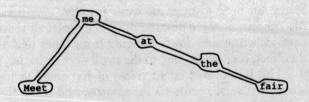

My bed was covered in a feast of information. I panicked at first, afraid. How had Tekún gotten all this? I ran out, checked the wrapping that sat next to my son. He had not moved. Nothing on the paper but my address and the return address in St. Paul, a book store. That, and the date of when it had been mailed, almost two weeks ago.

I retreated, closed my bedroom door.

An hour later a knock. "Are you okay?" asked Mamá.

"Fine. Just reading." I faked a yawn. She said that

Sergio had fallen asleep on the couch, and could I please carry him to his bed? Then she went to her room.

I couldn't let her see all this. Not with that drawing in the middle. And that autopsy report right next to it.

The details made it worse: Aprostadil, injected straight into the corpus cavernosum, the shaft of Jonathan's penis. Bruises around the shaft showed possible struggle during the injection. According to the medical examiner, Aprostadil, a drug used for male impotence, should begin at 1.25 micrograms. 60 micrograms had been shot into Jonathan.

No drugs were found in my sister.

There were no medications found in the bodies of the Mastersons.

The three stockbrokers in Memphis had all been slipped Flunitrazepam, an illegal drug here in the States but used to treat insomnia in other countries. Also known as the date-rape drug. The men all must have woken upside down, hanging from ropes tied to their feet, their wrists tied to the small of their backs.

The Pitbull had latent traces of Ketamine in his blood, a general anesthesia for animals. And again, the sodium phenobarbitol, used to put him to sleep.

I found the FBI agent's conclusion long after I had made one: the Whisperer had access to prescription medicines. He also knew how to do injections. None of his victims had died from an embolism created by an air pocket from a hypodermic needle.

Medical profession. Nurse? Veterinarian?

And why "the Whisperer?" It seemed here the FBI was at a loss; they merely tagged on that name as a reference. This, even after running the words from the notes through a computer, through the internet, and finding vague, indirect references to literary fig-

ures, medieval beliefs, Greek myths. Gallehault and
Cerberus: The latter was a three-headed dog from
The Aeneid who guards the underworld. Gallehault,
according to one agent's report, was a traitor in King
Arthur's time.

Our dog from Mississippi was not named
Cerberus, but Popeye, the main character of
Faulkner's *Sanctuary*. Popeye is one bad boy; he rapes
a woman with a corncob. Was that a clue to the Whis-
perer? Did *he* hate women? That didn't seem likely.
Out of his seven victims, only two were female.

He wasn't merely a misogynist. All his clues and
killings had a hint of moral purpose to them: child
abuse, adultery, and now I saw, in Memphis, according
to the drawn note, gluttony.

The Whisperer believes he has a purpose.

He believes in what he does.

Popeye lays dying on the collar. That got us to
Mississippi. That got us to follow him.

Meet me at the fair. Blatant. He's going to St. Louis.

He wants us to know.

He reads the papers. He watches the news. He's
left clues. Where is he going?

Waves of logic crashed over my brain, and for a
moment some of it made sense. But then another wave
crashed down and washed away the collecting story. I'd
lost the thread. It was way past midnight, and dawn
would be over the Cumberland Plateau soon. The papers on my bed, the medical reports, photos of the
crime scenes, the cryptic messages, all fell out of focus.
All except one thing: the federal seal of the FBI,
stamped on each paper: Tekún's printer had put them
on the page in their full colors, the blue background,
the circle of gold stars, the red and white striped shield
saddled between two thick olive branches. Obviously

he had downloaded all this from a computer, somehow hacking into the FBI's network.

That seal made sense. That seal warned me.

Some places in Nashville were still open, twenty-four hours a day. A Kinkos blazed bright on a side street just down from Vanderbilt University. A few students were up late, working on last-minute essays. A young woman played with her glasses until they fell off her nose. She checked the clock every minute.

I was done in half an hour. I paid in cash, tried not to look the copy shop employee in the eye. Less eye contact made for less likelihood of recognizing me.

I always carry stamps. I'm that kind of girl. I stuck a few on the new large envelope brought from home, along with the address taken off one of the old emails, and mailed the package to the only person in this town I could trust.

At home I curled up with my boy. He slept soundly. That was a sign of convalescence: the past few days, he had hardly been able to sleep. I should have slept too, since I had been up with him so much. But my eyes were wide. Tonight gave us a full moon, just outside Sergio's window. It blazed over Nashville like a beacon, just like, I knew, it glowed over the entire country. Over every single one of us.

But keep your eyes below us, for coming near
Is the river of blood, in which boils everyone
Whose violence hurt others

The Inferno, Canto XII

MARCH 9, 2001

He wonders if he's planned too well. They're not getting it.

Either that, Bobby thinks, or they're not letting it out. Nothing in the papers about Kansas City. No updates on the FBI public website about the one they have so blithely called the Whisperer.

And nothing at all about his words and his drawings. Ones he has spent so much time on. It's as if they've never existed.

He exists. Look at this hand. Turn it and see it is a hand with no wounds, no flaws. The light from that full moon makes shadows between his fingers. This is his hand. He is a part of it, it, a part of him. Nothing broken nor separated; he is whole. It seems, with each city, he becomes more whole, more himself. He recognized this the first time, with the Mastersons. Even though it was a mess, he had come out connected, for the first time in a long while, feeling as if his fingers were a part of him, that his very skin was his own. This memory still thrilled him. He understood it more, though he could not claim ownership of the entire mystery. This whole plan is mystery.

A mystery born in fear, in the separation. Those days in Bristol, waiting for answers, waiting for something to hit him. Waiting for a letter or phone call from the university in Chapel Hill, accepting him into their medical school. All that work training as a paramedic would pay off, he believed; yet he still had to wait, and hope for their positive response.

Waiting. He was not waiting for that department in Chapel Hill to answer him, this he now realizes. He was waiting, really, for the Mastersons.

When the news broke about their alleged child sexual abuse ring in their daycare, and the way that Mrs. Masterson was allowing her husband to bed the children in his private computer office upstairs, Bobby collapsed on the floor of his bathroom. There, taking a dump, reading Merwin's translation of *Purgatorio*, and the news coming over the local public radio station was enough to topple him. He lay on the linoleum for he knows not how long, the stench of his own shit lingering behind him. He shook. Strange, to have a radio report affect him so. He's thought about it, wondered if perhaps it was the stress of waiting on the med school's acceptance or rejection letter, or was it the simple knowledge that a married couple in town had created a breeding ground for fucking children? And why while he was on the toilet? He's read a number of books by Freud, but little there, except to say that shitting is a daily, ritualistic trauma none of us can escape, ever. And he shits daily, but at least he can see that. He can control it, as long as he can see it.

He needed to see the Mastersons.

It was a hunt and it was messy and from time to time he still reprimands himself for such sloppiness. Yet he also knows that he made up for it, learning that even chaos can be put in order. Which is why, after twisting the broken bottle into Steve and Eileen, he sat on the bed and stared at both of them awhile, both tied to the bedposts, their mouths duct-taped silent. His gun drooped in his left hand, from his middle finger, dangling there, never shot, used just to keep them quiet while Eileen tied Steve to the post. There: he *was* thinking more clearly than he gives himself credit for: he had Eileen tie Steve first, tie down the man, the one who could overpower him in a slipup. And he had brought along the duct tape, though he hadn't thought about bringing his own bottle. After they were dead, he squatted on that bed, with the bloody bottle before him, and he muttered, "Ah shit, what a mess . . ." Fear of getting caught? No; it was something else that bothered him. The mess. The chaos. The lack of order. There was an aesthetic involved, or there should be, one that he had not bothered to respect.

Which is why, in his apartment, after bathing and dropping his soiled shirt and pants in the wash (how did blood get on his underwear for God's sake? Mixed with the semen that he had not expected) he sat at his desk and pulled forward the old VT Corona, the one that belonged to his father's secretary thirty years ago, and typed out that first poem. It did not work for him at first, for it was all over to the left, too formal. It took awhile, but he could see that, even with planning, he could be creative, free. It was the formality itself that allowed for the freedom of movement, the taking of the entire page.

The writing took over two hours. Somewhere

around four in the morning he woke from the spell of the studies, the books that surrounded his antique, yet well-oiled typewriter, the old, classic (so realistic!) drawings by Doré. That book of classic woodcuts given to him by his aunt, long ago.

His aunt. And his mother. His sister and then the father and there's really no reason to go there now, is there?

For if there is any need for memory, it is to look at how the road of the past has brought him here, to this small snow-covered chalet, where he's free to open a can of Spam and cut it into cubes and toss it in a sauté of onions and pineapple chunks. And here he is, overlooking the Rockies that are so very different from his set of mountains from childhood. These mountains tower over the flat valley as if ready to crush it any minute now. And that full moon, how it just sets the shadows deep into the crevices of the mountains; shadows that are themselves huge, shades that engulf entire towns.

The only mistake he may have made that dark morning in Bristol was the way he delivered the poem. Yet it was a mistake born out of ignorance: he knew nothing about DNA samples, how they are collected, how you can find them in just about anything human, a hair, blood, a teardrop, and, of course, saliva. He had been careful in wiping down fingerprints throughout the house. He had even wiped down the poem and its envelope. Before the sun rose that morning in Bristol, he made one last trip to the Mastersons, but he did not go in the house again, having locked it up and left the keys inside. Rather, he opened their mailbox with a gloved hand and, after licking the envelope and sealing it, dropped the poem inside.

Now he knows that some scrapings of that enve-

lope glue, wherein lies his dried saliva, are in an FBI
database in Quantico. He has made it into the BSU Hit
Parade. Still, he wonders how bright the folks at the
Behavioral Science Unit are: they've not made heads or
tails of his notes. At least, that's the impression they
give to the public.

He's made other mistakes, of course, ones that could
have been much worse than the mess he left at the
Masterson house. Returning to Atlanta two years after
Catalina—that was a bad decision. He sees this now,
staring at the Doré woodcut of that young, adulterous
couple, spinning and turning in that human conveyor
belt of sinners. Francesca turns her head away from
Paolo, toward Dante. Yes, to tell Dante of their sin of
lust, but is she not also trying to pull away from her
lover's grasp, an embrace that has become an eternal
stranglehold? There they swing, forever stuck together, hurtling, two bodies javelined into one sprawl-
ing mess of limbs and pulled torsos. Doré managed, in
this chaotic corner of hell, to freeze-frame Francesca's
face. So beautiful, even in her obvious look of regret,
the same regret Catalina gave him in the end.

   Bobby loved Catalina. She was the only one he had
multiple feelings for. The others evoked only the clean,
simple emotion, a righteousness of clarity. Catalina had
confused him; she had smitten him. That's why he
keeps the Doré painting, wherever he goes. Better to
remember Catalina through Francesca, rather than
make mistakes.

   One mistake was trying to replace Catalina with
her little sister. Romilia, who had been a summa cum
laude student at Emory but lost that academic recognition the semester following Catalina's death. Romilia
had managed to graduate. Later she got accepted into

the Atlanta Police Force. By the time he met her, she was already six months into training. Her grades were up. The shadow he had seen in her, in the old newscast, had turned purposeful.

It was clumsy but it worked, pushing a grocery cart near hers in Krogers, then, as she reached for coffee, taking her cart away. "Hey. Hold up," she had said, "that's my cart." He, looking confused, even a little beleaguered, asked "Are you sure?" "Yes I'm sure. I don't eat Spam, and I sure as hell don't drink soy milk." He had laughed, though through melancholy, the one emotion he believed would attract her. He had a lie ready, though he worried it would be too blatant. "You all right?" she asked. There. He had her.

His lie worked: a younger brother who had died of Leukemia just two weeks ago. Having it a sibling brought it close; death by disease pulled it away. A balanced lie.

They ordered coffee in the small shop in Krogers. She listened as he spoke about his fake brother and how Steven had passed after an agonizing six months of failed chemo. It was tiring to make up all this, especially with her sitting there, looking at him so intently. Now he could see she was not a carbon copy of her bigger sister. Still, Catalina was there, all the time, in her eyes. He knew this once he turned the conversation toward her, "Did you say you lost a brother too?"

"Sister," she said. "Older sister."

He listened to her, though she did not go into details, only to say that it was a double murder a year ago, perhaps he had heard about it. "No, I hadn't, I moved here just this summer." He responded to her sister's story with words used in this world, this transient sense of order, *Oh God, so terrible, that must be hard on you, on your mother.* She quickly pulled the story to the present, "So now I'm in the police academy."

"Wow. So when do you become an officer?"

"Four more months."

"Then you get your uniform?"

"Yeah. But I'll move on."

"To what?"

She did not smile. "Homicide. Of course."

"I see. So you want to find your sister's killer."

"Always."

He saw Catalina in the hard pools of her eyes.

"And what will you do when you find him?"

"Kill him, of course." She leaned over the table. "Why do you think I want to be a cop? It puts a gun in my hand legally."

He shook his head, understanding.

She shifted. "Oh, you didn't hear that from me," she said. She laughed. But it was uncomfortable. A concern over incrimination, that someone would dig this guy up, and he would bear witness to this conversation in the coffee shop in Krogers.

It was over soon after that. She had paid for the coffee, treating him, as his loss was the more recent. No chance of asking her out. Vengeance blinded her from any chance at love. This he regretted. But regret and sadness, loss, could all be swept away quickly by the swirl of concentric, infernal circles. Those rings have guided him all these years; they guide him now. All these are his decisions, and he knows this. No God nor Devil telling him what to do; come on now. He knows. He knows that his love of Doré and his desire to read one Canto after another, over and again, is not something laden upon him by some supreme being that dictates all his moves. Please. Let's not be childish.

The pineapples. They are ready. Get them out

before they soften too much, or caramelize. Then the Spam: have to cook the diced pieces of meat until they brown, just enough to be crisp. The crispy Spam up against the softness and sweetness of the pineapples, you really can't get much better than that.

He hurries now, for his guest needs to eat. He places the plate of rice and sautéed Spam on a platter, takes it in, serves it before the young man. Bobby puts a small leather bag of scalpels on the side of the plate, right next to the fork. He checks the knots in the chair, especially those that hold the young man's head rigidly to one side, that stretch the dark neck muscles wide. The boy is deep asleep. He'll wake soon. He won't be able to move around at all, with all that duct tape layered over his bald head and holding him tight. Bobby opens a book and turns to Canto XII and waits.

Bobby has kept up with Romilia. She moved, from Atlanta to Nashville. This makes sense: she lost her sister in Georgia, in the town where she worked. She married, a year or so after that coffee break in Krogers. Then her husband ups and dies on her in a car wreck, leaving her pregnant and a widow. Atlanta must be a hell of memories for her. Does she feel safer in Nashville, taking that lower-paying job, acting as a translator for the other detectives? And even with her solving that very big case, the one called the Jade Pyramid Killings, she's still who she is: a Hispanic woman in an all-white force that's not going to make her Lieutenant overnight. Bobby knows the difference between acquiescence and survival. This girl, she means to go on. She's got a son; she's got reasons.

Bobby reads *The Cumberland Journal* website. An article written by the editor himself, Anthony Stapleton, about that same young homicide detective storming a methamphetamine lab house, because her son took an accidental overdose. Dressed up like a prostitute, forced her way in, wounded a resident of the house in the process. The local chapter of the ACLU is on her tail, and thus the tail of her boss, Lieutenant Patrick McCabe, about illegal entry into a private domicile. But the town leaders, even the mayor himself, lauds young detective Chacón for her act, and even though they cannot condone the bending of rights, the mayor recognizes the bind that law enforcement sometimes is in when it comes to the drug war.

Detective Chacón offered no comments.

There is a side-bar article on the meth-lab house unlawful entry: A Memphis police officer named Darla Taylor claims to have watched Detective Romilia Chacón beat a man from Mississippi in order to get information regarding the Whisperer.

Mississippi. She found Blevins. And she beat him up.

Bobby smiles. Those old articles were right. She loved Márquez, and thus knew Faulkner. She's got Bobby's trail, followed it to Blevins. Bobby can imagine Blevins' rough, mean voice, the shadows of his eyes. Bobby can take that voice and imagine it pleading, frightened, a mean Bubba racist with a Latina woman beating the shit out of him, God! It must have been something to see. Bobby just has to create the scene, just like he's done before: taking the voices, heard through walls, making the scenes.

Enough of that.

She's behind him. Much better than any of the fellows at Quantico. Bobby's glad he didn't kill Romilia back then, in a panic. After the coffee he just left town again, wagering that she would, somehow, play an integral role in all this.

But she didn't meet Bobby in St. Louis. At the fair . . .

Be flexible, he thinks. *Once they find the note in Kansas City, she'll connect the dots.*

He writes this poem, paraphrased, then restructured, from Canto XII.

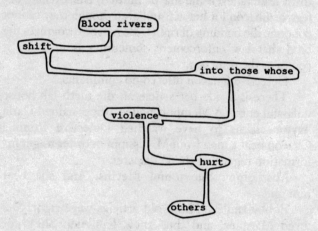

It's a temptation not to stop; this is such a beautiful canto. So he gives into temptation.

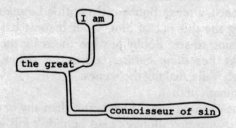

Yes, that's way over the top, he thinks. But what the hell? The Feds need help. Time to wave a flag.

Still, it's not enough. Romilia hadn't shown up in St.

Louis, and Bobby had to move on. He makes it easy for them to follow right along. Bobby takes the envelope, licks his tongue right across the seal. It takes his breath, smearing saliva over the glue, like a hand smearing its prints over oil. Exhilarating, this tempting of fear. And within that very breath, the fear becomes his. Bobby absorbs fear, and will turn it on them. Others will know fear. Others will mistake him for God.

MARCH 10

The DEA used a cell in the offices of the Tennessee Bureau of Investigation in downtown Nashville in order to hold Raimundo Salgado. In a week he would be processed and sent to DC. I had to talk to him before they took him away.

It didn't take as much arm-twisting as I thought. For the moment, I was in the public's good graces, and the ACLU was having a hard go at it bringing charges against me. But such moments, I knew, are fleeting.

The agents at the front desk let me in. There I checked my gun and clip. "You've got to go down to the cell," one of the agents told me. "We don't have a visiting center here. Harold will escort you."

Young Harold didn't say much, except to warn me to stay away from the front of Raimundo's cell. "He hasn't been violent. Just standard procedure. We don't want an inmate grabbing you, using you as a shield."

Raimundo was doing pushups when I came down the hall. On his tiny desk was a copy of Philip Roth's novel *Sabbath's Theatre*. I don't know why that bothered me.

He was surprised to see me. He actually smiled while standing up. The gray T-shirt showed the perfection of the pushups, the sharp curves made by the set. When he was in Tekún Umán's direct employment, I remembered him as more threatening. The only time I really looked him straight in the face was when I arrested him just a few nights ago, and now. Both times he smiled, either with his hands up or a set of bars between us. He was a handsome fellow, a thick-necked weight lifter from Guanajuato. He was a good head taller than I.

"Señorita Detective Chacón. How you doing?"

"I'm fine, Raimundo."

"I see you can't stay out of the papers." He smiled. "Good thing I put my hands up as fast as I did. Wouldn't want to get on your bad side."

My quick visit to Mississippi had hit the papers the day after the article on me entering Raimundo's house. McCabe was right: I regretted not calling Stapleton earlier, giving the editor a friendly interview after the Jade Pyramid Case closed. And how had Stapleton found Darla in Memphis? She must have come forward. Her statements to the press had tarnished me. I went from maverick anti-drug heroine to half-cocked cop in two issues of *The Cumberland Journal*.

Some would tell me not to blame Darla.

"I'm looking for Tekún, Raimundo."

"Yes?" Raimundo sat on the wooden chair next to the desk, lit a brown cigarette, tossed the pack atop the Roth novel. He sat back and studied me. "What do you need from him?"

"He's got to answer for some things."

"Like what?"

"Like that meth you were cooking up in your house."

"Now you know I can't make any statements about that. I'm surprised my lawyer isn't out there with you, reminding you of my rights. Then again," Raimundo glanced over at Harold, who stood at the door at the end of the hall, "once DEA gets a hair up their ass about you, you're fucked."

Harold didn't hear that. He was busy listening to his earpiece. The Feds were so serious, wearing those microphones all the time, even to the toilet.

"So you blame DEA for your trouble," I said. "Talk about denial."

"And you blame Mr. Tekún Umán for your kid's overdose. Talk about an overdeveloped sense of vengeance."

It seemed strange, hearing such words, no matter how cliché they were, coming out of this one-time bodyguard.

"I heard little Sergio got sick because he was dipping his hand in somebody's purse."

Hearing Sergio's name coming out of Raimundo's mouth didn't seem right; it gave him ownership over part of my son. "He's a four year old boy who was looking for some rock candy. And that girl's stash of meth came from your lab."

"Tenuous."

"Fuck you."

"Please. Don't make empty promises." He glanced at the Roth novel.

I turned away. The days were harder, with my boy coming back to the world. I prayed that all of him would come back. It was easy for Raimundo to trip my anger into gear.

Still, it was better that Raimundo believed I searched for his old boss because of my boy's overdose. It allowed me to hide the other reason; maybe Raimundo didn't know about the package. I asked him if he had heard from Tekún. He blew smoke out easily, said no, not since Tekún had left Nashville in a private plane, with gunshot wounds in his chest. It seemed Raimundo knew nothing about Tekún after that, that he did not know Tekún had contacted me. This jail visit was a dead lead.

The nicotine of his cigarette, while waking him, also seemed to relax him. "*Mire, Señora Chacón,*" he said, using the formal *Usted* on me, "I'm sorry about your son. I hope he gets better, and quickly. That shouldn't have happened. But you can't blame my old boss for that."

"Yes I can. And I can blame you too."

They had taken my gun upstairs. I itched for it.

"Anything else, Detective?"

"Yes. If you do talk to your boss, remind him that Doctor Juvenal Urbino died while reaching for his pet bird."

"Juvenal . . . do I know him?"

I walked away. He asked again for clarification of the name, and I yelled over my shoulder, Dr. Juvenal Urbino. That satisfied me, though I wasn't exactly sure why. Just the fact that I had something on Raimundo, or at least, I had walked out with the last word. It was important for me, these days, to have the last word. Important to have some control over a life that, though I didn't see it at the time, was losing all control. I had a son who was alive, but who stared vacuously over the dinner table, as if trying to remember something very important. I had promises from Dr. Clancy, who said Sergio would be okay, that even though he is a child, I shouldn't worry about having an illegal substance, one known for drilling holes into teenagers' still-forming brains, floating around in my boy's skull. I had a mother who smiled at her grandson, who tried to hold him as she always held him, putting him on her lap, stroking his hair, saying "*Ay, mi corazón, rey de mi vida,*" holding back tears when she saw that he did not smile anymore. I had a house, one that was mine, that demanded monthly payments, payments I made, every single first of every single month. And in that house I had a packet of documents that had told me more about my sister's killer than I had ever known before. So there: perhaps there was control in my life.

"Detective Chacón?"

"Yes?"

To my left was the front desk. I almost walked right by it. I smiled at the agent, who smiled back. I had to retrieve my gun, sign out, and thank him for his help.

He made a calm, gentle move with his open hand, palm down, over the record book, keeping me from putting down the time, "Please don't sign out yet, Detective."

I looked at him. Then I asked for my gun. Calmly, I thought.

"Yes . . . I've just gotten a phone call from upstairs, and they've asked to have you wait just a moment, if you could please."

"Why? What's up? I've got to get back to the station."

"Yes, just . . . Special Agent Pierce will explain it to you."

Special Agent. That was the agent in charge. And

upstairs, I knew, was not TBI, but the ones really in charge, FBI. "Explain what to me? What's going on?"

Harold, my escort, gently touched my elbow. "Take a seat in there please, Detective."

Harold's voice was soft, supple. There was no mistaking the authority in it. An authority so strong, one that came from above, that there was no need for him to put a rough edge to his words. His voice could rest in kindness.

It was a good twenty-five minutes before anyone walked into the room, which meant one thing: a shakedown. As much as the Feds and the Tennessee Bureau wanted to keep relationships smooth between their offices and local law enforcement, I knew they always had the right to revert to old tactics. It didn't take twenty-five minutes for a man to come down an elevator. They were sweating me.

They did a good job. I had part of it figured out before they walked in. This was their tactic: give me time to work on an alibi before they walked in, knowing, if I were guilty of anything, I would stumble over my own endeavor at clarity, would hone a lie so sharp that I'd cut myself on its edge. But I had nothing to lie about: the incident in Mississippi did happen, and I would be straight up about that. Blevins had a record, and Blevins hated anyone not white. These boys should understand that, especially Harold, being African American. He was just outside the door, watching the hallway. The door was closed, though I could see the blue blazer of his shoulder through the beveled glass in the door.

Something else picked at me. But I decided to deal with that once I got home. I had a little bonfire to build in the back yard.

A little late. The kindling of that bonfire walked into the room, along with Special Agent Pierce. The contents of the package that Tekún Umán had sent me was now tightly wrapped in a plastic bag, sealed, with a tag on it. It was not in the original envelope, which I had thrown away, one which I later looked for in the garbage. Before me now was the downloaded, color-printed seal of the FBI.

Tekún's letter was not in there.

Pierce walked with a limp. He was once very handsome. Blonde hair, and his blue eye was very blue. That one eye once had another; what was behind that black patch? And why a patch? Why not a glass prosthetic? And why, though he must have been in his early thirties, did he wear a face like a man who has seen war, who has regrets? A crooked scar ran underneath the strap of the patch, like a path crossing a black river twice, three times. "Here you go, Sir," said another agent, another white guy who pulled Special Agent Pierce's chair out for him. Pierce thanked him, still looking at me. He smiled only slightly, as if that were something his mother had taught him long ago. Then the smile disappeared, behind the memory of that regret, that eye patch, the limp. He placed the package next to him. The package that, just this morning, had been hidden under my bras.

They had been in my home. My mother had to

open the door to them, my son had to watch them open cabinets and check under the furniture and pull the refrigerator from the wall. Had Sergio responded? Or did he just keep watching television? My mother, God knows: she responded.

Pierce's blonde hair was so short, I'm sure he didn't ever need to brush it. Just wash and wear. He probably spent little time prepping himself for the day, what with two prosthetics to deal with; the way he limped, I could tell that was an artificial leg.

I realized my left index fingertip was running along my scar.

"Detective," said Pierce. "I believe we need to talk." He glanced at the package between us, at the large metal clip that held together the illegally downloaded papers. I had placed that clip there. "Our prints girls are very good. They'd be able to lift some clean latents from the paper itself. But you know what? I bet there are some fine thumbprints on that clip."

I really didn't need to say much, as Pierce was more than happy to put it out on the table. "Last month our computers in DC showed a blip of a hacker coming through. Someone was downloading files, someone who had access to some pretty sophisticated virus software. They also had a Swiper, which allows you to clean out your connection to the internet, leaving no trace or trail. So we had no leads.

"We send out memos all the time: all our people in the field got word of this, to be on the lookout for individuals who might have some connection to the specific downloaded files. I got a call from one Agent Burkett, from Memphis, who said you stopped by recently, asking for some information.

"That fellow you pistol-whipped in Mississippi, Greer Blevins. We brought him in for questioning. He

confessed to selling an attack dog to a stranger seven
months ago. You went to him on a lead that you decided not to share with Agent Burkett, or anybody in
the Bureau. You can see why our local District Judge,
the Honorable Renee Menster, had no qualms in handing the local Nashville Police a search warrant for your
home.

"Would you mind, Detective, telling me how these
downloaded files came into your possession?"

When my son Sergio has gotten caught with his
hands in something that is not his (the sweets jar, the
matches above the sink, my purse) he looks at me in the
same way that I now looked at Special Agent Pierce.
And he too, says nothing.

"It's a federal offense, to hack into the Bureau's
files."

"Have you checked my computer yet?"

"No. That's our next step."

"Then you'll see that I did no hacking. I have no
idea how to do that."

"Then how did you get these?" He placed his palm
on the top of the plastic wrap.

I was just about to say to them, *Tekún Umán, one
Rafael Murillo, the man who got out of here just a few
months ago, he's the one*, but Special Agent Pierce added
to his question, "and could you please tell me who is
Doctor Juvenal Urbino?"

That's why it took them twenty-five minutes to
get to me. They were questioning Raimundo. And
Raimundo told them the only answer he had: he had
no idea who the good doctor was. Only that he was,
supposedly, dead.

And for that reason, I told him, "I'm sorry, but I'm
not at liberty to say."

Pierce sighed heavily. "Look, if you paid someone

to hack into our files, that in itself is illegal, and you're in a lot of trouble for it. But I'd need the name of the hacker. You should understand that, Detective Chacón. We can't have a loose cannon geek out there, breaking into our files. That's just the beginning of chaos."

"Yes. I know. I promise you, I paid no one to hack into your files."

"Then how did you get these?"

"Would you believe me if I told you they were mailed to me anonymously?"

He knitted his fingers together before him. Then I noticed that his right thumb was gone; only the left lay atop the web of fingers. "Then I'd have to ask myself, why didn't you hand them over to us immediately? These downloads are dated over three weeks ago."

"Because, Special Agent Pierce," I said, "it was all about my sister."

I placed the ball in his court of empathy. He was a wounded man. Those wounds either had hardened him or softened him, depending upon whom he was interrogating.

He looked down at the table, putting it all together with quick words. "So someone anonymously sent you a packet of illegal documents, to help you out with your ongoing, private investigation of the murder of your sister. We're left with the simple question, who could that someone be?"

You would have thought he was finished with questioning. But he wasn't. "Of course, then I'd have to ask myself why a woman in the Homicide Squad of the Nashville Police Department is spending so much of her free time looking for Catalina Chacón's killer. Is she out for justice, or revenge?

"And then, I'd have to ask what this tells me when I realize that that same detective, upon receiving such highly charged, top secret files as these, did not return the files to their rightful owner, the Federal Bureau of Investigation. I have to wonder about how clearly that detective is thinking."

He paused. He looked at the packet, then back at me. "Then I have to think about the information you now have on the Whisperer. I have to think about that information."

He stood up, walked to the door. "I could have charges on you right now, Detective Chacón. But for now, I've decided to put in a phone call to your superior. You need to report to him right away."

He held the door for me. I walked out. I was free to leave the building. I walked to the front desk and, without really thinking, signed out and asked for my gun. The agent at the desk glanced behind me to Special Agent Pierce. I realized then I'd not get my gun back, not today. It came to me right then, how lately, I hadn't really been thinking. Not as clearly as I should have been.

ou're on suspension for an indefinite period of time. You'll receive half pay, all your benefits. That, because I argued on them for that. Your gun, you've already surrendered it to the Feds. They will turn it in to me. You're up to your ass in problems."

"I realize that."

McCabe leaned back in his chair. His left hand wiped automatically over his face, as if to wake him from this nightmare. He rubbed the bald of his head, pushed down the laurel of thinning hairs. "Romilia. You're one of the best. And you've been a pain in the ass since you got here."

"Excuse me?"

"Come on Romilia. You've got a short fuse, and all I see is it's getting shorter. You've got hell of good instincts. But that quick temper is going to get the best of you someday."

He paused, then turned the conversation another way. "I can understand. Your sister. Trying to figure out what happened there, put it to rest, somehow . . ." it was a voice of compassion, and from it rose his question, "Those records give you much hope?"

I did not hesitate to answer, "I'm not at liberty to say."

He smiled. "Good. That's the way you should be thinking." He poured himself coffee, and this time didn't offer me any. "Stay nearby. The Feds are pulling apart your computer. They'll probably press charges, but maybe they'll be easy on you, since you're local PD. But don't give them any more reasons. Stay close to home."

"Yes sir."

So, I went home and disobeyed. I helped my mother pack, put together a small suitcase for my boy. He was actually excited about this: he hadn't seen his cousins in several weeks. The excitement was good to see. Perhaps this would be good in a number of ways: maybe going to Atlanta to visit relatives would help pull Sergio out even more. And I was suspended; I had nothing I could do. I had no gun, had to put away the badge.

Before leaving, I made one more stop in Nashville.

Jacob "Doc" Callahan lived in Bellevue, a private house that he kept even though his wife had passed away three years ago. Before going there, I drove around other parts of Nashville until I reassured myself of no patterns of cars behind me. Then I drove to Bellevue. It was night. Doc opened the door, let me in, and quickly closed it.

"You shouldn't be doing this, Romi," he said.

"Just give me the package, Doc."

He sighed. He walked to another room, muttering

to me about how much trouble I could get in. Then he brought me the envelope, unopened.

"So. You weren't curious?" I asked.

"Of course. Damn curious. But I read your note on the front, the one that screamed 'Do NOT open.' What's going on?"

"The less you know, the more honest you can be."

"Romilia," he said. His tone carried my name like something sacred on a silk pillow. Only harder. "I would lie for you."

"Oh Doc, you're sweet." I tiptoed to him and kissed him on the cheek. That, I know, was manipulation: he wasn't always good at hiding how he felt.

Early next morning my family and I piled the luggage into the car. I called McCabe's message machine and told him to call me anytime if he needed anything, that I'll be out with my boy but leave a message and I'd get back to him right away. Then we drove to cousin Mirta's house in Atlanta. We ate supper, had a beer, talked about the latest gossip in the family.

The next morning, of course, I drove straight to New Orleans.

Life had changed in Tekún Umán's hometown. This was the first he'd seen a *New York Times* in Chattanooga. And the Starbucks were as ubiquitous as McDonalds.

No comparison, of course.

Still, the cappuccino was not as thick or as creamy as the ones Tekún made at his ranch in Ixaba. It was the cream. Which cream you bought made all the difference in the world. Starbucks couldn't have a cow in every establishment, with workers learning to skim the top layer off the bucket for the thickest cream. Some things from the old country you just couldn't mimic.

It took him a few mornings to get accustomed to wearing a warmup outfit into a public establishment. Normally, in the States, he wore suits at all times, light worsted wool Italian double breasted, with no tie, just an open cotton shirt, wing tip shoes from Brooks Brothers, the suit a Versace. But they'd be looking for that right off the bat. Of course, they'd be looking for a fairly tall, thin, black haired, bearded man with olive skin. Which is why he shaved his beard off in Mexico, and had Beads dye his hair a sandy brown. Beads had complained all through the rinsing that this was a bad idea; returning to the States at this time was simply a mistake. With his head in the sink in Mexico, closing his eyes so Beads could rinse out the excess dye, Tekún Umán said, "Beads, you worry too much."

But Beads did not worry too much, and Tekún knew it. This was not risky; it was beyond reason. The James home in Chattanooga was one obvious place where the DEA would have their men. Not in the premises themselves; he had already verified this, driving around the perimeter of the estate in a rented Hyundai in a quick reconnaissance of a piece of land that he knew so well. No Feds anywhere. But no doubt they were in Chattanooga, at least a few, and they had the James telephone tapped.

He was not beyond reason. He was careful in his plans, thorough. But he did have to see his mother.

The trick was not to be in Chattanooga for too long. He stayed at a Holiday Inn Express near the airport. The Radisson downtown beckoned him, but he knew, for this to work, that some sacrifices had to be made.

Four days in Chattanooga. Four days of continental breakfasts and no room service. But one can only give up so much: he made a Starbucks run every morning, early, and read *The New York Times*.

From a pay phone he called a house in Nashville, but Raimundo wasn't answering. On the third try someone did answer, but it wasn't Raimundo. It sounded cop-like. Tekún Umán hung up.

They had caught Raimundo. Another meth lab closed for business. He had his others, of course, in the Clarksville area, north of Nashville. But no one made a batch of meth like Raimundo.

The New York Times was his only delight each day. Here he could read about world events, national news, what the president was up to today. He could read about that killing in Denver, a young man who was the head of a newly formed gang that distributed Ecstasy on the school grounds and at the teenage rages. His name was Joaquín Champ. Twenty-three years old, a member of the Crips in Los Angeles, Joaquín had moved to Denver to form a satellite force there. He was known for his heated temper and a quick reliance on an old Luger his grandfather had given him. Charged with two counts of murder of rival gang members, Joaquín was found dead in a chalet in the hills surrounding Denver, having been kidnapped and held for several days before authorities found him. He had died by a tiny neck wound, a deep nick that made him choke on his own blood.

Tekún looked above his reading glasses at the Starbucks clientele. A black woman with a poodle in her arms. An older white gentleman in a jogging suit, done with a fast walk. The regulars.

Tekún had to use his laptop to find other news, such as the latest on Detective Chacón. *The Cumberland Journal*'s web site was a bit clunky, slow. Late one night in the hotel room he finally pulled it up on his screen. Lo and behold, there she was again, making the press. Federal charges brought on her. Breaking and entering? Computer hacking . . . He pulled up articles from the past two weeks. Meth lab found by homicide detective Romilia Chacón, Raimundo Salgado arrested for suspicion of operating the lab. Emotional homicide detective almost loses her son to an accidental overdose of methamphetamine, also known as ice or crystal. A probable cause of her heroic, irrational behavior.

Still, Sergio's overdose did not explain that other article, about a pistol-whipping in Mississippi days before. And now, a smaller article, though on page one: Romilia Chacón suspended from her duties. Lieutenant Patrick McCabe had no comments.

Again he looked at the federal charges placed on her. She had said nothing about how the stolen files had come into her possession. She had not mentioned him.

She had received his package. Had studied it. Had tried to keep it from the Federal agents. She had not mentioned the name Tekún Umán.

Her son overdosed.

"Well now, this could go a few different ways," he said, closing the laptop. "And it's going quicker than I thought." He stood up, zipped his dark blue warm-up suit, slipped into running shoes. It was cooler tonight.

As a boy in Chattanooga, Tekún was called Rafael, or Rafie. He was a wiry child who liked to do foolish things to worry his mother, such as jump out of the second-story window of his bedroom and grab hold of the oak branch just outside. He didn't merely jump: he launched himself out the window, trying each time to look more like Superman. Some of his Tennessee relatives called him "Squirrel." "Squirrel's gone and done it again," Uncle Peter from Knoxville once said during a cookout. "I just saw that boy jump out of his window. Looked like he was diving into a pool!"

That was enough for Ruthie to run around the corner of the house and scold him while he came down the tree. As he jumped from one branch to the next, then shimmied down the trunk, she told him how he would be the death of her, worrying about him breaking his neck. He just smiled at her, and with that smile broke her scolding like so many thin twigs. "Come here, Rafie. Have some chicken," she'd finally say.

Looking at those trees now did something to him that he didn't care for. He touched the trunk of one of them, then wished he hadn't. This was no time for memories.

Which made him ask himself, *Then why are you here?*

It was springtime. The ground was still moist from an afternoon shower. The blossoms on the dogwoods had yet to break open. He had not spent a springtime here in twenty-five years.

Enough.

He knew his mother was sick. When he had last seen her, she could still recognize him. Tekún had read that as the disease worsens, the person recognizes few things. A man may shave a mirror-image of himself, brushing the razor over the glass. A woman may stare at her daughter and call her *Usted* instead of using the intimacy of *tú*. Still, he had a hard time of it, imagining his mother acting these ways.

The city was quiet. As far as he could see, there were no threats anywhere. He had parked the Hyundai down the street, two blocks away. No traffic drove through the neighborhood.

After wandering the grounds for a few minutes in a useless act of nostalgia, he decided to be formal about it. He knocked on the front door.

It took awhile. He thought he heard someone on the other side. The peephole went dark. The door opened, and Carlita, the maid, looked up at him and smiled. *"Señor,"* was all she said, then *"Pase adelante. Que alegre es, verle . . ."*

He kept with her in Spanish, put his hand on her shoulder, leaned down and kissed her cheek lightly. They made small talk. Carlita asked about a cousin of hers back in Flores, four hours north of Poptún. He reported that Jaime worked for a petroleum company, and was looking good, *"pero que panza!"* said Tekún, making a round gesture before his thin stomach. She laughed, then made a comment about his dyed hair, his clean-shaven face. *"Pareces a Mel Gibson,"* and again she giggled. She talked more than he remembered, and it was pleasant; indeed, she seemed happy to see him. Though obviously nervous.

"I've come to see mamá," he said finally.

"Sí, como no."

She moved toward the stairs, slowly. He followed. "Where is *Tía* Kimberly?" he asked, to which Carlita said that *la doña* Kimberly was out for the night, Wednesdays were her chance to get away a bit, see a movie.

He heard his heartbeat. His mother was upstairs and it had been several years and Alzheimer's is merciless.

Once Carlita opened the door to Ruthie's bedroom, Tekún breathed out. This was his old bedroom. They had moved her here, Carlita said, a couple of years ago, as it was on the second floor, closer to the kitchen than her old room on the third floor. He breathed in and smelled the room where he had slept through childhood. This was home. One of two homes, of course; this smelled nothing like the *finca* in the jungle, but rather had the air of humidity that is uniquely southern Tennessee. They had moved no furniture. The cherry dresser was still in the same place. Tekún's light blue handprint, made of plaster when he was five, still hung on the cream-white wall. It hung right next to his favorite window.

His mother wore new pajamas. This was good, he told himself. Keep her in clean, new clothes. Keep her clothed in dignity.

She was well-kept. Her hair, nicely bunned, though of course more gray. She lay in bed, her head propped up on three pillows. She stared beyond him, toward the door, where Carlita stood. But she did not see Carlita. What did she see?

"Hello, Mom."

A pause, then a solid, "Benjamin, you have got to take care of this rascal dog of yourn."

Tekún turned to Carlita, tried to remember. Benjamin. A great uncle in Memphis, he believed. Died in '72, wasn't it? Hardly ever mentioned, as he was so distant in relation, in geography.

Which dog did she refer to? There was a lineage of dogs, both here and in Guatemala.

"It's me, Mom. It's Rafael. It's Rafie."

"You should know better, stealing my coffee."

He smiled at that. He always loved coffee, since he was nine. He would take sips of hers when she wasn't looking.

He had read a lot about the disease, so he followed through, "Sorry Mom. It just tastes so good."

"Where's Ben? Benjamin!"

He sat on the edge of the bed, took her hand. "Uncle Ben's not here now, Mom. I'm here, taking your coffee."

"Chulo's flown away again. Probably hunting."

The name of their macaw bird, back on the *finca*. Again, hopeful; but how did they keep up with her, the way she skipped about? Still, Chulo was a point of reference, "He'll be back soon. You know how he flies off."

Ruthie turned silent.

He turned to Carlita. "How is she?" he asked.

Carlita rubbed her left thumbnail with her right thumb. An old habit from way back, whenever she got nervous. And she had reason to be nervous, with his sudden return, with his mother, sicker than before. He remembered how Carlita never wanted anyone to feel hurt. "She goes in and out," said the maid. "Sometimes it's much worse. Once she hit me, because she thought I was a robber or something. But then she calms down."

A car passed outside in the neighborhood, followed by a second one. Other than that, all was quiet. He remembered the quiet of this place, and how he preferred the sounds of the jungle, the macaws squawking and the women constantly chatting outside about gossip from Poptún and the men who worked with the livestock. This was a rich neighborhood, and the wealthy of this town demanded a certain peace, a quietude. He preferred Poptún; but he could see how important this silence was for her. The two cars turned. All was quiet again.

"Chulo, he chased the robber away."

Tekún turned to her, smiled. "Well. At least she can associate a little," he said quietly, looking back at Carlita. Carlita was staring at Ruthie. He turned. It was Ruthie's eyes. They spasmed just slightly, then rested, barely, on Carlita.

It was a spasm of sentience. A look of recognition, the snapping of a façade.

Tekún, though he did not realize it, moved slightly back. He stared at her. He studied her. This he could do: he could study, whenever the enemy reared.

"Aunt Kimberly," he said.

She did not move.

Outside a car door closed, ever so slightly. It was a

late model. Its slam was muffled with the tightness of
being new.

He reached forward, grabbed the bedridden
woman by the neck. He barely squeezed. All fifteen
knuckles of his left hand locked. "Aunt Kimberly," he
said, as if calling her forward. She came. She looked
straight at him.

"Don't hurt me," she said.

Her body pulled inward to protect her neck. Her
hands shot up to his wrist. He did not contract the grip,
but he held her, like a clamp locked.

"Where is my mother?"

"Not here. We just had her put in a home."

The front door of the house opened, slammed
against the wall. Tekún turned. Carlita was staring at
him. She yelped, a plea, something in Q'eqchi' about
not killing her *patrona*. A call rose from downstairs. A
man's voice. Authority, laced with rage.

"Why did you do this?"

"Rafie. I saw pictures of that poor young man, the
DEA agent, what you did to him. You had no right to
do that."

"They have no right to hunt me."

His voice ground low with the statement. He
turned, still holding his aunt's throat. He gave an order
to Carlita, his tone so dark, no one could disobey it.

"Abre esa ventana."

She obeyed, seeing that he placed just the slightest
pressure on her employer's neck. She opened the window wide. At his demand, she unhooked the screen. It
fell to the bushes below.

We can return to our old bicycles and pick them up
and reach through decades to the days when we rode
off, free. The handles feel the same; and we know the
exact amount of pressure needed on these, our brakes.

We can follow paths in old forests, as we have forgotten nothing. Though trees grow, they do so slowly, and we know them, we know our favorites in a forest of them.

In crisis, we can reach for anything familiar, anything that will help us escape.

He let Aunt Kimberly go. She caught her breath, more from the fear than his grip. She screamed. But he had already jumped the bed, took two quick, solid steps across the old bedroom. Then Carlita saw what Uncle Peter had witnessed a childhood ago.

It was not as perfect as when he was nine. He was bigger now. He grabbed hold of the old branch. It held him. But he swung, pendulum-like, and his ribs slammed against a thick branch that he remembered being farther away. A stretch of ribcage muscles crunched under the round, rough wood. He made it quicker to the ground than he anticipated.

But he could run. And he could hear, clearly, through that open window, the official shout of the federal officers, demanding him to halt, followed by a curse that was all too human, stripped completely of governmental training. One of their own, he had hurt one of their own. Someone gave an order, to shoot the fucker down. The maid screamed. Within the minute he had the Hyundai on the road. He checked his ribs. They were tender to his touch.

There was nothing in the Holiday Inn Express. He had paid with one of Bead's fake cards. There was nothing in this town, not anymore.

Chattanooga turned into Georgia mountains and those turned into the flat of Alabama and Mississippi and from there it's a long slide to New Orleans.

MARCH 12, 2001

Supposedly there was an exotic bird store in the French District off Bourbon Street, but in my first day in New Orleans, I didn't make it there. I drove straight into the city, and was lucky to find a Motel Six with a vacancy. They still charged me higher than what I wanted to pay. Just the first in a long string of things that would not go my way.

It was two in the morning when I arrived. I trembled from the caffeine overdose and reeked of nicotine. The young man at the front desk didn't act surprised. I fell into a long line of self-beaten travelers who had survived the freeway and made it to his front desk.

It took another two hours of bad porn and an unmeasured amount of whiskey to get me to sleep. Still, the porn must have been working, even though it was obvious who the target audience of this little film was. If I ignored the silicon-hardened chick and focused on the man's sharp jaw and his thin, swivelling hip bone and oh-so-cute ass, I could feel something. I didn't undulate under the blankets like those couples did on the cable station, but my middle finger did find its way under my panties. And that was about it. Too drunk for anything to happen. Too stinky from the long drive and the pack of cigarettes and double pot of coffee to get loosened up. Not until the next morning, around eleven o'clock, when the sun was already hot over New Orleans, did I decide to do something. I crawled into the filled tub, floated awhile before reaching back down there and rousing a few thoughts, plugging in different faces for the man and the woman who undulated, what a word, undulate. It works when you keep fiddling with it, playing with the images, ashamed to tell anybody whose face you put on that man's body, especially when you think about why you're here, in a city you've never even considered visiting before.

Afterwards I just lay there, long enough for the water to turn cold. How long had it been since I was last with a man? Too easy to answer: I hadn't had sex since my husband died. My middle finger and I had gotten really close in this past year and a half.

The day was already half gone. But I needed to move, needed to run. I put on old shorts, a T-shirt, and stepped out into some of the worst humidity I've ever felt in my life. It was noon. People looked at me strangely: both off-pink and ebony faces watched this young brown woman burst into sweat a block from the Motel Six and figured real quick that she was from out of town.

But I kept running. I ran as hard as I could for half an hour. Back in the hotel room I left a stain of sweat on the carpet, where I did push-ups, sit-ups, leg stretches. I didn't watch the television. I lifted my thigh and counted until the burn made me drop my knee against the other. Then I went for the other leg.

Something needed burning out of me.

Half a minute of staring into the bedroom mirror, turning sideways to check the bulge in my tummy (it was almost period-time, I could tell), I rationalized that I hadn't gained any weight, just some water pounds from all that sitting in the car yesterday. I turned to my right, because all that exercise had turned the edge of the scar slightly red, something I really didn't need to see that morning.

Applebees was the closest restaurant to the motel. I sat there and ordered a salad and ran through the day's *Times-Picayune*, one somebody had already read and had tossed on a side table in the breakfast area of the motel. The waiter brought my salad. He was nice enough, with a good smile, good teeth. Maybe he'd make my next dream trip to the tub.

I stopped glancing, stopped turning the pages, upon finding the article that had come out of Colorado. It was a longer article, an analysis on a recent murder.

Though his neck had been slit, Joaquín Champ had died due to drowning. His own blood filled his lungs and had choked him to death. But that's not what stopped me. The killing was strange enough, the fact that a young man who was the head of a satellite drug-running gang out of Los Angeles was carefully murdered in a chalet just on the edge of Denver. The title of this article was "New Evidence on Champ Killing." It was a leak: they had found a note at the crime scene.

Notes had been on my mind these past few days. Three in particular. None of which I could make much sense out of.

"Shit," I muttered aloud, "I'm in the wrong city."

And then I thought, of course: he's killed again.

This, however, could be jumping to conclusions, and I told myself that while scanning the article for more information, which it didn't have. No details on the note itself, what it said, whether or not there was any bubble-like drawings on it. Though it did say something about being a photocopy, which made me doubt my quick theory, that this was the work of the Whisperer. According to the stolen FBI notes, the other letters had been written on thicker, twenty-four pound paper, slightly off-white, a cut above the regular typing or printing paper you'd find in a business office. The UPI reporter clarified that the Denver note was indeed a photocopy, they could tell from a slight smudge on the paper, like the shadow from a photo-copy machine's dirty glass.

That was not like the Whisperer. But this was not like any other gang killing. You think gangs, you see young guys storming in and shooting the enemy right in the face, or driving by and raining bullets sideways through the house with high-powered automatics. Whenever I thought about the Whisperer, I thought about well-performed slaughters. The article made this killing in Denver sound like a surgery gone awry. Which meant it didn't fit either scenario.

Still, something about the Denver case made me question what I was doing. Looking for exotic birds in a city I'd never visited before. Tekún Umán left clues that only he and I could follow. Who would remember a secondary character in a novel, and where she lived? Only people who had read *Love in the Time of Cholera*, in the original Spanish, so many times, just to feel that Spanish on your tongue (yes, I read it aloud whenever I could; did Tekún do the same?). Doctor Juvenal Urbino is one of the three main characters of that book, one corner of the love triangle that spins that novel forward, pulls you right into the world of geriatric erotica. He and his wife Fermina have a daughter named Ofelia Urbina, a young woman who, whenever she thinks about the love trysts of her elderly mother, retreats in disgust to her home in the United States: New Orleans. According to Gabriel García Márquez, Ofelia Urbina lived here, over one hundred years ago. In a city I knew nothing about.

Tekún's note, the one I pulled from my luggage in the hotel room, left a clarity of clues regarding how to find him. *"The freedom of the quetzal, it is no longer mine,"* meaning he had been in Guatemala (the quetzal being that country's national bird), but had left there. *"I've decided to retire to Ofelia Urbino's hometown."* Meaning New Orleans. *"Perhaps there, I'll be able to touch what was out of her father's reach."*

That last line is what I had fed back to Raimundo, down in the contemporary dungeon of the Nashville FBI offices: Ofelia's father, Dr. Urbino, dies in the first chapter of *Cholera*, falling from a step ladder while trying to grab hold of his escaped, smart-mouthing parrot.

In order to find Tekún Umán, I was to look for some place in New Orleans, Louisiana, that houses parrots.

And why was I looking for Tekún Umán? Because the bastard's drug dealings had come home to me, to my son.

A lie, or half-truth. I was here because he had given me more information in one book rate mailed package than I had ever been able to acquire in six years. If he could do that, maybe he could give me more.

Which meant I was associating myself with a felon, a fugitive from the law. The same law that was ready to press down on me with charges I didn't really deserve.

The law that was doing its job, something that, in six years of investigation, had gotten them and me diddly.

"Parrots?" said the older woman at the newstand. She smoked a cigarette. Which reminded me to buy a pack from her. "We got your parrots here, sure enough. All over the place." She laughed. "Back about seven, eight years ago a small family of them escaped from the Audubon Zoo, just across town. They did what every other animal and human in this town likes to do: fornicate. Now we got parrots all over the city. Our weather's just perfect for them, hot, wet. All the time. Other day I was walking by the river with my dog, and a green blanket covered over me: an entire flock of parrots. Never seen anything quite as beautiful as that."

I smiled, but it was faked. "Do you know of any place where they might sell parrots?"

She thought about it. She took a puff too many on her cigarette, as if I, like she, had time on my hands. "Off Bourbon Street, in the French Quarter. I believe there's a specialty shop of some sorts for birds. You know, the exotic kind. You might try there. Or then again," she puffed, smiled, "you need to find yourself a parrot, just try looking up."

I didn't go into The Green Plume. That would have made me too easy to find. I spent the better part of that afternoon across the street and down a few stores, in a coffee shop that had large, dark windows, ones that protected the clientele from the sun and allowed me to look out and watch the women walk into the pet store. Rich women. Most of them looking just a little bit older than me, women in their mid thirties who had somehow acquired enough money, either through their own businesses or through marriage, to walk into a store like that and buy a Tibetan Terrier or a Macaw from Nicaragua or a boa from God knows where. Just in their thirties, looking trim and well-kept and, no doubt, well-fucked. Here I was, jealous of women I did not know, just because they wore fine clothes, thin dresses that hugged them, with faces that revealed the satisfaction of either cunnilingus or at least an expensive vibrator.

I have dresses that hug me. I can make a skirt and a sleeveless top look really nice. Just ask Peaches back in Nashville. Of course, he was looking at my outline, at night, and not the details within the borders of my body.

It was just one cut.

It hadn't taken everything away.

I wanted to believe that. Wanted to believe I was the woman that some of the guys in uniform back in Nashville didn't mind sizing up, one of them once calling me the Lady in Red. It had made me angry at the time, knowing he was whispering something lewd to his partner. But rarely do emotions make their appearances in purity: pride was laced alongside it. I did look good. I worked out daily, watched my weight, kept a size six in my more expensive clothes (okay, size eight in my Sears jeans), and filled fairly well a 34B cup. Before I had gotten married a model instructor at Emory University had approached Catalina and me in one of the school's cafeterias. He wanted to shoot us for the local school magazine. I declined; Caty, of course, did not. Next thing I know she was on the front cover of *Emory Monthly*, all smiles and Latina-gorgeous, wearing a barely modest, ever so skimpy blue dress (her best color), and all I could think was what Caty had said, "Girl, you could have been on the cover with me!" And she was right. We were sisters, no one missed that. And she was a beautiful woman.

Somehow this cut made me forget all that.

My mind must have drifted at the coffee shop, because suddenly the young barista was beside me, asking if I wanted anything else. This was a Starbucks, in a busy part of town. They liked making sure the turnover turned over. I ordered another cappuccino.

For the entire afternoon the only people who entered The Green Plume were the well-kept, satisfied women (a couple of them with kids) and a few men who darted in quickly, left quickly, none of them Tekún, which of course made me realize that this was one long wild goose chase and I was nowhere near grabbing any geese.

My mother reported feeling fine. And she did sound happy over the phone. In the back I heard a number of children playing, Sergio and his cousins, though it sounded like a lot more kids than that. "You won't believe who's in town," said Mamá. "Your Uncle Chepe."

"You're kidding?" I smiled, and suddenly longed to be in Atlanta. Chepe was my mother's baby brother, a good seventeen years younger than Mamá. He lived in Los Angeles, ran a fairly large catering business that made most of its money on the lots of Warner Brothers and Universal. Sometimes Chepe called us with the latest version of "You *won't* believe who I met today." He never got tired of running into the stars, having seen most of them as a kid, watching movies that would finally arrive to San Salvador with poorly subtitled translations. The last I heard, Dennis Hopper was munching on Chepe's carrots on a film lot in Ojai.

Chepe had worked first on his business, then he and his young wife Sarita (my age) started having kids and didn't look like they were going to stop. Five boys, all under the age of eleven. That sounded like hell, I used to tell Mamá, but now, hearing them all screaming in the background while my mother and I talked, it sounded more like heaven.

Chepe had always been my mother's favorite of the

four siblings. Now Chepe was her one and only. The rest had been killed back in the old country. Getting Chepe out of the country was my mother's doing, paying for the best *coyote* she could find, a man named Ignacio who took my mother's money, drove all the way to San Salvador, sneaked her teenage kid brother out of the capital and delivered Chepe to her doorstep in Georgia. He liked Atlanta, but he had always heard of Los Angeles, and the moment he turned eighteen he was gone. A year later he started sending my mother a monthly check, and has never stopped doing that.

"You want to talk with Sergio?" she asked me.

Of course I did. She put him on. He was too busy for me. Though he called out to me, "Mamá! How are you?" I knew his eyes roamed the living room in Atlanta, searching out his cousins, keeping up with whatever game they played, like tearing up the house with a soccer ball. It really didn't matter that he didn't want to talk away the night with me, because that excited voice told me everything that I needed to hear: he was not only alive, but he was a boy again. He was not staring silently out of a dark and toxic world, but rather looking for his cousins through eyes that were free of the meth. He was playing like a four year old should play. That's why I cried.

Just one shot of whiskey with ice. No cigarettes. I had a book with me, and I was tired enough to read it in bed. The long drive from the previous day had done me in more than I realized. Sitting in a coffee shop the entire afternoon had not necessarily rested me. The run this evening was much better than the one in the morning: I found a long park, where others ran or walked their dogs, where Spanish moss hung out of trees and where no one looked at you strangely for sweating buckets. Then a decent meal alone in the Applebees, a salad, some sea bass. And a decision, of course: to hell with eating alone. This goose chase was about to end. I'd head back tomorrow. Back to Atlanta. Nothing awaited me in Nashville except a suspension; I might as well enjoy what my mother and son were enjoying. And I could work from there, in my aunt's guest room, much better than here in this lonely hotel.

I'm sure I snored.

The book fell against my chest, and lay there, no doubt, for a good hour before I felt the pressure against my mouth. That smell: he wore the same cologne, and it mixed with the natural odor of skin on his palm, which now pushed against my nostrils.

He reached up from the side of the bed with his other hand and turned off the reading lamp.

"Don't think about going for your gun."

No emotions come out pure, alone: that very statement, though it frightened me, also angered me. I had no gun. The prick had to remind me of that.

He stood up from the side of the bed. I couldn't see very well, but still could make out his shadow. So I punched it, as hard as I could. It was useless, I know; but if he was going to kill me, it wouldn't be without a fight.

But it wasn't useless. He fell over. I lunged out of the bed, stumbled for the lamp on the other side of the bed, flicked it on, and retreated to the opposite corner of the room.

There, on the floor, slumped Tekún Umán. The man who had de-testicled a DEA officer, who had avoided capture all these months from two federal agencies, now clutched at his ribs as if I had slammed him with a baseball bat.

He'd changed his hair color and style. He'd shaved off his well-groomed beard. Those changes weren't for me.

A knife tumbled onto the floor. His knife.

So this was a setup, getting me to New Orleans. Though for what, I wasn't sure. To kill me? Or just to take me?

It didn't matter. I took the knife. Reached around him quickly, stood again, held the knife up so he could see it. You'd think I had kicked him in the balls, the way he held his side. He made to get up. "Stay down!" I said. He hesitated, then disobeyed me.

How I wished that knife had been a gun. I've never operated with blades. He seemed to know this, maybe by the way I held it. Or maybe by the way I shook slightly. Either way, somehow the rest of his body pulled out of the pain and he was on me. The knife, though still in my clutch, was far from me, stretched to my far left. He pushed me onto the bed. His face was right above mine. His body, flat against me.

So this was all about rape. This was all he wanted.

"Drop it," he said. My hand dangled over the edge of the bed. He shook my wrist with his strong grip. "Come on Romilia, just let it go."

Finally I did. It clunked to the carpet. Though he still looked at me, his face turned exhausted, as if the pain had come back. He lifted off me, turned, picked up the knife, stood and lifted his jacket with his left hand, then reached back with his right, straining against pain. He slipped the knife into an unseen lumbar sheath. He tried to keep himself erect, but the pain was becoming too much. He sat down in a cushioned chair in the corner, like an old man.

"*Ya completamente rotas*," he muttered.

"What are you talking about?" My voice trembled, but I tried to sound more angry than frightened. "I couldn't have hit you that hard, to break bones."

"I had a little accident a few days ago, busted up my ribs. You may have just finished off the break."

"What happened?"

He smiled. "I was playing in the trees." He looked over at the table next to him, at the spread of papers, the death notes, the reports. "I see you received my package."

"Yeah. I received a lot more than that."

"What do you mean?"

I told him, in four sentences or less, about my suspension.

"So they confiscated the package?" He reached over, picked up one of the pages, the one with a Medical Examiner's report from Bristol. "Then this is a copy you made."

I didn't say anything.

He clicked his tongue at me in a mock-reprimand. "Naughty girl. Making copies of government documents. I think the charges could be deeper than a mere suspension, or loss of job. Federal offenses, that sort of thing. My my, Romi, when you sin, you sin boldly, don't you?" He glanced over the papers. "So what have you made of all this? Anywhere closer to catching the Whisperer?"

"Why should you care?"

"Why should I care?" The pain was leaving his body, his face relaxed, enough for him to smile. "I care because this Whisperer fellow is driving my favorite Homicide Detective to drink." He didn't have to glance at the bottle on the table. "Seems he's gotten under your skin and has stayed there."

"He's not the only thing under my skin." I stared at him hard. "My son. My son almost died because of your damned drug running."

He sighed. He turned away slightly, but then leveled his eyes right back on me. "No. Sergio did not almost die. He had a shock to his young system, yes. He had an episode. And I don't doubt he fell into a delusional depression, confusion, all of which is frightening, especially to a mother and a grandmother. But he is not hooked, Romilia. He is no addict. You prevented that. And as long as he stays away from the ice, he'll be fine."

"To hell with you."

"No. I'm sure it's been hell for you. I'm sorry it happened. How is your mother?"

I said nothing. He knew my mother. He almost once fooled my mother into believing he, Tekún Umán, was a good candidate for son-in-law.

He moved his fingers slightly over one side of his own neck, but looked at mine, "Are you doing all right?" he asked.

This, for some reason, I answered. "I'm fine."

"Let me see."

And I did: I turned slightly, as if I were merely avoiding his sight. But it was enough to show him the scar.

He leaned forward in the chair, made a slight wince from the pain in his ribs, but kept his eyes on my neck. He looked at it square, studied it; his facial muscles did not move, showed nothing. A neutrality that, for some reason, felt reassuring.

"It's healed well. But it bothers you, doesn't it?"

I stood up, paced toward the window. "Why did you tell me you were here?" I asked.

"Why did you follow?"

"You. Answer my question first."

He breathed hard again. "I owe you one. You saved my life."

"You owe me three."

"Come again?"

My arms had been crossed over my chest. I was wearing my robe, but I didn't remember putting it on. I must have slipped it on somewhere between punching him in the ribs and losing the knife. I uncrossed one arm, clenched my fist but allowed three fingers to punch upwards in explanation, one at a time. "You owe me for saving your life. You owe me for what happened to my son. You owe me for me losing my job."

"You haven't lost your job yet. By the way, why didn't you show them the letter?"

I said nothing.

"You didn't show them the letter because you don't trust them. Do you? You don't trust them because the Federal Bureau of Investigation has failed to bring down your sister's killer. You blame them for letting the Whisperer get away.

"So," he said, "why did you follow?"

"I want more information."

"On what? What you have is all I could get."

"How did you get it?"

"My dear, I hacked it."

"Then hack again."

"No, that's too risky, getting back into the FBI's mainframe. Now they know someone's been breaking in, they won't let . . ."

"Forget the FBI. Hack into St. Louis and Denver."

"Oh. The killing in Colorado. You believe he did it?"

"There was a note left."

"So I read this morning. A photocopy of a note."

"I'd like to see it."

"If you suspect that was the work of the Whisperer, the FBI will be all over it too."

"Can you get into the Denver and St. Louis PD's databases?"

"Of course. Why St. Louis? What happened there?"

"I don't know, but I want to find out." I turned, grabbed my clothes, walked toward the bathroom. But I was getting ahead of myself. I turned, looked at him hard. "How do I know you're not fucking with me?"

"Such language."

"*How do I know?*"

"Come on Romi. You just finished telling me how many times I owe you."

"Then swear."

"Swear what?"

"Swear that you owe me."

"Okay. Fine. You have my word." Then, as if it wasn't enough, he said it again, *You have my word.*

He introduced me to a man called Beads, an older gentleman who smiled at me and welcomed me into the condominium. We all spoke in Spanish. "Ms. Chacón. It is a pleasure. I've heard wonderful things about you." He smiled, invited me into a large bedroom that had been transformed into a place that looked ready to launch the Space Shuttle. Three computers ran at once. Wires ran from one to the other. Beads had me sit on a side chair while he took the main chair in front of the middle monitor. Tekún excused himself to make us coffee.

"Looks like some high-powered equipment," I said. "Are you planning to take over the stock market with all these gadgets?"

Beads chuckled. He put on a pair of reading glasses, then leaned toward the screen. "That would be a fine idea. But no, this is just regular computer programming that helps me keep up with Mr. Murillo's finances."

Beads was working the mouse quickly, which showed me how deft he was behind the computer, how those FBI files had been downloaded so nicely, before being sent to me. I kept my mouth shut.

He worked quickly, but it still took some time. Tekún was back with three cups. Beads took his, muttered "*Gracias, compa,*" sipped, put it to one side. I took mine and said nothing. But it was good. Freshly ground. Maybe freshly roasted.

"Anything?" asked Tekún.

"It's . . . weaving," said Beads. I wasn't sure what that meant. I couldn't help but get the image of a computer virus or bug of some kind, burrowing its way from New Orleans toward Colorado, cutting through a few websites along the way. Every few seconds Beads moved the mouse or punched a command into the keyboard. It seemed he had to manually maneuver the virus toward its destination. Was it a virus? Or did Beads have much more sophisticated devices, ones that helped drug runners stay ahead of the federal agencies, that always allowed them to win the drug war?

Drug war. Drug market was the term. Not a war. A supply and a demand. And Tekún knew it.

And I knew that, right now, sitting before this computer in this front of a condo, I was becoming more and more illegal. I'd have to make up for all this. Somehow.

"There. I believe we have something," said Beads. He turned to me, his eyes gentle and elderly behind those reading glasses. "Denver Police Department's mainframe. Homicide Division. Joaquín Champ. Under the name of one Sergeant Darrell Beckman."

"All right," said Tekún. "Open it up."

"Not there," said Beads. "We're inside their frame. Opening it might set off some whistles. I'll bring it home."

Whatever that meant. He fiddled more on the keyboard. The screen changed, but there was the file, with the victim's name on it. He clicked it open. A report came up.

There was no photocopy or facsimile of the note. But there were plenty of references to it, "Closed envelope found on the victim's lap, after passing through fingerprinting, Detective Beckman opened said envelope and found a note with the following inscription, written in a broken manner: 'Blood rivers///shift///into those whose///violence///hurt///others.' After which follows a second, separate passage: 'I am///the great///connoisseur of sin.'"

According to the report, the Denver division of the FBI had asked that copies of all homicide reports be sent to their state offices. A day after receiving the Joaquín Champ report, FBI in Denver asked to see both the note and the envelope it had come in. The moment FBI had taken a DNA sample from the glue of the envelope's seal, they ordered that the entire case be handed over to one Agent Sarah Preston in Denver.

DNA sample. The only thing they could compare it with was the envelope found in the mailbox of the dead couple in Bristol, the Mastersons.

They had compared the DNA and found a match. That's why they took the case.

Between the time they took the DNA sample and waited for the sample to come back positive or negative, Denver Homicide had an autopsy done on Joaquín Champ. He had ample traces of the sedative Alprazolam in his blood, heightened by the amount of whiskey he had consumed that night. Blood filled his lungs: the perpetrator had performed surgery on Joaquín, using a fine scalpel to open his neck, paralleling the Langer lines of the dermis. The cut was three centimeters long, though the thin blade (a razor? A scalpel?) had slipped easily through Champ's neck muscles. After that the perp used surgical tweezers underneath the skin. He somehow snaked a quarter inch of Joaquín's carotid artery into his trachea. It acted as a tiny hose that filled both lung cavities. Joaquín, his entire body duct-taped to a large, steel chair, his head pulled back and wrapped in solid silver-gray tape to the chair's back, had drowned in his own blood.

Blood rivers shift.

The Whisperer was not whispering so much now. His symbols cried out a little more each time.

It took another half hour for Beads to break into the St. Louis site. But we found nothing there, no reports of strange ritual killings.

Beads printed all of this before cutting off the connections to Denver and St. Louis and wiping the trails with yet another program. He handed me the hard copies. "Thank you, Beads," I said, perhaps too quickly. I thanked Tekún for the coffee. I readied myself to leave.

"Where will you be going?" asked Tekún.

I stopped in the middle of the front room. "I'm going to follow up on this." I held the papers up to him.

"This, I take it, means we're even."

"Yes. Yes it does. Thank you. We're clear now." I made a flat gesture with my hand, sweeping it before me.

"So. Do you need a ride?"

"No, no more favors." I forced a chuckle with that, reminding him, this had to end, right now. "I'll catch a cab. Thanks." I was out the door.

• • •

On our way in, as Tekún had driven us to his condominium, I had spotted a pay phone a block from his neighborhood. I thought to call from there. A cab, of course. But after calling the cab, I couldn't wait. I pulled out my phone card, punched in my account, and made the call to Nashville.

"Romilia? Where in hell are you?" McCabe sounded more worried than angry. But he was angry too.

"I'm okay, Lieutenant. I'm fine."

"I've called your house half a dozen times in the past forty-eight hours, don't you check your messages? That Pierce fellow over at the Bureau, he's breathing down my neck, wants you to come in for another interview."

Interrogation, you mean. But I said, "That's fine . . . no. Listen, Lieutenant, I've got new information on Tekún Umán. They can pick him up if they want."

"What, you know where he is?" More incredulity, laced with a little more anger, realizing that I had been on Tekún's ass more than I should have been.

"Yes, he's right here, I've got his address in . . ."

The paralysis was strange. I thought it began in my head, then I confused it with the sting in the nape of my neck, under my hairline. Then I wasn't sure where the numbness began, for it was everywhere. My voice froze. I dropped. The phone piece fell with me. Its steel cable jerked it up and slammed it once, then twice, against the phone box. It dangled two feet above me, an arm's reach away. If only I could reach up with my arm, touch the phone, say to my boss what I needed to say.

Tekún stood above me. He held an ornately carved, smooth, polished reed in his hand. Was it a reed? Was it a hollowed stick? My eyes watered, but the lids did not close. I heard him blow out a thick sigh. Lieutenant

McCabe yelled out of the phone piece. Tekún picked up the piece, looked at it as if it were my conspirator, then hung it on the cradle.

He leaned over, squatted above me. He cradled the flute-like instrument in his fingertips, then reached behind my head with the other hand and uprooted something from my neck. I felt nothing, though my head jostled. He held up a wooden dart, flipped it like a miniature baton before me as an explanation.

"It won't last long," he said.

Then he got on his knees and put his head just above mine, as if he meant to kiss me. But he did not kiss me. He spoke. His breath smelled of coffee. So I was breathing, though I did not feel it. I did not feel my heart.

"You know how I feel about you. But you should also know better about having them find me. Don't ever do that again.

"You can't have it both ways, Romilia: you can't break the law, then go kissing up to the cops, handing me over as some sort of sacrifice of appeasement. They are not my gods. They should not be yours."

He pulled out his knife. I had not gotten a good look at it before, even though I had held it. It was a strange knife, hooked at the end. My body wanted to jerk, but it did not; so the desire to jerk vibrated in me, in my skull, like a scream locked in an airtight box.

He placed the knife against the skin of my neck, on the unharmed side. The side I showed the world.

"I am very sorry for what happened to you," he said, glancing at the cut. "But you don't want a matching set now, do you?"

He sheathed the knife behind him, stood up quickly.

"Don't ever try to narc on me again."

He was gone.

I could not move. I wished to scream, wished to will even my toes or my thumbs to obey me, but nothing did. My throat could not cry out, my lips did not move. I was dead and I knew it; I had left the world and could still see it. He said it wouldn't last, but I could not believe him. He had killed me. I was just waiting for the final part, my consciousness, to snuff itself out, for darkness to fall over my eyes, a thick darkness blowing out the sounds of wind and a distant car that still seeped into my ear.

Then my left thumb moved. It pushed through the air like working its way through cold mud. But once it moved, the hand and arm followed, and the movement of the living pushed its way through me until it found my throat and I yelped an ugly yelp.

"You okay, lady?"

The cab driver stuck his head out his window. He looked about, perhaps searching for the gunman who had brought me down, wondering if he'd be the next victim. Finally he opened the door and helped me up, then tossed the envelope of papers and my purse next to me. He moved me to the back of his car. "Where to, ma'am?" I slurred out the name of my hotel. "You okay? You been drinking?" I said no; I slurred no; I actually slurred that monosyllabic word. The moment he pulled away and made a slightly sharp turn to the left, I slumped over the entire back seat. My head slammed against smoky, blue upholstery.

After calling New Orleans' finest, I regretted it. I regretted watching them as they teamed up with DEA and surrounded the house that I had pointed out and tore into it as if meaning to rip the first floor out, buckle the building and kill Tekún Umán with the weight of his own home. They had followed procedure, had called in SWAT teams and had sent in men and women to the four points of entry and had set up at the front door and had called out his real name, Rafael Murillo, then they had given him scant seconds to show himself before battering down the door. But the procedure was filled with an emotion that drove them forward like rabid dogs on leashes. They had found nothing. How did Tekún and Beads clean out so quickly? How had they managed to break down their computer equipment and load it all up and drive it away, wiping down the walls and doorknobs and oven racks of all fingerprints before leaving New Orleans?

Then I realized that they hadn't. Moving his own furniture wasn't Tekún's style. He always appeared in solitude. Whenever meeting him, I met him with only one of his hirelings beside him, never a group. Yet no doubt an invisible retinue of men and women were at his beck and call. Tekún didn't do the heavy work of hauling computers to the trunk of his Jaguar. They left in the Jaguar, or were driven away; then his people came in and took care of erasing his presence, his time, in the rented condo, which was paid for by one Dr. Juvenal Urbino.

"Son of a bitch!" yelped an agent, ripping off his gas mask. He stomped toward one of the parked police cars, where a colleague stood with a speaker-horn cradled in his hand. They talked. The agent glanced at me, still angry. But he did not blame me for a wild goose chase. "Not the first time," he said to me, finally calming down. "He's been getting a step on us. But we'll haul him in soon. No way Carl's gonna have to wait long for us to bring him in."

I had forgotten who Carl was.

They reminded me of Carl Spooner, their man in Guatemala, who came back home emasculated and tattooed in Tekún fashion. Then the agent went on, which surprised me, as DEA usually wouldn't give me the time of day. The story about almost catching him in Chattanooga seemed strange, as if, on that occasion, Tekún had indeed worked on his own to meet with his mother.

So he needed his mother. Ironic.

"But he never saw her," said the agent, and he laughed for the first time. It was an acrid laugh, "We had it set up with the old lady's sister." He told me about Tekún's aunt imitating her sister's Alzheimer's, then shook his head.

"Come on, Jack," said the other agent. Perhaps he was concerned Jack was saying too much to local law enforcement. Especially local law enforcement that was not local. Yes, that's exactly what he was saying. He turned to me, "Young lady, I think you better get yourself home. To Nashville."

He didn't have to say the name of the city. I knew where my home was.

It was a long drive home. And home was empty at this point, with my son and mother in Atlanta, safe, away from all this. A long drive of coffee and cigarettes and fiddling with the scar that Tekún had looked at directly, asking me how I was doing. When he had leaned over me, after pulling that dart out of my neck, he had looked at it once again, only to threaten me. The threat was real; this I believed, enough to put my entire hand to my neck and rub it, protect it here in the car while driving through and out of Meridian.

But he had also looked at me. When he was right over me, talking, telling me how I'm so good at kissing my precinct's ass while also wanting to follow my own way, I'm not sure . . . were those tears that lined his eyes?

He threatened to slit my throat and warned me never to expose him again. But the look he gave me was like nothing I have ever seen.

Is it possible, to show love in the moment of the kill?

Home was not home because it was lonely and silent and childless and grandmotherless. Home was in Atlanta now. This was just a construction that held photos and cast iron skillets and a scattering of toys in every room. How does one boy scatter so much?

I called. They were fine. Having the time of their life. Though my mother did ask when I was coming to pick them up. Not to take her back to Nashville necessarily, but merely to join in the festivities that were daily: the children making bigger messes, the women making bigger meals, the gossip at the kitchen table, growing more elaborate by the second.

"Soon," I promised.

The spread of evidence on my queen-sized bed had grown larger. All those scribblings on yellow legal pads, across the list of credit card numbers on the PriceRight Auto Rentals sheet, were my notes, taken down in the car on I-40 or scratched across a loose sheet in the middle of the night, between dreams. Nothing was coming together. I cross-referenced the tourist names from the PriceRight list: James Scarpetti, Claudio Sanchez, Dale Kolonsinski, Jamey Lei Yamanaka. They all checked out: legitimate names and numbers. So did the more familiar, or urbane names, Smith, McCaugh, Ryan. No dirt on any of them.

The Whisperer's little death notes were pissing me off. I made it easier on myself: I typed them out on one page, hammering them onto the sheet as if, in doing so, I could hold their meaning between my fingers. All that floating-over-the-page bullshit might have just been that: bullshit. A way of keeping us off guard.

It did help to line them up.

Bristol: *She made their own lust legal and used their lands to bed the children well*

Atlanta: *Nothing nor any Gallehault shall go between these two. Now they rest not from pain*

Memphis: *You blame Cerberus for his hunger. Fill your gluttonous mouths with gobbets from the hollowed earth* followed by the reference to St. Louis, *Meet me at the fair*

Denver: *Blood rivers shift into those whose violence hurt others. I am the great Connoisseur of Sin*

I took that last one first. He was telling us who he

was, the Connoisseur of Sin. Someone who knows sins. Who? God? Jesus? A priest?

Merriam Webster helped out more than I thought.

A connoisseur is an expert. Someone who knows the details of art, one who can be critical about a certain aesthetic.

A connoisseur of wines appreciates with great discrimination the subtleties of different vintages.

So my sister's killer enjoys with discrimination the subtleties of different sins.

Those other references, Gallehault, Cerberus. I had no idea who they were. My computer was gone, still broken down and packaged at the FBI local offices. So I went the old-fashioned way: the Vanderbilt University Library.

The librarian was an older, white woman, probably widowed, who loved her library. "Those sound more like mythological figures," she said, leading me to a section of the library farther back. "Especially that Cerberus fellow. I think he's a character in Virgil's *Aeneid*. You may want to start looking there. I'll try to find Gallehault through the library's web engine."

She went off to her computer while I leaned over an annotated copy of *The Aeneid*. The little old lady who looked as if she had walked out of a door from two centuries ago placed her dry, paper-like fingers on the keyboard and typed faster than Beads did in New Orleans. I bet she could match his hacker skills. Still, her typing was in clicking bursts, and she, like the rest of us, had to wait for the computer to download information. But unlike the rest of us, especially me, she waited with patience, staring at the monitor with calm eyes.

I found Cerberus. She was right: he was in *The Aeneid*. But he wasn't a man. He was a dog. A three-headed dog who guards the gates of Virgil's underworld.

You blame Cerberus for his hunger

Why did we blame Cerberus? Why a three-headed dog from Roman myth?

The men in Memphis, their throats torn open by a dog named Popeye.

Popeye lay dying
You blame Cerberus

Nothing came together. Virgil and Faulkner, *Sanctuary* and a dog. Shit.

And then little-old-librarian added to the mess. "Now this is interesting. Gallehault is French for 'pander' or 'a go-between.'"

"What's a pander?"

"You know," she said, looking over at me, her reading glasses down slightly on her little nose, "someone who runs between two lovers, setting them up."

"Like a matchmaker?"

"Not really. More like a pimp." She chuckled. "Someone who exploits others' weaknesses."

Was my sister weak? Falling in love with a married man. Why would that be a weakness?

"It says here," continued the librarian, "that Gallehault was the guy who sent messages between Lancelot and Guinevere during the time of King Arthur. Lancelot was Arthur's best knight, best friend in fact, but he got in bed with Arthur's wife, which made the whole kingdom go to hell in a handbasket."

So now I had a dog's name from *The Aeneid*, a real, dead dog who was named after a Faulkner character, and a reference to the Knights of the Round Table. None of them made sense together.

I turned back to the book about Cerberus. According to it, the three-headed mutt guarded the gates of the underworld, and the only way to calm it down was to throw it some honey cakes, which is what Virgil did.

Honey cakes. According to the Whisperer's note, we should stuff our mouths with dirt. Which is in fact what he did with Popeye: he stuffed the dead dog's mouth with clay from the pit in the shed. No honey cakes were found at the crime scene. Not even a Twinkie.

I had to use the bathroom.

When I returned, she was still typing away, then clicking the mouse onto other Websites. I looked over her shoulder at a series of paintings on the screen. "Oh. Sorry. I get to surfing and the time goes by."

"That's fine," I said, looking at the multi-colored photo of a painting that looked composed in medieval times. A woman and a man sitting on an ornate bench are about to kiss. A book dangles from her fingers.

"Look at him," said the librarian, "making the move on her."

"Yes, and she doesn't seem to mind it," I muttered. "So that's Guinevere?"

"Oh no. It's a woman named Francesca."

"Who's that?"

"I'm not sure. When I was surfing around for Gallehault, I stumbled across a number of websites with her name in it. Then I saw this one that said something about Francesca through the ages in paintings and murals. I love old paintings, especially from the Renaissance. But most of these are from the pre-Renaissance, medieval times."

I was tired, and didn't know how long my civility was going to last. Not that she was doing anything wrong. If anything, she had the gift of the greatest librarians: insatiable curiosity. I glanced at her older face, a woman in her early sixties, with a beauty that had never left her. "I'm sorry," I said, "but I never introduced myself. I'm Romilia."

"Oh I know who you are, Detective," she said,

smiling, but still looking at the screen. "You're the reason our city is safe. My name's Nancy."

That sounded oh-so-corny, the way she referred to the publicity around my last case. But she was kind.

"Is all this research on old mythological figures a personal hobby, or a case?"

From her tone, I knew she hoped it was the latter.

"It's a case," I said.

"Well then, I should stop playing around," she said, laughing slightly as she pulled the mouse over to the cornered X to close up the site. She clicked, just as her computer was pulling up a photo of a meticulous black and white drawing.

The face of the woman, turned away from the man, was what caught me. But then the computer pulled the website down and I was looking at the Home menu of Vanderbilt Library.

"Wait a minute, Nancy," I said. "What was that?"

"Oh I'm not sure who it was, but it was done by Doré." She was about to move on to the Search Box to look for something, anything, that I asked for. "You can never mistake his work, of course."

"Find it again, please."

She did. As we waited for it to pull up I asked who Doré was. "Gustave Doré. Nineteenth century. He was a French painter, but known more for his engravings."

The computer pulled up the engraving.

A beautiful young woman, horrified, turned her face toward us. Her lover's head was buried in her neck. The man was on top of her, the entire weight of his body pressed against hers. He pinned her, but not really: they were not lying down on the ground or on a bed, but swirled in a tornado of other people, other couples, thousands of them. They were all stuck together, in pairs. The woman's face was the clearest,

with the most details: she was scared, exhausted, from
the weight of her lover. She turned away from him and
toward two men who stood to one side on a rock. The
men watched the human tornado from the shadows.
Both men wore laurels on their heads. The woman,
frightened, spoke to them.

I had seen this before. Not the painting. But the
position.

The photos from the FBI website, the ones Tekún
had sent to me, the ones that had gotten me in hot water with the Feds: they had plenty of shots of my sister
and Jonathan, tied to the bedposts, the iron javelin
puncturing them both, holding them together.

In that photo, Catalina's head is turned directly to
the lens. Jonathan's face is buried in her neck, his entire
body pinning her to the bed. Catalina's eyes, though
rested in death, looked at me, at the Feds, at the cam-
eraman, as if wanting to tell me something.

Did he spend time adjusting their faces after killing
them? Did he carefully turn my sister's face to one side,
and then move Jonathan's head until it rested neatly in
the curve of her skin?

Did he have this engraving in his hand? And did his
copy of the Doré say, underneath it, *Francesca speaks to
Dante in the Second Circle of Hell?*

"Detective, are you all right?"

I turned and looked straight at Nancy. She startled.

I asked her to show me more pictures of Doré's
work, especially with a copy of the engraving of Paolo
and Francesca.

"We've got a lot on him," she said. I followed her
to another section of the library, passing numerous
Vanderbilt students along the way. "A number of our
departments have filled the collection of Doré works,

Art Department, Literature, Classics. And our Dante collection is quite thorough."

"Good." Something was coming together, but I wasn't sure what. The leap from Gallehault in the Camelot legend to these two Italian adulterers in Dante's hell was still beyond me.

"Here. This is one of my favorites." Nancy pulled a large, yellowed tome from a shelf. She had to lift it with both palms. At a table she opened it, started carefully flipping through the crisp pages and text. "This is the entire *Divine Comedy*, translated by, let's see . . . a fellow named Lawrence Grant White. I bet our two little lovers are early on. You won't find them in Paradise," she laughed. "Dante wasn't too kind to adulterers. Here it is."

She spread open the book and showed me in full the engraving that we had both seen on the internet. There were Paolo and Francesca, swirling away in the second circle of Hell. Looking just like my sister and Jonathan looked.

I had read parts of Dante's *Inferno* in my freshman year in college, a long time ago when I preferred to read only novels. Poetry at the time didn't catch my attention, even narrative poetry. Now my eyes scanned quickly over this text, but found the wording, the syntax, difficult. This was an old book, no doubt a very old translation, in an English that was not very attractive today. It frustrated me, not knowing the story. I flipped the pages of the book and looked at the other engravings, like a kid who's just learning how to read, who still relies on the pictures to tell her most of the story. There again was Dante and Virgil, only this time, Virgil's up front, tossing something at that three-headed dog.

Cerberus.

And under this engraving: *Virgil throws gobbets of*

earth at Cerberus. The gluttonous demon receives the dirt with great enthusiasm.

Enthusiasm. Those three heads looked ready to rip Dante's throat out.

This was Cerberus. Just a few pages away from Paolo and Francesca. Cerberus protected Virgil's Underworld, and here, in Dante's story, he guards the gates of Hell.

"Damn," I said. I turned to Nancy. "What time do you close?"

She smiled. "It's exam week, Detective. See all of them?" she gestured toward the students, all bent over tables. "You think they visit me this much during the rest of the semester? We keep the door open until one A.M. Take your time."

She left me with Dante.

I sat and started reading. But it was tough going. The older English threw me, and I strained to find something in the poetry. But in all those lines I saw a word that was familiar.

We read of Lancelot, by love constrained

This copy of Dante was annotated, thank God.

Dante was the true *National Enquirer* reporter of his time. Everyone he knew, living and dead, he put them into his depiction of Hell, Heaven, Purgatory. Paolo and Francesca were contemporaries of Dante. They had committed adultery. They were found together by Paolo's brother, Francesca's husband, Gianciotto Malatesta of Rimini. Gianciotto murdered them both. Francesca is confessing all this to Dante.

Confessing to Dante. Was that who my sister's killer thought he was? Was he taking on Dante Alighieri's laurels in order to decide who needed to die? This I believed for quite awhile, even as I turned to the shelves and looked for a more contemporary translation of the poem, one by Robert Pinsky. Lawrence Grant White's translation was way too hard for me, made me feel stupid in ways I haven't felt in a long while. Still, I used it, because it had the engravings that showed me more details of Hell than I had ever wanted. All those writhing people swimming in the River Styx, with muscular torsos and rounded bottoms. There was something innately sexual about Doré's engravings, and I was sure I wasn't the first person to notice this. Even that one demon, with the head of a crowned king but with the long thick tail of a serpent or dragon that wrapped around a clutch of sinners, had shoulders that you could find on any decent *Gentleman's Quarterly* advertisement. That was how I read *The Inferno*, staring at the engravings of one book, reading the translation by Robert Pinsky in the other. Pinsky, he was still alive, had just retired from the position of the country's poet laureate. His was a much kinder translation to my eyes. And he gave me something not only understandable, but familiar, way too familiar: where White told me, "discerner of transgressions," Pinsky gave me, "great connoisseur of sin."

Nancy and I walked out of Vanderbilt Library together, only after she had checked out both books under her name for me. I promised her I would have them back as soon as possible. She told me not to worry, that she could check them out for a semester at a time. "And I'm the librarian. What will I do, give myself late charges? They don't pay me enough." She laughed. I added on to my promise a cup of coffee someday. She liked that. It was one fifteen in the morning when we left the university. She, no doubt, fell fast asleep within the hour. I would not sleep until dawn.

At nine o'clock I would shower and drive to my boss' office and tell him the real name of my sister's killer.

What does Minos mean?" asked McCabe.

"He's the demon in hell who decides which circle you should suffer in for the rest of eternity."

McCabe shook his head. It was time to teach him some classic literature, at least, whatever I had learned in an overnight binge of reading.

I placed the copy of Pinsky's translation of *The Inferno* on McCabe's desk, and the book of Doré engravings next to it. "This is his map."

He first picked up Pinsky's book, then glanced at a Doré of a devil slicing a man down his stomach. "His map, what, of where to go?"

"Of where to go and who to kill."

"You've lost me."

I showed him my notes. They were detailed. The details seemed to bother him as much as the Doré did.

"In Bristol, Minos killed a woman and a man

accused of child abuse. In *The Inferno*, an old queen named Semiramis legalized incest in her nation. She's burning in hell, along with a lot of other sexual sickos.

"In Atlanta, Minos murdered my sister and her lover. In the second circle of the Inferno, this couple, Paolo and Francesca, are 'welded' together by their adultery, stuck together for all eternity. Just like Caty and Jonathan looked when they were found." My voice cracked only slightly. I continued.

"In Memphis, Minos killed three men who worked in the stock market. In *The Inferno*, a dog named Cerberus eats the Gluttons and the Hoarders. Greedy people.

"It took me awhile to find any match to the Denver killing, but I did. Farther along in *The Inferno*, you get to what Dante calls the Violent Sins." I opened up Pinsky's book, which had, in the prologue, an organized classification of souls, sins, and demons. This made the text easier to follow. "Look here, in the seventh circle of hell. People who do violence toward others, they boil in a river of blood. See this?" I showed him a very clear engraving of Doré's in the other book: People choking in a thick river, one that you could imagine as crimson. "That's how Joaquín Champ died: Minos had cut a river into his throat. The young man drowned in his own blood.

"It's all very clear, once you look at it from the right angle."

I looked at McCabe, who was looking at me from a cockeyed angle.

"What's the matter?" I said.

"How did you get into this?" he gestured toward the two open books.

"It was an accident, really. Serendipity. I was looking up words that the killer left in his notes. They led me down one path, but I stumbled onto another one that took me right to here," I pointed at the books.

"Why do you call him this Minos guy? Why don't you call him Dante?"

"Because our killer has referred to himself as *the great connoisseur of sin*. That's an exact translation of Dante in reference to Minos. In fact, I wouldn't doubt he's carrying around a copy of Pinsky with him."

"Who's Pinsky?"

"He's the poet laureate who's trying to make poetry more accessible to . . . never mind. He did this book," I turned the book over, showed him the cover, the translator's name.

McCabe turned his eyes to one side. He looked lost. I suspected why: surely all this seemed way off base to him, all of it coming at him at once. And no doubt I was too darkly enthused about it all, steamrolling him with information that I had gathered in the past several hours of reading and studying the engravings. I sat down, and was pulling out some cigarettes while I talked. "There is one problem," I said. "He's skipped a couple of sins."

"What?" McCabe leaned over slightly.

"Well, every city where he's killed, he's taken on a specific sin, following Dante's footsteps from one Canto to another. Dante's *Inferno* is filled with all sorts of sinners, and Minos, our Minos, doesn't take on every single one. He was consistent there for awhile, picking one from each Canto. But he started in the second circle of hell, not the first. I think I see why: In the first circle are people who can't be blamed for being in Hell, because they lived before Jesus. They're not baptized. So they're in Hell, but in the cushy part. Plato, Aristotle, even Virgil's got his digs there. So our killer started with the second circle. But later he skipped two basic sins: the wrathful, or sullen, and the Heretics. It seems he went straight from the greedy sinners straight toward the sinners who do violence to other people, right from the three stockbrokers in Memphis to Joaquín Champ. I'm not sure why. Maybe he just picks the sins that are easier to spot. I don't know if you could find a heretic today. And to kill someone who's sullen, or down in the dumps, well, you could do in every American who's not on Prozac."

I smiled at my own little joke, then lit up. I was feeling pretty good about myself. McCabe was so bowled over by this new information that he didn't even ask how I had gotten ahold of the letter from Denver. In fact, he seemed to know that there *was* a letter from Denver, which should have been my first clue. I kept talking, "My guess is that our killer thinks he's Minos, and he plans to keep on killing until he gets to the bottom of this map of Hell. That means a lot of killings. And he's doing them more often. A few years passed between the Mastersons and my sister. But now, they're coming at quicker intervals." That spoken thought tired me out. I looked at McCabe. He finally looked at me. "What's the matter?" I said.

"He didn't skip two sins."

The cigarette drooped from my lips.

"What?"

McCabe fessed up. "Pierce at the FBI told me. He ordered me not to say anything, especially to you." He paused, but then seeing how I was looking at him, almost rushed to explain, "Kansas City. Six weeks ago. The KC Police received a letter, which they handed over to the Bureau. Another letter from the Whisperer—your Minos, no doubt."

"Who did he kill?" I asked this slowly.

"They don't know if he did. But the letter came af-

ter the disappearance of four people from a small
church there. Some cult group that had made the news
there the past few weeks. Kind of a hippie commune, I
guess."

"They're missing."

"Yeah. No bodies have turned up. Just the letter."

"And St. Louis?"

"Pierce didn't say anything about St. Louis."

"But he told you to keep this from me."

At this, McCabe turned a bit more forceful, reminding me I really had no right to question his decisions. "It's a federal case, Romilia."

"Then why did he tell you?"

"Because I'm the head of Homicide for Christ's
sake. I talk to the Feds a lot, whether I like to or not."

What words could I use to express my surprise, my
pissed-off-ness?

"So you're telling me a religious group has been hit?"

"No, not a religious group. Some commune of
middle-aged hippies. I don't know the details."

This left Minos with one undone sin: the sullen.
That seemed more slippery than the Heretics.

I was too angry to think straight, learning how my
boss had withheld information from me. How much
more data was out there that I didn't know about?

"Has Pierce made any of these connections?" I
gestured harshly to the two books.

"He didn't say anything about Dante. No."

"So. Maybe I know something he doesn't."

"Which means you should report it to him."

"Why?" Did I shout that? "Why should I tell
Pierce anything? He and the Feds have their heads up
their asses on these killings."

"That's why you need to tell him." Then he added,
"It might be helpful to you, Romi, if you did."

I wasn't sure what that meant. I stood up. "I have to go now, Lieutenant."

"How was New Orleans?" he asked.

"I wasn't in . . . it was fine."

"Keep in touch."

"Are you going to ask me anything else?" I said.

"I don't want to know."

Someone once told me about the civilized manner of wolves. Supposedly, in the wild, wolves have a strong, clear code of community among themselves. They travel in packs, take care of their own. They have a hierarchy. Sometimes the chain of command may be questioned by one of the dogs on the lower echelon. They will fight. A bystander may believe the two wolves mean to kill each other, that it's not over with until one of them drops in a heap. It won't happen. Once one of the wolves knows it's lost, it shows its neck to the winner. It will stretch its head back so the other one can chomp down and, in one solid bite, snap the loser's neck bone.

Which the winner does not do. The winner sees the full of the neck and knows that the fight is over. He walks away.

I decided to show my neck to Special Agent Pierce.

A bad pun, I know, considering the scar. But he had scars too, more than I. So call it what you will: laying the cards on the table. Clear the air. Show your neck.

"I received the package of downloaded FBI files from one Rafael Murillo, aka Tekún Umán."

Pierce leaned over his desk. His one eye seemed to relax; did the hollow behind the patch do the same?

"Can you prove this?" he asked.

I handed him the letter from Tekún, the one that had come with the package.

"Why didn't you give this to me earlier?" he asked.

"Because I thought it would ruin my chances of acquiring more information regarding the murder of my sister and the other victims. I meant to make contact with Tekún Umán in order to see if he had more information."

"So you're saying you were prepared to gather more illegal documents from a known felon? Instead of having it fall into your lap, you were ready to go out and seek it."

"I was about to say, Agent Pierce, that yes, I was not thinking clearly. At all. It's not been a smooth few months here," I tried not to say it with any weepiness; that was not this man's style. More, I hoped to engage him in the field of familiar losses, his eye and leg, my neck, our body parts victims of on-the-job mutilation. "This . . . fucking scar has not been my best friend." I barely raised a finger to it.

He paused a moment, considered that. "Have you made any more contact with Mr. Murillo?"

"Yes I have." I knew he would already know this. He was a Fed. I told him in complete detail what had happened with Tekún in New Orleans. Sans the download of the Denver Police Department Web Engine, of course.

I meant to be honest, but not stupid. I wondered if those wolves in the woods, did they, while showing their neck, keep one paw with claws out, hidden under the snow?

And I could tell Pierce about Minos without having to refer to Denver. Using the words Gallehault and Cerberus was enough to show him how the perp was using Dante's *Inferno* as a guide, a map, for his killings. I opened the books on his desk, showed him the Doré engravings.

Pierce, after listening to my explanation and staring at the translations of Dante's work, sat back in his chair. He looked suddenly tired. "We need to send this to Quantico."

"That's what I thought."

"If this is true, this is one sick killer. I've never seen anything like it." Pierce rubbed his solid jaw with his fingers.

"I know," I said. "It doesn't necessarily fit within the profiles of a serial killer. Most of the victims are men, and they don't seem to be sexually related, as in most serial killings."

"Not true," said Pierce. "In Bristol, we found a semen trace on the carpet, near Masterson's body, the husband. It didn't match Masterson's DNA. Later we found that it matched the DNA found on the licked envelope, on the first letter." Pierce spoke to me now, knowing not only that I'd seen the documents, I had no doubt memorized them. "And where the semen was found, it's as if the perp had secreted it at the moment of the killing. He gets off on the kills. Probably masturbates, or maybe just 'naturally' orgasms at the moment of his victims deaths."

I didn't know this. "Part thrill-seeker, then. But in my mind, more a goal-oriented one."

"No doubt. Especially with this," Pierce gestured to *The Inferno*.

"Still, he's getting off on the power. He's having a sexual response to his killings." I thought about him standing over my sister and his lover, he, sending them to hell for their sexual sins, no doubt getting his rocks off at the same time, depositing the evidence into a condom. He had learned, by then, how his own body responded to killing. His own violence felt ecstatic, powerful. He had learned and he had planned.

Pierce was staring at me. It was not malevolent. He was trying to figure something out. About me, or about himself, I was not sure.

"Tell me, Detective. Why are you here?"

I didn't hesitate. "I found this new evidence, this theory," I gestured to *The Inferno*. "Considering what I had unintentionally learned about the case through Tekún's information, I knew I had to bring it to you."

"Yes. I see."

He turned away from me. He looked at his computer screen, paused barely a second, then started typing. He was putting in a password. This I could tell by the line of asterisks that filled the search box. He clicked around, found what he was looking for. Then he made a copy of it and gave it to me.

On the top it said, "Kansas City:"

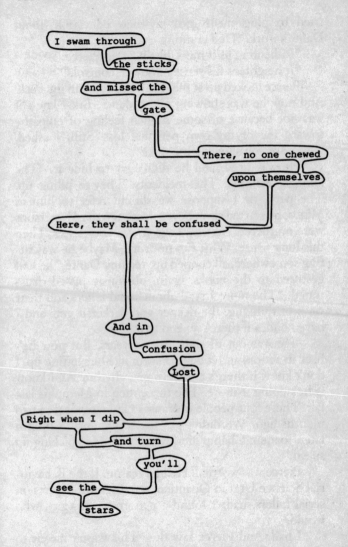

I swam through

the sticks

and missed the

gate

There, no one chewed

upon themselves

Here, they shall be confused

And in

Confusion

Lost

Right when I dip

and turn

you'll

see the

stars

"He's leaving signatures," I said. I stared at the note, the obvious clues that were abstract, even when I tried to plug them into my new education about Dante's work. "He's taunting us."

"Ridiculing us is more like it," said Pierce.

"It heightens his sense of power, control."

Pierce looked up at me. I had showed him my neck. And now he was showing me evidence. But I knew it was not because of some sudden feeling of empathy toward me or my own personal loss. Still, I asked, "Why are you showing me this?"

He was tired, and he didn't try to hide it. "The killings, Romilia. The incidents. They're piling up. The perp, or I suppose we should refer to him as Minos, he started slow. Seven years ago the Mastersons were murdered. Six years ago it was your sister. Then this long pause. Why, I'm not sure. Maybe he was sitting somewhere, all cooped up, reading Dante," he half gestured to the books again, obviously pissed, frustrated. "The more I read about serial killers and their ways of thinking, the deeper and darker it gets and I have no idea if there's an end to it.

"He was out of sight for six years. But now he's back in action, and it doesn't seem like he's letting up. I don't know if there's a pattern or a rhythm. All I know is he's doing it more. The three men in Memphis last fall. These four people in Kansas City disappeared two months ago. We didn't get the letter until a month later. Joaquín Champ dies this month. He's picking up speed."

Pierce was worried. He had reason. If the Behaviorial Science Unit in Quantico, the foremost experts on serial killers, hadn't found a pattern to this guy, who would?

I had. And Pierce saw this. This wasn't meant to shine my badge any: BSU had its hands busy with a multitude of killings all across the nation. I had the luxury of spending all my days, while changing Sergio's bed sheets or fixing him a hot dog wrapped in a tortilla or cleaning the dishes with my mother, thinking about who had killed Catalina. I had the luxury of obsession.

"I've had some conversations with your boss. Lieutenant McCabe thinks very highly of you. He went to bat for you, Detective Chacón, he explained to me about your sister. He didn't need to fill me in about the Jade Pyramid killings. I'd kept up with that case at the time." He paused, looked at me straight on with that one eye, then laid it out. "You're ahead of us all, Detective," he said, handing me the photocopy of the death note from Kansas City. "I don't have the luxury of time to take a course on medieval literature."

This took me back. I took the paper, looked at it as if it were a Christmas gift. I asked, "Does this mean . . . my boss, Lieutenant McCabe . . . could he, with your permission, lift my suspension?"

"Lift your suspension. Of course." He looked down at his desk, looked back up at me. "And I may ask for more than that."

I wasn't sure what that meant. But I took it. He dismissed me, as if he were my boss.

McCabe called me later that afternoon. "What angle, may I ask, of ass-kissing did you do?"

"I tried honesty this time."

"Whatever it was, it worked. You're back on the force."

I almost squealed, but decided not to. Not over the phone, to my boss. He'd think I was just another example of womanhood: that inherently, we're all giddy and high-strung or whatever else men thought about us. So I didn't squeal.

"But there's something else," he said.

"What?"

He hesitated, then went right for it. "You won't be coming back to work here for awhile. Pierce wants to borrow you."

"You're kidding."

"I don't kid very well, Romilia. You should know

that by now." He cleared his throat. "Pierce wants you on the case. We've done this before, had some of our own join up with the Feds on a very temporary basis for cases such as this one."

"And what did you tell him?"

"I told him that it was fine with me."

Still, I couldn't help but hear some regret in his voice. I wasn't sure where it was coming from.

"Thanks, Lieutenant."

"I don't think I really had a choice. Romi, listen. You did good, walking into Pierce's office like that. It's been a bit of a stumble lately, the incident in Mississippi, and the way the meth lab went down. . . ."

He spoke in the passive voice, never pointing a finger at me. This was good, I supposed.

"I can understand why all that happened. Why you did it. And I'm afraid it's all going into your record. But this is going into your record as well, your cooperation with the Feds. That's good. I just want to suggest you keep that attitude."

"I'm not sure what you're wanting to say, Lieutenant."

"Now see? You've got that tone in your voice. You get pissed off, Romilia, and when you do, you either blow up and damage the property around you, or you channel that anger to whatever it is you're trying to investigate. Do the latter. It'll take you farther. The other will drag you down."

It sounded preachy. I needed it. I thanked him for the advice, trying to sound sincere.

The note from Kansas City was broken into four sections, four complete thoughts. The thoughts worked alone as full, complete sentences, but they also hooked together in their own logic.

I swam through the sticks and missed the gate
There, no one chewed upon themselves
Here, they shall be confused and in confusion lost
Right when I dip and turn, you'll see the stars

I began with the third line, as it seemed the most decipherable. *"Here"* had to be Kansas City, where the note was found, at the door of the bohemian church where the missing people had last been seen. They're lost, lost in their own confusion. He had "lost" the victims, had kidnapped them and made them disappear from the public eye.

Swimming through the sticks sounded to me like he had made his way through some southern country territory, out in the sticks. Then Dante and Doré's drawings straightened me out on that one: In Canto VIII, a demon named Phlegyas puts Dante and Virgil in a boat and takes them across the River Styx, popping the heads of the sinful with his oar.

So Minos swam through the River Styx.

If the kidnapping in Kansas City were in fact the immediate act following the killings in Memphis, then I could imagine it fairly easily: the River Styx. The Mississippi.

My mother had an old road atlas tucked away somewhere in her bedroom. After a half hour of searching and cursing, I found it under a pile of books atop her small, cushiony bench that no one had sat in for years, due to the pile.

The first two pages had a spread of the United States. Between Memphis and Kansas City, there were a few bodies of water: Lake of the Ozarks, Cache Lake, several smaller rivers. But the largest of them all was the Mississippi.

He crossed the Mississippi River. He missed the

gate. Because at the gate, no one chewed on themselves.

Why Kansas City? Why not Des Moines or Lincoln or St. Louis? And Little Rock, that city was much closer to Memphis, and just a couple of hours from Memphis. . . .

He didn't go to just any city because he went to a city with a gate. And there is a gate, to the midwest, or to the new frontier, or whatever it was they called the Arch back then. The St. Louis Arch?

According to Mamá's map, St. Louis was almost due north of Memphis. And the Mississippi River ran between the two cities. Connected them.

According to the FBI reports, no ritual killings in St. Louis. *He missed the gate.*

In *The Inferno*, the River Styx runs between a tower and a gate. The gate comes second. I knew of no tower in Memphis, but there was that huge pyramid building, what was it, an arena of some sort? I was grasping at anything.

Still, I had to be careful. Minos had not left any other hints of architecture or of geographic locations in the previous notes. The first notes were found on or near the bodies. This note, in Kansas City, had been left behind. It carried more abstract arrows in it, hints toward a sense of place, or places.

I turned back to Dante, reread what I had spent the past few days getting to know, to the point that I had memorized certain lines from Cantos V to XI. The images at times escaped me, but others clung to me. No wonder Doré did such a good job of drawing in the details.

In Canto VIII, Dante passes one of his many named spirits,

"Come get Filippo Argenti!" they all cried,
And crazed with rage the Florentine spirit bit
At his own body. Let no more be said
Of him . . .

Pinsky's notes said that Filippo Argenti was one of Dante's enemies in real life, known for his savage temper.

Sometimes I slipped into believing that my sister's killer was trying to be Dante. But the more I read of the poet's work, the more I believed, with more clarity, that he was not Dante. For Dante was humble and careful and clear. This bastard, now roaming around in the middle of the United States, thought of himself as Minos. The great knower of sins. An arrogance beyond human imagination.

It took a couple of days to get used to the idea of being on the Bureau's dole. That meant I could call Pierce and ask him questions about the case. When I asked him to confirm about St. Louis, and if any incidents had occurred there that would send up a flag, he checked, called me back an hour later, and said that no, according to local FBI in St. Louis, no homicides that fit our perp's description had occurred there.

"But now that I've got you on the phone," he said, "how about making a trip with me?"

I also wasn't used to Pierce's amiability. But I rode it. "Where to?"

"Denver. I told Quantico that I've got an angle on the Whisperer. They were more than happy to hear that, so I've got clearance to head to Colorado."

"It's that easy with the FBI, to jump from one region to the other?" I asked.

"No, it's not," he said. "But with me, they give me a little latitude."

The way he said it, I could almost picture him tapping his prosthetic leg.

"On the plane I'll give you a copy of the Kansas City file, so you can study up on it. Maybe your Dante angle will cut another line into the information."

He told me to be ready before nightfall, that we'd leave from the Nashville airport at six.

In Atlanta, when I was a younger cop in blue, a psychologist once suggested to me that I take one of the popular SSRI drugs. Prozac or Zoloft were easy on the system, she said. This, of course, was the psychologist whom the Atlanta department had appointed for me after I had taken a pistol butt to a rape suspect. The psychologist said I wasn't depressed, but anxious, that I was always on guard, waiting for an attacker to come around the corner. I never rested. My seratonin, she said, that river of tranquility that allowed other people to rest in the dens of their existence, was dry in my brain, leaving my nerves crackly, snapping in the wind, looking for an enemy. Zoloft could get that river running again.

I had never used it, so now, even with Agent Chip Pierce welcoming me into his bureau, giving me files and free frequent flyer miles to Crime Scenes, I didn't trust it. He was the guy who had holed me up in his interrogation room and asked about the packet of downloaded files. He had had me suspended. Now he was treating me like a subordinate, someone in his chain of command.

And what really rattled me was that McCabe seemed all right with this.

When I went in to collect my badge and my gun, McCabe made sure that my temporary transfer to the Bureau would happen quickly, that they would know the make of my parabellum, its number, the number of rounds in my possession. This was a temp job, so no need for the Bureau to issue me a weapon when I had my own. Now that weapon was out of Nashville Homicide's jurisdiction, and under the wider parameters of the Federal Bureau of Investigation.

It rattled me the way McCabe signed the papers, had them delivered to the offices downstairs, who would then send them on to Washington. It bothered me, the way McCabe, who I had come to like, to trust, now avoided eye contact with me. He said little. Though he did, as I left the threshold of his door, wish me good luck.

Agent Pierce handed me a temporary FBI badge. It was cardboard, with my name typed over a line, just above the federal seal. Not even laminated. Even with a temp, I expected a little more from the Feds.

The file from Kansas City kept me busy most of the flight. Pierce drank scotch and later slept as I read. I wanted to join him in a drink, wanted to order a bourbon from the young man who attended the few agents on board the small, federally-owned jet. But I didn't want to give the wrong impression. I didn't want to give any impressions. All I wanted to know was what went down in Kansas City.

It wasn't really a church that had suffered the kidnappings, but rather a nonprofit company that made organic juices. Landley Brothers Inc. had been making carrot, tomato, and fruit juices for independent stores throughout Kansas City, and had spread its business from the organic food stores to the mainstream grocery markets. All this in seven years of business. What had caused a scandal was a newspaper report that came out early in the year, accusing one of the proprietors of Landley Brothers, George Landley, of growing and harvesting a variety of hallucinogenic mushrooms on the outskirts of their little farm. Landley had tried to argue that the mushrooms were not for public consumption or sold for profit, but rather used in the small yet ongoing spiritual services that he and his fellow workers had been performing for almost as long as the business had been open. In fact, they had attracted a number of followers to the Landley Fruit Juice Farm. George had gone to jail; the mushrooms had all been torn out of the ground and confiscated by the DEA; the company was shut down. But the folks who had been munching on mushrooms and praying to the spirits of the carrots and the god of the tomatoes kept on gathering at the farm, without the help of the party fungus. Much of Kansas City was surprised by this; some were outraged, and wrote editorial comments to the local paper. Others praised the Landley Gatherers (as they called themselves) for following out their religious beliefs, showing that, though the mushroom was an aid to their spirituality, indeed a sacrament of their beliefs, they could still commune with nature without it.

The disappearance of four of their members, one woman, two men and a twelve year old boy, at first proved the naysayers right: the four people had split town, no doubt afraid of repercussions from the law. But then the note arrived, the FBI swept in, and nothing else was heard about the incident in the local newspapers. Probably because the FBI shut the story down.

The Federal Agents out of Oklahoma City acted quickly. They got profiles on the four missing people. Sarah Green and her son, Taylor, had been part of the Landley farm and its church for three years. Taylor, age twelve, had, according to Sarah's ex-husband, never partaken in the mushroom rituals, though Sarah was one of their main priestesses ("I guess that's what you'd call them," the disgruntled, obviously upset father had said). Regis Landley, George's younger brother, had been dating Sarah for the past year. She and little Taylor had moved in with him in his private home on the farm. Sean Cotto, the most recent member of the Landley church, had been enjoying dinner with the Landleys the night before he, along with the others, disappeared. When asked more about Sean Cotto, George had told the agents that he was a good kid, had been in their employment for only a month or so, but had taken quickly to the Landley Gatherer ways. "He even switched over to vegetarianism, though we don't enforce that. But he did it. Except for one thing: he just couldn't give up his taste for Spam," George had said.

The agents had checked out Regis' house, but found nothing out of order. Sean Cotto's apartment in town was what got them to thinking: it was empty. Only the furniture stood there, along with the pots and pans that the landlady had provided to the tenants. But Sean Cotto was gone. Not only was the apartment empty, whoever had last been in there had polished all the wooden furniture, the handle on the toilet, the rims of the skillets. He had taken his time, no doubt working from the very back room to the front door with rag and dust spray. They didn't find one print.

The feds figured that, if they ever found the bodies, they'd find not four, but three.

I teased out a crude theory about all the cases: Minos faked friendship. He brought his victims into his web of trust. Then he closed the web.

It's in a dorm room at UC Denver," said Pierce. We were in the back of a large Ford. An agent, a fellow who looked a little younger than I, drove.

"A graduate student named Theo Simon checked in just this semester, took some classes but never showed up for them, and checked out. He's pulling a straight F at the University of Colorado. He also likes to dust his room completely of fingerprints. What they found in the room made them call the police. Denver PD took one look and called us."

I was doodling on a pad, a way of keeping away from cigarettes. I hadn't smoked in a couple of days. And even though it was a recent habit, I missed it. I had written in a scrawl the name "Theo Simon," and quickly started switching the letters around in the name. It was an easy anagram. "Minos" appeared in three consonant movements. And didn't "Theo" mean "God"?

Pierce glanced at my pad. "Yeah, I thought that too, once you told me your theory."

"What did they find in the room?"

Pierce looked out at the downtown of Denver, then up, toward the Rockies beyond the city. "Drawings of some sort. Not drawings, but photocopies. I'll not crowd your head with what they said to me, so you can work from your own first impression."

He talked to me as if I were a profiler.

Like most dorm rooms across the country, this one was depressing. Cinderblock walls. I had lived in a similar room at Emory years ago. These cinderblocks were not painted off-white like mine were, but rather a very light brown that tried to make the cinderblocks more welcoming. But you couldn't miss those horizontal and vertical lines criss-crossing the wall like a very clean minimum-security prison.

The one desk bolted to the wall was made of pressed wood, hard sawdust glued together and covered with a veneer of fake oak. A blue plastic chair shoved under the desk did not match. The room was clean, the light gray linoleum floor had been scrubbed, no doubt by our suspect who wore gloves as he washed down the walls, took a mop across the floor, stripped the single bed and wiped down its metal frame. I didn't go into the bathroom now; Pierce had told me nothing was in there, though I would still look, once I gave a good, long stare at the six photocopy prints taped in a row across the wall.

One piece of clear tape held each sheet of paper to the painted cinderblocks. The sheets were in a row, one after the other, in a succession that bothered me the moment I glanced at them. At first the naked men, from a distance, seemed to be standing in dance poses, their heads turned to one side, their arms outstretched only slightly or bent, with a finger pointing toward the ground or to the sky.

These were photocopies out of a book of black and white engravings from another century. This I could tell by the background: simple rolling hills with a small village nestled between intricately drawn trees, round, arched doors of another country. Was it France? Spain? Those were pastoral landscapes, peaceful. The church steeples and tiny windows offset the dissected men filling the foreground.

Each page had one man. Was this the same man, drawn in succession? Or were these six men in different poses of mortis? And were they dead? The artist had depicted each man as standing, holding himself upright, as if walking, naked and skinned, away from the village, toward me.

These were as detailed as any of Doré's engravings of the buffed, suffering souls of Hell. The one difference was that these were drawn up close: whoever had held the pencil and the pad had stood over real bodies to get the details.

The first man looked the closest to the living: his body was missing only skin. All his muscles were intact, and his face was neutral, as if he stood still while someone sliced all those parallel lines over his body, lines that flowed over him, following the sheet of abdominal muscles that plunged toward his groin, or curving around his flank.

The second man looked more in pain. The lines were gone. His face turned upward, toward the sky, his lips slightly parted, as if too weak to describe his pain. More of his muscles showed: the bulk of the forearm looked like a chicken leg that my son Sergio loved to chew.

Pierce left me alone with the pictures. He gestured the other agents away. Just the photocopies and me, standing right here, where Minos once stood. He and I, sharing the same space.

The third man is more flayed. A thin, almost transparent layer of flesh shows his ribs and sternum. A string of cut muscle that once ran from his fingers to his elbow now falls like a long, thick drop from his fingertips toward a patch of bramble on the ground. He turns to his right, his neatly half-torn skull showing surprise at a sheet of muscle pulled and twisted, like a fan, from his upper arm. Strips of muscles slip from his upper leg, though still attached at the knee; they half-fold over the ground. A blade has sliced his penis off neatly, like bologna; two large circles that once filled with blood during an erection are now empty: they sag over one small oval that once held his urethra.

The fourth man stands in a weak pose of surprise, one arm bent and barely pointing upward, the other swooping down. Shoulder bones pop out, still attached on one end. His teeth show forever, as his lips are gone.

The fifth man is more open: his left leg shows the shinbone, the calf muscles flap about it like thick curtains. His jaw, bifurcated and torn to both sides, looks like the open prongs of an insect. His entire tongue is a lump, falling over his trachea. He has no eyes.

The sixth is fully gutted. The intestines are gone. You can see the full of his backbone. Two tubes have been severed, like plumbing on the back wall of his ribcage. He hangs from a rope: the rope, tied to his skull, holds him in a slump. You stare up his nostrils. His jaw is gone. A strange shell-like object hangs next to him, with two severed pipes. His diaphragm.

Small, cursive letters mark each muscle on each body. They are letters written long ago, in a style that beckoned the Renaissance. Greek letters mark some of the bones.

The men are all alive. Though they are dead.

"Detective Chacón?"

Pierce's voice felt like an abrupt awakening. I turned to him.

"What do you think?" he said.

I turned back to the photocopies, looked at their corners, at the numbering. I cleared my throat. "From a book, obviously. They're in succession, page 178, 179, then they skip around a few pages, to 184, 187, 190. There's some text between the drawings. No doubt the text lines up with these letters on the muscles. It must be some sort of anatomy book." I said this as clearly as possible, but again, the words rattled out of me. It seemed my voice knew something before my head did.

"No prints on the pages nor on the tape," said Pierce. "Wiped clean. Just like the rest of the room. The paper looks like your regular twenty pound type from any photocopy store. Nothing special about it, though we'll have it run through the girls in lab."

"I have an idea, Agent Pierce, if it's okay." Again, my voice was working through something; I had never had this happen before, that somehow my words trembled with knowledge that my head had yet to confirm. "I'd like to fax these to a friend. I think he could give us an idea where they came from."

The FBI carried basic equipment wherever they went: laptop computers, small printers and faxes, cell phones, scanners, and an agent who knew how to run all the machines. I called Doc Callahan. He was awake, reading a novel by Antonya Nelson and drinking a Cabernet Sauvignon from the Santa Ynez Valley that he thought I'd like. "Buttonwood, 1997. I'll save you a bottle, Romilia, if you promise not to leave us."

"Thanks, Doc, I'd . . . what's that supposed to mean?"

"McCabe tells me you're a card-carrying fed."

"It's a temporary card."

"Fine, fine. So you didn't get in trouble."

"No. I'm okay." I smiled, embarrassed, holding the cell phone. Pierce was next to me, talking with another agent, but hearing, I knew, everything I said. "I need to fax you something. Some drawings."

"I don't have a fax here at home. That's so terribly

yesterday, Romi. Do you have access to a scanner hookup?"

"I don't know."

"Put your agent on the line."

Pierce and he spoke. Pierce said "Yes" a lot to whatever it was Doc was asking him, regarding modems, hard drives, scanners, color codes. Then he said "Good. Thanks, Dr. Callahan, talk to you in fifteen," and hung up. He turned to me. "We'll scan them to him. He'll have them immediately, and they'll be clearer. I gave him my direct line. He'll call the moment he gets them."

Pierce had the assistant, the same young fellow who drove us around Denver, do his tech magic. The agent had hair like caramel. He handled the pages of the gutted men without gloves, which meant his would be the only prints now on them. He lay each page on the small scanner, covered it, pushed buttons. A light like that of a photocopy machine leaked out from under the lid. He made a file in his computer, pressed Save, then put another dissected man on the scanner plate.

This took a few minutes. Pierce and I walked away from the portable office in the back of the Federal van. I lit up. I offered Pierce one. He took it.

"So. What do you think?" asked Pierce.

This still took some getting used to. But I told him. "I thought at first this was a clue to what he did to the people in Kansas City. That he's kidnapped them and cut them up. But there are only three victims in Kansas City, and this is a series of six pictures. They're here, in Denver. Has there been any other report on people disappearing or getting killed here besides Joaquín Champ?"

"Just local homicides. Drunks, a crack house on the east side. Local cases."

I smoked. The nicotine helped. "I'm trying to figure out whether these are drawings of one guy getting dissected, or six individual men in different points of dissection."

"There hasn't been any reported cases of six people being killed at once. The three men in Memphis. The two victims in Atlanta. Two in Bristol. Three disappeared in Kansas City, and Joaquín Champ, here, in Denver. That's eleven altogether. But no one case of six."

"Which bothers me." I looked up at him. "I'm afraid this is a tease. He's showing us his next one."

"I was thinking that too."

The caramel-haired agent called out from the van. He had sent all six scans by email. Doc had called back, saying he got them and was opening them into his hard drive. He was on DSL, which meant his computer was not hooked to his telephone. He could talk to the assistant and work his internet system at the same time.

The assistant handed me the phone. "What do you think, Doc?" I asked.

"Just a second, I'm lining up the files, let's see. Did you say they were in a row, taped to the wall?"

"Right. Like in a progression, from one to six."

"All right, I'll do the same, see if I can fit them on this screen . . ." He must have had the phone cradled between his head and shoulder, because I could hear the keys of his computer getting tapped. "Here we go. Oh. Goodness, I haven't seen these since med school. *De Humani Corporis Fabrica Libri Septem.*"

His southern accent had a way with Latin. "What does that mean?" I asked.

"That's the title of the book where these came from. *On the Fabric of the Human Body.* It's a classic."

"Okay. Who wrote it?"

"Andreas Vesalius. French fellow. Sixteenth century doctor who was also an artist. He did these drawings, as well as wrote the text of his books. I think this is from Book II, on the ligaments and muscles."

"So an anatomist from four hundred years ago did these?"

"Yep. He was an amazing man, ahead of his time. He used regular, everyday tools to do his trade, but was a self-taught artist in the skill of autopsy. And a great drawer, as you can see. I have him to thank for the advancement of forensics. Gray used Vesalius to do his own anatomy book, but of course, by the nineteenth century, Gray didn't have to deal with all the hocus pocus superstitious beliefs of the Europeans three hundred years earlier. He could cut more freely, with even more accuracy. But Gray knew about Vesalius, all right."

"What about Doré?" I asked.

"The engraving artist? Oh yes. He, and most artists of his time, had to depend on Vesalius and other forensic doctors of the ages to draw the way they did. Of course, Doré couldn't have done so well without studying Michelangelo's art."

I didn't have more time for the history lesson, though Doc was obviously enjoying this. "You couldn't tell me, Doc, if these pictures are of one man, òr six men?"

"No. I don't have a copy of *Fabrica*. Much too expensive, even for my tastes. And I have to look at this every day anyway. No need to come home to it too."

"Where could I buy a copy, at Borders?"

"Lord no, girl." He laughed. "This is a specialty book, for certain libraries only. Universities may have them, especially their medical schools. And maybe some art museums. But you won't find it in a book store."

"Thanks Doc. This helps a lot."

"Romi. When are you coming home?"

"What? Oh. Soon."

"Why do I doubt that?"

"I don't know, Doc. I've got to get home. I've got a kid to feed."

All he said was, "Be careful, girl."

"We need to check the university library, see if anybody checked out a copy of this book," I showed Pierce the name on my notepad.

"We can do that, but don't expect them to give us a name. Privacy act. But they can tell us if someone checked it out."

He got the caramel agent on that. Then he dismissed me for the night. "Get some sleep. We're at the Radisson, I'll drive you over. We'll get up early tomorrow."

"Where will we go?"

He sighed. "I'm not sure. He's come a long way in a short time. I thought I saw a pattern there for awhile, between Bristol and Kansas City. Kind of a half-circle. Aren't circles part of that book?

"What, the autopsy book?" I referred to Vesalius' work.

"No no," said Pierce. "The Hell-book. *Inferno*. Dante. Doesn't that have a bunch of circles in it?"

I paused. "Yeah. It does."

"Maybe he's swooping," said Pierce, "Moving up north, to form a circle. But now he's jumped over here to Denver. So I don't know if there's a real circle pattern or not. Either way, I'll call a couple midwest offices to give them a head's up."

• • •

I couldn't sleep. And I couldn't drink either: the bar downstairs was closed. I had no car to drive around town, looking for a liquor store. So I looked at the television and didn't see it. All I saw were those six drawings, and all their details.

And here I was in Denver, a city I had never visited. I didn't want to tour. The skiing here was some of the best in the world, and I had no desire for it. Out the window I could see the full side of the mountains. They looked ready to topple our way.

No liquor. So I spread what I had out on the bed: the file from Kansas City; the notepads, now two, that I had filled with my own writings; photos of crime scenes.

Then the description of the man we thought was Minos: George Landley back in Kansas City told the Feds that the new member of their commune, Sean Cotto, was a man in his early to mid thirties who had black hair, somewhat olive-white skin, no beard or mustache. He was in good shape; he ran every day while living on the premises, did push-ups and sit-ups and used a thick tree branch to do his pull-ups. Landley thought he was a Hispanic. "But he talked like he was from the south, you know, a southern twang, just barely. And a Spam eater from the get-go."

Spam. I couldn't help but think southern. That was a staple in many southern homes.

The clerk at the front desk of the dorm building also described Theo Simon with almost the same words: Hispanic-looking, but white. Big. Strong. Southern.

That bothered me. There were few Hispanic serial killer suspects on file. Recently they had caught one man who was raping and murdering women on the

Texas-Mexican border. But they had fried his ass last year.

A Hispanic with a southern accent was not impossible. I had met enough of them in Nashville. Even in some ways I was that, though my English had more of an NPR lilt to it. Perhaps from living in the cities all my life.

Theo Simon and Sean Cotto were not Latino names. Then again, they were not his real names either.

My road atlas was open to the map of the entire country. I looked at where I was, in Denver, then looked over at Atlanta.

I was far from home.

Mamá answered after the second ring. "*Hija!* I was wondering when I would hear from you. Where are you?"

I hoped my aunt didn't have *69 to trace back this number. "Oh I'm in Nashville, still working on this case."

"Are they still mad at you at the office?"

"No. Not at all, I'm happy to say."

She believed me. She usually knew when I was lying. But she was so happy about me not losing my job that she must have blipped over my lie about being in Nashville.

She started telling me about Sergio and the cousins and the latest gossip about a distant relative back in El Salvador who's thinking about making the trek through Mexico and into the States, buy the fake papers in Houston then make his way toward Atlanta. I asked more about Sergio. She was glad to fill me in on his antics. And he was doing antics. He was in bed now, fast asleep after a day of running around the park near Peach Tree and seeing some movie at the theatre and eating pizza. He was very alive, that's what she meant to say: no aftereffects of the meth anymore, as if it had worked completely out of his body.

I let her talk. I needed her chatter. As she spoke I doodled, first on my pad, then on the map: I circled, with half-thought, each of the cities of the Crime Scenes. Bristol, then Atlanta, then Memphis, Kansas City, Denver. Then my hand, seemingly, on its own, drew lines between the cities, connecting the dots of murder. What the hell: talking with my mother, listening to her go on and on about the little man we loved the most in the world, had a way of clearing out my mind, even clearing it of the desire for whiskey. Though a cigarette sounded good now. But I held off lighting up, and drew lines. Pierce wasn't exactly right: it wasn't so much a half-circle, but a dipping from Bristol to Atlanta, then cutting over, before jumping across a state or two and landing in Kansas City. I lifted my pencil: my stick drawing looked like a broken ladle that had snapped at its rim. There they were, all five places where Mister-Whisperer-Now-Minos had been, and we had no idea now where . . .

You haven't been to five places.

You've gone to six.

You missed the gate. You didn't kill there. But you went there.

Mamá kept talking. I kept saying "Uh huh, oh *¿sí? ¿De veras?*" All the while erasing the line from Memphis to Kansas City and drawing two new lines, from Memphis to St. Louis, and then from St. Louis to Kansas City, and muttering in English, "Oh shit."

"*Qué pasó?*" she asked.

"Mamá, can I call you back?"

"What happened?"

"Oh I left the damn water running in the tub, and I'm on the old phone, I'll call you soon, mami, bye."

"Oh, all right *hija, te quiero.*"

You too, *adios.*

Did I say that? Or had I already hung up? I was only sure of what I saw before me, and of the final words he had left us with.

Right when I dip and turn, you'll see the stars.

I was seeing stars. A collection of them. But I wasn't sure. I was in a hotel room with no access to any books. Time to make another call.

"Romi, I don't mean to complain, but I *was* in bed."

"Sorry, Doc. I need help. How many stars are in the Big Dipper?"

"What?"

"Please, Doc."

He put the phone down, rummaged through his library. "Let's see. Got a world atlas here, I think it's got a map of the constellations, yes. Okay, Orion, Draco, where the hell's the North Star, oh yeah, right in the middle of the page. There it is. Big Dipper. It's got seven stars. Yeah. Last one's called Alkaid."

"How are they shaped?"

"What do you mean how are they shaped? Like a dipper."

"I know, but the handle part, does it go straight, or does it bend any way?"

"Would you please tell me what you're up to? That may help explain what you're looking for."

"I think he's drawn a map, Doc. A map of the places he's hitting. He's using stars . . . look, in *The Inferno,* I mean, in all of Dante's work, every section ends with the word 'star.' At the end of Hell, Dante see the stars. Same with Purgatory and Heaven, according to my notes . . ." I flipped through my pads, looking for that footnote where Pinsky had written about Dante's patterns.

"Slow down, Romilia. Listen. I can try to explain to you what the Big Dipper looks like. But I suggest you just walk outside and look up."

He was right. After he told me how to find the constellation, we hung up. I put on a coat over my pajamas and walked outside.

It was cold, the air crisp, dry. At first the lights of Denver put a glow over the sky, but as I stared long enough, I could make out the stars. The longer I looked, the clearer they became: they were beautiful, crystals that I had taken few moments in my life to look at.

Now I looked at them, not for pleasure, but for information.

The Big Dipper's front end, made of two stars, forms a trajectory that points straight to the North Star. Four stars in an opening square make up the bowl of the constellation. Three more trailing behind make for the handle. I stared at it, long enough to keep the image in my head. Funny, I always had an idea what it looked like, but the more I studied it, the more I realized how my memory of the Big Dipper was off. The handle: I always thought those three stars were in an exact straight line. But I was wrong; the real Big Dipper has a handle that is crooked, as if the cup itself were heavy with some liquid, one that made the handle bend. I could see the fairly straight line between the last star of the cup and the first two stars of the handle; but then the handle dipped down, to the very final star of the constellation, the one at the end of the handle, the one Doc had called Alkaid.

I ran back into my hotel room and placed the new memory of the Big Dipper down on the map, which was too easy to do. He had made it much too easy to do.

Bristol, Atlanta, Memphis, and St. Louis made for a perfect image of the dipper's bowl. St. Louis, Kansas City and Denver made for a fine copy of the handle. There was only one star missing.

Which city was Alkaid? Which city was the final star?

And would it be the final star? Would his killing spree end with just one more city?

I lay the pencil on the map, its eraser on Denver, and pointed its lead tip into the southwestern states. Straight lines from Denver could lead to Las Vegas or Los Angeles. If I turned the pencil to San Francisco, the handle straightened out too much. If I dipped it toward San Diego or Tijuana, it seemed, in my mind, too bent.

"Shit. This is still guessing. Still could be crazy." But the more I moved the pencil around, the more I thought this was right. And having a trajectory was better than having no pattern at all. He wasn't circling toward Chicago, or Minneapolis, or Des Moines. He was heading toward the southwest; somewhere in lower California six people would die and their skin, their muscle, would be flayed and . . . Shit. Jesus Christ.

Dante. I picked up *The Inferno*, split Pinsky's translation down the middle, cracked its spine. The next sin, what was the next sin?

He left off in Denver with a man who drowned in his own blood. A man, Joaquín Champ, who was a suspect in a number of drug-related murders, who had come to Denver to set up a new market for his gang. Violence toward others, that was his sin.

The next Canto, number XIII: violence toward the self.

> *... and through the mournful wood*
> *Our bodies will be hung: with every one*
> *Fixed on the thornbush of its wounding shade.*

I almost didn't want to look at the book with the Doré engravings. But I did. I rushed to it, threw the book open, found Canto XIII. The Forest of the Suicides.

Vultures, with the heads of women, sit on the tree branches, plucking away at the wood that bleeds. A man with a beard is a tree. He turns his head away, trying to escape the claw of the harpy that sits on his skull. But he can't, so enwrapped in the tree is he, as if someone had knit him into the wood. His bellybutton is a knot of oak. Below him, another man writhes on the ground, his arms and legs pure roots that push into the earth. Others, as I stare at the engraving, emerge from the dark woods, all of them either wrapped within the bark or made of the bark, the wood, itself.

Six plates from *On the Fabric of the Human Body*. Andreas Vesalius' bodies, all flayed and stripped of skin, muscle.

Unfortunately, I could put the two images together, and imagine.

Pierce was asleep, but he woke immediately, with no complaint. I told him what I imagined.

When the fierce soul has quit the fleshly case
It tore itself from, Minos sends it down
To the seventh depth.
The Inferno, Canto XIII

MARCH 17

This is probably really stupid, calling. Stupid, just an idiot. Crazy. It's the only decision I've made in two days. You get these calls all the time, don't you? I'm really not this way, you know. I've thought about it. Yeah, who the hell doesn't think about it in this town? Everybody's so fucking beautiful and pumped up with plastic in their tits but they're all thinking about it. We're thinking about it. All the time. It's like it'd be a decision, you know? It'd be a choice to make it stop, I could make it all go away. Because it never goes away. This time around it's not gone away, at all. I wake up, it's already near lunch, and I feel it, it swamps me, it's this curtain or something, it sucks me in. And *she* doesn't see it, of course. She'd have to be around to see it, wouldn't she? I don't get it, I've taken all her shit, eaten her Xanax, I, well, I sneak her wine when she's not around. Plenty of chances to do that, right? There it comes again, see? Fucking buckets . . . just the wrong word, I say something that brings it on and I don't know what the fuck it was that I said, and I'm crying like a damned baby, shit!

"You hear this, don't you? All the time. Somebody like me on the other end, doing more crying and sobbing than anything else. How many of us nutsos you think are out here . . . what did you say your name was?"

"Bobby."

"Bobby. So Bobby, how many phone calls you get in a day?"

"Right now you're the only call I care about, Karen."

"Oh yeah. All on me. Ready to save me . . . You want to save me, Bobby?"

"I want you to choose to live, Karen. That's what I want."

"I like your voice. You seeing anybody?" She laughs.

He chuckles, embarrassed. "No. Not now. Karen, it sounds like your mother isn't in the house much, is that right?"

"Understatement, man. She couldn't give a shit about this place. Like I'd want her around."

"Do you want her around? Karen?"

"I just want to die, Bobby." She sobs.

"You've thought about it. You've thought about suicide."

"Yeah. Yes."

"Sometimes it gets so hard, that you just want it to go away, or you want to go away, right?"

She agrees.

"I can understand that, Karen. I can. It's understandable, here, in this town, anywhere. Sometimes suicide seems to make sense. But you know, Karen, there are alternatives. And when you look at them, you might see a way of getting out of that darkness you're talking about. Karen? Are you there?"

He hears a whimper, a "Yes." It sounds promising.

"Good. Now, you said something about your mother's medication. Is she suffering depression or anxiety?"

"Oh shit, if that's not an understatement!" she laughs.

"Lots of stress in her life, I take it."

"You could say that. Though sometimes she brings it on herself. You can blame a town for only so long, you know Bobby."

"Does she drink?"

"No. Believe it or not, she doesn't suck it down as much as I do. But she's got to have it in the house all the time, right? Never know who's going to stop by. It's good shit, too. None of this under ten bucks a bottle stuff that you can get at Costco. She put up with that for years. But not now. No way. She has Maya go out and buy the best at a market near the Promenade. Yes sir, nothing under thirty bucks now. Hey, I get shit-faced only on the best, Bobby."

Bobby chuckles. A chuckle of acceptance.

"You drink, Bobby?"

"Not much. No."

"You're better off. Funny, I always think of my friends at the raves, you know, they suck down the coke and take the Ecstasy, they get bent on heroin. *They* were always the addicts. But I just can't make it to noon without stealing into Mom's cabinet." Again, the tears.

He is patient, and he follows the rules of training. But he also needs information regarding location, schedules. She mentioned the Promenade, which, he figures, is the Third Street Promenade. Santa Monica. But he must narrow it.

"How old are you, Karen?"

"Seventeen." She sniffs. Maybe she's reaching for a tissue. Or a bottle.

"So you're a Junior, right?"

"No. Senior. I cut ahead."

"Oh."

"Oh yeah. I'm one of the Starlette Intellectuals at Brentwood High." Again, a self-deprecating laugh.

He writes that down. "There's something to live for."

"You kidding? Starlette Intellectuals is a way of making the Geeks feel better about themselves. I tried to fail the Calculus exam last week, just to get pulled off that roster."

"But it shows something about you, doesn't it?"

"What's that?"

"You're smart, Karen. You can think things out. Even when it's the worst time, you've got a strong mind." Over the top, he thinks, but he needs to pull her in.

"You're nice, Bobby." She pauses. That must be a sip of wine she takes. More of a gulp. "Do you know who my mother is?"

"What? No, I don't. But I don't need to know every . . ."

"Rigoberta Allende."

Oh goodness. But he doesn't say that. He just thinks it. Goodness gracious.

"You've heard of her?" she laughs, as if that is a ridiculous question. For it is, in this town.

"Oh yes. The movies. Of course."

"The movies. You must spend a lot of time on this phone, Bobby." Again she laughs, "She's just the first Mexican American from East L.A. to win the Oscar, remember that?"

"Oh yes, I think I heard something about that, yes." Of course he remembers. Cameron Scott's now-famous *The Cruelest Month*, which swept the Oscars. He had seen it, had loved it. Rigoberta Allende was marvelous. An older woman, and a Latina at that, getting the part. Older woman; that seemed a strange way of referring to her, as the press had done. She was in her early forties. But in this town, for a woman, that was old.

Bobby wonders how much Karen looks like her mother. He learns that Karen has her mother's last name. Perhaps she was another man's daughter, or perhaps Rigoberta demanded it, that her child carry her name. Anything was possible here. Rigoberta Allende had been married to her husband for twenty years, that had made it into the press as well. Happy couple in Hollywood, both in the business, who have remained together for two decades. But now here is Rigoberta Allende's daughter, talking for over forty minutes to a stranger over a suicide hotline.

He keeps her on the phone for another fifteen. This is against the rules, he knows. Their rules are stringent, clear, designed to protect the callers as much as possible, to help them move toward the decision of living. Even here, where the murder rate is, like New York and Baltimore, one of the highest in the country, suicide is even higher. Only the best can become suicide hotline volunteers. Bobby has made their rank.

"Karen, how are you feeling?"

"I'm better, I think. Thanks, Bobby. Thanks."

"Listen, I want you to remember something. You can always call me. And you can go to others. Maybe not your mother, not now, I can see why you may not choose to talk with her. But someday, maybe you and she will talk."

She begins to cry again. He waits until she calms. He is getting tired, but he knows he must wait and let her emotions empty out, in order to fill her again. "For now, Karen, look around you to others you can trust. Someone you can talk with. Friends in your life. Your friends at school, do you all do things together? Do you hang out?"

"Sometimes, we, yeah . . . we'll head to the Starbucks, get a Frap."

"Yeah, the Starbucks on the Promenade?"

"No, it's the, the one in Brentwood, off Barrington. . . ."

He writes that down. "Right. Wherever it is, you hang out. And you talk about all sorts of things. Don't be afraid to talk with them about this."

"What, about wanting to kill myself?" she turns afraid.

"About you. About who you are. About how hard it is." He wants to quit, as he's about to fall over with exhaustion. This one has taken more planning than any other city. And he needs to get to her soon. The other five are all ready, but he can't hold them forever. Still, he must not rush. How this phone call ends will determine how they will meet.

"Thanks, Bobby. I think . . . I think you're the best thing that's happened to me, in a long time."

He means to blush.

"No, I mean it. Thanks."

He responds, tells her don't hesitate to call. He hangs up, then, on his yellow notepad, circles twice the collection of words, *Starbucks/Brentwood/Barrington.*

The following steps, in comparison to phone counseling, are much easier: *The Los Angeles Times* website gives him photos of the last Oscar ceremonies, when Rigoberta Allende stood to accept the Oscar for Best Female Actor in a feature film. A beautiful woman, whose beautiful daughter claps for her mother, with a shimmer of tears around her eyes, due to the occasion, the stress in the Shrine Auditorium. Auburn hair, a black dress with a necklace, and a bust that looks like something she had disparaged over the phone: made-to-order in a plastic surgeon's clinic in Beverly Hills.

Easy to spot her in a crowd. But it's not crowded in the Starbucks at two thirty this afternoon. The students at Brentwood High are still in class, except for the few seniors who have the last period free. She walks in with three other girls. They order Frappuccinos. He has ordered tea. But he needs honey in it, so he stands next to her at the sugar counter and drops a dollop in and casually pops his knuckles against the cup and out spills the tea, over his own hand. "Oh goodness," he says. "You okay?" she says. He laughs, says he'll be fine, he's just clumsy, isn't thinking as straight as he should be, and he'd come to have a cup of decaf tea just to settle down, isn't that ironic?

She looks up at him, stares at the face of that voice. "Excuse me, do I know you?" She does know him, and at first she looks as if she's made a mistake to say it. But she wants to say it.

He introduces himself. She is shocked, but she smiles.

"I'm Karen. Karen Allende. We met, over the phone."

She has something to say to him. At first he balks; this is not conventional, he says, though they never mentioned this in training. She kindly dismisses her friends; they walk out, drink their drinks at a table outside, just across from the Brent Air Pharmacy. Sometimes they look at Karen's male acquaintance, wondering who he is. They whisper and giggle, questioning his role in Karen's life (boyfriend? He seems a bit older, but buff!). Then they turn to their own conversations about school and boys and tailored drugs; for Bobby and Karen seem too adult now, the way they talk.

As Karen speaks to him about her loneliness, how she has been able to deal a bit better since they spoke on the phone, Bobby listens. He takes what she says about the desire, the need to escape, how the thought of doing it, over taking her mother's sleeping pills and washing them down with the wine, oh that's so crazy I know, you probably think I'm crazy. He does not think that at all. Before they depart she offers him what he needs: on his notepad, she writes her phone number down.

In his room, he carefully takes her name and her number and writes it under those five other names.

The following day, when they meet at the coffee shop, she orders a regular cappuccino. She touches his arm, smiles at him, "I'm sorry, I've got to hit the lady's room, do you mind waiting for my coffee?" Not at all. She rushes off. The barista is efficient. And Bobby is quick.

Midazolam Hydrochloride is known for its ability to disable a person with a "conscious sedation." Unlike its date-rape cousin Rohypnol, which puts the body in a state of aroused amnesia, Midazolam acts as a sedative, a hypnotic. It's the drug of choice for Colombian kidnappers. It also looks similar to the vanilla powder that Karen mentioned putting in her drink. He holds his thumb over the top hole of a straw, pushes the straw to the bottom, into the espresso, and carefully pours the powder through the straw. He sprinkles vanilla and three sugars atop the foam, then hands it to her as she walks out. "You may want to make sure there's enough sugar," he says.

"Thank you. That's sweet of you." She tastes it. "Oh. Well, that's *really* sweet!" She laughs. He apologizes, says he can buy her another one. "No, that's fine," she says. "Thank you." She looks at him like she could fall in love. And she could; he knows this, knows it from the suicide prevention training.

They sit down, talk. She gets tired. She stares at him, her jaw slack. He's more than happy to help her walk out of the shop. No friends have come with her today, no one to see the make of the windowless van he puts her in, nor to notice how fast it drives away, east on Sunset, toward the 405.

• • •

He's tired. This one has taken much more planning, many more steps. But it's been worth it, because he knows it's going to turn out just beautiful.

The traffic in this town doesn't help his weariness. Still, it was better to use the Warehouse Storage Center in Van Nuys, away from the center of the city. It's a clean storage building, fairly new, and the cubicle that he's rented is a bit larger than in other warehouses he visited. The walls are thin, just raw, gray cinderblock between his cubicle and the one next door. But he's rented a room wedged between two others that are already filled, which was what he hoped: a lesser chance of someone new putting their furniture into storage and by chance hearing a moan from that middle room.

But they don't moan much. The liquid Versed that he keeps injecting in them every three hours keeps them quite passive. It's a perpetual amnesiac sleep, which he will maintain in them until the appropriate afternoon, when he will stop the injections and make sure their muscles, though flaccid, lift slightly from the inducement, taut enough to receive the blade.

This is tiring, having to feed and water them every day. They remember nothing. They stare at him as he feeds them spoonfuls of gelatin. They chew, swallow, stare up at the metal rafters. Then they sleep. A couple of them have already shown signs of weight loss. But it's only been a week since he got Raul, that man from Venice who was the first to call him. They won't starve to death. Bobby makes sure they get enough water.

Cleaning up after them is another issue. But he keeps that as proper and as efficient as possible. As they are all naked, he has no clothes to wash. Just the floor where they lie, and their skins, which chafe.

All the care takes time. A good hour and a half with

each visit. He's moved in a cot, where he sleeps at night.

He needs a rest. He makes time for himself. He's heard about the new Getty, the one that stands on a hill in Brentwood, just above the 405. *The L.A. Times* wrote an article on the Getty's Research Library. One of the best in the country. Art historians from all over the world arrive and take out a carrel and spend months poring over the original documents of Picasso letters, or sitting for hours in the Special Collections room, turning the pages of an 1842 first edition *Incidents of Travel in Central America, Chiapas, and Yucatan*, by John L. Stephens, with a pair of tweezers.

He just wants to see what they have on Dante.

The air-lifted train ride up from the underground parking garage is meant to separate the visitors from the din of L.A. traffic. It works; merely sitting in the second coach while the train pulls smoothly up the hill over an electric rail allows him to relax. A little girl with a tiny stuffed doll shaped like a rhino looks out at the skyline. The purple rhino limps in her fingers. "Is that Hollywood?" she asks her father. He says no, it's Beverly Hills. Hollywood is farther out.

Bobby looks the other way, toward the Santa Monica Mountains, at a small college campus nestled like a quiet kingdom, standing even higher on the mountain than the Getty. Someone else sees it as well. "Mount St. Mary's," says the older gentleman. "Those nuns built there before any of this was here, when Brentwood was forest. Now their property must be worth, I dunno, a good billion."

All this is nice. It is a quiet place, in the most sprawled city in the country. He leaves the train with the rest of the tourists, walks across the large patio of marble and granite, follows a map and takes the steps up to the library. It is a round edifice, built of the same Italian stone of the museum. The entire museum seems to have been born out of the Santa Monica Mountains.

At first they do not allow him into the main part of the library. "Unless you're planning to do research here," says the guard at the front.

"Oh yes. I'm a professor."

"I can give you a temporary pass. After that you can apply for a permanent reader's badge. Which college do you work at?"

"I'm your neighbor," says Bobby, smiling. He gestures toward the campus on the hill. "Mount St. Mary's."

The guard writes the college name over a line. Bobby signs his name on another line, hands the guard his license.

"Here you go, Dr. Yamanaka. Just clip it to your shirt."

Before he sits down at a computer terminal, he looks at the interior of the building. He chuckles, wants to laugh out loud but doesn't, not with all those serious scholars bent over tables and studying piles of art books. The building: it's made up of rings. One ring after another, concentric. Perfect circles. He follows the curved walkway to the second floor.

There is no limit to Dante references. He finds a vein of books, many of which are the drawings by Blake, which he does not care for. Then there are the Doré prints. He pulls out a thick book, *The Complete Doré of the Inferno*, puts it under his arm. There are several others. One spine catches his eye, *The Inferno: A Translation With Paintings* by Thomas Phillips. He flips quickly though it: more contemporary stuff, using cartoon characters and Andy Warhol-like images to explore the rings of Hell. *Inferno* with twenty-first century irony. He places it under his arm as well.

There's Vesalius' *Fabrica*. Take that one too, just for the fun of it. A review of sorts. Volume II, of course.

He recognizes the passing of years. When he first started reading the *Comedy*, when he first stared at the old books his aunt had in the house, those engravings by Doré made something in him vibrate. They were frightening; but they were also very clear, concise. Now they do not hold that same power over him. Perhaps it is because he has gone beyond Doré, he has been in the circles themselves, he has made the circles real. This one, of Minos, for instance: it is almost quaint. Funny, in a dark way. Minos sits on a stone hill as the newest group of sinners comes before him, some of them bowing. One naked soul falls to one knee. A devil with thick, upright wings stands to one side, also nude, leaning on a pole. Minos is huge; he takes up most of the engraving. We cannot see his eyes, as he is turned toward the sinners. His crown is pressed over his head, tucked into thick blonde curls that flow into a beard. His left leg is crossed over his right thigh, effeminate, relaxed. A constrictor-like tail snakes over and under his body, though we don't see how it connects to his buttocks. It curls over his left forearm; he holds the end of the tail in his right hand. The fold of his back muscles, the vein of his bicep. Doré knew the human body. Minos waits to hear what the penitents have to say, which sin they must confess. This confessor is calm. We see him now, before he wraps his tail around them and flings them into their appropriate circle.

Bobby has outgrown this depiction. He's bigger than it is.

Vesalius' notes and drawings are much more interesting to him these days. This list, and the drawing, of the Instruments that can be Procured for Performing Dissections. Vesalius had no fear, did he? It was the Renaissance, of course, which allowed him to perform autopsies that his predecessor of centuries previous, Galen, could never get away with. Galen had to rely on animals to learn about the human body; at least Galen used apes. Vesalius, while careful in not insulting the previous mentor of human anatomy, quite thoroughly rectified the numerous mistakes Galen had made regarding tendon positions, flexion, the difference between quadrupeds and bipeds. Regarding tools, Vesalius made do with what he had. Just under the drawing of the table filled with utensils, Vesalius has each article labeled with a letter, followed by a complete list of tools.

Image C is of various holes through which we pass nooses to immobilize its legs and arms.

D are rings for tying the animal's hands and feet to.

E: To this ring the upper jaw (but not the lower) is bound with a small chain to keep the head still; thus the voice and respiration are not impeded by the use of chains.

F: Different types of razors, with a sponge lying above them.

N: Curved needles along with thick thread used for sewing fascicles.

X: Forceps

The Italians use crude knives with large upstanding hilts or handles, and these hilts tend to be a nuisance in making curved incisions, and they also get in your way and prevent you from bending your hand as you might wish.

He has better equipment. A visit to a medical warehouse in Orange County got him all he needed.

He falls asleep while turning the pages of Vesalius. When he wakes his mouth is dry. He finds a water fountain, returns to the small carrel, opens the book of

Tom Philips' renderings of the Inferno. How can this be Hell? Images of Superman flying over a collage of a dark city. A Post-Modern Inferno.

Still, after a half hour of looking, there is something about the prints that make him pause. His aunt used to teach him that: take time with art. If it's good, it will seep into you.

His aunt. So good and so gone and far away from all this.

She was right. Philips starts to make more sense. Maybe not make sense, but play upon the senses. There is repetition in Philips' work: arrows all pointing one way but going nowhere. A thick pistol lying in shadows. Words sprawled, over and again, across a folding of bright colors. Colors. He's never thought of the Inferno having color.

Then there is this Minos. Oh. This is Minos.

The profile of a skull, cut in half, down the middle. The mouth open, though no teeth show. The eye, just the socket, hollowed out. It's the image of a skull, really, not a complete rendering, not a snapshot. But it is a skull, no doubt. And in it lies the tail: wrapped over itself, again and again, the tail turns into a swirl that does not end. A small box covers where the tail would become a complete vortex: in the box, tiny figures slam against each other, nude sinners, all in a row.

It's the tail that stops him now. Not protruding from his backside, but taking the place of the brain. Bobby stares at the coils, how they wrap into themselves, tight inside this skull. If the tail expanded any, if the sinews pushed the wrong way, the skull would crack, bone would fly everywhere, and scatter across this second floor of this library in this museum.

Bobby blinks. Again something snaps, like a whip: he is in a closet, his head pressed against the wall, where he can hear the moaning sins of a father and a sister.

Maggie.

Later, Maggie in a tub. Maggie staring at him, her arms bobbing in red water.

He cannot breath. Something pushes through him. It's just a painting, just some fucking painting, some guy's idea of an old myth but I can't breathe.

"You all right sir?"

Bobby's eyes are open, but he does not see. The voice rouses him. The name on the librarian's badge is Joshua. He's got a beard, kind eyes. "Let me help you up."

Joshua puts his hands under Bobby's arms, tries to pull him from the floor. He stands now on his own. Outside it is dusk. The sun sets toward the Pacific. Joshua says something, but Bobby does not hear him. This is strange; he looks around, sees the open book of Philips drawings, turns away again. Joshua offers advice, something tepid like get some water or a bite to eat. Bobby thanks Joshua, walks out of the library, shuffles across the Getty's large outdoor patio, down the white marble steps that follow a cascade of water. He does not wait for the next train. There's a path, a road, running away from the Getty, and he sprints over it, all the way down.

MARCH 18

Pierce had called ahead to the FBI offices in Los Angeles, giving them the details of the Minos killings. They now used the name, though that information had not leaked to the press. There was no need for leaks; if what we knew were true, we had a possible location and a target of victims. Pierce told the L.A. FBI to look out for medical, religious, and private institutions that dealt either with suicide prevention or patients who had tried suicide and were now in a rehab program. LAPD also should be involved, keeping the Bureau apprised of any recent disappearances. If there were any connection between those two, especially if there were six connections, we would follow that direct lead.

"Though the disappearance angle may be frustrating," said Pierce. "This is L.A. People get reported missing all the time, then they show up two days later, or someone finds them at a girlfriend's house, or they're runaways. I don't know how we'll keep up with that."

I was listening, but I didn't answer him, because I watched as our small jet banked over the city and headed toward LAX. I had never been to Los Angeles before. The city went on forever. It never ended.

The Los Angeles FBI offices were huge. There were more women here than I had seen in any other crime prevention office, local, state or federal. Everyone dressed sharp. I felt dumpy; I hadn't had a shower in twenty-four hours, hadn't changed my clothes since before Denver. I, along with the other agents, including Pierce, had tried to get some sleep on the plane flight from Colorado, but that proved difficult, with the new lead in my mind. A new lead that made me believe this was the closest I had gotten to him.

Pierce shook hands with the head of the FBI in Los Angeles, one Special Agent Leticia Fisher. She greeted Pierce with a smile, "Good to see you Chip." Though she knew him, she must not have seen him in a couple of years, no doubt since before his loss of eye and leg.

They made quick, familiar small talk. Pierce introduced me, then asked me to give the details of the case.

I repeated pieces of information that she already knew, but then dovetailed into the theory that had brought us to Los Angeles. "The perp has a thing for Dante's *Inferno*. He's using it as a map. He's also creating his own map: all the killings and the references to the cities that he's been in show an exact outline of the Big Dipper. The outline points to the southwest now, and the major cities in the trajectory are Los Angeles and Las Vegas."

"Have you contacted the Las Vegas branch?" asked Special Agent Fisher.

"We have," said Pierce. "They're following through with the same possible leads regarding suicide cases."

She already knew we were looking down the suicide angle. "That's a real tossup, between L.A. and Las Vegas. Two cities of broken dreams. Just a different dream in each."

"That's true, Special Agent Fisher. But my hunch is with L.A."

"Why's that?" she looked straight at me. I liked her for this. She could look directly at me and expect straight answers. She could do that here, in this huge city, where she was the boss of the regional Bureau, the largest FBI offices outside of New York. She was either Latina or African American or both. And she was a she.

I said, "I think he's here, because he needs some dark woods. Las Vegas is a desert. He needs trees."

"Explain that, please, Detective."

"He's very meticulous with his killings. He likes to leave behind blatant symbols, signs of how his victims lived, and thus how they died. The three men in Memphis were killed with a dog, just like Cerberus, the three-headed dog in Hell. Joaquín Champ drowned in his own blood, just like the violent people of the Inferno who hurt others. My sister, Catalina Chacón, and her boyfriend were stuck together with a javelin-like instrument, held together when they died. Just like the couple, Paolo and Francesca."

Special Agent Fisher was listening. I felt strange, almost childlike, giving her this information, as if, somehow, I was guilty of the way Minos killed. I, the messenger of his actions, felt tainted by the very message I had to give. But that's not why Fisher' eyebrow lifted.

"One of the victims was your sister," she said.

A mistake. But I said, "Yes, yes ma'am. She was."

Fisher turned to Pierce. "Could we have a word, Chip?"

They walked away.

Pierce met me in the coffee room. I turned on him, obviously afraid, but also not ready to deal with bureaucratic shit. Perhaps the first time he had seen that complexity of emotions run across my face.

"It's okay, everything's fine," he said.

"Then why'd it take so long?" I asked, looking over his shoulder, "What, was she checking up on me?"

"Detective Chacón, you are now an agent, and though it's temporary, you don't talk like that with your superior." He looked down at me. I hadn't heard that type of authority before. It was a simple authority: one man's voice backed up by one entity, which happened to be the Federal Government.

"Detective Fisher will allow you to continue on this case in her jurisdiction," said Pierce.

"Reluctantly?" I asked.

"Yes. But I talked with her. We go back a few years. Look: Lettie's got a lot on her plate, more than most of us in the regional offices. This is L.A. Ruby Ridge and Waco are mere sneezes in comparison to what can happen in this city. We've had black eyes in the past, and we're trying our damnedest to keep from getting another one."

I couldn't care less about their public eye, how much they'd screwed up in the past. That was their issue. My issue was Minos. But they had gotten me here, so I kept quiet, making no snide comments that floated to the top of my thoughts.

"Just keep doing what you're doing, Romilia."

• • •

Background checks on recently employed nurses, Candy Stripers, and resident students at local hospitals, particularly those that also had suicide prevention programs and suicide watches, did not bring up much. A couple of nurses had done drugs in their past; one had a charge on cocaine possession, which, Agent Fisher muttered, was like getting caught drinking coffee in this town.

Pierce asked, "What about suicide hotlines?"

"There are three in the area," said Fisher. She was at her desk, clicking her mouse over the laptop. "Two have been here a long time, very well established. The Suicide Prevention Center gave us names of all their volunteers, along with a checklist of their backgrounds. Nothing set off alarms there. Same with the Hope and Hands Clinic. We're waiting to hear from this third one, let's see, the 'Reachout Hotline Services.' They've been a bit more reticent. The gentleman in charge there likes to remind us of his rights." Leticia Fisher looked at me, her eyes almost ready to roll with cynicism. "It got started a couple of months ago."

The thought of following up the hotline angles exhausted me. It seemed tepid: Minos would want to see his victims, have them all together. I imagined a different scenario: Minos posing as a nurse (he could do that; he knew medicines, drugs, how to use syringes), getting a job at a local clinic, getting to know some of the patients in the mental health ward. Perhaps he'd drug them all, put them in an ambulance, drive away one night during the change in shifts.

The disappearance angle was just as weak. So far four different LAPD precincts had reported a total of seventeen alleged disappearances, people who were reported missing in the past forty-eight hours. Most of those would show up soon enough, either passed out in a hotel room after shooting up, or wandering home after an all night drinking binge. Only a few would end up becoming open-file cases of Missing Persons. And according to Special Agent Leticia Fisher, only one, at this point, would get any special attention from the police.

"Karen Allende, daughter of Rigoberta Allende, the actress. Reported missing by her mother last night."

"You're kidding," I said. Had I sighed? One day in L.A., and already I was coming into indirect contact with its Hollywood glitter. And not just any glitter: Rigoberta Allende. She was one example of when my mother packed up her prejudicial bags concerning Mexicans and sat in the theatre, glued to every movement Rigoberta Allende made, every single word she uttered.

"The boys in Brentwood will be all over that one," said Fisher. "But they won't let it leak out to the press yet. The girl's probably driving around in a Ferrari up the Pacific Coast Highway."

Everyone had a job to do: even Chip Pierce, who, though not in his office, was on the phone constantly, checking in with, I suppose, Nashville or Quantico. And here I was, far away from home. Los Angeles. I looked out the large window, from the twelfth floor, out at that city that seemed to have two, no . . . three skylines. I thought about calling my uncle Chepe, but that would light a string of fire between here and Atlanta. He was probably back from visiting the family in Georgia. If I called, it wouldn't be thirty seconds before Mamá called, and then, "*Hija*, you won't believe who just called me with the strangest piece of news." and it'd be downhill from there.

I just kept staring at L.A., in this aquarium of a

Federal Agency, while all the other fish in here, every one darted back and forth with something important to do.

A nice young woman with an earpiece plugged in found me an empty desk. I spread out my file, the one that was perpetually with me, the one that I stuffed into my shoulder bag every day. The pages had become ragged around the edges, though I had managed to keep them intact. Of course, the bag had become even heavier with me heaving around two copies of *The Inferno*.

The Forest of the Suicides. People who had gotten lost in their own despair. This was an old world way of thinking about death. Though Dante's vision was harsh, Dante comes off as a broken, emotive character: he speaks with the damned, asks them why they are in Hell. They explain, as if in a final confession. At first I thought our killer meant to see himself as the Italian poet, until I got to know Dante more. Dante wept over these suffering souls. Minos did not: Minos did not hesitate to throw them where they remained forever.

I looked at the faces of these people, locked into the very bark of these trees. Their wounded, self-mutilated souls had fallen like seeds into Hell, and like seeds, Minos had tossed them here. They grew into twisted, gnarled trees where Harpies sat, picking away at their woody flesh.

A warning. Dante was warning his own world: don't do these sins, or this is how you'll end up.

A warning to our world? Was my Minos trying to warn the world of its evil doings? A religious perspective, bent and twisted until it committed murder?

The Doré engraving depicting the souls of the suicides was enough to help me form a picture that I did not want to see. This engraving melded with the Vesalius dissections. Men and women, stripped of their flesh. Minos was literal: he couldn't make his victims grow into trees; but he certainly could skin them and somehow pin them to the bark.

I could think like Minos. I could see the logic of his kills, the way he did my sister and Jonathan, it made sense to him. It made sense to me.

I rubbed my eyes. A drink would have been good now. Not this coffee, as good as it was; but whiskey, pure, straight turkey. Wild.

I flipped through *The Inferno*. After awhile, the Doré images ran together, one after another, gutted corpses, beheaded men, women with their hard bosoms floating in a sea of blood. Then at the end, that horrific drawing of Satan, stuck in a solid lake of ice. He's chewing on three men with his three mouths. He's pissed off. He's huge.

Would Minos keep killing until he got into the final circle? What did this mean: would he end up somewhere in Minnesota? There could be a lot of Cantos between now and then. How long could he keep this up?

Pierce came up from behind, "We've got something here. One Ethan Coleridge, twenty-one years old, junior at UCLA, has been reported missing by his roommate. The roommate, Elijah Reed, said that Coleridge had been missing for three days, and he was worried because he once walked in and caught Coleridge staring at a bottle of sleeping pills. Let's go."

W hat, you guys are *FBI?*" said young Elijah Reed. He gazed at Pierce's eye patch.

Pierce ignored the question, and moved the thin, white nineteen year old down a line of questions, "Was your roommate, Mr. Coleridge, known for taking off for days at a time?"

"No way. He was solid whenever he wasn't down. Always showed up to class on time, liked to get up early and study, that sort of thing. And he didn't do drugs or anything like that. Didn't even drink. He was a good guy, from some small town out in the desert. I'm sorry, but I got to ask, why is the FBI involved in this? Isn't this a local case?"

He must have taken a class in judicial law. Pierce answered him, "Sometimes the Bureau has to involve itself in possible missing persons cases."

"Only if it deals with crimes that have crossed state

borders. Are you all after somebody in particular?"
Though nervous, he also showed a hint of glee.

"You want to join the Bureau someday, son?" asked
Pierce, smiling. Good move, I thought, because Elijah
grinned with embarrassment. "Keep that up, you and I
might end up working together someday. Listen,
Elijah, you mind if we look around?" Pierce motioned
to the small dorm room.

Elijah moved out of the way. Pierce and I looked
around, asked which desk was Ethan's. I studied it
while Pierce looked through Ethan's closet. Elijah sat
on his bed, nervous, though it seemed he had little if
anything to hide.

As I looked around, I asked, "Tell me, Elijah, what
would those 'funks' be like, that Ethan fell into?"

"Pretty strange. He'd just get really sad. It was like
he was trying to keep his whole life together by studying hard, getting up early, diving into his classes. But
then he'd get tired. He'd dread the weekends, like he
had too much time on his hands. I'd ask him to get out,
you know, go to a movie or something. But he'd lie in
bed and sleep til noon, which was something he'd
never do in the middle of the week. He'd stay in his pajamas all day, wouldn't even watch television, even if I
had it on. And he wouldn't get on the Web or anything.
He'd just get kind of, I don't know, catatonic. Well, just
really really sad."

Ethan had a clear, precise handwriting. Too precise
for someone his age: it almost looked scripted, like
something that would come out of a list of fonts on a
computer. Notes on his class schedule, reminders to
himself about certain books to check out, a detailed
listing of expenses written down the margin of a
notepad. Nothing at all lascivious or questionable,
which in itself was strange: he was nineteen. Didn't he

have any thoughts that were just a little out of kilter?
No journal or diary, only work notes, class notes, and a
few phone numbers. But one of the numbers was familiar; I had seen it on Pierce's notepad earlier.

"Agent Pierce."

He stepped over to the desk. I pointed out the one
number.

"Yeah. Good." He wrote it down, then looked at
the dorm room telephone, wrote it down.

Once I met Mikey Farrell, I understood Special Agent
Leticia Fisher's cynical remark about Reachout Hotline Services.

Mikey Farrell was the ebullient administrator of
the new depression and suicide prevention service. He
was also its fundraiser, and when we met him, he was in
a meeting with two well-dressed women from a very
large corporate foundation. It seems our arrival spoiled
the meeting.

"I'm sorry, but couldn't we talk another time?" said
Mr. Farrell, his mouth splitting into a smile and his
thick curly hair almost trembling with an emotion that
could have been ebullience or rage, take your pick.

"No we really can't, Mr. Farrell, because we're investigating a missing persons case that has led us to
your offices."

"I don't know what you're referring to."

"You got a call from my superior, Special Agent
Fisher? She wanted to talk with you about your new
program here."

"Yes, and considering the delicacy of the program
and the clientele we work with, I told her to make an
appointment and I'd be glad to speak with her." Again,
the splitting smile.

"Do you mean the delicacy of your fund-raising?" I asked.

"What are you insinuating?"

This went way too fast: he seemed a bit high-strung for a suicide prevention director.

"Please, call my assistant and come back later." He turned back to his office door and began to pull it open. His mistake.

Pierce reached over Mikey's shoulder, pushed it closed again. He looked Mikey straight with his eye and his patch, smiled, and said, "Mr. Farrell, we're the FBI. We don't come back later."

I liked that.

Within three minutes the two women were kindly dismissed and asked to arrange another appointment, due to some very important circumstances that I did not hear because Mikey made sure to close his door. The women left, neither of them smiling. They looked at us with that distant disdain; then the first woman's eyebrows shot up as she first saw Pierce's eye and then, swiveling to me, my neck: the Mutilated Hit Squad.

We sat before Mikey's desk. He sat behind it, rubbed his eyes, pushing his glasses up his forehead with the back of his fingers. "Okay, so I guess you've come to ask about Bobby."

We had come to talk about Ethan Coleridge, who may have called this place before disappearing. But Pierce didn't miss a beat. "Tell us about Bobby."

"Well I don't know where he is!" Mikey looked at us both, then looked down. "I feel just as bad about it as anybody. And I'm *very* conflicted about not reporting it. But I, I don't know, I figured his family would do that. I just thought he got a better paying job."

"Pay?" I asked. "I thought this was a volunteer organization."

"It is. Bobby was my assistant, my only staff. Sometimes, whenever a volunteer wouldn't show, he'd take the phones. He was good about that, always pitching in wherever I needed him. Really courteous. Had a real, you know, pastoral voice to him. That's good on the phone, when you're talking with suicidal people."

"Do you have a lot of volunteers, Mr. Farrell?" I asked.

"No, not yet. We just started up a few weeks ago. Don't get me wrong: I've got some really good patrons. Those women who were just in here, from the Slake Foundation? They're planning to give us two years' worth of start-up funding. Well, I hope they do. . . ." He stared at the door. "You know, there are only two other hotline services in southern California. They need some competition to cover more area, keep them on their toes."

Competition for suicide prevention. *Scam* came to mine. "These volunteers, do they go through training to do this work?" I asked.

"Of course. I train them."

"I see. You're a psychiatrist?"

"No. I've got an MBA from Illinois State."

Pierce asked, "How does having an MBA prepare you to run a suicide prevention program?"

"I don't *do* the prevention, Detective," he said, crossing his arms over his chest. "I just make sure it's done well. I'm an administrator. That's the problem with most nonprofits. They have good people with caring hearts, but they don't know poop about how to run the thing."

"So do you have a professional counselor on hand?"

"Yes! Bobby!"

I asked for Bobby's employment file. Farrell sighed,

reached back, thumbed through a cabinet, and handed a thin file to me.

Bobby was now a possible Missing Persons. Maybe Minos was looking for people who reached out to depressed individuals, who wanted to help them. That may have been against Minos' theology, or whatever you'd call his warped sense of thinking: suicidal people shouldn't be helped, but they should burn in Hell. Or more accurately, grow like trees in Hell.

The file had a photocopy of a diploma from a university in Georgia, one I had never heard of. It seemed legitimate enough, that Bobby Green had a Masters' Degree in Psychological Counseling. A closer look revealed something that I had seen in the package sent to me by Tekún Umán: the slight, filtery signs of a downloaded file, the thin streaks through the university's title of an ink jet printer. I pointed this out to Pierce.

"How long has Mr. Green been missing, Mr. Farrell?"

"Today's Friday . . . he came in on Tuesday morning, then left for lunch. I expected him back in half an hour. He always ate here, where I could make fun of him." Farrell grinned, the first time he looked sincere.

"Excuse me?" I asked. I smiled too, baiting it out.

"Oh, that stuff he loved to eat. You know. Sushi. I'm not from southern California, we never ate much raw fish in Illinois."

Pierce was not perturbed, but he didn't see the humor. "What's so funny about sushi?"

"Nothing, except for what Bobby ate. You know, that fake meat . . . what's it called?" He scratched his head. So I said the word, perhaps too quickly. "Yes! That's it. Whoever heard of Spam on sushi?" he laughed again.

I looked at Pierce, and he glanced back at me. We made our exit, with Bobby Green's file in hand.

In the car Pierce corrected Mikey Farrell, "It wasn't sushi. It was musubi."

"What?" I barely heard him. My mind started connecting dots quickly: in Kansas City, the young man who disappeared along with the others from the hippie church ate Spam. Lots of Spam.

"Musubi," said Pierce. "It's a Hawaiian dish. Looks like sushi. Some rice and Spam wrapped in a leaf of seaweed. I had some while visiting the island once. Nothing to write home about. But the Hawaiians love it. Hawaii is the Spam capital of the world. Ever since we introduced it to them in World War II, they've kept the Spam corporation in business."

"It's Hawaiian?"

"Yeah. What?"

I grabbed my bag and dropped it on my lap. While Pierce drove us back to the FBI headquarters, I riffled through the bag looking for one document: the printout from the rental company in Memphis. PriceRight Auto Rentals, where all the names had checked out. But there was a name on the list that I had not readily recognized when first reading it, and now, was not sure I'd get the pronunciation right.

"Yama . . . Yamanaka. Is that Hawaiian?"

"Hawaiian, maybe Japanese. Yeah. Why?"

"Minos rented a car in Memphis, drove into Oxford, Mississippi, to buy the dog. This is the sheet of names and credit cards from the rental company, for those days when he may have been in the area."

Pierce glanced at it, but he had to be careful, unaccustomed to Los Angeles traffic. But he did glance at me. "This come from your little jaunt into Mississippi?"

"As a matter of fact, yes."

He smiled. Did this mean I had shaken off one less hook?

"So you think there's a connection to this Jamey Lei Yamanaka?"

"I don't know. I only checked to see if the credit cards were fake. I didn't find out who owned them."

"None reported as missing?"

"No. People were honest in Memphis that day. At least they were at PriceRight." I paused, thought it out. "Does the FBI have a way of contacting the owners of credit cards?"

"Of course."

"And how about finding out if the cards have been used recently? Like here, in Los Angeles?"

His chuckle was the answer.

I didn't mind. I just thumbed the file that little Mikey Farrell had been forced to give us. I touched it, pulled my fingertips over it, knowing now that Bobby Green was no Missing Person.

At the Bureau Pierce gave instructions to a young fellow at a computer terminal: find Jamey Lei Yamanaka's phone number, and find out if the credit card had been used in the southern California area. The young man said the phone number would come quicker, but it'd take a while to trace the card's activities.

I had felt victorious in the car, knowing that my escapade in Memphis and Mississippi, one that had gotten me docked at the department in Nashville, had now come through with a possible lead. But now a wave of failure washed over me. Why hadn't I followed through, found out where the credit card had been used? I should have done that. Then I reminded myself that I couldn't: I had been put on suspension, with all my rights in the department temporarily revoked. I didn't even know if the Nashville Police Department had access to credit card databases. I asked Pierce about this.

"It's hit and miss," he said. "Some Homicide Departments have the capability of getting into a larger database more directly, like here in the LAPD, or the NYPD. But smaller towns, like Nashville, have more limits placed on them. Nashville has a lower homicide rate. You don't have as much a need for high tech equipment."

"I never thought of Nashville as a smaller town."

He laughed. "Live there awhile, then travel the country, and you'll see that it is. Don't get me wrong, I like Nashville. Good place for family and all. Good schools, nice people, and the music industry brings in good shows, decent entertainment. But I don't have a family."

He paused only slightly; was that regret I saw, crossing his face? Had he once had plans, now blown away, along with his body? Perhaps someone who once loved him couldn't love him in this new state, handicapped, broken but still standing. But after being with him these few days, I had grown used to the eyepatch, the limp. They seemed more a part of him, something integral to who he was. And he was a looker still, once you grew accustomed to those coverings: His blonde hair, cut short, still could drop a lock down over the black strap that ran over his forehead. He still worked out, I could tell that through his suit. And that eye: sometimes I caught it glancing at me, just casually running down the side of my arm, hoping to catch the curve of my back, perhaps? Perhaps.

The young agent came around, handed a card to Pierce. "Here you go, sir. Dr. Jamey Lei Yamanaka, she lived in Knoxville, Tennessee."

"She?" Pierce was as surprised as I was.

"Yes sir. She was a professor at the University of Tennessee."

"What, she's dead?" I asked.

"Yes ma'am. She died seven years ago."

Seven years ago, just a little less, the Mastersons were killed. I looked back up at the young agent, "How did she die?"

"She had cancer. That's all they told me. Sounds like she was very popular at UT. The secretary still talked about her like an old friend."

"So this is the university number?" Pierce held up the card.

"No. Her widower. Barry Sanford. I didn't call, figured you'd want to do that."

The kid agent walked away. I had had the thought before, that some of these agents looked younger than me. But now I just thought about that card. I must have looked at Pierce right, because he handed it to me.

"Get on this," he said.

Barry Sanford sounded like an old man. Maybe seven years wasn't enough to forget about his wife. Still, he could say it, "I'm sorry, Jamey died a while back. Who'd you say you were?"

"I'm Romilia Chacón," a hesitance, and then, "I'm with the FBI."

"FBI? What's the matter?"

"I'm sorry to bother you sir, but we're following up on some questions involving a case."

"What case?"

"I'm not at liberty to say."

"Oh." He was tired, it seemed, from living alone, but my response was enough to perk some questions in him, some obvious concern. "How did you come by calling me?"

I told him about the credit card. He listened well. Then I heard him breathing. A sad breath, like that of a widower, something I recognized.

"That's Bobby's card."

"Bobby?"

"Bobby Green, my nephew."

"Do you know where Bobby is now, Mr. Sanford?"

"I'm sorry, I haven't seen Bobby in what, three years now. No, two. He came through, yes, around this time a couple of years ago. Just to stop in, but he stayed awhile, a couple of days. It was good to see him. I've wondered how he's doing."

"So you haven't had contact with him for awhile?"

"Oh, he sends me cards from time to time. Keeps me up with where he's been traveling."

"Does he travel a lot?"

The old man chuckled. "Bobby loves to travel."

"How does he afford that?"

"Money's no issue for Bobby. His aunt made sure of that, before she died. Jamey worked it all out. Bobby's set for life."

I was still confused. I poked a few gentle questions around the elder man.

"You've got to understand, Ms. . . . what was it? Chacón. I'm sorry. My short term memory tends to fizzle. Bobby, he had a rough one. His father and all. It was sad, in that house. Jamey did everything she could to get Bobby out of that house. That was after her sister was killed, and that man got away with it. Jamey did it. That brother-in-law of hers, he had us on the hot plate for years. The only time I ever thanked God for someone's death was the day Frank died.

"I'm sorry, Ms. Chacón. Some of these memories, they'll make you say what you feel. Old age does that too. . . ."

It took a second, but he spoke again, slid into memories way too deep. "The things that man did to his kids when their mother died. God-awful. And Frank had money. No one could touch him. Drove the girl to suicide. Maggie was her name. Beautiful little thing. Bobby's the one who found her, in the tub. That boy's seen too much."

I needed more data. "So, the credit card, Mr. Sanford. Bobby uses it?"

"Yes. Jamey opened that card for him, under her name. She used to take care of his bills. Once he went to Italy, spent a summer there, just put it all on the charge card. That was the biggest trip he ever made. He'd use it, she'd get the balance statement, pay it off from his estate. When she died, I took care of it. He doesn't use it as much now, but we still keep the system. I've thought about asking him to come home, take over the trust fund, maybe do something with it, start his own business or something. But then I think about all that happened, and I figure, let him go on and live his life. He's put in enough time, and doesn't need to work."

As calm and as sad as this old man's voice was, my voice had a hard go of it breathing evenly. "Mr. Sanford, when was the last time you heard from Bobby?"

"Let's see, he called me, oh, about two months ago. He was up in Alaska, fishing."

The hell he was. "Do you have a way of contacting him?"

"He left a number, let's see. No, it's the number of the lodge where he was staying, but he said he wouldn't be there after the first of the month. I'm not much to be on the phone anyway, so I never did get around to calling him back." A pause, and then, dark illumination, "He's in trouble, isn't he, Ms. Chacón?"

"Mr. Sanford, if you hear from him, I need for you to call me. For now, I need a favor from you: I need for you to get a photo of Bobby to your local police. Please give me your address, I'll have them come to you."

"What's happened, ma'am?"

"I really can't say, sir." I was about to move toward ending the call, when it occurred to me, "I'm sorry, but one more question: what was Bobby doing in Italy?"

His fear turned back a moment, to a more pleasant time. "Oh, his aunt got him on a Dante kick. She was a medievalist, one of the best in her field. She used to laugh about how nutty Bobby got about the *Divine Comedy*, it was something. . . ."

After getting his address, I hung up too quickly, I'm sure, with a speed that may have frightened that old man.

"Chip! Agent Pierce." He turned to me.

"Jesus, girl, what's the matter?"

It took the young agent another ten minutes to pull the information on the credit card's use. Pierce had left us to speak with Special Agent Fisher. I was alone with the youngster. He looked a bit nervous, with me standing over his desk. But he was good at ignoring me.

"Okay, here we go," he said, watching the computer screen open one page to another, until it pulled up the credit card number of one Dr. Jamey Lei Yamanaka. Doctor and Jamey: I'm sure our Minos had no problem going under those auspices, posing as a male Jamey with a Ph.D. Anytime he was asked for identification, no doubt he showed a fake ID with his face glued next to that name.

"Not much action on this card," said the agent, "just a couple of gas stations in Des Moines and Indianapolis . . . a rental car company in Des Moines, Buffalo, something in Dallas. And a couple of restaurant bills. One in Montreal."

Why did he do that? He must have figured we could trace the card sometime. Those cities were nowhere near the sites of the killings.

Montreal . . . that meant he had to have a passport. We'd have to look for a passport for Bobby Green or one for Dr. Yamanaka, with his photo on it.

"If he's going to all those places, he must be using the credit card for plane flights," I said.

The agent-hacker kept clicking the mouse. "He pays for a lot of things in cash. Here's a holding code for the credit card, see? He's put the card down to reserve a room, but the amount wasn't charged to the card. He paid in cash. And here, at a travel agency in Chicago: He buys his plane tickets there. They've got his card number, but they've never charged it. He pays in cash."

Which means he has access to a bank account. Another lead, perhaps. But one that I didn't want to follow yet. I wanted to milk this damned card for all it was worth.

"Look," I said, leaning over the kid's shoulder and pointing at the screen, "this 'holding list,' or whatever you call it. It's long. Roll down, let me see where else he's used the card just to hold reservations."

"'Roll down?' Don't you mean 'scroll down?'"

I just looked at him. He scrolled down. Far enough for me to see some other reserved places, like a storage warehouse in some place called Van Nuys, California. But nothing in Los Angeles. I said this aloud.

The kid agent smirked. "I take it you're from way out of town." He was clicking away, making the list go up and down.

"What's that mean?"

"Van Nuys. It's in the Valley. It's part of Los Angeles. But most of us think it's the armpit of the city."

I had been leaning, breathing down his neck. Now I stood up straight, enough for my head to swim. "Print that, print that business name. Now."

This new information got us a helicopter ride.

It was two o'clock. Flying over the city, I could not believe the knot of traffic below us. That good-looking green Jaguar, sitting in the middle of all those other cars: how long would it sit there? Until the sun set?

I turned to the photo that Mr. Sanford in Knoxville, Tennessee had given the local police there. They had scanned it into a computer file and had sent it to FBI here. It was not a good photo: very grainy, and out of focus. It was of a woman, with brown skin and black hair and a kind smile. She wore a smart dress, professional. A large man, young, stood next to her, holding her in a huge grip of a hug. Short black hair, but thick. He was smiling. Lighter skin than hers, but just a little. He could have been a cross between white and Latino. But she was not Latino. She must have been the real Dr. Jamey Yamanaka.

It was difficult to stare at him. For this was the face of the man who stood over my sister. But something else bothered me. His face drifted in a steam of thought, vapors from a long time ago. As if I had known him. Had I met him before, had my sister known him well enough to introduce him to me in a quick passing? It could be; those months around her death had blurred themselves in a chalky plaque of memory.

The chopper followed the clogged freeway, past a large, off-white construction that jutted out of the mountain, what I would later learn was the Getty Museum. We flew by the skyline of Beverly Hills, then over Mulholland Mountain. The more it banked, the faster we flew over the low forests. Then, on the other side, another city greeted us, an urban spread they called the San Fernando Valley. To me, it was just more of Los Angeles, slightly interrupted by Mulholland.

Pierce sat next to me, but he was not dressed for the occasion. He had handed me a bullet proof vest, one that matched the vests of the two other agents who sat in the chairs behind us. He didn't have to explain: he was on this possible raid, but he couldn't enter it with us. The helicopter would touch down near the warehouse, where another vehicle would be waiting for us. Pierce would get in the vehicle and, with the earmikes that he gave me and the two agents, would keep in touch with our movements.

They had radioed ahead to the local LAPD, who had gone to the warehouse, had found the landlord's office, and had passed the credit card number to the secretary. She had verified it: a hit. One Dr. Jamey Lei Yamanaka. The good doctor, who she had seen only once, rented a large, eight hundred square foot cubicle. Yes, she had a master key, which she handed over to the police, who then handed it over to Pierce.

And Pierce handed it to me.

The vests were necessary. Though I had never been on a checkout of a warehouse, I had heard from other cops how dangerous they could be. In larger cities, and even in smaller ones like Nashville, individuals, mostly men, lived inside the storage rooms. Some were poor folks who just found it cheaper to rent a cinderblock-walled cubicle by the month. Others, however, were suspected local terrorists, questionable people who had an interesting supply in their little rooms, such as semi-automatics and dynamite sticks, ready to defend an array of causes: drug trafficking, right-wing terrorist groups ready to take over the country, left-wing vegetarians ready to storm a nearby chicken slaughterhouse, Muslim fundamentalists. A couple of cops had been wounded in a checkout gone bad: they hadn't expected to run into a human being behind the door, some sweating, gaunt fellow with a hollow look to him who had spent too many days closed up in the windowless storage unit.

We had prepared for that. But we also had to be prepared for our particular vagrant: Minos had planned too many murders too well not to be prepared for a sudden, unexpected knock at the warehouse door.

It was hot here, a hell of a lot hotter than back at the FBI offices, where we had boarded the chopper. There, a cool wind blew over us, and it smelled like the sea. Here, the air didn't move, and though it was dry, I started to sweat before we got inside the warehouse. Maybe the heat, or maybe it was simply waiting for the cop to click open the lock. He had to be quiet. We had to push ourselves against the walls to either side of the corrugated tin door. This was an FBI move, something I wasn't accustomed to. I was used to yelling out my position, the name of my office. They didn't worry about that. They worried only about surprising whoever was inside.

Which was nobody. The cop undid the lock, grabbed the handle, flung the door upward and open before jumping to one side to let us enter. I was the first in, my gun raised before me in both hands. "Freeze!" said one of the other agents, to no one.

But there was plenty inside, plenty to tell me who had been here.

"Report," Pierce said through the earpiece. The other agents checked quickly, thoroughly, for any

booby traps, bombs. Nothing. But we all reacted to the
smell. It was a mix of putrid things. But nothing to
threaten us. Just those six strange stains on the cement
floor, the one cot at the other end, the work table next
to the cot, with its lamp, still on. A large black book
stood open under the lamp. It was turned to two full
pages of text, no pictures. But I knew there were pictures, especially when I lifted the front end of the book
to read it's title, *On the Fabric of the Human Body*. I carefully placed the book back to the pages of text, where
he had taken a pencil and had underlined important
phrases,

> . . . you must proceed, using a small knife or a
> thin razor, to detach the beginning of the
> obliquely descending muscle of the abdomen
> from the right (sixth) rib by making a light cut
> along the remaining ribs toward the spinal col-
> umn and along the top of the ilium to the mid-
> dle of the pubic bone. Make this cut so lightly
> that the present muscle is the only thing sev-
> ered . . . I think it is impossible to remove the
> tendon whole and completely undamaged and
> uncut all the way to the white line that appears
> in the middle of the abdomen because there is
> no flesh under it, however sharp a razor you
> use (and you will achieve nothing with a blunt
> one).

He hadn't left this for us. This was his study hall.
The six stains, almost in a row upon the cement
floor, looked moist. I reached down; they were. The
entire floor was wet, though the porous cement had
started to absorb the moisture. Mopped. Just mopped.
But not enough. Judging from the confusing stench in

the room, those were the stains of human waste, ones he had tried to clean with a lemony disinfectant. Judging from the cleanliness of the cot, that was where he slept.

Pieces of clear tape still clung to the wall. One held a corner of torn black paper, with a drawing of something brown right at the rip. The agent began to lift it. The other side was also black, but with the top of a white letter. S or C.

"I'm coming in," said Pierce. He clicked off the mike.

"I need some gloves," I said to the other agents. The woman had a kit with her. She pulled out a pair of off-white surgicals. I pulled them on, then turned to the book.

He had taken copious notes. He wrote reminders to himself, about what type of razors to buy, and more, which medications would be best for this exercise. "Check Phenergan," said one note, in pencil, and under it, "Vioxx, COX-2 inhibitor (pain)."

This was not looking good.

I flipped through the pages until I found the original prints of the dissections. It was difficult to turn the pages with gloves on, and with the blood that pumped hard and made my hand shudder. But there they were, all in a row, one page after another, starting on page 170. The man with the missing skin, standing before those lovely woodlands, with a small European village behind him. And under his feet, written with a pencil, *Carol*.

The second man, looking more in pain, as the muscles, each and every one, showed so clearly. And under it, pencilled in, *Fred*.

The third, flayed, with ribs and sternum sticking out, with muscles dripping from his fingers. *Ethan*.

Ethan Coleridge, the college student. I had no doubt.

The fourth, with shoulder bones popping, the lips, gone. *Gerald.*

Raul will have his jaws broken neatly down the middle, spread out like an insect. He will have no eyes. His calf muscles will flap loose from his knees.

Karen will be gutted completely.

Or they have been, already.

Pierce stood beside me. He said nothing. He had seen the last three drawings while I flipped the pages.

"Agent Pierce," said the woman detective. Her voice was hard, clear. I had yet to learn her name. Pierce and I turned. When I did, the thought that things couldn't get much worse became a horrible joke.

She pointed up, to the garage door that was now above us, up against the ceiling.

He had stuffed and taped thick pillows to the garage door, a way of sound-proofing the room, so that the moans or yelps his victims made were well-muffled. That was bad enough, of course; but the map taped to the metal frame of the door, covering a large portion of the pillows, became too clear.

"Kimberly, pull down the door, shut it," said Pierce. The agent did, with us inside. Then she reached over and turned on a switch that lit the lone bulb above us.

It was a Rand McNally map of the United States: five feet wide, four feet high. Though tattered on the edges, the map itself was intact, with the details of mountains and rivers and major roads across it. The two agents with us did not understand the stick drawings that covered most of the individual states, nor the cryptic words written around the drawings. But I understood them, which at first should have bothered me, that I could figure out, so quickly, what Minos had in mind, how well-planned all this was.

He had drawn constellations all over the map. The cities and towns stood for the stars. The first collection I saw was the Big Dipper, stretching across the country: Bristol, Atlanta, Memphis, St. Louis, Kansas City, Denver, Los Angeles. Just like I had accidentally done in the hotel room in Denver, he had drawn, with a ruler and a thick, red marker, a clear, neat depiction of the Big Dipper. But he didn't call it that: in the bowl of the dipper, in thick black letters, he had scrawled, *Ursa Major*.

Doc had taught me how to find the North Star: follow the outer edge of the Dipper's bowl, make a straight line, and you'll hit it. Here, the North Star was Montreal. And that's where the constellation Ursa Minor began, covering several states that surrounded the Great Lakes: Montreal, Sault Ste. Marie, Wausau, Duluth, Sioux Falls, Des Moines.

I had heard of Draco, but did not know what it looked like. Now I did. This Draco's body began in the Midwest and ended in the Rockies: Cincinnati, Indianapolis, Springfield, Topeka, Lincoln, Council Bluffs, Winona, Green Bay, Thunder Bay, Hibbing, then a long stretch of the dragon's neck to Cheyenne, Pueblo, Escalante, Salt Lake City. There it was: the dragon's head, neck, body.

Draco's head rested atop Hercules' body, which took up the entire western states with San Francisco, El Paso, Idaho Falls, Rawlins, Sundance, Chappell, Salina, Amarillo. Then Hercules' legs and arms: Springfield, Missouri; Jonesboro; Little Rock; Williston and Bismarck in North Dakota; Three Forks, Great Falls, Chester, all in Montana; before going to Hercules' hand, Lethbridge, in Canada.

The Corona Borealis covered the east coast: Buffalo, Harrisburg, Washington, DC, Richmond, Raleigh, Charlotte, then ended in my home, Nashville.

Cancer covered the south: Dallas, Montgomery, Columbia, Miami.

Forty, no . . . over fifty cities.

He's far from over. He's just getting started.

You'll see the stars.

It's a joke. One big fucking joke for him.

My anger told me that. But the more I looked at this map, at this seemingly perfect set of constellations, I knew better. This was no joke for Minos. This was a mission. It made perfect sense to him. A destiny. Beyond purpose. It was, to him, the way things are. How they would be.

But he also taunted us: he left us messages. He wanted to be recognized.

Then the thoughts rushed at me, as if Minos himself were in the room and he rushed me, explaining it in one expulsion of clarity. I couldn't get it all at once, couldn't be in his head that long, though I had to. We had to.

"Start collecting this," said Pierce to his agents. They got to work. Kimberly opened the evidence kit again, worked on fingerprinting the tape on the wall, making sure to keep the torn black paper underneath it intact. Kimberly's partner worked on the book, the table, the lamp.

The torn paper and this map, the book left on the desk, opened to text, not to drawings. He had not left this for us. These were signs of rushing. He had moved out of here quickly.

"He's coming back here," I said.

Pierce looked at me. "Yep. He forgot his road map."

I stared out of the chopper's thick glass but saw little of the city: Los Angeles was a world, and I was in my own.

Why come back? Why return to the storage warehouse?

Map left on the garage door. Tape left on the wall, with a piece of torn paper underneath. Stains left on the floor, half-scrubbed with lemony disinfectant, but still, the smell of feces, of urine, in the air.

That lemon smell was strong. Still in the air, still fresh, like when Mamá just finishes dusting the living room. Still lingers.

The floor, it was still moist.

Shit.

He was in a rush. He had to leave quickly. Had to leave, because keeping six people in a storage warehouse, even if they're drugged, is too much. He had to take care of them, keep them fed somehow, watered, quiet.

The woods. Dark woods, mournful woods.

I pulled out my Dante. I read quickly, from the thirteenth canto.

We moved forward into woods unmarked
By any path. The leaves not green, earth-hued;

The boughs not smooth, knotted and crooked-forked;
No fruit, but poisoned thorns. Of the wild beasts
Near Cecina and Corneto, that hate fields worked

By men with plough and harrow, none infests
Thickets that are as rough or dense as this.

"If he's using that map as a literal path of killing," I said to Pierce, "he's also using this poem as a map." I paused, then looked at him. "He needs some woods. Dark woods." Then I read the passage aloud to them all, having to shout it over the chopper's propeller whip.

"Rough thickets," repeated Kimberly, "that could be almost anywhere. Santa Monica Mountains, San Gabriel area. My boyfriend and I hike all those places. They're full of desert shrubs, thick, brambly undergrowth."

"How about trees?"

"Yeah, they got trees." She looked at me as if I were a little slow.

I explained to her, loudly, fighting the *whup* of the chopper blades, "He wants to dissect these people and pin them to the trees. Kind of like this." I found the Doré engraving and split the book open for her. She stared at it.

"Got it," said Kimberly.

• • •

"He must be in a national park," said Pierce. He had a report in his hand, showed it to me. "That paper torn on the wall, under the tape? It matches the paper on a U.S. National Park map, which is set in a black background."

"How many national parks in the southern California area?" I asked.

"The two major ones are the San Gabriels and the Santa Monica Mountains. Agent Fisher has put agents out to each area, making contact with the local rangers."

That made sense with the torn "S" in the black paper.

He handed me other news. "This is a list of the people who, as of this moment, are officially missing in the area. Fifty-eight names now. Lots of Freds, I think there are, let's see . . . four. Three of those are kids, maybe runaways. But here are the names we're interested in."

I looked at the stats.

Four people named Fred. Three named Carol, though with different spellings. One named Ethan. That was our Ethan. Six Jerry's, or Geralds. One Raul. Two Karens.

Most of them sounded white, though that could have been a large presumption. But one was definitely Latino, Raul. I was sure of this, until Pierce corrected me.

"One of the Karens is a little girl who's probably wandered off in her neighborhood somewhere in Glendale. The other is Karen Allende. Remember that name? Rigoberta Allende is making a stink right now. She just had an interview with KABC-7."

My jaw may have dropped.

She lived on Carmelina Avenue, north of Sunset and just four blocks from where Marilyn Monroe died. A

maid let us in. Rigoberta Allende greeted us in the
foyer, which looked as large as my house. A spiral stair-
case snaked to my right. Paintings hung everywhere.
Was that an original Rivera?

We shook hands. I greeted her in Spanish, which
she acknowledged but did not smile about. This was no
time, for her, for cultural niceties. "What do you know
about my daughter's disappearance?" she asked.

"We're following some leads right now," said
Pierce.

"Yes, and what are those leads?"

"We need to ask you some questions, Ms. Allende.
When did you last see her?"

"Two nights ago. The following morning I reported her missing. I have heard little from the police.
You are, what did you say, FBI? Good. I want the best."

"May we see Karen's room?" I asked.

She led us upstairs. Something in me settled. Yes,
this was *the* Rigoberta Allende. Yes, she was an earthly
goddess in our home, as well as in every house of every
cousin I had anywhere in the States and back in the old
country. And yes, I was here, in her house, walking behind her up her stairs and thinking about how I'd relate
this to my mother.

But I settled down. She was a mother who had a
daughter who was missing. I had a son who I had almost recently lost. These were similar playing fields.

The room was huge, bigger than my den at home.
Some regular teenage stuff: posters of pop singers on
the wall, photos of her and her friends on a corkboard,
books toppled against each other in a shelf. A computer
with speakers and a laser printer and a CD burner and
at least three other digital machines that I did not recognize. No cell phone; she must have had that with her.
But there was a phone. I asked Ms. Allende if this was

the same number as the house phone. "No. Karen had her own line." I asked if they had Caller ID. "Of course. Just dial *69."

I did. A number came up on the digital readout above the touchtone buttons. It looked familiar, of course. And then Mikey Farrell answered, so sweetly, "Reachout Services, may I help you?"

What energy I had, I didn't want to waste on him. I hung up and turned to Pierce. He saw my look, and moved out with me to the hallway. Ms. Allende was still inside, looking at her daughter's empty room.

"He called her," I whispered.

"Yeah?"

"Yeah, unless suicide hotlines are calling around for business. Mikey Farrell just answered. Minos, or dear Bobby Green must have called her from there. So she had to have called him beforehand."

"And for him to call, she had to have entrusted him with her number. He knew her."

"Maybe got to know her, after the initial phone call."

Ms. Allende was at our side. She did not appreciate our whispering. She said, curtly, "Have you followed up on the man at the Starbucks?"

We didn't know anything about this. Pierce said, "I wanted to ask you, Ms. Allende, to give us more details on that."

"It is just as I told the officers. Her friends, Melinda and Jean, they had had coffee with her, but then she sat down with the man. They did not know him. They thought he was a new boyfriend that Karen was seeing."

"And what did he look like?"

"Tall, a large man. Lighter skin, with black hair, thick black hair is what they said."

"Had they seen Karen with this man before?" I asked.

"No. They ran into each other at the coffee shop. She left her friends. They saw her at school next day. But then she was gone. He is the one, isn't he? What has he done with my girl?"

"Ms. Allende, it's best to stay put until you hear from us again," said Pierce.

We moved to the door, ready to leave, when Rigoberta Allende grabbed my elbow and made me turn to her. *"Hallala, joven. Hallala,"* she said. *Find her, girl. Find her.* I couldn't tell how she said it, with anger, or just plain fear.

Something was wrong.

Something was wrong with me. Something had gotten inside, chewing under the root of my brain. It made the nerves connected to my lungs pop, crackle. My breathing rattled. At first I thought it was the helicopter ride. I wasn't used to such transportation, didn't even really like planes, preferred to prepare for long flights with a drink or two early on. A helicopter was worse: a thinner wall between you and the world, just some glass, slight layers of metal, the whopping sound of those very large propellers above us.

It didn't bother Pierce. He looked out over the Malibu beach, down at expensive adobe houses. The sun was still high enough to make you believe nighttime was a long way off. Which was a mistake. It was not long at all.

That was part of the problem.

He'll do it at night, I thought. *He'll kill them at night. Numerous reasons for this: no one will see him, no one will be out there. He can sneak in somehow, get past the rangers. Do it at night, in the dark woods. Symbolism. Practical. Night is in his favor.*

That, and the lemony odor of the warehouse storage room.

He had left there, this morning. Early. Before anyone came to the storage offices. He had spent the night there, had gotten up before dawn. By the time the secretary came in, he was gone. He had cleaned up just a little, so that the stench would not attract attention. But he was in a hurry.

He left this morning. He must be driving a large vehicle to carry six people in. Six drugged, or tied, individuals. A vehicle that you couldn't see into. Not a mini-van, too many windows. A large van, completely walled in, one used for company purposes. A business van? A moving truck?

The helicopter touched down in a park called Leo Carrillo. It was Friday. Some campers came in, parents with children in the back seat, with sleeping bags piled up behind them, along with ice boxes and blow-up rings for the beach. A boy pointed and shouted to his mother about the chopper.

We got out. I turned to Pierce as we walked away from the chopper. "He's going to do it at night," I said.

"Yeah? And?"

"So this doesn't make sense. We're not that far away from the storage warehouse, are we?"

"About twenty, thirty miles. Maybe forty-five minutes in light traffic over the mountains."

I looked into the woodlands. They didn't look right. Nothing here looked right. "I don't think this is it."

"Kimberly said some of the thicker areas of woods are right here, behind Leo Carrillo. We've got some boys hiking through now. And they've driven Jeeps up the fire roads." He looked at me. "Come on, Romilia. We've got to check it out."

"Just think about it a minute." I stopped, tried to shake out whatever it was that bit at me. "He's going to do it at night. If he did it here, he should have left the storage facility late yesterday, to do it last night."

"Maybe that's just what he did. Maybe, it's over with, and the bodies are in there," he gestured to the mountains. "But we've still got to look. He may be in the area."

"No. The smell. It was too fresh, sir. The floor, it was still wet. He had just mopped up, right before we got there." I looked out toward the beach. "I think he's driving."

"What?"

"He needs this as a drive day. He's taking them away from here." I looked back up at the mountains. "I mean, look at that. I don't see much in the line of trees. This is desert. He needs a forest."

"So what's your point, Detective?"

"He's not here."

Pierce turned, walked to me. He was frustrated, impatient. I had seen this in other men. They're on a trail, or have made a decision, and it just goes against their genitals to turn and look another way. But Pierce tried. "Then where?"

"How many national parks in California?"

He laughed. "Too many."

"How many with trees? All this is desert, arid. Aren't there those big old trees, what do they call them, Red Trees?"

"Redwoods. Sequoias."

"Yeah. Aren't they in California?"

"Yes, Romilia. They are."

He appeased me. He called the office, told them to put the word out to every single national park in the state, paying special attention to the parks that had the 'red trees.' The agent on the other end said, "Repeat sir?" to which Pierce said, "The Redwood Forests. Up around San Francisco, Yosemite." He clicked off his radio, held his hands up to me, as if making sure he had done the right thing.

"Thanks," I said.

Still, something was wrong. What the hell was it? The helicopter geared down. I walked back to it to retrieve my pack, to, once again, thumb through *The Inferno*, or read the notes on my pad or stare at Tekún's gift of files. There was the list of credit cards and their numbers. I considered throwing that out. But I wouldn't throw any of this out until it was all over with. And when would that be? When would this all end? I could carry all this around for another year, maybe two. I could carry it through a box of empty whiskey bottles, clanking against each other in the recycle bin. I could carry it with me, right next to Sergio as I drove him to a pee-wee soccer match. While he practiced with the other kids, I could flip through all this shit once again and look up and think about my sister and curse, curse, God damn you. You, in this photo, standing next to your beloved aunt, perhaps the only person in your life you could trust, an aunt who, before she passed on, made sure you would never have to worry about money again. You could live off the riches that your sadistic father, whatever he did to you, had accumulated. You could roam the world. I suppose that photo should have pulled out some sympathy in me, the way he smiled, the way she leaned into his large arms and her head tipped to his shoulder. But I had no room for sympathy, for I knew that he had made choices. Blame the sadistic father and the suicidal sister, blame the aunt for dying on him, abandoning him. Fuck him. I'll get him.

I'll get him.

The photo shivered between my fingers. I gripped it with both hands. It still flapped. My breathing, again, still, it was off. I was off. Something rushed through me, and meant to make its appearance in tears, right here, as I leaned on the helicopter portal. I would have cried, had not Pierce yelled out at the pilot, "Gear it up. Let's get out of here." Pierce tried to run, which made his limp more apparent.

"What?" I said. I wiped tears that had yet to come.

"Sequoia National Forest. North of here. They've got a dead ranger. And a stolen park vehicle."

It took the helicopter over an hour to reach the Sequoia Forests. Too much time. The sun was setting.

Too much time. But only an hour away. He was an hour away.

"The ranger's name was Anniston," said Pierce. "He was found about two o'clock this afternoon, just before our APB got to them. He hadn't reported in at lunchtime, which wasn't like him. They started walking the area he manned. Found him with a knife wound under the sternum. Sliced his heart in two. His vehicle was gone. They figured the perp had stolen the vehicle and had left the park without them seeing him. They didn't think to go deeper into the woods."

From their point of view, that made sense: why kill a ranger and then go into the area that the rangers know best? A killer would flee the scene, the park, get out of state.

"He's slipping," I said. "He's making mistakes. As far as we know, the ranger is the first killing he's done outside of his rituals."

"A ranger who got caught in his slip ups. Wrong place at the wrong time." Pierce looked down at the chopper's floor. There was regret in his voice.

Regret and, I would later learn, a certain fear. Pierce hesitated to get out of the chopper once we landed in a clearing next to the rangers' office cabin. Another larger helicopter landed nearby, filled with a team of agents, all geared up and ready to move into the woods. The rangers had already cleared the park of tourists. I still had to get a vest on, wire up, check my pistol once again, looking at a cartridge I already knew was full. I turned to Pierce. He stepped out of the helicopter and stared at the woods just behind the cabin.

"What's the matter?" I asked.

"I've got a thing about forests," he said. Then he looked at me, as if he hadn't meant for that to slip out. "Fall in, Detective. Get ready."

We boarded a large truckbed. I turned, looked through a set of trees. The sun winked at me, then went away.

Again, the doubt. And the fear. Sitting in a truck-load of FBI agents, one gun in my holster, my ear and mouth wired to Pierce. The agents looked out at the woods around us, just like I did; but they didn't see what I saw. They didn't see the Doré engravings, the references to the gnarl of forests, of people's souls reborn in the shape of wood, of trees that bleed. Bleeding trees. Trees, made out of the fabric of the human body. He meant to make beauty from his kills.

These agents saw none of that. They saw Sequoias, giant evergreens that towered over the truck, turning shadowy as night took the forest. They had on helmets

geared with high-beam flashlights that were now off. I
didn't have one; they hadn't planned on me coming. But
they didn't look at me. Each man wore what could pass
as civilian clothes, except they all had on the same black
T-shirt, the same make of running shoes. This was not
army. These were agents, ready to find an enemy of one.

I would have to stay behind them a few steps. This
was their specialty. Now, Dante was of no use to us. The
only thing Dante did was play with the images that
danced in front of me, of these trees, some of them as
large at the base as the length of the truck, others smaller,
but big enough to spread a man out on, fillet him.

The truck's light beams cut in front of us, threw
shadows through the woods, made things move.

The driver parked the truck where the ranger had
been found. He got out, vested and helmeted like the
rest. Another agent, from the passenger seat, gave orders, told them to form three V positions to sweep
north, west, and east. The men fell in line and walked.

Then he turned to me and said, "All right, Detective. You need to stay here."

"But Agent Pierce, he wanted me to . . ."

"I understand. You're here. But you're not trained
in our maneuvers." I could tell that he had received an
order from Pierce, one that he didn't like. He had
brought me here; but he didn't plan on following the
order completely.

I made to argue. But he set me straight. I shut up.
The men turned, got in their positions, and walked
into the woods.

No lights. They used the crescent moon for guid-
ance. After twenty minutes of standing in night, I could
too. I could see the trees, some of them glowing under
moonlight. Still, there were shadows everywhere. I

kept my eyes on the men in front of me, until their shadows blended into those of the trees.

I was alone at the truck.

Did I mess up, theorizing as I did in that park next to the beach in Malibu? But we had a dead ranger here, someone I had not known, in a park a good five or six hour drive away from Los Angeles, where there were woods, dark woods, these woods. Six hours of driving, during which he kept them well-medicated, lying in the back of a van . . .

Where was the van?

Why did he kill the ranger?

The ranger may have stopped him. Right here. Saw him driving up into this area, over a dirt road that was not for tourists, but rather was an access road for the rangers and their trucks, which were built tough enough to take these roads. A van would bottom out on a road like this.

Did he dump the van somewhere? Did he transfer the six people from the van to the ranger's vehicle, lose the van in the woods somewhere, and drive on?

That sounded way too cumbersome.

A thought verified by one of the agents, who radioed in with a whisper, "This is East Wing. We've found the ranger's truck."

"Roger," said the agent in charge of the maneuver who had ordered me to stay here. "We're doubling back behind you."

The other two wings of Vs would now move from the north and the west, to the east.

I followed moonlight over the road. Sometimes I looked back, toward the east, where the agents wandered. None of it made sense. Especially when I heard the noise toward the west, on the other side of that hill, where the old road lay.

Deer, perhaps. Or a bear. My luck. But no: those animals do not make the sound of a rope whipping through air.

I whispered into my mike, "There's movement, over here."

Pierce: "What movement?"

The agent in charge: "Detective, stay in the truck."

"What?" said Pierce. "Agent Bane, what is Detective Chacón's position?"

I let them fight that out. I found a flashlight from the truck's cabin, unholstered my parabellum and walked up the hill.

Again the sound of a rope whipping through air, then slapping against something hard, like a tree trunk.

I ran up the hill.

The road turned to the right, climbed over a saddle of earth made from two large hills coming together. But the sound didn't come from there. I stood at the curve and tried to place in memory a sense of location: the whipping sound had come from there, below the curve, in a valley of straighter, darker trees. I had yet to turn on the flashlight; if I did, I would become a beacon, easily seen. I walked carefully, sometimes stumbling on a rock, twisting my hips to right myself. My arms straight ahead of me, clutching the gun. I turned to the left, the right, pointing, waiting for movement.

Movement came. There. Between those shadows of trees. My eyes watered from straining. The shadow turned, looked at me, turned again and walked toward a hallway of Sequoias. A man, obviously, one arm longer than the other.

Not longer. Holding something long.

The ranger had died from a long blade sunk under the sternum, slicing his heart.

I held the gun in my right hand. My left hand

wrenched the flashlight from my back jeans' pocket, shook, found the switch, pushed it on. The light beam burst forward, cut through the woods like a laser, and burnt away my night vision.

"Freeze! Police!"

The forest swallowed my yelp.

For a moment, all I could see was the beam, which now danced upon the tops of branches. I aimed it to where the shadow had walked. He was gone. He had walked away into a hallway of trees. I turned the light every which way, but the woods were thick, and all I saw were tree trunks, huge boulders, the dark earth of a clean woodland. I ran forward until I was between the two trees where the shadow had first appeared, then disappeared. Nothing. Nothing.

Then the sound. Breath. A moan.

They were to my left, behind me. I had run by them, but had not seen them, as they were on the opposite sides of the trees. For that one second, shadows: tall Sequoias, but then there were those with dark bulks hanging from them. Flashlight, flashing it back and forth across them all, all six of them, hanging from the trees.

Hanging from their wrists.

Strapped, naked, against the large, flat trunks of redwood. Their heads hung to one side or another, like numerous male and female Christs. My rude flashlight showed their bent knees, pale slack thighs, their toes, half dug in the dirt.

I must have bellowed into the mike. They could not understand me the first time, couldn't hear my screams as I flashed the light from one body to the other, trying to make sense of what I saw. A woman's head swung to one side, then another, like a pendulum, or an animal with a broken neck. Lines over her breasts, running down her thick hips. Incision lines . . .

no. No blood. Lines made by a marker, positioning the place of incision. She was alive.

Alive, and intact.

Where was she, in the group? Was there a formality to their placement? Were they in line, following the sequence of Vesalius drawings? No. A man, the one who moaned, had blood sliding down his stretched armpit.

"Jesus Christ, Bane!"

The agents scrambled over the hill. Their flashlights lit up the area, and now I could see them: six people, all alive. Two of them bled. He had planned to dissect them while they were alive, while they could see him. They moved as if drugged; the medication, whatever it was, kept them in a stupor, but soft moans still fell from their mouths.

"Oh God," said Bane, looking at them. "Get them down!" he yelped at another agent.

"Through there," I said, pointing to the two larger trees that made an opening to another section of the forest.

"Stay here," he said. I obeyed. I stayed and tried to keep my breath from rattling. He murmured location, logistics, and orders into the mike. Five agents followed him through the trees.

The thick woods before us were silent. The agents behind me talked to one another, giving quick orders about slicing the ropes, loosening the slip knots from the victims' wrists and ankles, easy, watch it, she'll fall forward. He's tipping, get him. Carefully they caught the bodies, like good sentinels taking care of the crucified.

Then the gunshots came, from beyond the opening of trees.

There were three. With each one, my heart burst with a harder pulse. My lungs meant to collapse. On the third shot I whimpered. I saw my sister: I sat at our mother's kitchen table, doing homework as Catalina came by and gave me a noogie on the scalp and so I choked, here, in these woods.

And then, as the agents walked between those two trees, I ran forward. Their flashlights caught me. I raised my gun, pointed it at the body that they carried between them and I demanded, "Is he dead?"

"No," said Banes, and he looked at me. "Put that gun down, Detective."

"Why isn't he dead? *Why isn't he dead?*"

"Detective!"

Minos' head down, the thick top of black hair right before me, only twenty yards away. My arms were straight out in front of me, my pistol gripped tight and the hammer cocked back and my finger squeezing. His black hair was my mark; and I could hit that mark. Bane wouldn't even feel the wind from the bullet's passing and Minos would finally be dead.

Five, then six weapons cocked in a semi-circle behind me. Though I did not see them, I knew where those guns were pointed.

"Stand down, Detective Chacón."

I did not.

"Detective, we will shoot you if you do not lower your weapon and stand down immediately."

As if I could give a shit. As if it meant something to die, because right at that moment it didn't at all, not with the man who tortured my sister in my perfect sight, after all these years.

That's when Sergio came to mind. Like a shot.

The six agents escorted me out of the woods and delivered me to Pierce. The others took the victims away, wrapping them in blankets that the rangers provided. They were still drugged; the agents carried them out of the woods, had them placed on cots until medical helicopters arrived.

They took Minos, or Bobby Green, another way. He left in the second chopper, the one that had followed ours. He was covered in blankets. A Federal Agent, whose specialty was as a paramedic, worked on him. The bleeding stained the off-white blanket. Some agents moved him onto the helicopter; but other agents, the ones who had pointed their guns at me in the woods, watched me watching Minos being saved.

Assuredly Pierce knew what had gone down in the woods. He knew of his men needing to draw a bead on me. But he said nothing of it, since I finally did stand down, dropping my aim, slapping my nine millimeter against my thigh. He said nothing of that. All he said was, "It's over, Romilia." And this allowed me to cry.

Back in Los Angeles, I did not call my mother. It was late at night. Pierce planned to have me on a redeye back to Nashville before dawn.

"We can wrap it up here. I got a report from the UCLA Medical Center. He had sedated them all. They're weak from lack of eating, and partially dehydrated. Cuts and scrapes and rashes from the kidnapping and the holding in the warehouse. But they're going to make it. All of them."

I didn't say anything. Just shook my head.

"You did good work, Detective Chacón."

Again, just some head shaking. I said, "Your second in command, Agent Bane, may have a different angle on that."

"I'm sure he will. In the future, please don't point your weapon near any of my men."

I promised him I wouldn't.

"I'll be in touch," he said. We shook hands, parted.

In the taxi that took me to LAX, I wondered what he meant.

Somewhere over New Mexico I muttered, "Ah shit."

This, because I should have asked Pierce to put me on a redeye to Atlanta. That's where my family was. I could have rented a car from the airport, gone straight to my aunt's house, woken up my boy and hugged him until it hurt. I could have shown my mother, in the flesh, that I was in one piece. I could tell her that I had helped bring down the man who had murdered her daughter. We could have wept together.

Now I'd have to settle on calling her from

Nashville, then drive to Atlanta as soon as I got some coffee in me.

Delayed gratification. I never cared for it.

It was a full flight, even being a redeye. Or maybe because of being a redeye. Cheaper. Most everyone slept. Heading to the bathroom, I saw more folks covered in blankets, some up over their heads, as if trying to escape the very air of the plane. In first class, they had it made: one fellow got two blankets, and a seat that pulled out into a couch.

First class.

I didn't have first class, but I did have some dollars. The older stewardess brought me a couple bottles of whiskey. Then she made my night: "No charge, honey," she said.

It was still night when we landed in Nashville. The sun would be up in an hour or so.

Pierce was right. Nashville seemed small, after being in Los Angeles. Anything would seem small after that city.

Everything was quiet now, and I felt alone. One more long leg until I'd be with my family. The weariness of a lousy night of sleep made the loneliness even worse.

Tomorrow would be different. Tomorrow the FBI would make it known that they had caught the infamous serial killer the Whisperer, now known as Minos. Agent Chip Pierce would hold a press conference in Los Angeles. Would he mention me? Perhaps. Would it matter? Hardly likely. Not to me. Not now.

I had not been comfortable after my last case, when the media swarmed my house and whenever I walked across the Police Department parking lot. Unlike my older sister, I was not used to being in the spotlight.

Catalina would have sucked it all up, and would have made the world shine even more, for adoring her.

We all had adored her.

Would Pierce make it known to the public that Minos had planned to continue on a killing spree, no doubt for the rest of his life? He had several constellations waiting for him. He had it well-plotted. He had time and money and good health. He had the rest of *The Inferno* to walk through, with no lack of sins to interpret. He could have gone on for a long while. Not now.

There was some rest in that. Some.

It was a lovely morning. Saturday. Fewer cars on the road. Nashville slept in a little.

I opened the front door of the house, said *"Hola, ya estoy,"* to no one, tossed the keys on the side table next to the Aztec sun god. I placed my roll-on suitcase, which had been double-tagged due to me carrying a handgun, at the door.

It was habit to check the answering machine. I hit it, then went to the refrigerator. Milk. Juice. Something to fill my mouth with. The first message was Doc Callahan, made right after I left Nashville. The chirpy female computer voice said, *Monday, five-fifteen-P.M.* followed by, "Hello Romi. Just checking to see how you're doing. Call me when you return. McCabe says you're out of hot water. Glad to hear that. Just come home to us. Bye."

That was a little strange. Of course I'd come home.

Monday, eight-forty-three-P.M., "Hello Mrs. Chacón, my name's Jackie, could we interest you in coming back to AT&T? I'll call back at a time that's convenient. Bye!"

Erase.

Wednesday, ten-twelve-A.M., "Hello Romilia, Lieu-

tenant McCabe here. I don't know if you're checking
your messages while you're away, but give me a call
when you can, okay?"

That sounded more personal than professional. A
plea?

A couple more messages from the local newspaper
and a next door neighbor. Two for my mother, from
the old country.

Saturday, five-twelve-A.M.

Jeez. Half an hour ago.

"Romilia. Chip Pierce. Listen, there's something
wrong. Call me immediately, right when you get in.
I . . . just call me."

Oh shit. What? I dug through my backpack, found
his cell phone number, called it. "Agent Pierce, it's me,
Romilia. What?"

He was talking with someone else. There was a lot
of noise behind him, of people giving quick orders
about medications, room numbers, nurses' stations. He
was at the hospital. "A fuck-up, Romilia. I almost didn't
call, now that you're home, but it's better that you
know this."

"What?"

"He's out. He got away."

"*What?*" The breath, again it became separate
from me, as if my lungs were not my own. "What the
hell? He was shot, three times! How in the world . . ."

"That wasn't Bobby Green."

"What?"

"Raul Espinoza. He's the guy we shot. The guy
they pulled out of the woods."

Raul Espinoza. The fifth missing person. "What
are you talking about?"

He hesitated. Was this embarrassment, or his own

way of showing fear? "Bobby Green was tied to one of the trees."

I did not breathe.

"We're trying to piece it together now. He must have known we were right behind him. He was about to cut them all up, but heard us coming. He couldn't get away by running. So he switched places with Raul."

Switched places with one of his victims. The only one with black hair. A man. It was night. Lights flashing. Hard to distinguish. Perfect, for a magician's trick, a killer's escape.

My mind ran back to the scene, created the images. The whipping rope I had heard: that was not Minos tying up one of the victims. He was whipping it around the tree for his own wrist, catching the slip knot on the other side of the trunk, tying himself.

Raul Espinoza, dazed and medicated. Before tying himself, Minos had put the knife in Raul's hand and sent him on his way, maybe told him he was free, he could escape, take this knife, protect yourself, they're coming to kill you, get out of here.

Then the ropes, tying himself to the tree, pretending to be drugged. Cutting his arm with the knife before giving it to Raul. Just enough blood to freak us out, make us pause.

Minos standing there, stretched, as I walked by him, as I watched them pull the wounded Raul from the forest, as I aimed a gun at the top of Raul Espinoza's skull, ready to shatter, perfectly, his parietal bone.

Pierce filled in the rest for me. "All of them were checked into UCLA's hospital. They were going to clean out their systems, get them on glucose drips. One of the nurses came in, saw him standing next to his own bed. He even smiled at her. She told him to get back in the bed, he had to rest. But he swore he was feeling fine, and he wanted to check out. She said she had to pass that by her superior first. When she went to look for the doctor, the patient was gone."

"When? When did you figure out he wasn't Raul?"

"Raul's wife came to the hospital. They had called her, told her he was safe. She went to the empty bed. He was gone. They couldn't explain it to her, except to say he left on his own. She was hysterical. She wanted to see the kidnapper. She insisted, started yelling. So they let her look through a window. Then she told them all, that was her husband."

Shit.

Shit.

"Romilia?"

"Yeah?"

"Romilia, you know he may come after you. He saw what you did, aiming your gun at Espinoza. He knows who you are, your sister, he knows you now."

"Yeah. Yeah I know that."

"Don't worry, we'll put you under watch. Witness protection, the best. We'll keep you hidden until we track that bastard down."

Keep me hidden. Protect me, my mother, my boy. For how long? Another six god damn years? But all I said was, "Yeah, good. Thanks." And I hung up.

I had time. I was awake. I'd drive to Atlanta, pick them up, we'd stay somewhere else. Where, I wasn't sure. The man knew the country too well. He had stars all over the nation, places that he had checked out well in advance, from Montreal to San Francisco, all the way over to Miami. That's what he'd been doing all those years, between killing my sister and finally reemerging to kill the three businessmen in Memphis:

he had been planning. Getting to know each city, using his entire estate, his funds, to hunt.

I knew few places, besides Atlanta and Nashville. Maybe we'd move back to El Salvador.

I went for the phone to call my mother, but hesitated, trying to calm my voice, wanting to tell her not to worry, everything was fine, we just needed to make some huge changes in our lives. That hesitation was enough to allow the phone to ring. I picked it up. "Hello?"

"*Mi amor.*"

I paused.

"Who . . . ?" But I knew.

"Well now. You don't sound like a person who's traveled all night." He laughed good-heartedly.

I was confused, but cleared up real quick. "Tekún." I was actually happy to hear that voice. Though that mellifluous tone added to my tremor. "Where are you?"

"I'm just around to make sure that you got home okay. Friends on the west coast told me you were heading back. It's good to see you made it. I take it you bagged your bad guy?"

God no, no I hadn't. I hadn't bagged anything, but I said, "I'm all right. Yeah. I'll be fine."

His voice turned lower, more honest. "What's the matter?"

"Nothing, I . . ." I tried to calm down. Shit. What was it with this breathing of mine? Couldn't catch my breath, couldn't take a deep breath. I reached into my backpack, the one filled with the Minos files, the Dante books. "It's just been, a rough investigation, you know?" I stumbled across Tekún's files, tossed the books to one side. The photo fell out.

The photo of Bobby Green with his aunt.

Perhaps it's panic that can clear away the steam of

memories. Memories that hover around your sister's murder like a fog that means to protect you, until the very fog itself, at the wrong time, will help bring you down.

First year in the academy. Shopping somewhere in Atlanta, in Krogers. Someone took my cart. His had Spam and soy milk in it. Spam, for God's sake.

Coffee, with him, sitting with him, telling him I'd kill him whenever I found him.

He's kept up with me. All these years.

"Romi?"

Tekún's voice, bringing me back, or trying to.

"I want to tell you, I've been thinking a great deal about our last encounter . . ."

He hesitated for too long. "Listen Tekún, if you want to apologize, I'm not really ready to take that on right now. I don't get into people wanting to cut my throat."

"And as I told you I'm not into people turning me in . . ."

Shit. Like a lover's quarrel. "Look, Tekún just say what you want to say and get out of my life."

He said nothing.

Great, I thought, now he's pissed again.

"Hello?" I said. "Are you there?"

"Romi. Get out of the house."

"What?"

"You're having a visitor. Second floor. Sergio's window."

I heard, through the phone, a car door slam. Tekún's car door. He was nearby.

A visitor.

Someone was trying to open the back door, at the porch. In the phone Tekún cursed. Then he hung up.

He said the upstairs window. But I heard the back door.

The back door was Tekún.

Upstairs. How?

Me, downstairs. In the middle of the kitchen. That door to the back of the kitchen, double-bolted. My keys, on the small oak table near the front door.

I ran toward the keys. That's when he punched me between my shoulder blades. My head hit the wall. The small table rattled. The Aztec god fell and shattered.

The pain meant to run off my fear. But the two fought in me, especially when Minos started singing.

Meet me in St. Louis, Louis
  Meet me at the fair.

Don't tell me the lights are shining
  Any place but there.

Then his voice, right in my ear, though I could not see him, "You didn't."

He flipped me onto my stomach and locked my wrists together with his one hand while the other wrapped a rope around them.

He kept talking, about me meeting him in St. Louis, why hadn't I shown up? At the gates, the gates, I waited for you, girl. The Gates of Dis. You didn't catch up with me. I thought you were right behind me.

A window shattered. I turned, could see Tekún's face in the space of broken glass. He was looking in, right at me, then at Minos. He reached into the back of his tailored coat and threw something through the window. Minos aimed a small gun at Tekún, shot; did it hit? Minos wasn't sure either, so he followed Tekún to the window, then ran to the den to look for him.

Tekún's green-handled Harpy Knife slid across the wood floor toward my chest.

It stopped two feet away.

I rolled. I turned, found the blade, cut two fingers, found the handle, snatched it in a bloody grip, and worked on the rope. It split apart.

My gun, in the luggage, next to the door. The house keys, gone from the table. Either he had taken them or, when I had hit the floor, I had popped the table and had knocked them down behind the wall heater.

The luggage was locked with a small padlock.

Shit shit shit shit shit

Cursing, while turning to look for Tekún's knife. Finding it, then plunging the knife into the thick suitcase, tearing open a ragged door, ripping through a red bra and a pair of jeans, then reaching in with my uncut hand, the cartridge under and to the left of my jeans but where had I packed the gun? Behind me around the stairs the wood floor creaks with his weight and his hammer clicks back and I pull the parabellum out of the gut of the suitcase and snap the cartridge while whipping around. Blood droplets fling from my hand.

When he shoots I feel nothing. When I shoot, neither does he. Though his neck blows open.

I can feel the floor under my buttocks, the wall against my back. I lean my head against that wall, look up, at the wallpaper that Mamá and I have meant to strip since the day we moved in here.

Sirens wail toward me.

... we came forth, and once more saw the stars.

The Inferno, Canto XXXIV

EPILOGUE

According to an article jointly written by Doctor Laslow Menkin, Director of Studies on Medieval Literature at Illinois University in Champaign and Dr. Bryan Lemough, Professor of Psychiatry at Notre Dame University, Bobby Green probably meant to kill me in St. Louis at the "Gates of Dis" (the St. Louis Arch) for my sins of sullenness and wrath. After a thorough research of the Minos case, Drs. Laslow and Lemough surmised that Bobby Green, who had followed my career ever since the day he and I met in the Kroger's in Atlanta, saw in me not only a threat, but a clear case of vengeance that could only be defined as wrathful. They argued that, since the wrathful in Dante's Hell tear one another to pieces, he would have found some appropriate end for me, though neither professor wished to be responsible for assuming any details concerning my demise.

This would be printed in the *Journal of Dante Studies* just six months after I killed Bobby Green. But much had already been made of the case. Someone had gotten hold of a copy of the map that we had found in the storage warehouse in Van Nuys. It hit the World Wide Web. Psychiatrists, Forensic Psychologists, Medievalists, novelists, all had a field day with it. Some universities predicted a spike in the interest of Dante studies come the next fall semester.

Mikey Farrell, the Director of Reachout Suicide Prevention services in Los Angeles, lost all his funding, and was sued by the city of Los Angeles for negligence in business ethics. He tried to sue the FBI, and lost that as well. He left town one night, and hasn't been heard from since.

All six victims returned to their homes. Bobby Green had indirectly helped them through their own healing: Versed, or Midazolam Hydrochloride, like its date-rape cousin Rohypnol, knocks out memory. They all had amnesia. Sometimes I wondered, though, if this were worse: to have the world tell you of your experience, leaving you to make up the images. I decided not to dwell on that too much.

I heard from Raul's wife. She thanked me. She would never learn how I lowered a gun barrel right at his head.

The others I would not hear from. Except, of course, for Rigoberta Allende. Though we knew nothing of each other, I was her latest best friend, and she insisted I come and visit her and her daughter Karen again sometime soon.

• • •

The three people from the Landley Farm in Kansas City have never been found.

Special Agent Chip Pierce moved from the Nashville offices to become the second in command at the FBI offices in Los Angeles.

Tekún Umán disappeared again. I never figured out who his narc was within the interior circles of the FBI (the "good friend" he referred to, who lived on the west coast), or even if he has a narc inside the Bureau.

I have received thank-you letters from the mayors of thirty of the fifty-six towns that were marked on Minos' map. Bismarck, North Dakota, which was one foot of Hercules' body, has invited me to come to their town as their guest, receive a key to the city. I've not taken them up on that yet.

My mother and son did not return to Nashville right away. I had a lot of cleaning up to do. That's where I last saw Pierce. He flew in immediately after the shooting, and they verified the body of Minos as that of Bobby Green. I'd never call him Minos again. He was a man with a real name who made choices, and giving him a literary pseudonym only gave him the power he wished to have forever.

After they worked over my house, found where he had entered, found in his pocket the first class plane ticket stub from the same flight that I had taken home (had that been he underneath the two blankets on the pullout couch?), Pierce took me out for a cup of coffee. He asked if I was all right. He wondered if I wanted an escort, someone from the Bureau to stay with me awhile, make sure I settled in. I thanked him, but preferred not. I just wanted to get with Sergio and Mamá Celia. He offered to have me flown to Atlanta. That, I took him up on.

"Have you spoken with your boss yet?"

"McCabe? Just on the phone. He said he was coming over, but he hasn't yet." I looked out the window of the restaurant near my home. Agents still walked around it.

"They never found the knife," said Pierce.

"What?" I was smoking a cigarette.

"The knife. The one you used to cut open the suitcase. How'd you do that?"

"I, I had a knife."

"Yeah I know, but where'd it go? Had to be a hell of a knife, to cut through that cloth. And your fingers." He pointed to the two bandages on my hand.

I just shrugged. That shrug tossed a curtain of a lie over him, so he would never see my memory, of how, after I killed Bobby Green, Tekún Umán had put his hand through the broken window, undone the latch, and crawled into the house. How he had hovered over me, put his hand on my head, then my shoulder, and asked me if I was all right. How I cried, right then, belched with crying in front of him. Tekún had leaned over, carefully hugged my neck, my shoulders. *It's okay*, he had said, *He's dead. It's over*.

It was the most clear voice I had heard in a long time.

So when Tekún Umán tilted my chin up to him to check my face, to see if I had been hurt, I couldn't really tell you who had kissed whom.

He had stepped away from me as the sirens grew louder. I was about to raise my gun to him, some crazy instinct, I suppose. But I didn't. He smiled.

He was gone, and I watched him go. And so now,

in front of Pierce, I shrugged and feigned ignorance. Amnesia. Pure stupidity.

When I reported to McCabe, he was quiet. Almost like a kid on the playground who hasn't been asked to join the game.

"So. Has Pierce called you back?" he said.

"What? No."

"He will."

"Why?"

"Oh don't bullshit me, Romilia."

"I'm not, what are you talking about?" I was chuckling. Maybe too much.

He shook his head. "Romilia. You get a taste of the Feds, it's hard to go back to local gravy."

Ay, I said to him. My pat answer, whenever I need to avoid something.

Sergio looks up at me and smiles like he's done something wrong but he knows I'm in one of those mother moods that won't let me reprimand him. He could drop whole rolls of paper into the toilet and right now I'd just snatch him up and cuddle him until he squirmed.

"You home early?" he says.

"Yeah. I've got me a few days off."

He's playing with his hair, twirling it, as he does whenever he's nervous or excited. He must be excited. Here I am, coming to pick him up in Atlanta, take him and Mamá home. In Nashville the window's been fixed, as has the one upstairs in his bedroom. McCabe had one of the boys patch the bullet hole next to the front door. The cops also scrubbed Bobby Green's blood off the wood floor.

Sergio's happy to see me; but he'll be sad soon,

when he knows I'm planning to take him back to Nashville, away from this gaggle of cousins, away from the mix of my mother with her sister and the neighbors. But he doesn't know beyond that. He doesn't know that the cousins will leave soon as well, return to their home in Los Angeles. And he doesn't know how big their house is there, how it could easily hold three visitors for awhile. I mean to surprise him.

"Hey *hombrecito*, how'd you like to take a trip?"

"Where?"

His smile, how can it get so wide?

I tell him. He rattles off names: Disneyland? Universal Theme Park? The beach? My eyes open big to all that. He attacks with one of his slam-dunk hugs. And then of course, he has the last word in surprises. As only a four year old can do, he kisses my mouth, my cheek, and then my neck, his lips not hesitating at all as they land a wet smack on that long scar.

My mother sees all this from the kitchen door. Triumphant grandmother, watching her grandson take hold of her daughter, healing that girl's wound in a way only he can do, of course.

Of course.

ACKNOWLEDGMENTS

Thanks to the Nursing Department of Mount St. Mary's College, Los Angeles, for all their help regarding anatomical and medical procedural questions (Keloid scars, the art of giving injections, etc.). Also thanks to the pharmacists of Brent Air Pharmacy, Brentwood, for their information on various medications. Any mistakes in the novel regarding these areas of expertise are the fault of the author.

Robert Pinsky's translation of *The Inferno of Dante* is a great pleasure to read, and I am thankful for all the work and years he put into that text so Romilia could carry it with her across the country. Thomas Phillips' work, *The Inferno: A Translation with Paintings* is to my mind the most fascinating contemporary interpretation on canvas of Dante's *Inferno*. The "bubbled notes" left by Bobby were partially inspired by Phillips' art.

The sage and patient librarians at the Getty

Museum Library in Los Angeles guided me through their holdings and allowed me time and space to stumble around their stacks and wallow in serendipity.

DeAnna Heindel is perhaps the newest best friend of my writings. A tip of the hat to her for her excellent editing.

Michelle, *Mi Vida*, must always be thanked.

ABOUT THE AUTHOR

MARCOS M. VILLATORO is the author of several books of fiction, poetry, and nonfiction. The *Los Angeles Times Book Review* listed his nationally acclaimed *Home Killings* as one of the Best Books of 2001. It won the Silver Medal from *Foreword Magazine* and First Prize in the Latino Literary Hall of Fame. His second Romilia Chacón novel, *Minos*, was released to high literary acclaim. His other books include the Pushcart Prize nominee *The Holy Spirit of My Uncle's Cojones* (also an Independent Publishers Book Award finalist), *They Say That I Am Two: Poems*, the novel *A Fire in the Earth*, and the memoir *Walking to La Milpa: Living in Guatemala with Armies, Demons, Abrazos, and Death*.

After years of living in Central America, Marcos attended the Iowa Writers' Workshop. In 1998, he and his family moved to Los Angeles, where Marcos holds the Fletcher Jones Endowed Chair in Writing at Mount St. Mary's College. A regular commentator for

National Public Radio's *Day to Day*, Marcos also hosts a book show called *Shelf Life* for Pacifica Radio.

He lives with his wife and four children in Los Angeles, and is now hard at work on the third Romilia Chacón novel, *A Venom Beneath the Skin*. Visit Marcos on the web at www.marcosvillatoro.com.

**Don't miss
Marcos M. Villatoro's
first novel featuring
Latina homicide detective
Romilia Chacón**

An *Los Angeles Times* Best Book

"One of the best novels—mystery or otherwise—
you'll read this year." —*Los Angeles Times Book Review*

"Well-crafted and unique . . . Romilia, her mother,
and her son would be welcome again!"
—*Kirkus Reviews, starred review*

"A slick, elegantly crafted mystery." —*Publishers Weekly*

"Twisty and clever in the extreme, will surprise even
the most experienced detective-story reader."
—*Hispanic Magazine*

Available from Dell Books

**Read on for a thrilling excerpt—and look
for your copy wherever books are sold.**

**And don't miss the new Romilia Chacón thriller,
A VENOM BENEATH THE SKIN,
available in hardcover in Spring 2005.**

MARCOS M. VILLATORO

"One of the best novels—mystery
or otherwise—you'll read this Summer."
—*Los Angeles Times Book Review*

A Romilia Chacón Mystery

HOME
KILLINGS

My first thought that night: I hate gunshot wounds to the head.

I leaned forward, placing my right foot ahead of the other and bending my right knee so as to hover over the dead man's face. This was uncomfortable. Still, I didn't use my gloved hands to balance myself against the red Honda sedan that stood two feet from the body. An old rule from academy days marched through the rear of my memory: "Always keep your hands behind your back when first approaching the crime scene."

I didn't need to hear that. I knew it well enough. Still, the rule played along, reminding me that this was my first case in this new city that I barely called home. Better to hear recordings out of the rule book. Rules helped me distance myself from the killing, but not for very long. This exit wound, right through the top of the skull, an inside-out, crumbly, bloody cradlecap topped with disintegrated brain tissue, shortened the distance between the victim and me real quick. But the killing didn't let the pistol in the man's hand escape my sight, the first thing that was wrong with this picture.

"*Carajo*," I muttered, "what a mess."

"What's that you say?" The voice came from one side. It was a southern voice, one of the common twangs I heard throughout Nashville. I looked up at an older man. He crouched next to me. He was the medical examiner. His name escaped me. I hadn't worked any big case since arriving here from Atlanta four weeks earlier, and up to now had had no need to meet the examiner. The dead man's doughnut head promised to bring that old guy and me together for a while.

"Oh. Nothing. Just a Spanish word," I chuckled, tossing my hair over my shoulder as if catching it on a hook. I sounded embarrassed. It wouldn't do to translate *carajo* to a stranger. Bad manners, my mamá would remind me with her scolding voice.

He didn't respond. For the moment he seemed too preoccupied for introductions. He had sliced a small opening into the victim's abdomen and was now shoving a digital thermometer into the slit. Then he crouched there, holding the thermometer still. "Gonna be hard to get an accurate reading," he muttered. "Too much blood gone from that head wound. The bullet must have sliced through the edge of the carotid. The blood pulls away the heat more quickly." He wrote a note in his pad regarding the incision.

Bulbs burst about us from the two uniform cops who took pictures of the area. They lit up the early-morning darkness with their silent flashes. While the doctor pushed the thermometer deeper into the man's gut, I walked away to look at the car. It was a small Honda, sporty red. The driver's door was open. The body itself lay in front of the car to the right side. The car straddled two parking places, covering one of the lines with its midsection. It appeared that the victim—if he had been the person driving—had pulled in quickly, paying little attention to the lines of an empty parking lot.

The short, buzzing sounds of an unhooked telephone chirped in the grass. I was surprised no one had noticed that. Perhaps the scene-of-crime technicians had decided to leave the cellular phone there, waiting for Prints to come by and dust it. I shined my handlight into the grass. The thin, new cellular was the type that fits easily in a breast pocket.

Behind me, the M.E. pulled the tiny, thin rod away from the man's abdomen. He had to stand to hold the thermometer up to a streetlight and read it. He turned away from me momentarily. The man was much taller than I, and skinny.

I wasn't sure if he wanted to know me or not. He seemed busy, too busy to take time with me. Yet I walked as if I had no place here. I was one of two or three women in the area. Perhaps that was what made me hesitate to take my position—which was the main position—at the crime scene.

Then there was the kill itself. I couldn't keep my eyes on the wound too long. I had to stand again and take a couple of steps back. Beyond the Honda, in the background of my vision, a large riverboat floated in the Cumberland, its ornate bridge protruding above the flood wall. On the other side of the river stood the black outline of old buildings, a small, antique skyline that had been overshadowed by the new skyscrapers standing on this side of the water.

Two police officers wrapped the area with yellow tape. I kept my hands in the small of my back and walked toward them. They muttered to each other about how strange it was to find a suicide in this part of town. "Right downtown, on River Park, in the middle of the night. Can you figure that?"

I introduced myself as the primary detective. Actualy, I was the only detective, but I wasn't about to tell the uniforms this. One of the cops turned and looked down at me. I could feel his eyes float quickly down my body, which made no sense, considering I wore a long black trench coat that covered me from my neck to my ankles. These cold November days demanded such protection. The cop seemed familiar. Then I realized it was his eyes. They had floated over me before, in the hallways of the Main Police Squad downtown. One day the previous week I had walked by. He had looked me up and down, then had whispered to his partner, "Check out the lady in red."

My mother would not have liked that statement. Yet she would not have scolded the officer for his soft, lewd comment, but would have berated me instead for wearing my favorite color. "*Demasiado* sexy, *hija*," she would have said. "You are giving messages that do not befit a lady."

As always, she was right. And yet I never had the desire to send ladylike messages. I was a homicide detective, not a damned debutante who waited on her fifteenth birthday at the church doors for the perfect man to come by and sweep her away. I'm Latina, but damned if I'll be that Latina.

"I'm Detective Romilia Chacón, Officer. And you're . . ." I looked down at his nameplate and almost chuckled. "Officer Beaver. First name?"

"Henry."

"Mind if I call you that?"

He didn't answer.

"One of the other blues tells me you've got the notes on this. What can you give me?"

The beaver walked away from me and the tree branch where he had been tying the yellow tape. He approached the car. "Pretty cut and dry. Suicide."

"Why do you say that?"

"Because of the gun in the man's hand, Detective." Beaver looked at me with that Some-things-are-just-too-obvious-look. I wanted to give him my Go-screw-yourself-up-the-ass-with-your-own-nightstick look, but decided to turn my attention to the body. He continued, "It's a forty-five caliber. Once we lift it, we'll check the numbers to see if he owned it. I got his wallet from him, got his name and address. That's why they called you, Detective." His voice was deadpan.

"What's his name?" I asked, knowing that it was a Spanish name, and ready to see how this gringo cop was going to butcher its pronunciation.

He had to flip through his notebook to read it phonetically. "Diego . . . uh . . . Diego Sinus, something like that."

"Sáenz," I corrected, looking over his shoulder at the spelling. "Diego Sáenz." My clipped Salvadoran accent made his very voice sound stupid.

"Yeah. Whatever. Not like we need to practice our Spanish here in Nashville." He closed his notebook. "Anyway, Prints will dust the weapon and lift it in a minute."

"His name sounds familiar. What about legal time of death?"

"It's 3:11 a.m. I arrived here at the time and called it in. I had driven through here an hour earlier, but hadn't seen the car, so he killed himself sometime after I moved on. I came back around, and here he was."

"You got an estimated time?"

"You'll have to ask Doc about that."

"Right. By the way, what's Doc's name?"

"Jacob Callahan."

Before dismissing him, I asked Beaver for any other information on the victim. He gave me the run-down: Name: Diego Sáenz. Age: twenty-four. Weight: one hundred sixty-five pounds. Race: Hispanic. Height: five feet nine inches. Eyes: brown. All of this was from his driver's license, of course. It told me very little.

"I also found two credit cards on him. VISA Gold and MasterCard Platinum. Oh yeah, also a press card."

So Sáenz was a reporter. "May I see the card?" I asked Beaver.

He handed it to me. It seemed legit: Sáenz worked for *The Cumberland Journal*, the second-largest paper in Nashville and the surrounding areas. This wasn't going to be a commonplace killing among a few drunk migrant workers. I bet my boss McCabe didn't expect my first case to be a victim who carried around ten grand in plastic money.

I gave the press card back to Beaver. He took a step away, blatantly ignoring any chance of my dismissal, not even remaining by my side for a "Thank you, Officer Beaver." Maybe he would appreciate "Up yours, Officer Beaver" more. He angered me. But he also emptied a hole in me. I had a sudden urge to call home, wake my mother, and ask her how my son, Sergio, was. She would tell me, of course, that he was asleep, he was fine. Yet she would understand the lack of logic in my phone call, and would assure me that my *hijo*, my *querido*, was safe. It would be enough to fill the edges of this hole.

Beaver walked back to his tree branch. He said nothing, though I could hear the other uniform walk up to Beaver and whisper something through a barely controlled, manly giggle. Something about ladies wearing red, perhaps? I had spiked platform shoes back home that could slice their quick erections right down the middle.

I walked back to the body. Dr. Jacob Callahan leaned over Sáenz. He moved his gloved hand over the head, then pulled back, as though he had merely waved the dark air between him and the victim's wound to clear out an opening where he could see. He wrote notes onto his pad.

I offered a rubber-gloved hand and a fairly large smile to the squatting man. "Excuse my bad manners. Here we are working together, and I haven't introduced myself yet."

Callahan stood up. With his full height it looked, from my point of view, like the lone streetlight was just beside his left ear. He gave me his gloved hand. "Jacob Callahan," he said. "Most call me Doc, even though it's not a very creative nickname. And you should excuse me," he said, chuckling. "I got right to work without saying hello. Just wanted to get the temperature. Not good to wait around for that."

Though it was dark out, I could see parts of his figure. His graying hair was once honey brown. He kept it short. Wrinkles tried to cut into what was once a perfectly smooth, tanned face. Callahan looked very good for his age, even handsome. His jaw was a strong one, and though the years had caused a slight sag in the muscle and skin, the jawline still looked like well-sculptured marble. Doc smiled. It seemed sincere enough. "You're new in the unit, aren't you, Detective?"

"Just a few weeks old. A babe to the Nashville scene."

He liked that, grinning a little more. "Welcome," he said, motioning his hand like an emcee, back toward Diego Sáenz.

We approached the small car together. "Did you get an ETD?" I asked.

"Yes," Doc said, his Nashville accent turning to a get-down-to-business quickness that I appreciated, sensing that the elder southerner was ready and willing to work with me. "The loss of blood concerned me. But there was still enough heat in his abdomen to get a reading. Then I compared notes with Officer Beaver. Sáenz's body had dropped two degrees. With this cold night and the blood loss, I'd say the estimated time of death to be 2:15, 2:30, more or less."

"That's pretty accurate."

"I'll shoot for the best I can."

"By the way, what day is today?"

Doc held his watch up to the light. "Let's see . . . November second."

"Ah. *El dia de los muertos*," I said, mumbling it.

"What's that, Detective?"

"The Day of the Dead. Yesterday was All Saints' Day. Today's All Souls' Day, or The Day of the Dead."

"Oh. I see. So you're a religious person."

I laughed. "Oh, yeah. I never miss a Christmas or Easter mass."

The air felt colder. I wrapped my coat tighter around me and leaned over again, staring into the man's still-intact face. Another uniform cop approached Doc Callahan and gave the examiner a flashlight. "Thanks, son," Doc said, then flicked the light on and shined it down over my right shoulder. A spark reflected off the victim's left ear. Sáenz sported a diamond earring. Then the light fell upon the full of the wound. It was too much for me to say anything in either of my languages. I tipped, and almost placed my left fingers on one of the blood spots next to Sáenz. After several seconds of composure—still not enough, as I could feel my voice quiver—I asked "What do you make of this?"

"Well, lots of suicides stick the barrel in their

mouth. That's usually pretty efficient. They either shoot upward, at an angle, and blow out their brains like this young fellow appears to have done. Or they shoot straight back, missing much of the brain but destroying their esophagus and the whole upper region of their respiratory track, drowning or bleeding to death. This fellow's way of doing it worked pretty well. He apparently put the gun underneath his chin, tucking it right up against his Adam's apple, aiming upward. I'd say the bullet destroyed his sinuses, then cut through the brain, probably slicing up the medulla oblongata before ripping through the cerebral hemisphere and exiting here, between the frontal and parietal bones, right through the coronal suture."

"So he literally blew his brains out."

"Exactly."

One doubt dangled over me. "You think it's a suicide, then?"

He grinned slightly. "Notice I've said the word 'apparent' about a dozen times. Though I'm willing to bet it was."

"Strange area of town to do yourself in."

"Maybe he liked fishing," said Doc, motioning to the river, "and they weren't biting."

"Then what about the gun in his hand?"

Doc knew exactly what I was referring to. "It's a sure bet that his was an instantaneous death. His hand muscles were in work at he moment of death. He could have had a cadaveric spasm, which is like a pinch of early, quick rigor mortis. When that happens, the victim's hands clutch whatever they were holding, permanently."

I raised my eyebrows, then shined my flashlight over to the body, directly at the hand. Even in the night I could tell that the back of the hand looked somehow stained.

"What are those blotches on his hand?" I asked.

Doc looked over at it. "I'm not sure." His brow furrowed. "I'll need to make a note to check that . . ."

I stood up and looked around, my eyes falling back upon the car. I looked at its driver door. "By the way, was this door open when you got here?"

Beaver, who had walked over to us, answered, "Yeah. It was open. I guess Sáenz left it that way when he got out of it."

Which means he was in a hurry, I thought. I studied the positions of all the objects. Car parked over two spaces, as if done quickly. Door opened. Body found on the right side of the car, just two feet from the front passenger wheel. Cellular phone found directly to the left of the car, just before the front driver's wheel. He either dropped the phone while walking over to this side, or flung it behind him once over here. Maybe he flung it the moment he shot himself . . . but that gun in his hand, it was all wrong.

Doc asked Beaver to help flip the body half-over. "I just want to see if there are any other opening wounds in the dorsal region," he said. The men turned Sáenz forty-five degrees, resting him on his right arm and pelvis. Though Beaver cradled the right side of Sáenz's head, the skull tipped slightly, showing me once again the smaller hole in the tuck of his neck and mandible. A bulb flashed almost directly in my face. The cop with the camera had just taken another shot of the body, then moved away. "I don't see anything. . . . Okay, that's good. Let's put him back," instructed Doc. He and Beaver lowered the dead man onto his back again.

A man and a woman, the ones from Prints, separated and took different parts of the car to dust. The woman took the phone. The man worked on a door handle. He aimed a flashlight from various angles upon the handle, then twirled a fluffy fiberglass brush between his palms. He dipped it into a fine black powder, then brushed the dust delicately over a print. The woman did the same with the phone.

I asked her for the phone once she was done with it. Cradling it carefully in my right hand, I hit the "redial" button with my left forefinger. The weakened phone barely chirped out three tones: one high and two low. The last two were the same sound.

Nine-one-one.

I walked away to give them more room. Doc followed me. We walked beyond the yellow boundaries of the plastic police line. I pulled the thin, tight rubber gloves from my hands. Doc did not, as if accustomed to functioning most of his day with them on.

"So, you're not so sure it's a suicide?" he asked.

"I'm sure it's not a suicide. This dude was murdered."

"Really?"

"Yep." I let my bravado sink in a good five seconds before telling him about the last call Sáenz made. "Why call nine-one-one if you're ready to kill yourself?"

Doc shrugged his shoulders. "Maybe he was reaching out, looking for anybody to talk with. From his point of view, it was an emergency."

"Maybe. But I bet those blotches on his hand will tell you differently."

Doc raised his eyebrows at me. He smiled politely. Then he excused himself. "I'll have a report for you in a few hours. If you want, I'll give you a call when it's done."

"Great. I'd appreciate it."

He folded his tall body into a Jaguar and drove away. I turned back to the scene, where Beaver was telling a few of his uniforms to wrap it up because this suicide case would be quickly closed, and they would be leaving the area soon. My pleasantries with Doc ground into hot anxieties as I watched this jerk hand out orders that were mine to give. It was time to show him the size of my spiked heel.